The Shelly Beach Writers' Group

June Loves is the author of over one hundred non-fiction books for both children and adults, and she has been a newspaper journalist, freelance writer and teacher librarian. She now lives near the beach in Victoria with her husband (but no Dog).

The Shelly Beach Writers' Group

JUNE LOVES

VIKING
an imprint of
PENGUIN BOOKS

VIKING

Published by the Penguin Group
Penguin Group (Australia)
250 Camberwell Road, Camberwell, Victoria 3124, Australia
(a division of Pearson Australia Group Pty Ltd)
Penguin Group (USA) Inc.
375 Hudson Street, New York, New York 10014, USA
Penguin Group (Canada)
90 Eglinton Avenue East, Suite 700, Toronto, Canada ON M4P 2Y3
(a division of Pearson Penguin Canada Inc.)
Penguin Books Ltd
80 Strand, London WC2R 0RL England
Penguin Ireland
25 St Stephen's Green, Dublin 2, Ireland
(a division of Penguin Books Ltd)
Penguin Books India Pvt Ltd
11 Community Centre, Panchsheel Park, New Delhi – 110 017, India
Penguin Group (NZ)
67 Apollo Drive, Rosedale, North Shore 0632, New Zealand
(a division of Pearson New Zealand Ltd)
Penguin Books (South Africa) (Pty) Ltd
24 Sturdee Avenue, Rosebank, Johannesburg 2196, South Africa

Penguin Books Ltd, Registered Offices: 80 Strand, London WC2R 0RL, England

First published by Penguin Group (Australia), 2011

1 3 5 7 9 10 8 6 4 2

Text copyright © June Loves 2011
Illustrations copyright © Kat Chadwick 2010

The moral right of the author has been asserted

Cover and text design by Marina Messiha © Penguin Group (Australia)
Illustrations by Kat Chadwick
Typeset in Fairfield by Post Pre-Press Group, Brisbane
Printed and bound in Australia by McPherson's Printing Group, Maryborough, Victoria

National Library of Australia
Cataloguing-in-Publication data:

Loves, June, 1938–
The Shelly Beach writers' group / June Loves
9780670074853 (pbk.)
A823.3

penguin.com.au

FSC
www.fsc.org
MIX
Paper from
responsible sources
FSC® C001695

For my daughters, Elisha and Natalie

July

Wednesday 1 July

The small, scruffy Dog was sitting by my side on the verandah. It had started to rain. We watched the misty rain falling from the grey sky.

'I'm guessing this is standard Shelly Beach winter weather, Dog?'

The Dog ignored me.

We watched the rain change to a steady downfall.

'Well, that's it, Dog. I'm now an official house-slash-dog-sitter.'

The Dog stared at me with his beady eyes.

'What do you see, Dog? A barely-50-something woman with tear-streaked mascara, angsty green eyes and birds' nest hair badly in need of a good cut?'

The Dog shifted his head to a cute-dog pose. He kept staring at me.

'Reality check, Dog. We're on our own. And we're not getting teary! I'm teared out!'

No comment.

Only minutes before, the Dog had been bouncing and barking around the car in the driveway while Adrian, his owner, stowed luggage in the boot. Then the Dog was told to sit with me on the verandah, and we watched Adrian slide into the passenger seat of his daughter's car. Tania was driving her dad to the airport to catch Flight 678 to London. We watched as the car backed out of the drive and disappeared down Sea Spray Street.

A chilly sea wind blew in from the bay. I pulled my Armani trench coat around me and adjusted my scarf. 'It's freezing. Time for coffee. And I suppose you want water.'

The Dog followed me inside the minus one-star beach house with the pretentious name of Sea View Cottage. If I was a twelve-foot giant bouncing on a trampoline I might be able to catch a view of the sea from here.

The Dog waited while I filled a bowl with water. I watched him drink, then shooed him out the back door. I brewed myself a cup of coffee using the excellent coffee beans I found in Adrian's cupboard.

A folder labelled *The Shelly Beach Writers' Group* and my contract were lying on the kitchen table. I'd co-signed the contract with Adrian Fraser, owner of Sea View Cottage. As a reformed non-reading-contract signer I'd carefully read every fine line.

'It's for insurance and for your protection, Gina,' Adrian had said.

I looked at Adrian-with-the-friendly-eyes. True. I nodded in agreement and signed on the dotted line.

As his house-slash-dog-sitter I have six months of rent-free and bill-free accommodation – on condition I look after a cottage . . . and a dog. I gathered up the contract and stuffed it in a kitchen drawer. The Shelly Beach Writers' Group folder remained on the kitchen table.

Just an hour before I'd untangled myself from my three long-time friends' air kisses and body-crunching hugs. Clare and Hester wrangled over who was going to sit in the passenger seat on the journey back to the city. With the dispute settled, Eva did a zappy reverse in Adrian's drive. Her red Jag sped down the unmade street. Clare's last 'Ohmagod – I can't believe we're leaving her' lingered in the salty air.

I'd told my three friends my decision on Monday when we were lunching in the city at Louie's Riverside Cafe. 'I'm moving to Shelly

3

Beach. I've decided to become a house-slash-dog-sitter.'

'You can't be a dog-sitter. You're not a dog person. You don't like dogs!' Clare was her usual glass-half-empty self.

I put on my professional positive-plus voice. 'You don't have to like dogs to be a dog-sitter. You feed a dog, give it some water and take it for walks. How hard can it be?'

'You hate exercise.'

I ignored Clare.

'What about vet bills if the dog gets sick?' Friend Eva, aka the financial wizard, was on the ball.

'The owner, Adrian Fraser, has arranged to settle any bills that occur while looking after the house or the dog. I have to take the bills to the bank in Sea Haven.'

Quiet, competent Hester looked uneasy. She and her husband Paul are part-time animal lovers – no pun intended. They have a hobby farm where they keep an assortment of token animals: sheep, cows, a goat and ducks. 'What breed is the dog, Gina?'

'A small one with piranha-type teeth.'

Adrian had shown me a photo when we'd met just a few days before and he'd first presented his proposal.

'Small dogs can be snappy.' Consoling information from Clare.

'Adrian still has ten fingers. He says the Dog doesn't bite.'

Then Clare turned practical. 'Gina hasn't got a choice, really. She's turned down a brilliant offer from Julia.'

I ignored the comment about the offer from my daughter Julia, former accountant of the now defunct Laurel-Scott Corporation. I knew Eva and Hester would approve of my decision to decline the offer. They'd been taking turns to provide me with emergency accommodation since *it* all happened, but neither needed a long-stay tenant, and I didn't want to be a long-stay tenant. I wanted my own cave. I needed my own space!

Clare was right. I had no choice. Two weeks ago, 17 June to

be exact – my barely-50-something birthday – King Rat Kenneth, husband of twenty-seven years, executed the classic dumping. He dumped me for Clever Angela, his oh-so-caring personal assistant. My dumping also came with the news that the Laurel-Scott Corporation was bankrupt. As a silent joint-owner, and as the result of years of recklessly signing any document Kenneth put under my nose, it turned out I'd signed away my upmarket home, my (leased) Audi, my access to multiple credit cards and a high-end lifestyle.

Back in the kitchen of Sea View Cottage, the Dog came inside through the pet door. He stared at me with his beady eyes.

'Too early for dinner, Dog.'

The Dog didn't look happy. Was he missing his owner already? Could dogs get depressed? 'Don't you dare get depressed, Dog. You'll be on your own. Suicidal dogs were not mentioned in my contract.' I walked to the calendar (sponsored by Rupert's Butchery, Shelly Beach) fastened to Adrian's kitchen wall and ripped off the months until I arrived at July.

'See, Dog.' I flipped through the pages for him and counted the months to December. 'Only six months – *six months* – and your owner will be back.'

The Dog's ears looked different. They'd gone droopy. 'At least you've a kennel, and food, and know Adrian will return in December. How would you like to be me? I have to get a new life by December.'

No answer. I opened the back door and shooed the Dog outside again. 'Fresh air will make you feel better. Go do whatever it is you do. I'll call you when it's time for dinner.'

I made myself another cup of coffee and contemplated the folder with *The Shelly Beach Writers' Group* written in large print on the outside. A large envelope with *Key* scrawled on it was attached to the folder. I tried to remember the verbal instructions and superfluous information Adrian had given me before he left.

The Dog reappeared in the kitchen again through the pet door.

'I think a key keeper person is calling in soon to pick up this folder for Adrian's writers' group.'

The Dog feigned ignorance.

'You heard me tell Adrian I'm not interested in joining his writers' group . . . didn't you, Dog? I'm not wasting another year of my life – longer counting the time spent in revision and editing – to write another unsuccessful novel.'

The Dog lay down on the worn mat in front of the empty fireplace.

'No way am I going to be part of any writers' group, Dog. It's not in my contract.'

The Dog thought Adrian's writers' group was part of the package that came with caring for him and looking after Adrian's house.

I ignored the Dog and left him staring at the empty fireplace.

My two Louis Vuitton suitcases containing most of my remaining worldly goods stood in the middle of Adrian's living room. They looked like objects from Mars. My friends had salvaged what they could for me – anything that might escape the eagle eyes of the receivers and bring in cash. A 'financial stimulus', Eva called it. 'It's an income, Gina, to last for a few months until you can get on your feet.'

Clare's mantra was still ringing in my ears: 'I know what's happened to you is tragic, but you have to move on, Gina. You have to move on.'

Clare had done an excellent job of packing for me. One suitcase for clothes, the other for necessities. I selected one of Adrian's two basic bedrooms and trundled Suitcase Two to it. According to the label, Suitcase Two contained linen, towels and other bits and pieces.

The Dog appeared at my side and watched me unpack. A leather-bound journal rested on top of the towels. It had been a birthday gift from my friends, a gift I now intended to dump in the nearest charity shop bin. I flipped through the opening pages. They were filled with

6

entries I'd written at two painful writing workshops with Clare only weeks before.

Over the past year, Clare had been disturbed by my radical change from professional woman-in-a-power-suit to eccentric writer-in-an-attic. 'You have to get out, Gina. Meet people. Have fun!' She'd organised some self-improvement stuff for us, and I remember enrolling in French for Beginners. But Novel Writing for Beginners? No way! Claire said it was an administration glitch. 'I know you're not a beginner novel-writer, Gina, but the classes will be fun.'

Next to my journal in my suitcase, thoughtful Clare had also packed Sweet-Scary Tutor's best-selling book, *Journaling: a pathway to your novel*, a valuable epistle that was included in the cost of Sweet-Scary Tutor's ten-week writing course.

'Thank God I don't have to attend another single one of those workshops. What do you think, Dog? Will my journal entries about a classic dumping make a must-read opening for a tragic romantic novel? Maybe I could write a book about a protagonist who meets a knight in shining armour and is rescued from a life of poverty and drabness?'

No comment from the Dog.

'Or maybe a Scott of the Antarctic survival-type journal is more appropriate for a Shelly Beach sojourn. Don't you agree?'

The Dog left the room. I looked at my watch; probably time for his dinner.

I found him waiting in the kitchen. He watched as I measured and poured his prescribed ration of vitamin-packed dog pellets into his bowl.

Ever-thoughtful Clare had stocked Adrian's ancient fridge with a range of frozen dinners-for-one. I heated the organic chicken on a bed of wild mushrooms and rice. I ignored the stick-on recommendation: *Best eaten with a green salad*.

After dinner I battled with Adrian's vintage hot-water system.

Eventually I managed to get a stop/start supply of lukewarm water. But afterwards I couldn't light the fire.

'I haven't had to do this in years, Dog. All I had to do in my last house was press a button. Magical gas-fuelled flames would leap up and radiate heat.'

The Dog wasn't interested in magical gas-fuelled flames. I guess if you have fur it doesn't matter if it's hot or cold.

I selected a book from Adrian's crammed bookshelves. I wouldn't be short of reading material at Shelly Beach. I located my Prada handbag, comfortingly stuffed with medication for blood pressure, insomnia and high cholesterol. I escorted the Dog to his kennel on the verandah. Inside I blocked the pet door with a chair, and locked up for the night. Mental note: buy lock for pet door.

I'd decided to keep a Shelly Beach journal to record my riches-to-rags journey. Maybe it would be discovered one hundred years from now. It could be registered as an historical document – evidence of a barely-50-something female's survival in tough economic times. Maybe not.

Thursday 2 July

I don't know what woke me – the Dog howling, the storm or the steady stream of water pouring on my face. I brought the Dog inside and we watched the rain escaping from the ceiling onto my bed.

I grabbed some blankets from Adrian's hall cupboard and made a bed on the couch in the living room. The Dog and I watched the spectacular storm from Adrian's front windows. Eventually we fell asleep.

We were woken by hammering on the front door. Clutching a blanket around me, I hobbled to the door to answer it. Three characters were standing on Adrian's verandah. I stared at a woman dressed in corporate clothes, holding a small child. An older child was standing beside her. The woman juggled the small child on her hip while she nudged the older child forward. This was a perilous thing to do as the child was clutching a casserole.

'I'm Joan Waters, Sam and Terri's mother. We live next door. I apologise for not coming over to say hello to you yesterday. Sam' – she indicated the small child – 'had a fever. Adrian said you'd be happy to keep an eye on Terri until she goes to school this morning.'

Bloody hell, Adrian. Was this in my contract?

'And Adrian usually picks Terri up after school every Thursday,' the corporate female rattled on. 'I'm sorry to put this on you. I've a 9 o'clock client and I had trouble arranging alternative childcare. Adrian said he was sure you'd help out.'

The older child came alive. 'Didn't Adrian tell you about me? I'm Terri. T–E–double R–I. He said I had to show you how to use the computer.'

In Adrian's endless stream of instructions I vaguely remembered him mentioning a Terry. Terry with a Y? An adult Terry?

'Adrian lets me stay here every Thursday morning until I go to school. Then he picks me up after school; we come back here and Adrian cooks me dinner. When Mum comes home and settles Sam she rings Adrian, and he hands me over,' the older child finished. I stared at the small child straddled on the woman's hip. 'Sam doesn't stay here. He goes to Grandma's.'

'Right.'

'Can I come in? Mum's running late.'

Bloody hell, Adrian! 'Yes.'

Joan looked relieved and handed me a card with a business address and a handwritten telephone number. 'This is where you can contact me if anything happens to Terri, and this number here is my mother's phone number. She cares for Sam during the day. I've contacted the school, so they know to expect you. Can you go to the office? Do you mind? You have to sign Terri in when you drop her off, and sign her out when you pick her up.'

I nodded. The older child followed her mother to the car. I watched Joan as she kissed her daughter goodbye, strapped the toddler into his car seat and drove off.

What kind of mother leaves her child with a madwoman who talks to a dog? Wrong call, Gina. Adrian had already told her that her child would be safe with me. Of course he had.

'Can I put the casserole in the fridge?'

'Yes.'

'Adrian usually makes dinner but Mum thought you mightn't be ready to cook yet.'

I clutched the blanket around me. 'Right.'

The competent child ignored me and set about making coffee. She was obviously familiar with Adrian's kitchen. 'Do you like "real" coffee?'

'Yes, I do.'

'Adrian says the other stuff is crap.'

'Right.'

'Have you fed Hugo?'

'The Dog? No. Not yet.'

A condemning look. 'Hugo likes to be fed at the same time every morning – 6.30.'

Bloody hell! I clutched the mug of 'real' coffee handed to me and watched the child feed the Dog.

'If you hurry and get dressed, you can walk Hugo and me to school. It only takes fifteen minutes. Mum's a bit paranoid. She likes to know I'm safe at school. You'll have to go to the office first because you're not a regular parent.'

'Right!'

'Can you do that?'

'Yes.'

'Cool. You'd better hurry. It's getting late.'

Bloody hell! I needed a Bossy Child in my life like a hole in my head, but I dressed on cue, ran a comb through my hair and put the Dog on his leash.

At the school gate, this alarmingly independent child took the Dog's leash. 'You have to sign me in at the office. I'll wait with Hugo.' After due signing, I collected the Dog from Bossy Child.

'I'd think about an emergency meal for tonight if I were you. Mum's tuna casseroles are frequently feral. Sometimes they're brilliant, other times she just misses. If she misses we give them to Hugo.'

'Right!'

'See you after school. Adrian and Hugo always pick me up at 3.30.'

I nodded, feeling shell-shocked. The Dog and I walked home along Beach Road.

Beach Road is the hub of Shelly Beach consumerism. The one-sided shopping strip (across the road is the grassy foreshore with a few trees, sand and sea) consists of three operational shops – a general store, a hairdresser's salon and a butcher's shop – bookended with an old bakery under renovation on one corner and a pub on the other. The four remaining shops in the strip are boarded up – ghostly reminders of a once flourishing seaside town.

The wind-up Dog stopped abruptly outside Rupert's Butchery, which suited me. I needed to buy something for an emergency dinner. What does a nine-year-old – or maybe twelve-year-old – like to eat?

I checked the specials' board. 'Tender lion cutlets' were on special. Should I query Rupert about the sourcing of his 'lion' cutlets? I decided not to go there.

'It's okay to leave Hugo on the step,' Rupert called from his butchery.

I tied the Dog to a rail in front of the shop. The last thing I needed was a lost dog. The Dog dropped onto his paws, and watched me as I entered the shop.

'Guess you're Adrian's house-sitter?'

The butcher wasn't Rupert. Rupert was his dad. His dad passed away last January. The butcher was Harold.

Introductions over, I explained my problem. 'I need to feed a child.'

'Young Terri?'

'Yes.'

'Adrian cooks Terri schnitzels when he's looking after her.'

'Right.'

I watched Harold expertly slice meat for schnitzels.

'And you'll need bones for Hugo.'

I smiled my thanks. I bought a few basic ingredients from Jenkins' General Store next door. Robot Dog followed. No need to introduce myself this time either. The whole bloody town already knew I was living in Adrian's house – but just for six months.

At 3.30 I met Bossy Child near the school office. She held the Dog while I signed her out.

When we returned home Bossy Child made a quick survey of Adrian's property. She raced into the kitchen to inform me of my gross neglect. 'You forgot to feed the Girls!'

'Excuse me?'

'Adrian's chickens.'

Was caring for three chickens in my contract?

'Haven't you checked the garden? Didn't you see Adrian's henhouse?'

'No.'

I ignored Bossy Child's look of frustration as she marched me to the henhouse to collect the eggs, and feed and water the Girls – Myrtle, Hilda and Gretel.

'They could have died of starvation – or thirst.'

'But it's hardly even been one day.'

Rolled-eye look from Bossy Child.

I was then shown a once magnificent wrought-iron fountain, now frog and fish pond. Fortunately frogs don't require feeding and goldfish only require feeding three times a week. However, I was to check regularly that the wire mesh stayed firmly over the pond. The odd seabird had been known to add frogs' legs and fillet of goldfish to its menu.

Later that evening Terri located Adrian's manual and took me through it. 'Adrian's written everything you need to know about looking after Hugo and Sea View Cottage here. He must have told you about the manual?'

I ignored Bossy Child.

Chicken-feeding instructions were under G for Girls. Where else? Tomorrow I could fill the bird feeder for the doves. Instructions for feeding doves were under D for Doves, not B for Birds.

We struck it lucky with the tuna casserole. At 7 Adrian's phone rang. Joan was home and Sam was in bed.

It had started raining in buckets again. Bossy Child located Adrian's raincoat, gumboots and a torch on the back verandah. Clad in said raincoat and gumboots, and aided by the torch, the Dog and I walked Bossy Child next door. A relieved mother met us and took the parcel of meat I handed her. She looked at Terri. 'Everything okay?'

Terri nodded and smiled. 'The schnitzels are for tomorrow night's dinner.'

Joan smiled again. 'Thank you. Will it be all right if Terri comes next Thursday?'

Bloody hell, Adrian! I heard myself say, 'That'll be fine.'

The Dog and I made our return five-minute walk to Sea View Cottage. Bossy Child's repeated screams of 'Thanks for everything!' carried over the noise of the torrential rain.

Friday 3 July

I had a reasonable night's sleep due to moving into Bedroom Two. I fed the Dog, but we decided it was too cold and wet for a morning walk. I went back to bed and listened to the rain, which I hoped was hitting the roof and trickling neatly into Adrian's gutters and downpipes.

When I prepared the Dog's dinner I found a box of gourmet chocolates and a touchy-feely card that Clare had left in Adrian's pantry: *Enjoy your life-changing journey, Gina*. Bloody hell, Clare! How can you have a life-changing journey when you haven't had a life for the past few years?

The Dog followed me outside to the C-for-Compost bin. 'Clare's the friend you don't need to have, Dog. Last year I covered for her every Wednesday for a month. She commuted on the breakfast business flight to Canberra to spend the day with her mystery lover in the Hilton's honeymoon suite, but on the fifth Wednesday she got the guilts and cancelled further romantic assignations.

'She'd asked, "How would it look, Gina, if there were an engine failure and the plane crashed? I'd be the only female in an airbus packed with middle-aged suits."

'You know, Dog, it had never crossed my mind that if the bloody plane crashed, I'd have to explain the tai-chi-classes-with-me lies to James, Clare's husband.'

The Dog wasn't interested in my story about the friend you didn't need to have, probably because he hasn't got any friends. Did dogs have friends? The Dog's eyes were fastened on Clare's gourmet chocolates as I tossed them, one by one, into the compost bin.

I relented and we shared one coffee crème walnut cluster.

'If I did decide to write another novel, Dog, I could write about betrayal and life. I could write about a protagonist who suffers the consequences of avoiding choices. When she finally decides to meet her deadline and choose between Life A and Life B, she finds her choices have disappeared.'

The Dog wasn't interested. He has no trouble making choices. It's easy. When you come to a fork in the road you take the left turn.

14

Saturday 4 July

Bossy Child called in to check on the Dog ('I promised Adrian'). She made me a cup of coffee and a hot chocolate for herself.

'The old bakery on the corner of Beach Road is going to be Adrian's bookshop cafe. We named it Piece of Cake. We called the flat above the shop Crow's Nest Flat. When you look out the windows you feel like you're in a crow's nest on top of a sailing ship's mast. It's got a 360-degree view. Alf is doing the renovations, and Adrian said you'd help Alf with stuff.'

Did I agree to assist an Alf person with renovations? Is it in the contract? Bloody hell.

Bossy Child checked the clock. 'I have to go home. If Alf's working at Piece of Cake today, tell him about the leak in Bedroom One.'

'Right.'

After lunch I took the Dog for a walk. We walked to Piece of Cake and I yahooed at the door. A sun-weathered, smiling, sixty-something man wearing a sleeveless Shelly Beach Lifesavers T-shirt met us. 'You're Gina. Adrian's house-sitter.'

Amazing deduction.

'I'm Alf.'

Alf invited us to stop for a cup of tea, a bowl of water and biscuits, and I reported the leak in the bedroom ceiling.

'Adrian never sleeps in the bedroom with the leaky ceiling. You must have been sleeping in Bedroom One. Adrian sleeps in Bedroom Two.'

Of course he does. Was this bedroom information in Adrian's unending string of instructions? Or was it in the manual? Probably.

Alf continued very slowly with further instructions for the incompetent house-sitter. 'If the ceiling leaks again, I'll repair it.'

'Right.'

'Keep a bucket under the ceiling where you think the leak is.'

'Right.'

15

When we arrived home the Dog helped me find a bucket. We shifted the bed in Bedroom One and placed the bucket where the bed had been. I moved the bed in Bedroom Two closer to the window.

The Dog wanted to know why I kept moving beds and buckets.

'I thought it would be pleasant to lie in bed and look out the window at Adrian's garden. I couldn't do that in my last house. I was locked in the attic writing a novel.'

The Dog accepted my explanation for moving his owner's furniture and playing with buckets. He raced off to go on guard duty – he'd heard noises in the garden.

Sunday 5 July

Last night I dreamt I was still living in Montpellier Place. Could I start a novel with that opening sentence? The Dog said no. He thought a similar opening sentence had already been written.

Anyway, I dreamt I was living in my former too-clean, too-perfect, luxurious cocoon – the elegant Montpellier Place in tree-lined Montpellier Avenue. I woke to reality. I was living in a seaside holiday cottage with direct access to the elements through the walls, windows and ceiling.

I lay in bed and watched the rain pelting down on Adrian's garden. I thought back to the day not long ago when I had to leave Montpellier Place.

My three warrior friends were firing. They were revelling in the idea of a rescue operation for their friend Gina. Eva had suggested I do a last check through the house to see if there was anything I could salvage; the receivers were due the next day.

As I walked through Montpellier Place there was no indication Kenneth had ever been an occupant; wardrobes, shelves, cupboards and desks were skinned clean. I remember noting the space on my desk where my new laptop had rested. Had Kenneth purchased it for me with this snatch in mind? Probably.

The safe was empty. My jewellery had vanished. There were blank spaces on walls where paintings I'd selected had once hung. Kenneth's nineteenth-century silver collection, the one he'd bought in one huge expensive auction lot and used as a talking point, had vanished too. The King Rat had taken the lot.

At Sea View Cottage, the Dog wandered into the bedroom. Time for breakfast. He watched me as I shivered and shuffled into my robe and slippers.

The rain let up later in the morning, so I took my coffee and joined the Dog in the garden. When I'd met Adrian-with-the-friendly-eyes last week he showed me photos: one of the Dog, and picturesque Sea View Cottage and Shelly Beach. I can't remember if there was a photo of the bakery, his potential bookshop cafe, but I do remember there were a lot of photos of his garden.

Adrian's garden does not resemble, in any way, the garden in his photos. No roses, no blossom trees, no wisteria. A huge leaf-free mulberry tree, a small orchard of lemon trees, all bearing fruit, and a jungle of overgrown plants dominate the large space.

'I had a designer garden in my last house, Dog. I owned a mini orchard designed to hide a city landscape, with a collection of citrus trees in imported designer pots.'

The Dog wasn't interested. For a small dog with short legs he can dig impressive holes. He'd been able to transform Adrian's vegetable garden into a war zone over the last few days.

I whistled for the Dog to leave his impersonation of a meerkat and join me to explore Adrian's property. I remembered Adrian mentioning his Shelly Beach property included three bungalows that were holiday lettings in the sixties or seventies. The bungalows had private outdoor areas where I imagined holiday tenants congregated at the end of lazy summer days. Adrian plans to renovate and holiday-let them again as part of his grand retirement plan.

I checked the interiors of the bungalows through the windows.

They were basic – one or two bedrooms, a small living area, kitchen and bathroom – and all in need of repair. The rooms were stacked with boxes. I deciphered labels through the dusty windows. Each seemed to contain books.

I'm in awe of Adrian's sea-change retirement plans. 'That's what I need, Dog: plans. A Plan A and a back-up Plan B to take with me when I leave Shelly Beach.'

The Dog wasn't interested. He thought plans were things you had while other stuff was happening. He prefers dreams. The Dog has a dream that one day he will excavate a dinosaur bone.

Adrian's garage housed his 1987 Ford. It was not a pretty sight. It was on its last legs. Wheels? Next week I'll give it a run. A 1946 MG was up on blocks next to it. How much help do you need to get a vintage sports car down from blocks and on the road? I'll check with Alf.

The rain looked like holding off so I decided to walk the Dog to the general store to buy the Sunday papers. Jody, who presides over the point of sale, looked frazzled amid a tangled pile of artificial flowers and pieces of cardboard house cut-outs. The gap-toothed grin I'd observed on Thursday was missing.

'We're closed, luv. Don't open on Sundays. I have to get this display up for Monday. Adrian cancelled his paper order, but I'll place a new one for you. Sunday papers come with Monday orders. Some locals even save them to read the next Sunday.'

I smiled a thank you. Jody looked like she was being strangled by artificial apple blossom.

'Do you need some help?'

Help was graciously accepted. The apple blossom and the cardboard house cut-outs were for a *Constant Heart* promotion.

Jody held the apple blossom while I tacked and glued the cardboard house together.

'Do you watch *Constant Heart*?'

'No.'

Jody registered absolute disbelief and handed me a competition entry form. 'Monday nights are appointment television nights for locals. You won't get anyone to answer the phone between 8.30 and 9.30 while *Constant Heart* is on.'

I promised to catch *Constant Heart* tomorrow night. If I watch tomorrow's episode, I can enter the competition. First prize is a real *Constant Heart* house.

'Lee Wang, he's the cook at Rosa's pub – a nice young man – mentioned he was going to call at Adrian's tomorrow afternoon. Adrian lets him borrow books. I said it'd be fine with you.'

I smiled agreement. If Adrian's operating a library for Shelly Beach locals it's nothing to do with me.

The Dog and I decided to walk back along the curling beach track. Stretches of grey sea filled the gaps left by clumps of tea-trees.

The Dog eyed the competition slip in my hand warily.

'Don't worry, Dog. When I win the *Constant Heart* house I promise I won't leave until I find a responsible new dog-sitter.'

The Dog was relieved.

That night I got the guilts about not calling Julia, daughter and former company accountant. I attempted to call her but failed. My mobile access has been cancelled. The service is seriously dead and buried together with the now defunct Laurel-Scott Corporation. In a former life I couldn't bear to have my mobile out of sight or sound – now I tossed it into the garbage bin with only a smidgen of regret.

I shifted the Shelly Beach Writers' Group folder to the middle of Adrian's kitchen table to clear some space while I ate the last of Clare's frozen dinners.

'Hopefully we'll get rid of the writing stuff tomorrow, Dog.'

The Dog wasn't interested. I shooed him onto the verandah and watched him do his weird walk-in-tight-circles thing before he settled. Inside the kitchen I propped a chair against the pet door.

Before I went to bed I recorded my medical details in my journal. Palpitations, stomach cramps and reflux have lessened. Hopefully my medical issues will disappear once I dispose of the Shelly Beach Writers' Group folder. If I did have plans, writing another unsuccessful novel wouldn't feature in Plan A *or* Plan B.

Monday 6 July

The Dog barked the arrival of Lee Wang returning some of Adrian's books this afternoon. A handsome young prince riding on a bicycle?

'Adrian said it's cool to borrow from his library while he's overseas. Do you mind?'

Of course I didn't.

Lee is a very personable young man – tall and lean with a ponytail. 'Hot' is the one-word description that Eva, my ferocious man-eating friend, would use to describe him.

Lee made coffee and we talked books. Lee's reading his way through Adrian's collection of Pulitzer Prize-winning books. We decided Adrian must've begun his collection when he was lecturing in modern American literature. I'd just reread Adrian's copy of Annie Proulx's *The Shipping News*. I suggested Lee borrow it.

'I usually get through a book a week,' he said. 'Not much else to do at Shelly Beach.'

I agreed. Lee was happy working at the pub for the present. 'Rosa is a reasonable boss.' Monday is his day off.

'Maybe we can discuss *The Shipping News* next Monday?'

Maybe.

The Dog and I watched the lean-and-muscular-complete-with-a-cosmopolitan-Hong-Kong-accent Lee cycle off. Well, I watched and the Dog chased. I waited for the Dog to return, exhausted from running after elusive whirly silver bicycle wheels.

'Lee's an intelligent young man, Dog.'

The Dog was out of breath, defeated and depressed by the speed of the bicycle wheels. He wasn't interested in a hot, intelligent young man.

I decided to check sometime to see if Adrian had a bicycle hidden in his garage. It would be a better transport option than Adrian's old Ford, assuming the tantalising MG is an out-of-bounds vehicle.

I pushed the Shelly Beach Writers' Group folder to the end of the table. I needed room to chop the vegetables I'd dug from Adrian's garden. I resurrected a past culinary skill and chopped the vegetables for soup. Considering I've been harvesting only frozen produce from supermarkets for many years I was pleased with my effort.

After dinner I recorded the day's exciting events in my journal. In a lapse of judgement I read an early journal entry – the one from my second and final writing workshop. It was one of the writing tasks Sweet-Scary Tutor set us: *Write about a significant event in the not-so-distant past*.

This had been easy. I wrote about the not-so-distant past and my bloody significant barely-50-something birthday. A birthday I'd planned to ignore. I'd decided to ignore anything connected with numbers: weight, sizes, ages, chapters or pages of a novel.

I'd returned from my compulsory birthday luncheon at Louie's – a warm, fuzzy afternoon spent with my three best friends. I'd showed suitable appreciation of their combined thoughtful gift of one over-the-top journal I planned to deposit in the nearest charity shop bin – but which I was now using to record Shelly Beach survival stuff.

'Marriages are unique institutions, Dog.'

The only institution the Dog knows is the Lost Dogs' Shelter.

'Every marriage operates in its own unique way. Every marriage has its own set of rules.

'One of our marriage rules was that I play the corporate-wife role for Kenneth. I assisted with entertaining – organised catering, smiled, remembered names of clients, etc. In return Kenneth played

21

the corporate-husband role for me. He accompanied me to functions and sometimes conferences, so I didn't look like a cormorant on a rock when I was outside my workplace.'

The Dog had no idea how a marriage worked but he was aware of rules, particularly *No Dogs Allowed*.

'I existed in a marriage of convenience and it had become very inconvenient, Dog. It was a messy marriage. A dog's breakfast.'

The Dog couldn't relate to this metaphor. He enjoys his breakfast of vitamin-packed pellets.

'Anyway, not only was my marriage a mess, but my whole life was one big mess. When I was made redundant at the beginning of last year, I decided to put my career on hold for twelve months. I spent a year – obsessed, possessed – writing a novel in the attic, and then a few more months in the editorial process after the book was contracted. But then my novel did a dead-cat bounce when my publisher went under, and I decided I had to change my life.

'So . . .' I checked the Dog was paying attention. He was.

'So I gave up cigarettes, chocolate bars and thick crusty peanut-butter sandwiches. I was just ready to give up Kenneth – find a new job, a new life, maybe a new partner – when my King Rat husband beat me to it. He gave me up.

'It was the night of my barely-50-something birthday. I had long since realised it wasn't worth the emotional energy arguing with Kenneth and was resigned to the fact he used the company for aspects of our personal life, such as asking his personal assistant, Clever Angela – now Kenneth's life partner – to organise a cake and flowers for my birthday.

'Kenneth enjoyed playing the role of caring husband occasionally. Lately he'd been into karaoke. Singing tacky love songs! Kenneth said it created good vibes for the company. Board members and favoured punters loved the personal touch. Like celebrating your wife's barely-50-something birthday. Not!

'However, Clever Angela's choice of the Green Ginger restaurant that night was perfect. The food was excellent – particularly the dessert: individual matcha pavlovas with an azuki bean cream and fresh raspberry coulis. And Clever Angela had taken note of my email: *Candles on cake will not be necessary!*

'I looked good too, thanks to Clever Angela discovering a designer boutique selling frocks that float past out-of-control parts of the body. (I'd put on weight from sitting for months at a computer in the attic, eating chocolate bars and thick crusty peanut-butter sandwiches while writing an ultimately unsuccessful novel.)

'After our dinner, Kenneth and I were having a nightcap in our lounge at home. Kenneth enjoyed the afterglow of an event that went well. He poured me a Scotch and produced a gift for me from his pocket. Surprise! A diamond ring. At least four carats! Instantly I smelt a rat.

'Kenneth had done this many times before – especially in the early years of our marriage. Bought me diamond rings when business was not going well. He knew I hated flashy rings, but diamonds were an excellent investment. And whenever we needed extra cash I surrendered the rings without a quibble.

'I remember Kenneth sitting down beside me and taking my hand. "I've bad news, Georgy."

'Another warning sign. Georgy was his pet name for me. Whenever he wanted something he used it.

'"The company's going into receivership. It's a tough call. We have to sell Montpellier Place, the other properties, and we're losing the leases on the cars. You'll be fine!" He gently patted my hand.

'I remember wrenching my hand from his grasp, and Kenneth taking it again as if we were playing an absurd child's game.

'"Georgy, while I'm delivering bad news, I have more to tell you. You've been a wonderful, supportive wife over the years . . . but I have to tell you I don't love you any more. I'm sorry, but I'm leaving,

Georgy. I'm moving in with Angela. It's best for everyone. Don't worry, you'll be fine."

'I stared at Kenneth's irritatingly unlined, tanned face. Had Clever Angela been booking him tanning sessions? I pulled my hand from his grasp and focused. Kenneth continued.

'"You're not to worry, Georgy. Julia and I have sorted the financial stuff. You'll be safe and comfortable."

'Safe and comfortable! Had our daughter Julia, our company accountant, helped Kenneth map his escape? Bloody hell! Kenneth had beat me to it. He was escaping before I had my escape plan on the drafting board.

'"Julia will meet with you soon and walk you through what's happening."

'Then Kenneth gave me a hug. "How about one last walk down the garden path, Georgy?" Translated: screw.'

This was the moment when the shit hit the fan. I remember I enjoyed writing the five graphic words in my journal – *the shit hit the fan*.

'I screamed as I've never screamed before. "Sod off, Kenneth!" Such a satisfying phrase.

'I sloshed my Scotch in his face. Then I threw the crystal glass at him, followed by the whole bloody bottle. Finally I threw the ring.

'When Kenneth started scrabbling on the floor in search of the ring, I seriously lost the plot. With perfect aim I threw every cloying, pristine piece of Limoges porcelain in the room at him until he ran out. God, how I'd hated those knick-knacks! They kept appearing, piece by piece, after Kenneth's overseas trips. The collection I didn't want.

'I remember grabbing another bottle of top-shelf whisky from Kenneth's atmosphere-controlled cellar and pouring myself a full glass. Then I vomited. Never could hold my alcohol.

'After a while I felt better, and dragged the whole bloody case of

Glenlivet up the cellar stairs to the kitchen. I smashed the tops and emptied each bottle down the sink. I fell asleep on the couch in the north-facing sunroom. I remember waking early in the morning and checking the lounge. It resembled a war zone. Kenneth had gone. He'd left Montpellier Place for good.

'I didn't read my journal entry to the writing workshop attendees, Dog. I mumbled something to Sweet-Scary Tutor about having root canal treatment and escaped.'

The Dog agreed it was probably not advisable to read my journal entry about King Rat Kenneth to workshop attendees. However, the Dog could relate to rats. The breed of dog he belongs to were very useful rat-catchers in the past.

The Dog watched me while I carefully counted the pages in my journal, pages that recorded 'a significant event in my not-too-distant past', and ripped them out – one by one. I tore each page into tiny, tiny, tiny pieces. The Dog didn't want to sleep outside tonight. He wanted to sleep inside on the worn mat in front of the no-fire fireplace. He hated the wind and the rain. Fair enough.

Tuesday 7 – Thursday 9 July

Already I've lost the habit of keeping a daily journal. I would have stayed in bed hiding under a goose-feather doona the last three days, except I could only find a heap of miserable blankets in Adrian's linen cupboard. And I needed to action the devious unwritten contractual stuff Adrian had left behind re: his writers' group.

A letter I found pinned to the front door declared I'm now official key keeper of Adrian's Shelly Beach Writers' Group. (Adrian's stand-in key keeper has flown the coop. Flown away to look after grandchildren while her son's incapacitated with a broken ankle.)

I'm responsible for confirming the seven potential members of Adrian's writers' group still want to take part.

Bloody hell!

ARGYLE

And the inaugural meeting will take place on 22 July.

According to the letter, Adrian's writers' group is the first community education program Shelly Beach has ever had. It's been touch and go, like pulling hens' teeth, to even rally seven members.

I put aside the enclosed list of potential members for Adrian's writers' group and opened the folder Adrian had left on the kitchen table. According to the enclosed instructions, as the newly anointed Shelly Beach Writers' Group key keeper I have to:

- Liaise with local author and tutor Bill Kruger (make sure Bill receives his fee and do whatever photocopying is required for the following meeting)
- Check the members on Adrian's list are still keen and remind them of the first meeting
- Open the community hall at 7 p.m.
- Switch the heater on
- Fill the urn and prepare the tea, coffee and supper
- Lock up

And there was a P.S.: *Don't lose the community hall key! Another one is being cut.*

Bloody hell!

On either the seventh or the eighth – the Dog and I can't remember which date – we trekked up McIntosh Hill to visit Pandora Papadopoulos (no. 1 on Adrian's writers' group list).

According to the letter that was pinned to Adrian's front door, Pandora Papadopoulos is renovating her deceased father's home (turning it into a B&B) and is suffering from burnout. She had a top corporate job and lost it. It was a piece of luck that her father passed away at the same time as she lost her job, since he left the house to her.

Pandora greeted us in overalls, protective helmet, industrial goggles and gloves. Minus helmet and goggles, her thirty-something – maybe forty-something – dazzling good looks managed to shine through a layer of plaster dust and paint splotches. For a woman who was burnt out she looked amazingly uncharred.

Pandora was happy to be a member of the writers' group and attend meetings, although she doubted she'd get much time to write. She was racing to complete renovations before the summer trade began. She wanted her B&B up and running by then.

I'm green with envy. This infuriatingly in-control woman has a plan and a deadline. She knows what she has to do by this summer.

The Dog was not happy about another potential trek up McIntosh Hill. We'll have to visit Violet Harris (no. 2 on Adrian's list) when she returns home from a cat show to remind her of the date of the inaugural meeting.

Today the Dog reminded me that it was Thursday so I was ready and waiting, dressed and in control, when a relieved neighbour left Bossy Child this morning. No wild woman wrapped in a blanket this time.

The child Adrian has bequeathed me is skinny with red corkscrew curls and a flat smile. She's numerically twelve years old – in reality an indeterminate age – and abrasive with an I-can-conquer-the-world attitude. I wonder how long it will take before she realises she can't?

Bossy Child made 'real' coffee for me, hot chocolate for herself.

'Adrian usually helps me with my homework.'

I listened to her spelling homework.

'Adrian usually cooks schnitzels on Thursdays. Can we have schnitzels tonight?'

'We can.'

'Good.'

The Dog and I walked her to school.

I signed Bossy Child in at the school office. On the way home

I called into Rupert's Butchery aka Harold's Butchery: 'Since Dad passed I haven't had the heart to change the sign.'

We bought some schnitzels – and some bones. 'Snitzels' are on special at Rupert's Butchery every Thursday.

'Should I tell Harold he has an issue with his spelling, Dog?'

The Dog thought it best not to go there.

At 3.30 we walked along the beach track within sound and sight of grey Shelly Beach bay to collect Bossy Child from school. Raining again. Bossy Child said Shelly Beach is always like this in winter. Very damp!

Later that evening: 'Your schnitzels were nearly as good as Adrian's, Gina.'

I took this nearly-compliment on board. 'Have you got more homework to do?'

I received a rolled-eye reply.

Bossy Child settled to do her homework and the Dog snoozed at her feet. With only a dog and three chickens to look after, plus child-minding (8–9 a.m., 3.30–7 p.m.) on Thursdays, I'm confident I can survive – and live within my budget – at least for the next six months until Adrian returns. I need time to develop a Plan A and B so I can move on with my life. And I can be key keeper for Adrian's writers' group – but I'm not writing another novel.

Friday 10 July

Bossy Child called after school to check how the Dog and I were progressing. 'Did you remember to feed the Girls?'

'Yes I did. Proof – no dead chickens lying in the henhouse.'

Rolled-eye look from Bossy Child as she made coffee for me and hot chocolate for herself. We sat on Adrian's front verandah and watched the rain as it pelted down. Bossy Child reminded me to tell Alf the verandah guttering was leaking and needed repairing. 'Did you check the leak in Bedroom One? Was there any rainwater in the bucket?'

'Yes. Just a few centimetres.'

Bossy Child loves to ask questions. She fires questions like bullets. Adrian apparently told her you learn by asking questions. 'Have you got any kids?'

'A daughter. She's grown up.'

'Where does she live?'

'In the city.'

'Do you see her?'

'Not very often.'

'Do you talk to her?'

'Not lately.'

'You could talk to her on the phone. Mum talks to me on the phone when she's working.'

'My mobile doesn't work.'

I received a disbelieving look. 'It should. Where is it?'

'In the bin in Bedroom Two.'

'Whaaat!'

Bossy Child returned with the discarded mobile.

According to her my mobile is 'retrievable'. Amazing. I just need a new plan. I agreed to drive to Sea Haven and take out one.

Bossy Child walked me to the phone on Adrian's desk in Bedroom Two. 'You could always use this one too. Didn't you read P for Phone in Adrian's manual?'

'No.'

'Have you got any friends?'

'Yes.'

'Don't you want to talk to them?'

'Not particularly.'

Accusingly: 'You should give them Adrian's phone number so they can phone and see how you're going.'

'I'll do it later.'

'You don't like talking to people, do you?'

'Not particularly.'

'I'll do it for you. Adrian lets me do his phone stuff. Where's your address book? I'll ring up your friends and leave Adrian's phone number. Do you want to write down stuff for me to say – or can I make it up?'

Bloody hell. 'Make it up.'

I found my address book. Bossy Child in her I-can-conquer-the-world voice dialled Hester, Eva and Clare's numbers, plus my daughter Julia's number, and left her message on their answering machines.

'Hi, I'm Terri Waters. I'm ringing for Gina Laurel-Scott who cannot come to the phone now. Her new number is 272 8349. You're welcome to contact her at your earliest convenience. Thank you. Goodbye.'

Bloody hell! Half an hour later, the phone rang, interrupting our game of Scrabble. It was Julia. I indicated to Terri to stay put. We listened to the answering machine pick up.

'Hi, Gina, it's Julia. Received your new phone number. I hope you're settling in well. Keep in contact. Speak soon, bye.'

Bossy Child smirked. Then her mother rang to say she'd settled Sam, and the Dog and I walked Bossy Child next door.

The wind and rain were lashing the trees. It felt like Sea View Cottage was going to do a *Wizard of Oz* take-off at any moment. The Dog was wimpy. He definitely doesn't have a Toto temperament. I let him inside and made myself a hot chocolate. From the window we watched Adrian's winter garden bending and twisting in the wind and torrential rain. The sound of the waves swallowing up the Shelly Beach foreshore added to the feeling of gloom and doom.

The Dog wanted to know how I'd ended up as his sitter. He wanted to hear a story so he could take his mind off the storm.

I thought back to my last meeting with my daughter.

'I didn't score a good report card as a mother. Martha, my perfect mother-in-law, was always there to take my place. I never took my daughter to school. I never picked her up from school. I missed her starring role in *Bye Bye Birdie* and a major speech night. I probably missed a bunch of other important occasions in my daughter's life that she never even bothered to tell me about. Her grandmother, my perfect mother-in-law, would have gone with her. And Julia was always her daddy's girl.

'Martha had style. She was the sort of grandmother a young girl would be happy to acknowledge. And my perfect mother-in-law, with elegance and ease, kept our home – using my income – running smoothly.

'I remember reading an article in a pop-psych mag in a dentist's surgery. It said men who are very close to their mothers do not make five-star marriage partners. I can vouch for this.

'My work–life balance was out of balance, Dog. For years I thrived and enjoyed a life that consisted of ninety per cent work and ten per cent life.'

The Dog appreciated the metaphor. If you don't have good balance you can't jump and catch a ball in your mouth.

I gathered up the Dog and placed him on my knee. 'Thunder and lightning can't hurt you. If you stop shaking like a battery toy, I'll tell you how I met your owner. It was after I'd left, or was forced to leave, my previous home – Montpellier Place. I stayed first with my friend Hester, and then with Eva. You've met Eva!'

The Dog remembered Eva's snippy red heels.

'Anyway, I was sleeping in Eva's study on a bone-crunching camp bed. The room was crammed with stacks of her latest boyfriend's car and fitness magazines, torturous gym equipment plus an electronic sound system. Hardly room to scratch yourself!'

No sympathy from the Dog. There's no room to scratch in his kennel and he doesn't complain.

I ignored him and continued. 'My daughter Julia had traced me to Eva's. She'd phoned and said I had to visit. There were papers to sign.

'I found appropriate clothes to wear – my Armani trench coat that covers a multitude of body and clothing sins.

'Eva with the snippy red heels was fluffing around trying to help me get ready.'

The Dog was keeping up with my tragic tale.

'She was raving on, "Thank God Clare packed for you! Have you got enough money to get to Julia's? Pay attention to every word Julia says. Listen closely. Take notes if you think you'll forget information. Be prepared for the worst, Gina. As a co-director of the Laurel-Scott Corporation you'll be taken to the cleaners. Do – you – under-stand – Gina?" For a childless female, Eva can do a good take on Red Riding Hood's mother but dressed in a stylishly cut pinstriped suit and wearing very little under the jacket.

'I understood what she meant, Dog. I was getting a clear under-standing of my carless, cashless and homeless place on this planet.

'In consideration of my newly acquired zero income and lack of status, I'd decided to avoid taxis. I'd taken up the challenge of travel-ling on public transport. Eva scribbled how-to instructions to Julia's place via bus.

'Like a pirate counting paces to buried treasure, I followed Eva's directions to my daughter's house. Julia met me at the entrance of the over-restored and over-renovated Victorian house she and her partner Simon call home.

'I could feel Julia's unease as I dutifully followed her into the sparkling stainless-steel kitchen where she made coffee for me and herbal tea for herself. She collected a pile of documents and we moved to the dining area. She said consolingly, "This must be a ter-rible shock for you, Gina."

'Julia calls me Gina, or sometimes Mother with a capital M. She started calling me Gina the first year we travelled overseas together. She didn't want people to know she was travelling with her mother.

'I ignored Julia's comment. We sat at the table in her stainless-steel kitchen while she delivered cold hard facts accompanied with small twisted smiles. Facts I didn't want to hear but already knew. Fact one: as a silent partner I was equally responsible for the debt the Laurel-Scott Corporation incurred. Fact two: my home, several other properties and their contents would have to be sold to pay Laurel-Scott Corporation debts. And fact three: the company's cars were leased and had been returned to the respective car companies. The good news was Julia didn't think I would have to declare bankruptcy.

'I remember tidying the documents in front of me while I registered the pathetic piece of 'good news'. 'Sign here' tags hung out like flags from the pristine pile.

'Julia continued, "Fortunately, I'm not a company director, Gina, and qualify as an employee." She indicated the tags on the documents I had to sign. "Simon and I are in the process of setting up our own accounting business. We'll do everything we can to see you're settled and happy." She indicated a page I'd missed.

'Julia waited until I'd finished my coffee. She wanted me to see a surprise she and Simon had planned for me.

'Dutifully I followed my stylish daughter across the tiled entrance hall to the stairs. Julia made hard work of the stairs. Her humpty-dumpty figure was slowing her down. I tried to calculate – she'd have to be around thirty-one or thirty-two weeks now.

'Julia's pregnancy has been a joyless journey. She set the boundaries for our motherly chats. She'd made it very clear, when she and Simon announced their unplanned pregnancy, that she didn't want constant queries about her state of health. No fuss. She was continuing to work as usual. Pregnancy was a perfectly normal function for women. Lesson over for her mother Gina.

'Upstairs, Julia stopped outside what had been the old servants' quarters a century ago. She opened the door with a flourish. We walked through a bedroom complete with sitting nook and side-street view, into a kitchenette, through a linking en suite, to a nursery. Bingo!

'My daughter thought I'd be happy living in the nanny flatlet helping to care for the new baby when it arrives. A feel-good solution for the problem of what to do with a dumped wife and a mother who needs something to do in her life now she's tossed her dream of becoming a novelist out the window and looks an unlikely candidate to re-enter the workforce.

'Julia explained she didn't expect me to be a full-time nanny. She planned to employ a night nanny for the first few months – until the baby settled. I could do the day shift. When Simon and Julia were home in the evenings, weekends and holidays, my time would be my own. And she'd still employ Lily to clean on Mondays and Fridays.'

The Dog knew nothing about nannies or babies. To his knowledge he's never fathered pups. That's a touchy subject.

More thunder and lightning. The Dog was keen for me to continue my tale.

'So Julia popped the vital question: *What did I think?*

'I remember watching her lower herself into an eggshell-white nursery chair, ready to receive my answer. What did I think? I thought quickly. I said that everything had happened so fast. I needed time.

'Julia was in her win-win negotiating role. She assured me there was no hurry. They could move me into the nanny flatlet whenever I made my decision.

'Thankfully the doorbell interrupted Julia's negotiating. We went downstairs to greet Adrian – your owner – and his daughter Tania.'

The Dog's ears pricked up.

'You've met Tania, one of Adrian's daughters.'

Of course he had.

'Tania is my daughter's best friend and handmaiden. Adrian had been staying with Tania in her city apartment to finalise arrangements for his trip to England – you know, to look after his older daughter's children during her chemotherapy. You must have known about that. Someone had to look after you while Adrian was away.'

The Dog feigned ignorance.

I continued with my cringe-inducing story. 'Anyway, Adrian was convinced we'd met before. I can't remember him being on the scene when Julia and Tania were growing up. Tania lived with her mum and her sister, and later a step-dad. Ralph? Rudolph? Maybe Adrian was beardless then?'

The Dog can't remember Adrian without a beard but he likes Adrian's friendly blue eyes that crinkle at the corners when Adrian smiles.

'Julia poured coffee for Adrian, and took Tania to check out the new nanny flatlet decorated in seamless shades of white. Your owner joined me on Julia's patio with the designer water feature. He said he'd heard I was moving in as soon as the baby was born.

'I told him I hadn't decided yet. And then like an angst-ridden adolescent, I launched into my tragic narrative. Did he know I'd been dumped for a personal assistant half my age? Did he know I'd been made redundant a year ago? Did he know that the Laurel-Scott Corporation had gone into receivership? Did he know I'd lost my Audi and had to move out of my home? And had he heard the contract for my novel had been terminated?

'Your owner sipped his coffee and listened while I poured out my inappropriate confession. Thankfully, his daughter Tania returned and saved him from making any comment. What could your owner say, Dog?'

The Dog agreed his owner was wise to say nothing.

'Tania and your owner offered me a lift back to Eva's. I accepted. A repeat journey on public transport didn't appeal.

'Back at Eva's flat, I tried to wipe from my mind that I'd told your owner, a practical stranger, my overly personal stuff. Instead I contemplated my future. To be or not to be a super granny?

'My baby-rearing record is not good, Dog. Martha, perfect mother-in-law, moved in with us and cared for Julia from when she was six weeks old. Cash flow from Kenneth's business deals was unreliable. My salary kept us afloat.

'What do you think, Dog? Was this new baby-rearing opportunity a gift from heaven? An opportunity to heal my relationship with my daughter? I know I've refused Julia's initial offer – but the nanny flatlet door isn't closed. I can still look after Julia's baby when I leave Shelly Beach. If I decide to leave early, I'll find a replacement dog-sitter.'

The Dog had fallen asleep. So much for his storm phobia.

Saturday 11 July
I woke early, fed the Dog and left at our planned time to visit Violet Harris (no. 2 on Adrian's writers' group list.) We followed Adrian's map with *V. H.* marked on it. It was impossible to miss Violet's farmhouse. Beside the *Moggy's Manor* and *Kittens for Sale* signs over the entrance gate, the house was virtually jumping off its foundations. We stopped to regain our breath, and waited until the final blasts of the '1812 Overture' ended, then I yahooed at the door.

Violet answered, a sharp-eyed seventy-something woman in a shabby cardigan and running shoes with a ginger cat twining between her legs. She had a bread knife in her hand: 'I just love conducting the "1812".'

She turned her hearing aid up, and we were ready for business. Violet fossicked in cupboards until she found a plastic container, and filled it with water for the Dog.

'Tie Hugo near the garage. He's nervous around the cats.'

Violet pushed cats off the kitchen table and chairs so we could sit down. I drank my tea, ate coconut slice and tried not to count cats. How many kittens were in the shopping basket in the corner?

Violet thanked me for alerting her to the date of the inaugural meeting for the writers' group.

'I only joined the group to make up the numbers – Adrian wanted to get a grant to run the group and needed a minimum of seven people. Another cup of tea? More coconut slice? I'm glad you're the new key keeper. Don't let Digby Prentice-Hill get his hands on Adrian's group!'

I looked puzzled.

'Digby Prentice-Hill lives in the house – well, more a castle, really – at the top of the hill. He and Adrian are always competing. Can't help themselves. Digby's all set for Adrian's writers' group. Now he's finished planting his olive trees he's looking for another project. Says he has a novel in him waiting to get out. Could have. Have you got a novel inside you?'

I indicated I had a mouthful of coconut slice and avoided giving a mind-your-own-business answer. Violet poured me a second cup of tea. 'Adrian will never get his writers back if Digby takes over.'

I stirred my tea, stopped counting cats and listened as Violet shared privileged Shelly Beach information.

'After Digby's wife, Annette, passed away he lost the plot. Did you read about the tragedy?'

I shook my head.

'Annette was a lovely woman. A good neighbour. It was in the city newspapers. Tragic accident. She fell from their bedroom balcony – instant death. The gardener found her body in the petunia bed the next morning. Had to wake Digby to tell him about it. There was an inquest. Verdict: no funny business.' Violet gave a sneaky chuckle. 'Excellent plot for a whodunnit!'

Violet's a prolific writer of whodunnits. She's written six – the Agatha Christie kind. 'Starting on my seventh! Keep them in a box under the cats' sofa in the front room. Always on the lookout for a new whodunnit plot. Another cup of tea? That's the last of the coconut slice. Only seed cake left.'

'No, thank you. I have to be going.'

We went outside and I untied the Dog. He seemed pleased to see me.

'You'd better carry Hugo. Hill's too much for a little dog like that. He's not a spring chicken, you know.'

Bloody hell! How was I to know Adrian's dog is classified as a senior citizen? He seems frisky enough.

Violet pointed out Digby Prentice-Hill's castle. 'Brilliant view of the bay from the upstairs balcony. Stunning homestead. It was his late wife's family home. Digby's worked hard restoring it to its former glory. Don't bother calling on him today. He's away at a conference. I'll let him know about the inaugural meeting date for Adrian's writers' group. You can count on him being there.'

Violet watched from her gate while I began the descent of McIntosh Hill. I carried the Dog and made plans for tomorrow as we progressed down the slope. 'I'll contact the shortlisted author-slash-tutor, and locate the other members of Adrian's writers' group.'

The Dog was asleep. Sleeping dogs are easier but heavier to carry than wide-awake dogs.

Sunday 12 July
Bossy Child called to check on the Dog and Adrian's chickens: a useless mission.

'Adrian's livestock is alive and kicking.'

Bossy Child gave me a cross-eyed look.

'Your eyes will get stuck if you keep doing that.'

My expert advice was ignored.

'You're going to be key keeper for Adrian's writers' group, aren't you?'

'Where did you hear that?'

'Everyone says you're going to be.'

'It's not set in concrete yet. And it wasn't in my contract.'

'What about Adrian's other folders? Have you delivered them yet?'

'What other folders?'

'Adrian said if you hadn't found them after a week I could give them to you.'

'Well, I haven't found them.'

Bossy Child returned with two bulky folders tied with string in a complex criss-cross pattern. 'They were on the desk in Bedroom Two. Right in front of your eyes, Gina! Here's a note Adrian left for you.'

Bloody hell! Is Adrian going to be my Macbeth's ghost? I read his note – more like a military command.

Dear Gina,
Ran out of time. Can you deliver these folders for me?
Terri can tell you where to find the recipients.
Regards,
Adrian

'Well?' I looked at Bossy Child. 'Who do I give these folders to?'

'The action committee folder is for Bianca. She's also agreed to join Adrian's writers' group. She owns Scissors salon. She's got gorgeous mermaid hair. The book club folder is for my teacher, Mr Colovich. He's going to join the writers' group too.'

Adrian runs a book club? Plus the writers' group and an informal library? 'Can't you give the book club one to your teacher?'

'No. Adrian said you had to give it to him.'

Bossy Child refused to draw me a map. 'You don't need a map. You can't get lost, Gina. You know where the school is, and you can't miss Bianca's shop. It's the only hairdresser's on Beach Road.'

'Right.'

Bossy Child went home to tidy her room. I fastened Adrian's living room drapes with safety pins to shut out the reflective inky blackness, and plugged in Adrian's antique room heater.

'Another mission, Dog. Two folders to offload. And two more writers' group members to meet and remind about the inaugural meeting.'

I decided to read myself to sleep as opposed to popping sleeping pills with their accompanying disturbing dreams. Adrian's bookshelves are loaded with enough eclectic reading material to satisfy the fussiest reader.

Monday 13 July

Panic stations. I decided to action the writers' group inaugural meeting.

The Dog listened while I phoned the Kingston Council. 'Is the local member for Kingston aware he's opening the Shelly Beach Writers' Group inaugural meeting? The meeting's on Wednesday week at 7.30 p.m.'

Reply from a bubbly secretary: 'Yes, he is. And he's looking forward to it.'

'Obviously, Dog, there aren't many Shelly Beach occasions where a local MP can star and spread bonhomie to small seaside-town taxpayers.'

The Dog ignored me.

I checked Adrian's list. I placed ticks beside Pandora and Violet. And I placed a tick beside Digby Prentice-Hill, writers' group member no. 3.

'Violet said Digby was a definite, didn't she, Dog?'

The Dog couldn't remember. Lee Wang, hot young chef, was on the list too. I made a mental note to remind him about the meeting when he dropped by later – if he dropped by. I grabbed the folders to give to Bianca and Josh – writers' group members numbers 4 and 5.

'We have to tell Bianca and Josh about the inaugural meeting, Dog. Remind me that I have to contact the author-slash-tutor Bill Kruger, too.'

I read the note beside Daphne Schwarz's name (writers' group member no. 7) on Adrian's list. Daphne is wending her way home from a birdwatching trek up north.

'Bloody hell! I'll have to check if Daphne Schwarz is going to be back in time for the meeting. Adrian's writers' group is driving me mad.'

No comment from the Dog. He thought I could be suffering from nicotine withdrawal. It hasn't been all that long since I gave up smoking.

I ignored him. I grabbed the two folders and the Dog before fast-pacing my way along Beach Road to Bossy Child's school. Josh Colovich, Bossy Child's 'fave' teacher, was umpiring a netball game. I waited until half-time, shivering in a cold wind straight off the bay, to hand over the book club folder and remind Josh about the writers' group meeting.

The tall, smiling teacher was wearing a Shelly Beach Lifesavers tracksuit and jogged over to meet me. Josh is an exceedingly pleasant young man. It seems Shelly Beach is a breeding place for smiling, pleasant people. 'I'm cool to look after book club meetings – keep them running smoothly – until Adrian returns. You'll have to join our book club, Gina. I'll let you know when our next meeting is. I'm looking forward to writers' group. I've found the novel I started writing at university. I'm keen to move on with it.'

I mentally ticked no. 5 on Adrian's writers' group list. Another budding novelist with a burning urge to put pen to paper.

Josh directed me to Scissors salon, although it's impossible to miss in Shelly Beach's one-blink-and-you've-passed-it seaside metropolis.

(The Dog says that if you like to drive with your head hanging out the window, one woof and you're through Shelly Beach.)

The Dog stayed outside on threat of death if he so much as took a paw-step away from the front door. I went inside and introduced myself to Bianca, owner of the hair salon with a brilliant view of Shelly Beach bay. I recognised her because of the mermaid hair. It was captured in a seaweed tangle on top of her head.

'I guessed you were Adrian's house-sitter because of the Dog. Isn't he gorgeous?'

The Dog had invited himself inside. He gave Bianca one of his fake grins and lay down under the washbasins.

Bianca was expertly finishing the last tweaks to a client's hair. I waited until the client left and we continued our conversation in the mirror while Bianca tidied up for her next shampoo and blow-wave.

'I'm so excited about joining Adrian's writers' group.'

I made a mental note to tick member no. 4 on Adrian's list.

'Bill Kruger, our tutor, was in for a trim this morning. He was telling me how to find the spellcheck thingy on the computer. You have to look for the red squiggly lines under words.'

I nodded.

'I'm a terrible speller.' Buzzy Bianca continued cleaning and chatting at a fast pace. 'Bill's prepared for the first meeting. He's so nervous. He's spent hours doing how-to-write-a-novel stuff. Everyone is so pleased you're looking after the writers' group. Bill is so grateful to Adrian for organising the grant to cover his tutoring fees. Things were getting tough for the family. You don't make a fortune as a writer, do you?'

I agreed.

'Except if you write books about wizards and vampires.'

I placed the Shelly Beach Action Committee folder on the mirrored bench. Bianca is replacement secretary for the action committee – 'just until Adrian returns in the summer'.

Her salon cleaned and tidied for her next shampoo and blow-wave, Bianca checked her reflection in the mirror. She released the pins from her mermaid hair and shook it loose. It floated around her. 'That feels better. I don't suppose you've heard yet, but I've just got the masseuse's job at Sea Haven Resort.'

Bianca, blue eyes dancing, explained that Sea Haven is the upmarket tourist town twenty minutes' drive away. 'It's got everything: cool cafes, shops and a cinema. Sea Haven Resort is five-star. Gorgeous views of the sea from each room. I could be late for some meetings because of work. Does it matter?'

I gave a comforting shrug.

Bianca lowered her voice to deliver secret information. 'Members are so glad Digby isn't key keeper for the writers' group.'

Another client entered the salon. Snippy goss came to a halt.

As we raced home in time to open up Adrian's library for Lee, I breathlessly questioned the Dog. 'Why can't Digby Prentice-Hill be key keeper for Adrian's bloody writers' group? Does it matter? Surely Adrian can get his act together when he returns and regain control?'

The Dog wanted nothing to do with small-town politics. He should. It concerns his owner.

Lee cycled into Adrian's driveway about 3. 'Would you like a cup of coffee?'

I watched mesmerised as the tall, young-enough-to-be-my-son Lee Wang made two cups and effortlessly stacked four new packets of Brazilian coffee in Adrian's cupboard. One answer to the question of Adrian's well-stocked store cupboard.

We drank excellent coffee and talked books. Lee borrowed another Pulitzer Prize-winning book from Adrian's shelves. We swapped fill-the-gap information.

In a former life Lee was the hot young chef at Lemongrass – a restaurant that's won endless awards. I'd actually dined at Lemongrass many times in my former life. I entertained important clients there. I'd probably eaten Lee's food – brilliant, stylish dishes.

We both agreed it's a small world.

Lee had assumed I was going to be key keeper for the writers' group as Adrian had mentioned I was a writer. Bloody hell! I checked if Lee was able to make it to the inaugural meeting.

Yes! He was confirmed for Adrian's writers' group.

I mentally ticked member no. 6 on the list.

Lee's writing a novel – a sexy crime thriller. Of course he is. He's finding plenty of time to write – as you do when you're stuck in a backwater like Shelly Beach.

'I'm looking forward to workshopping my novel. I've a friend who works in publishing. He's read a few chapters. Says I'm on track with the plot and action but my characters need more development.'

I looked at this stunning young man. He really was serious. He wasn't joking. He was prepared to workshop his novel – even the sexy text! Expose his writing to other people! Correction, Gina: not other people. Other writers.

I watched Lee cycle off, backpack full of Adrian's books and a head full of characters that needed developing.

'Do you think Lee has a partner, Dog? A girlfriend? He must have. She probably lives in the city. Lee would make a catch for any girl.'

The Dog hadn't the faintest idea about Lee Wang's romantic connections in or out of Shelly Beach.

The Dog pushed his way to his fave position in front of Adrian's antique heater. I moved my feet and stopped fantasising about a man young enough to be my son, and checked my list of things to do for Adrian's writers' group.

'I've confirmed six members, Dog.'

The Dog was impressed.

'What do you think? Will Adrian's writers' group become my

Achilles heel? My Moby Dick? Coordinating a small group of writers' can't be all that difficult, can it, Dog?'

The Dog avoided answering my question. He was standing, ready for guard-dog duty.

Tuesday 14 July

I had to get to the bank in Sea Haven as well as buy a new plan for my mobile phone. The Dog thought it'd be a good idea to drive – then he could come too. He's partial to any kind of travel where you can stick your head out the window and the wind blows your fur.

Was it safe for a dog to travel with its head stuck out a window? Bloody hell! I hunted in Adrian's shed and found a box. I decided the Dog could sit in the box, on the floor, in the back of the car. No way was I losing a dog from a car window.

I retrieved the car key from Adrian's meticulously labelled key board, the perfect set-up for a literate burglar. After wasting an hour trying to start the car we walked to Piece of Cake. Alf returned and helped me jump-start it. Riding a bike would have been quicker, but there's no bicycle in Adrian's Ali Baba shed. Not even a pumpkin.

I purchased a new plan for my mobile phone. Now I'm fully connected to society – if I remember to turn my mobile on. I checked that my new bank account had been set up successfully, which it had, and saw it included cash from the sale of my diamond ring – my fortuitous birthday gift from Kenneth. Eva found it among the pieces of broken Limoges porcelain when she was doing a final clean-up of Montpellier Place.

My bank account total also included the first miserly advance from my terminated novel. I was happy with my first advance at the time. I accepted that first-time authors couldn't expect huge advances, and anyway, I planned to become a bestselling author. I'd earn huge royalties so I could keep writing for years. When my publishing company went down and my contract was terminated, I decided to return my advance with a note – *Please donate this cheque to the charity of your choice*. Thankfully, I didn't, as I'm now a charity of choice.

And I'm eternally grateful to my friends for salvaging what they could from my train wreck of a previous life. I may be trying to avoid them all now (there's only so many pitying looks one can take), but that doesn't mean I'm not grateful. And especially so to Clare for her meticulous cataloguing and marketing of my designer clothes.

I recalled a recent phone message from Clare: *I've left your clothes at Silver Heirlooms, Gina. The manager says vintage clothes like yours are selling for a fortune.*

'Let's hope my clothes sell well, Dog. I never imagined a stacked wardrobe of designer gear – impulse buys for conferences and one-off events – could turn out to be useful. If I manage my survival cache frugally and continue to endorse the age-old habit of thrift, I should have enough cash to meet my goal: survive until Adrian returns.'

The Dog thought I sounded mean when I talked about my friends. Not that he has any.

'Don't misunderstand me, Dog. I'm really grateful for the support my friends have given me. It's just that I've lost my role in our group. I've always been the fixer, the smoother, the Mother Goose. I hate being on the receiving end.'

The Dog understood. He likes being top dog when he runs with the pack.

Wednesday 15 July
You do not have to apologise for not writing in your
journal – or for writing very little!
– Sweet-Scary Tutor

Today I did absolutely nothing of any interest. I would have wallowed in bed the whole day except the thought of a starving dog and dead chickens made me get up. I needn't have worried. The Dog was happy digging his little heart out and the Girls looked very chirpy. The Dog had let them out of their henhouse and they were dining on worms.

Thursday 16 July

After we collected Bossy Child from school we walked along the beach. Bossy Child had homework to do: seashore observations.

The grey sky was reflected in Shelly Beach's grey sea. The Dog and I survived arctic conditions, frozen eyelashes and fur for the sake of Bossy Child's homework. And the Dog entered a dancing duel with a crab, making a strategic exit just in time to avoid a nasty nip.

We had heated arguments on the way home re: how does a hermit crab decide which other crab's shell to live in? Does he wait until he finds a discarded one, or does he wait until another crab is leaving and take possession?

As soon as we arrived home, doubting Bossy Child wanted to use Adrian's computer to check the answer. 'I'll look on the internet. Can I use it? He always lets me use it.'

'Go ahead. If Adrian said you could use his computer while he's away it's fine with me.'

Bossy Child bolted to the computer and logged on. I followed her into Bedroom Two. She stared at me accusingly as emails flooded Adrian's inbox. 'You'll have to reply, Gina.'

'Open the last one. Delete the rest!'

'There's a heap of emails from Leonda.'

'Who's Leonda?'

'Adrian's friend.'

'Is she young or old?'

'Old, but not as old as you.'

'Delete them.'

'Gina!'

'Tell Adrian to tell Leonda that he doesn't live here now. He can send her his UK email address.'

'Is that all?'

'Yes. Send it.'

'Can I send Adrian an email?'

'Do what you like. He's paying the bill.'

When Bossy Child returned to the living room she found me channelling a hermit crab. 'I'm going to inhabit Adrian's shell. While he's away I've taken his shell over. I'll use his email and his car, and I'm throwing his junk out of my shell.'

'You can't!'

'I can. Just watch me!'

'You can't throw Adrian's stuff away!'

'I can.'

'But it's not exactly Adrian's stuff. It was here when he bought Sea View Cottage.'

I relented. 'We won't throw his junk away. We'll store in it the shed. Can you find some boxes?'

A relieved Bossy Child made several trips to the shed, returning with a stack of cardboard boxes. She found a notebook and a pencil. 'I'm making a plan of all the rooms in Adrian's house and marking where everything belongs. You'll have to put Adrian's things back before you leave!'

I ignored her. For the next hour I tossed Adrian's (or a previous owner's) junk to Bossy Child. She carefully packed, labelled cartons and drew her location map so we'd be able to replace Adrian's (or a previous owner's) stuff when I left.

I removed most of the eclectic collection of framed pictures from the walls. I kept two: a Utrillo street print and the ubiquitous Van Gogh fishing boats.

'Out of the way, Dog!' I cleared the floor to attack the hideous drapes covering the windows by some miracle and the use of multiple safety pins.

The Dog went into hiding.

'You're mean to Hugo.'

'No, I'm not!'

'He hates being called Dog.'

The Dog came out from under the couch.

'Dog is a good name for a funny-looking dog. It's a quirky name, isn't it, Dog? What breed are you, anyway?'

'He doesn't look funny. He's a terrier-cross: fifty per cent terrier and fifty per cent something else. We're not sure. You have to call him Hugo. If you don't he doesn't know you're talking to him.'

I ignored Bossy Child. 'Hugo's an extremely stupid name for a dog.'

'Adrian called him Hugo.'

I surrendered. 'Right, I'll call him Hugo. Hugo! See, he doesn't come. He prefers to be called Dog.'

'You're not saying Hugo correctly. It has to sound French. *Oooh-goh.*'

Hugo went into hiding again.

'Why on earth did Adrian give the Dog a French name?'

'Adrian was reading a book by a French author . . . something Hugo.'

'Victor Hugo?'

'Yes. Hugo didn't have a name when we brought him home from the Lost Dogs' Shelter.'

That would be right. Saint Adrian would never buy a dog from a pet shop. He'd rescue a dog from death row.

The Dog came out of hiding. He went out the pet door and returned with his leash in his mouth. 'See what you've done now,' Bossy Child said. 'He's totally confused. He thinks we're taking him for a walk!'

Then Joan rang and Bossy Child left. Very reluctantly.

'Don't worry, I'm taking full responsibility for the junk. I promise not to build a bonfire and burn Adrian's stuff. You won't get into trouble!' I called after her.

The Dog watched with interest while I spent most of the night moving furniture and scrubbing every surface, cleaning windows and putting order into Adrian's bookshelves. A satisfying librarian task.

I discovered a heavy cream bedcover in the linen cupboard to camouflage the lumpy couch. I found cream linen pillowcases to replace the ugly cushion covers. 'I'll invest in new curtains and cushion covers. I'll take them with me when I move out.'

The Dog thought that was a good idea.

I took a torch and ventured into the dark and rain to plunder leafless filigree branches from Adrian's mulberry tree.

Around the living room I placed a vase of elegant mulberry branches, a green glass bowl of eggs from the Girls and Adrian's emergency candles in empty bottles.

Last touch: I located the monogrammed hand towels and jasmine guest soap Clare had packed for me in Suitcase Two. I placed the soap and the hand towels in a fan pattern beside the washbasin in Adrian's dodgy bathroom. I'd taken ownership of Adrian's shell – for a short time.

Friday 17 July

I was lying on Adrian's lumpy couch staring out into the blackness of an early Shelly Beach evening. No city lights reflecting in the sky.

I was in my routine of 6.30 dinner – scrambled eggs tonight (from the Girls) – followed by a lukewarm shower. Adrian's ancient hot-water system takes all day to reach a bearable level of warmth. I was preparing to luxuriate in an evening of reading, wrapped in my fine-wool bathrobe. This had been a guiltless illegal purchase, along with sundry items like six pairs of fine-wool socks, a toaster, an iron, and towels and sheets. The last purchases I could make on my credit cards before Laurel-Scott Corporation accounts were closed for good. I collected a rug and filled a hot-water bottle. The Dog was snoozing near the antique radiator.

My sliver of peace was destroyed by a car pulling into the drive. Headlights shone into the room, I heard loud male voices, car doors slamming. I answered the door and shielded my eyes to squint at the male figure outlined by the headlights.

'Gina?'

Bloody hell! It was James! Clare's husband, James. Intelligent, charming James. Smart James, who'd been part of our original university group. When he married, he slipped away from our group, and Clare, his new wife, slipped in.

'What's wrong?'

'Not a thing. I was nearby and I promised Clare I'd call in to see how you were getting on. Is it all right if I come in for a while?'

'Of course!'

James returned to the car, spoke to the driver and collected a box from the boot. The car drove off.

I led James into the kitchen where he deposited the box containing two bottles of champagne and food on the kitchen bench.

'You look great, Gina!'

He had to be lying. I looked 'great' two years ago in my size-eight corporate-chic gear and with twice-weekly blow-dried hair. After my author-in-the-attic year, wearing the same clothes for up to three days running and existing on a diet of mainly chocolate bars, I was well aware I didn't look 'great'.

'Any glasses for the bubbly?'

I found glasses in Adrian's cupboard and watched as James expertly poured the Dom Perignon. Bloody hell!

'I asked the chef to rustle up a few nibbles for us.'

I gave a slight smile as I sipped my champagne. Kenneth always said, 'You can't beat French champagne to impress punters.' Damn Kenneth. Damn him for beating me to it. Leaving me dumped, flat broke and vulnerable.

I took a sip and put the glass down. Champagne has never impressed me. Where the hell had James come from?

'The company's holding our annual professional development seminar at Sea Haven. We've dumped the "adventure" stuff and gone with bonding instead. The board agreed with me that the staff need the bonding – especially as I've had to lay off so many people this year.'

'Right.' Now his visit made some sense.

'You really do look wonderful, Gina.'

Another faux compliment. I do not look 'wonderful' wearing a gown hiding an overweight body and with bird's nest hair that hasn't seen a hairdresser in months.

'Settling down? Enjoying life here?'

The Dog stirred in his sleep.

Lie, Gina. 'Yes, I am. Surprisingly. I like the quiet.'

'Bit chilly! Like me to light a fire?'

'Go ahead.'

The wood bucket was full of kindling, and logs were stacked by the fireplace. In about five minutes James had a fire blazing.

I looked on jealously. Fire-lighting practice is going to be top of my to-do list tomorrow.

James found his way round Adrian's kitchen and opened the chef's packages: cheese, paté, olives. He arranged them on a plate. He pulled Adrian's coffee table in front of the couch, carried the nibbles over and topped my glass up. He checked out Adrian's CD collection. 'Do you mind if I select something?'

I gave a noncommittal shrug.

My soothing Mozart was exchanged for cafe jazz.

An hour passed in the unbelievably pleasant ambience James created. No wonder Clare runs round him like a besotted cow with a long-lost calf.

Then came the pitch. I could feel it coming. James, my friend's husband, did not need to be here.

He pushed wisps of my hair behind my ear. His fingers travelled softly down my cheek to my neck. He gently stroked the side of my neck. Then his hands moved to my shoulders, carefully massaging them. My body relaxed at his touch. 'You're very tense, Gina.'

I watched, hypnotised, as he took my hand, his fingers tracing the veins. 'I can find a place in my life for you, Gina. We've always been good together.'

Silence.

Bloody hell! Always been good together? When were we good together? Twenty-nine years ago? James and I had been a couple at university, but for a very short time. Nothing serious. That was before Kenneth came on the scene. And it was B.C. – Before Clare. Before James became my friend's husband.

'I travel a lot. I can fly you anywhere in the world. We can meet up. Have a brilliant time together.'

Bloody hell! That woke the Dog up. Good Dog! He needed to go outside to pee.

I pulled my gown tighter around me. I moved away from James and took the Dog outside. I took deep breaths in the cold sea air. I was ready to face James again. Smart James with his tantalising proposition. I settled the Dog on the mat in front of the fire. I didn't return to the couch.

'Tea or coffee, James?'

'Coffee.'

'Italian, German or Brazilian blend?' Thank you, Adrian, for your cupboard of coffee.

James chose the Brazilian. I ground the beans. While the coffee percolated, I set out mugs, a jug of milk and a bowl of sugar on the kitchen table.

James was getting the message. I had to deliver a tactful no-go reply, yet keep his ego intact. And no way did I want Clare to get a whiff of his proposition.

'James, I'm extremely flattered.' (Lie.) 'I can't think of a more exciting proposal.' (Lie.) 'But I can't accept it. I could never live with myself. As much as I would like to be with you…' (lie) 'I couldn't do it to Clare – or your family.'

Immediately James fell back to a win-win position. His face shut down.

'Of course. I understand, Gina. Let's forget about it.'

He checked his watch, took out his mobile and excused himself while he made a quick call. He was no doubt contacting the driver at the Sea Haven Resort.

What arrangement did James have with his driver? 'Stay on duty till 9. I might need a pick-up. If I strike it lucky, collect me in the morning. About 8.'

I poured James another coffee.

'I'm being picked up in twenty minutes.' James smiled his practised rueful smile. 'Sorry I got it wrong, Gina.'

Time to fill. I smiled, changed the music and switched the lights back on. And James changed the conversation. We discussed Adrian's book collection. Thank you, Adrian!

In twenty minutes the driver arrived. I accepted James' lingering kiss and feel-up at the front door. It looked good for the driver (colleague or employee?) and would keep James' reputation intact with the guys.

The car noise woke the Dog. He started his 'stranger beware – don't come here' barking. Too late! But I was glad of his furry company.

'I'm angry, Dog. Bloody angry. That's the second time I've been caught without an escape plan.'

The Dog understood. He was angry with himself too when he found he was on death row in an animal shelter.

I put more logs on the fire and we watched the flames flicker and flare.

'If I did write another novel . . . could I write about a guy who hits on his wife's best friend? Maybe they have an affair. I'd change the characters' names . . . and the place . . . and the time. What do you think, Dog?'

The Dog thought I'd be paddling in dangerous waters. He's probably right.

Saturday 18 July

Hammering on the front door woke me. Bloody hell! Why can't Shelly Beach locals knock on people's doors?

Valiant guard dog was still asleep. I looked out the window. Violet Harris, the writers' group member who's channelling Agatha Christie, was standing on Adrian's verandah.

I couldn't ignore her. She looked as if she could be planted on the front verandah forever.

'Do you mind if I come inside? I'll make coffee. You look as if you could do with one.'

Another Shelly Beach inhabitant who's very familiar with Adrian's supply of coffee and the operation of his percolator.

Violet stood back and analysed my body, hidden beneath my bathrobe. 'You need to get some exercise. Start with the Strollers. They stop for coffee and get the bus back. The Walkers are well outside your fitness range. Adrian said you were a writer. It's probably all the writing you do that's made you so unfit. What do you write, dear?'

Bloody hell!

'I'm just keeping a journal at the moment. And keeping Adrian's writers' group afloat.'

Violet was examining the empty champagne bottles, the tired

remains of paté and cheese on a plate and the dead embers in the fireplace. 'You had a visitor last night?'

'Yes. An old friend.'

'Adrian has great coffee!' Violet finished her drink and I gently shepherded her out the front door onto the verandah.

'Nearly forgot why I came here, dear. You need to call in at Piece of Cake. Alf's got a problem.'

'Excuse me?'

'Alf has mislaid Adrian's colour charts. He needs to buy paint and he can't remember the colours Adrian chose. If the colour charts don't turn up – and Alf can't remember what colours to use or which colours go where – Adrian said he'd leave it up to you to make new colour choices.'

Bloody hell! 'You've been in contact with Adrian recently?'

'Yesterday, dear. Email.'

'Email?'

'Yes! Adrian's been sending you emails too. You haven't been replying.'

Was Violet a prison warden in another life? A school inspector? Maybe a bankruptcy investigator?

'You haven't turned the computer on, have you, dear?'

'I did. A few days ago when Terri was here.'

'Good. Adrian was worried you hadn't logged on. If you get yourself into a difficult situation, dear, yell for Terri's mum, Joan. She's a sensible woman.'

I murmured, 'Thank you. I'll remember that.' And to the Dog, 'Bloody hell, Dog! Do I have *victim* tattooed on my forehead?'

We watched Violet as she climbed into her van decorated with *Keep your cat in at night* signs.

One dozen red roses were delivered from the Sea Haven florist after lunch. I'd say it was the first ever delivery of a floral tribute to Shelly Beach by the way the delivery woman carried on.

I read the card: *Sorry. I got it wrong. Forgive me? James.*

I dumped the roses in the garbage bin. Then I had a rethink. I rescued them and took them next door to Joan.

'Thought you'd like these.'

'Thank you. They're lovely. Cup of tea?'

'No, thank you.'

'I feel good,' I told the Dog later when we went for a walk. And I did.

Sunday 19 July

Journal Writing Task:
Write an account of a boring person's day – an hour at a time.
– Sweet-Scary Tutor

8 a.m. Doves tap-dancing on the tin roof woke me up. Can't think of a bloody thing to do today. Would do the crossword if I had a newspaper. Maybe if I'd encouraged James he'd have escaped from his bonding with staff and whisked me away for a great meal in a secluded little restaurant? Maybe not.

9 a.m. Fed the Dog. Complimented him on his hole-digging. Fed the chickens. Cleaned their henhouse. Put chicken poo on vegetable garden as directed in Adrian's magical manual. Put out seed for the doves.

10 a.m. Coffee break. Would have read Sunday papers except they don't arrive at Shelly Beach until tomorrow. Checked tally of spending for the week. Doing well.

11 a.m. Rain stopped. Mooched in garden. Adrian's spiders build webs like trampolines. Checked netting on fish/frog pond. Impossible to count frogs or fish to see if any are missing as water too murky.

12 p.m. Kept mooching in garden. Did a little weeding in the vegetable patch and avoided spiders. Helped the Dog count his holes. Helped the Dog fill in his holes.

1 p.m. Lunch. Egg sandwiches.

2 p.m. Took the Dog for a walk. Did not meet a living soul. I could be living on Mars.

3 p.m. Back from walk. Exhausted. The Dog and I needed an afternoon zzzz.

4 p.m. Did more weeding and some digging in garden.

5 p.m. Getting cold and overcast. Went inside. Cooked dinner. Listened to news on radio. Unfortunately no scandalous reports of a city tycoon going bust.

6 p.m. Washed dishes and tidied kitchen.

7 p.m. Couldn't get a reasonable fire going. Freezing cold. Took a book to read in bed.

A totally exhausting and boring day.

Monday 20 July

A disastrous day for a dog-sitter. I lost the dog. When I struggled out of bed to feed Adrian's livestock, the Girls were having a wonderful time freelancing in the garden, but the guard dog was missing.

I herded the Girls back into their henhouse and searched every square inch of Adrian's house and garden. No sign of the bloody Dog. I panicked and raced down to Piece of Cake to find Alf. Alf heaped on the guilt.

'Adrian loves that dog.'

'What do you suggest I do, Alf? Where should I look?'

Alf checked his watch. 'School recess is in ten minutes.'

'Yes?'

'Go to the school. Ask permission to talk to Terri. She'll know what to do. If she can't help, you'd better ring the police in Sea Haven. The nearest lost dogs' home is in Kingston.'

Bloody hell! My stomach was turning cartwheels. I could see my wait-a-while Shelly Beach idyll disappearing down the plughole. Only twenty days and I'd failed as a dog-sitter. I had no dog to sit.

I raced to the school and arrived as the bell rang for recess. I explained my predicament to comforting teacher Josh. He sent Bossy Child to me.

'You've lost Hugo!'

'How did you guess?'

'Mr Colovich told me. You look terrible.'

'Right. Do you know where the Dog could be?'

'He'll be at Henry Shepherd's.'

'Who's Henry Shepherd?'

'Henry is a kind old man who has a poodle called Sally. Since Henry's wife died, Henry's looked after Sally. Hugo likes to visit Sally. Have you got your mobile?'

'Yes.'

I handed it over to Bossy Child. She punched a phone number in. I waited anxiously while she talked. 'It's okay. Hugo's at Henry's. Have you got a pen and paper?'

I searched my bag for a pen and notebook, and waited while Bossy Child drew me a map marked with a dotted line and a square marked with the initials *H.S.*

She pointed to the initialled square. 'This is Henry Shepherd's house. It's only ten minutes' walk away. Henry will have a spare lead so you can bring Hugo home. I bet you slept in and forgot to feed Hugo.'

I ignored the guilt from Bossy Child.

'If you looked up L for Lost Dog in Adrian's manual you would have known where to find him. Hugo often visits Sally.'

I ignored Bossy Child and left the school grounds. I followed the map and located Henry Shepherd's house and thus Henry himself.

He's another sun-weathered, talkative Shelly Beach local. The Dog was sitting close to a fluffy poodle in front of the fire – as innocent as a lamb. He avoided looking at me.

'Hugo and Sally are great mates.'

Henry made me a cup of milky tea with a few ginger biscuits and explained how Sally, the fluffy poodle, had belonged to his wife. (Henry left his sheepdogs on the farm when he moved to Shelly Beach.)

The Dog and I did not talk as we walked back home along the beach. We concentrated on avoiding the frothy crested waves as they bounced on the sand.

Hot young Lee was sitting on the step of Adrian's verandah – writing *the* novel. I apologised profusely for not being there to greet him.

'Not a problem, Gina. I knew you'd turn up sooner or later. Now I'm into writing, I grab every spare moment I can.'

Lee had brought the ingredients for a pasta dish and cooked up a fantastic meal. Over a glass, maybe two, of Adrian's wine, the day definitely picked up.

The Dog and I are not talking.

Tuesday 21 July

To: Adrian <bookstreet@network.com.au>
From: Gina <piececake@email.com.au>
Subject: Key keeper
I'm official key keeper for your writers' group.

I hope your daughter is doing okay and you and her family are well.
Gina

To: Gina <piececake@email.com.au>
From: Adrian <bookstreet@network.com.au>
Re: Key keeper
How did that happen?

My daughter is coping and the family and I are managing well.
Adrian

To: Adrian <bookstreet@network.com.au>
From: Gina <piececake@email.com.au>
Re: Key keeper

I'm surprised you're surprised as you evidently told all and sundry I'd be stand-in if anything happened to your previous stand-in key keeper, and it has. She's flown the coop to look after grandchildren. Her son has broken his ankle.
Gina

To: Gina <piececake@email.com.au>
From: Adrian <bookstreet@network.com.au>
Re: Key keeper
Congratulations!

To: Adrian <bookstreet@network.com.au>
From: Gina <piececake@email.com.au>
Subject: Collapse of writers' group

A thought: can your writers' group go ahead with just six members? I only have six definites: Pandora, Violet, Digby, Josh, Bianca and Lee. Haven't heard from Daphne yet. If your group can't work with six members I'm happy to do the cancelling stuff.
Gina

To: Gina <piececake@email.com.au>
From: Adrian <bookstreet@network.com.au>
Re: Collapse of writers' group

Writers' group can proceed with seven members, a convener and a tutor. Daphne's emailed me. She'll be joining. That gives us seven members. If you take my place as convener we'll be fine. This way we won't have to disappoint participants or cancel Bill Kruger's services, which would be a blow to his young family. He needs the money.
Adrian

To: Adrian <bookstreet@network.com.au>
From: Gina <piececake@email.com.au>
Re: Collapse of writers' group
As previously stated I'm fine with the role of key keeper/convener/
whatever – as long as it's understood I will not be participating in
any writing activities. I do not plan to write another novel.
Gina

To: Gina <piececake@email.com.au>
From: Adrian <bookstreet@network.com.au>
Re: Collapse of writers' group
Understood. Are you familiar with the change-over details for the
key?
Adrian

To: Adrian <bookstreet@network.com.au>
From: Gina <piececake@email.com.au>
Subject: Key relay
Yes! Gardening club key keeper delivers the key to me on Wednesday
morning so I can open up for writers' group. I take the key to Josh
at the school on Thursday morning so Josh can open hall for band
practice. If Josh isn't in his classroom I leave key at the school office.
P.S. Shelly Beach Writers' Group inaugural meeting is tomorrow
night, and yes, I've notified Kingston Council, local MP, tutor, and
members.

To: Gina <piececake@email.com.au>
From: Adrian <bookstreet@network.com.au>
Re: Key relay
Well done! I suggest you drive the Ford. It'll be safer at night. Do a
practice run. Take my torch. It's on the back verandah. The lock on
the hall door can be difficult if it's been raining.

Don't forget to take the folder I left. There's paperwork in there for Bill Kruger. He has to sign it to get paid. Make sure he signs it on the first night. Post forms to local council the next day. Address is in the folder.

To: Adrian <bookstreet@network.com.au>
From: Gina <piececake@email.com.au>
Subject: Trial run
Trial run to hall successful. Now know best place to park on foreshore and how to avoid craters so car doesn't get bogged for eternity. Will try to remember other stuff.
P.S. Your Ford is on its deathbed.

To: Gina <piececake@email.com.au>
From: Adrian <bookstreet@network.com.au>
Subject: Intro
Sorry about the car. Get Alf to look at it. Can you do the intro for Bill and the local MP? Can't remember his name. I've written an intro. It's in folder.

To: Adrian <bookstreet@network.com.au>
From: Gina <piececake@email.com.au>
Re: Intro
YES! YES! Dean Morris is name of local MP! Found intro!

Wednesday 22 July

Bianca and Pandora were waiting when I arrived at the community hall for the inaugural meeting of the Shelly Beach Writers' Group. They'd anticipated I'd need help: 'The hall door is tricky to open.' True. You need one body to turn the key in the lock, two bodies to push the door open.

Bianca and Pandora helped with brewing 'welcoming' cups of tea and coffee. As soon as members trickled into the hall they were put to work shifting tables and chairs. Did we want a behave-and-face-the-front layout or a friendly feel-good half-circle layout? We decided on the friendly feel-good half-circle.

The furniture-moving operation filled in time. This was fortunate because our tutor and the local MP were late.

Bill Kruger, shortlisted author and tutor, was laden with apologies. Hunter, Bill's two-year-old kid, scribbled over the writing tasks and Bill had to print a new set. 'And the printer's playing up.'

We understood.

The MP arrived soon after. He'd gone to Sea Haven community hall. Easily happens! He delivered his two-minute pitch – 'Kingston Council's delighted to provide funds to encourage ongoing life-learning in a small community like Shelly Beach.'

Then he excused himself and dashed off. He's obviously not a novel writer.

'Bigger fish to fry,' Violet said.

Bill Kruger is unbelievably fortunate with his collection of And Then There Were Eight docile, serious members. Some about to emerge, some emerged – and one who is submerged!

We did the fake-friendly, around-the-table introductory talk. Why we want to be here. *Why do we want to be here?* Why we write. *Why do we write?*

Bianca whispered, 'I've been working out the average age of our group.'

(As you do when you're in a writers' group and haven't a clue what to write.)

'It's forty-something.'

Bianca, Josh, Lee, Bill – maybe Pandora (Bianca's not sure if Pandora is thirty-something or forty-something) prevent our little writers' group from becoming an oldies' group.

'Although there's nothing wrong with oldies.'

Thank you, Bianca.

Everyone was quietly enthusiastic except the illustrious Digby, who was over-the-top enthusiastic. Dr Digby Prentice-Hill (not a real doctor – a literary doctor) is tall with a mane of silver hair. Charming. Charismatic. A silver knight in burnished armour in comparison to Sir Adrian's creaky armour. Digby is eloquent, and he uses humour deftly. We listened to him talk about his prospective novel for hours. Exaggeration – half an hour.

'I was going to write my memoir but decided to write a psychological thriller set in academia instead. I did a rethink after considering legal ramifications.'

I bet he did.

'Adrian suggested I take a wordwise segment each week. How does the group feel about this?'

No one objected.

Bianca mouthed 'B-o-o-o-ring.'

'It'll be about nouns and verbs and adjectives. Stuff like that.'

I'm glad I didn't give Dr Digby Prentice-Hill the opportunity to be key keeper. I'm guessing Digby's looks and talent, combined with luck, have been able to get him what he wanted and where he wanted to go all his life – with little effort. Maybe he's run out of magic power and a warlock has banished him to Shelly Beach?

Daphne, an energetic, attractive and tanned sixty-something, had returned from her birdwatching trek and was pleased she hadn't missed a meeting.

Bianca whispered, 'Daphne's lived in an old-growth forest on top of a tree! I'm not sure for how long. She was a chained-to-a-tree-hugger. She actually lay in front of a bulldozer to stop trees being cut down.'

Looking at Daphne it was hard to imagine her as an environmental warrior.

Daphne gave her three-minute intro. She's the social and

environmental reporter for the *Sea Haven Sentinel* – the local rag. 'I use colour when I'm writing pieces for the *Sentinel*, and make sure I document my sources when I'm writing a feature for a city paper.'

Shelly Beach writers were suitably impressed.

Violet whispered, 'She uses a different adjective to describe each deb's dress when she writes up the Sea Haven debutante ball.'

I was impressed. Daphne's obviously a writer who knows how to write for her readers. I passed on my three-minute intro – 'Have to get supper ready.'

Unsuccessful novelist and giggling hairstylist escaped to prepare supper. Bianca feels woozy if she has to read stuff she's written aloud to people.

I understood.

Talented, shortlisted author Bill gave us a writing task. By next meeting we have to write about our works-in-progress or works-to-get-in-progress.

Bianca was upset. 'What if I can't think of anything to write by next meeting? Can I write about a DVD I've seen?'

Bill gave a comforting reply in the affirmative.

As soon as Bill indicated that the inaugural meeting of the Shelly Beach Writers' Group had concluded, members made a quick escape.

Bianca stayed with me while I locked the hall. 'It's tricky being key keeper.'

I agreed. Spending hours battling with an ancient key and lock on a darkened foreshore while the sound of the waves and the spooky calls of plovers swirl around me is not my idea of fun.

Thursday 23 July
Bossy Child opened the email inbox. She called from the bedroom. 'There's an email from Adrian. Can I read it?'

'Yes.'

'He wants to know how the writers' group meeting went last night. You should have emailed him this morning.'

'Well, I didn't.'

'You should ask him how he's getting on in England. Ask him how his daughter's going! Cancer's horrible. My dad died of cancer.'

I had a fill-the-gap answer to a question I'd been wanting to ask. 'I have asked Adrian about his family. They're doing as well as they can. Come and get your dinner. I'll email Adrian later.'

Bossy Child concentrated on my 'nearly as good as Adrian's' schnitzel. When her mum phoned, the Dog and I walked her next door. As soon as we were outside, misty sea air surrounded us. Bossy Child absolutely loves the salty smell of Shelly Beach air!

To: Adrian <bookstreet@network.com.au>
From: Gina <piececake@email.com.au>
Subject: First writers' group meeting
First writers' group went okay – except for few hassles, i.e. tutor and local MP were forty-five minutes late. Everyone was ready to go home. MP went to Sea Haven by mistake.
- Did key relay thing successfully.
- Organised Bill. He's signed forms and posted them to Kingston Council to receive his tutoring fee.
- Group agreed Digby can do his wordwise stuff. They'll live to regret this.
- Lee, Violet and Josh have started their novels. Remaining members (except me) are thinking about writing a novel. Bianca hopes she'll know what her novel's about by next meeting.
- Members spent most of evening eating and drinking. Very little writing!

Gina

To: Gina <piececake@email.com.au>
From: Adrian <bookstreet@network.com.au>
Re: First writers' group meeting
Well done! How did Bill go? He's never done anything like this before.
Adrian

To: Adrian <bookstreet@network.com.au>
From: Gina <piececake@email.com.au>
Re: First writers' group meeting
Your author was okay – but very nervous. Looked like a rabbit
caught in the headlights. He needs to speak louder. Violet said she
couldn't hear him very well but she's going to turn her hearing aid
up next week. Pandora says if Bill stopped talking to fixed spot at
back of wall, his presentation would improve considerably.
Gina
P.S. You didn't tell me I had to bring a plate of food!

To: Gina <piececake@email.com.au>
From: Adrian <bookstreet@network.com.au>
Re: First writers' group meeting
Bringing a plate of food is accepted norm at Shelly Beach. Never
attend anything in Shelly Beach without taking food or grog. How
often did writers' group decide to meet?
Adrian

To: Adrian <bookstreet@network.com.au>
From: Gina <piececake@email.com.au>
Re: First writers' group meeting
Will store food and grog info for reference. Intend to avoid group
functions of more than one while here. Writers' group voted for
monthly meetings. However, Digby pointed out to the group we
have to meet twice a month in order to meet grant requirements.

Members sidestepped crablike during sharing time – except Violet.
She's offered to read a short extract from one of her whodunnits
featuring her Red Blaze detective character for next meeting.
Members left laden with homework.
Gina

When I returned to the kitchen Bossy Child played back my phone
messages.

> Gina, hi, it's Julia. Simon and I are planning to visit on Sat-
> urday 25 – about 11ish. There are more papers you need to
> sign. We've booked at the Sea Haven Resort so don't worry
> about accommodation. If Saturday doesn't suit, call me and
> we'll set up another date. See you soon – bye.

Bossy Child was waiting with her notebook for my reply instructions.
'Reply. I've got the plague. I'm dying. No . . . say it's not conveni-
ent. I've already made other arrangements.'
'You can't. You haven't.'
'Okay. Don't reply. I'll have to sign the bloody papers.'
I ignored the rolled-eye look from Bossy Child.

Friday 24 July
I fed and walked the Dog, fed the chickens, fed the doves, cleaned
the henhouse and collected the Girls' eggs.
Then I scrubbed and cleaned Adrian's house. Again. Picked
mushrooms (or are they toadstools?) growing in Adrian's bathroom.
I made a note to check the bathroom before Julia and Simon arrive
tomorrow morning.
I found ingredients to bake a cake in Adrian's store cupboard.
The Dog agreed that providing morning tea was a clever diversionary
tactic to stall answers to probing questions.

I told the Dog to remind me to wear make-up and respectable clothes for the visit from my daughter and son-in-law. The Dog did not understand how a mother could be so nervous and apprehensive at meeting her daughter. Being nervous and apprehensive at meeting a son-in-law he could understand – but not a daughter.

I ignored the Dog. He knows nothing of family relationships.

Saturday 25 July

Daughter Julia and son-in-law Simon arrived precisely at 11. The Dog and I wondered if they'd stopped somewhere in order to time the visit perfectly. Maybe they'd stopped at a must-visit coffee shop in a must-see town they'd discovered in What to Do in the *Weekend Guide*.

Simon chose to sit in the car in the driveway and use his BlackBerry.

'Sorry. Can't come inside just yet. Have email to answer. But I wouldn't say no to a cup of coffee.'

I felt like a drive-in attendant as I took coffee and cake to Simon sitting in his car in Adrian's driveway, and vaguely remembered a time when I was permanently attached to my BlackBerry. In a former life it was my lifeline. It was my connection, my communication with my all-consuming career.

Over coffee (herbal tea for Julia) I prepared for another round of document signing.

'Gina, Kenneth wants a divorce. If you sign these papers we can start the process. Kenneth is using his solicitor, so you won't have to foot the bill. You're not upset, are you, Gina?'

I looked at Julia. She was blooming in these last weeks of her pregnancy. Was I upset? I'd stopped loving Kenneth years ago. We'd existed in a marriage littered with betrayals. A marriage dotted with red flags. A marriage that was now well and truly broken.

'I should have dumped Kenneth after his affair with Francesca.'

Julia gave me a puzzled look.

'Sexy Francesca. Your father's PA. The one before Clever Angela.'

'Why didn't you, Mother?' Julia was distressed.

'I'd just been made redundant. I was comfortable and confident writing my novel. It didn't matter. I didn't care.'

The Dog clink-clinked into the room. Julia gave him a smile and bent to pat his scruffy fur. He'd been playing with the Girls in the mud and long grass.

The Dog smiled back at Julia. I seized the moment and offered Julia some cake, cut another piece and took it to Simon.

When I returned, I ignored the 'was I upset' question and opened with a diversionary question. 'Have you found a nanny?'

'Yes. We've been lucky. A wonderful woman – Nanny Anny. We found her through an agency. We'll employ a night nanny if we need one.'

'Good. I'm glad.' This time I carefully read, then signed, the flag-tagged pages.

'Don't worry, Gina. Everything will be fine. You've missed a flag.'

'Sorry.'

'It's a charming cottage. Delightful garden. Cute dog.'

The Dog smirked and wagged his tail at Julia. He rarely wags his tail for me.

'Yes, it is a charming cottage. I'm fine here.' Ridiculous four-letter word, *fine*. 'More herbal tea?' I refilled Julia's cup and thought of another diversionary question. I use fill-the-gap questions frequently when I talk to my daughter.

'Can you find out how I'd go about a name change? I'd like to be Gina Laurel – not Gina Laurel-Scott, especially as the company's in such a mess.'

Julia looked startled but didn't say a word. She probably knew I could do the name-changing stuff myself. But I'd thrown her with the fact I actually wanted to change my name – break every connection with her father. When Julia married Simon last year I was surprised my independent daughter took Simon's surname. Maybe she'd foreseen the Laurel-Scott Corporation's collapse and wanted to end all visible connections with our company too.

'Changing your surname won't be difficult, Gina. I'll send the papers to you.'

Julia gathered the signed documents into her briefcase. A visit to Adrian's bathroom – thank God I'd scrubbed it from top to bottom – and she was ready to leave.

'I hope the Sea Haven Resort is reasonable.'

'It should be. It has five stars.'

Thank you, God, for serious, suitable accommodation not far from Shelly Beach.

'Thanks for the flowers and fruit.' Of course Julia couldn't arrive empty-handed. 'Keep well. I'll come and visit soon.' (White lie.)

I don't imagine my pregnant daughter would welcome a walking-on-eggshells visit from her mother. We have a long way to go before we reach an amenable mother–daughter relationship.

'Let me know if the baby decides to come early.' I hoped this was a politically correct comment from a prospective grandmother to a daughter who was soon to give birth.

It must have been, because Julia actually smiled. She waved and blew the Dog and me an air kiss as she and Simon drove off.

'I need to walk, Dog.'

The Dog grumbled. It was too cold.

'If I'd left our marriage first I'd be feeling euphoric. I wouldn't need to walk off my anger. Bloody Kenneth! He had a well thought-out plan. He's wasted little time in shedding the old wife. Come on, Dog. Time for a walk along Shelly Beach.'

I ignored the Dog's 'not again' look.

'Don't complain. Some dogs never get a walk. They're locked inside stuffy little apartments all day long.'

We compromised and decided on a short walk along Beach Road. The Dog hates Shelly Beach when the waves take over the sand and he can't dig. We crossed over to the foreshore. I released the Dog from his leash and sat on the bench near the pier. I took deep breaths and cleared my mind while the Dog chased seagulls. He enjoys terrorising them.

When we returned we took Julia's flowers to Pandora. The exotic perfumed lilies overwhelmed Sea View Cottage's basic ambience; they added a funereal atmosphere. I didn't feel funereal. I felt cool.

Pandora was happy with the flowers. She agreed that lilies are funereal but she was happy with a funeral-parlour look while she's renovating.

'Cup of tea?'

I accepted Pandora's offer. We chatted about ships and seas, and sealing wax, men and divorce – but not writing.

Sunday 26 – Thursday 30 July

Five moochy Shelly Beach days highlighted by a Shelly Beach book club meeting, a fox warning and fine dining at Rosa's pub.

Each day the Dog and I walked in the wind and the rain along desolate Shelly Beach. The grey skies were reflected in the grey seas. And there were spaces in those five days for planning a new life – but I didn't get there.

The Dog thinks I have avoidance issues.

I'm ignoring him.

Josh, Shelly Beach's stand-in book club convener, had left a battered copy of *David Copperfield* on my doorstep as an invitation to come to book club on Monday. He also left a note to remind me to locate the two bottles of wine Adrian had left for the meeting. Josh would pick us up at 5.45 p.m. on Monday.

Sunday was spent skimming through *David Copperfield* and hunting for the wine. The Dog and I eventually located Adrian's hidden cache. The tagged bottles of wine were resting side by side, row by row at the back of Adrian's linen cupboard. I retrieved the two bottles tagged *July book club*. Two dozen bottles were tagged *December book club*. Obviously a wild breakup is anticipated for that meeting.

On Monday night the Dog and I were ready and waiting on the verandah of Adrian's cottage. Josh drove into Adrian's drive at 5.45 p.m. sharp. I noted hot young chef Lee and kindly old Henry Shepherd were passengers – obviously Shelly Beach book club members.

'Have you got the wine?'

I handed over Adrian's bottles of wine as the Dog and I slipped into the back seat, receiving the warning, 'Watch Lee's coq au vin. It's on the floor.'

Adrian's bottles of white and red wine (French vintages) were checked and approved.

Henry, fluffy poodle Sally and the Dog sat on the front seat. Henry handed over his chocolate mousse for me to hold on my knee until we reached Violet's farmhouse. (A French theme had been planned for the book club meeting but Adrian couldn't get multiple copies of *Les Misérables*. The members had voted to keep a French theme for the dinner although we were reading an English novel.)

Dinner is obviously the high point of book club meetings. There was very little book discussion that evening. Bianca said the meeting was mostly eating and drinking because Digby was at an interstate conference – but he'd be back in time for the next writers' group meeting.

Chirpy Bianca loves being a member of the book club. She just loves its no. 1 rule: you don't have to read the book!

Bianca said, 'Digby usually leads the discussion. If people can't think of anything to say about the book, or they haven't had time to read it, it doesn't matter much. Digby's happy to talk about the book and give out notes.'

And Adrian wasn't the only contributor of wine. Some excellent local vintages were tasted and appreciated during the evening. No wonder Shelly Beach Book Club (aka Shelly Beach Writers' Group with one extra member) has a full roll call each month.

I decided I would continue to attend book club meetings during my short stay in Shelly Beach. I need to bring Adrian's wine.

The Dog agreed. Even though he's not a particularly literary dog, he's very keen on literary dinner party leftovers.

The next day Pandora called to warn me about a fox she and Violet had seen skulking on their properties. I have to lock Adrian's chickens up every night. And she invited me to dine with a few locals at Rosa's pub the following evening.

'We always eat at the pub on a Wednesday night. Rosa makes Wednesdays a discount night for locals. Everyone's appreciating Lee's cooking.'

I reported Pandora's fox warning to the Dog. 'A crafty fox is on the loose and he'll be after Adrian's chickens.'

Although the Dog is a brave foxhunter we've arranged a signal. One bark from him when outside and I'll race out with the broom, a saucepan lid and spoon to assist in chasing the fox away. Consolidated forces work best.

By Wednesday night I regretted accepting Pandora's invitation. I didn't feel like eating out at Rosa's. 'It's too cold and wet and I can't waste money dining out.'

The Dog encouraged me to front up. He thinks it's extremely rude not to go to something you've said you would go to, and he didn't think dining at Rosa's would break my budget.

So on Wednesday night I walked along Shelly Beach's main road to Rosa's. It was a warm and welcoming haven from the biting wind blowing off the sea. Pandora had kept a place for me on a table with Bianca.

When Violet arrived we made room for her. She stowed her cat basket under the table. 'Brought some kittens for Rosa to choose one or two from. They'll be good mousers. Their mother is an excellent mouser. Serious mice problem in the pub's kitchen.'

I didn't want to go near the mice problem.

At this point the Dog gatecrashed and found his way to my table. I sent him daggers. He'd said he wanted to stay home. Everyone made a fuss of him. 'Poor little dog. Missing Adrian?' The Dog gave me his I-told-you-so look, and left to sit under Henry's table with fluffy poodle Sally.

Violet introduced me to the multitude of friends who stopped to chat at our table. 'Meet Gina – Adrian's journalist friend. She's the writing guru from the city who's staying in Adrian's cottage.'

Each time I smiled and attempted to correct the myth Violet was creating around me. 'I'm not a journalist, Violet.'

'But you're from the city.'

'Yes.'

'And you write?'

'Yes, I do. I keep a journal . . . but I'm not a journalist.'

'There you go.'

Pandora whispered, 'Give up. Violet hasn't turned her hearing aid up.'

Back home the Dog was amazed I accepted the title 'journalist'.

'It was easier than arguing with Violet.'

The Dog understood.

'What do you think, Dog? Am I a journaler or a journal writer? Maybe I can say I'm a writer. A writer who keeps a journal. If you keep a journal are you a serious writer? If you keep a diary, what kind of writer does that make you? A less serious writer?'

The Dog said that Adrian keeps a diary. The Dog wanted to know if you keep a diary, are you a diarist? If he started a diary, would he have to begin each entry with *Dear Diary*?

I ignored him.

When Thursday rolled around I was feeling good and in control.

No stuff-ups. The Dog and I walked Bossy Child to school and later picked her up. We also entertained one of Bossy Child's best friends until her mum collected her after school. I reminded Bossy Child that I'm not running an after-school kids' club.

Rolled-eye look from Bossy Child.

I'm sure I saw the Dog whisper to her to ignore me and invite her friends whenever she wants.

The Dog likes the Bossy Child's friends because they make such a fuss of him. He's not keen on children under the age of three, though, unless they have been dog-trained.

Friday 31 July

I lost the Dog again! I woke up this morning and went to feed the Dog. There wasn't sight or sound of him. I rang Henry Shepherd; he's a comforting old man. 'Yes! Hugo's here. He's in front of the fire with Sally. I'll walk him around when the weather breaks.'

Guilt! Guilt! Guilt! 'I'll collect Hugo, Henry. No problem. I have to collect some supplies from Jenkins'. I'll be around about 11.'

The electricity was off, probably because of the storm last night. I heated some water on Adrian's gas stove for coffee, and took a luke-warm shower. How can you tell if a portable gas container is empty? I made a note to ask Alf.

I waited for a lull in the rain and set off. I'm positive that treks to the Antarctic are very similar to walking along the Shelly Beach foreshore in winter – except there's no ice.

Locating dog food in Jenkins' General Store was like looking for a library book with seven decimal places. I fought my way up a crowded aisle of canoe paddles and fishing tackle. The pet food supplies were next to a chain of flip-flops hanging like tropical fruit. I couldn't resist the serendipitous find of a container of neatly woven balls of string. In my present life, a ball of string could prove to be useful.

It was when I reached Jenkins' new point of sale and Jody that I lost the plot – spectacularly, of course.

'Food for Adrian's dog, luv?'

I nodded and burst into body-racking sobs. I mumbled something about losing the Dog. Again.

Jody yelled across the store to her mother-in-law behind the post office sub-branch. 'She's lost the dog again, Mum.' The bulky woman perched on a stool received my message in noncommittal fashion.

I shook my head, blew my nose and tried to stifle the tears running down my cheeks. 'I haven't lost Hugo. He's at Henry Shepherd's. I'm going to collect him now.'

Jody yelled, 'She hasn't lost him, Mum. He's at old Henry Shepherd's place. She's going to collect him now.'

I blew my nose again and stared out the front entrance of the store. I concentrated on the torrential rain pouring down and forced myself to stop crying.

'Arnold!' Jody's mum screamed into the cavern of the store. 'Arnold! Make the writing lady a cup of tea. Plenty of sugar . . . and bring some ginger snap biscuits.'

Jody emerged from behind her point of sale; rubbing my back she led me to a stool at the post office counter.

'It's too wet for walking, luv. Arnold will drive you to Henry's so you can pick up Hugo.'

Arnold appeared from the back of the store with a tray containing mugs of tea and ginger snap biscuits.

'Don't you worry, luv. Hugo does this all the time. Leads Adrian a merry dance. He's got a bit of a crush on Henry's poodle, Sally.'

Mum and Jody nodded in sympathy. We sipped our sweet, milky tea and crunched on ginger snap biscuits in companionable silence.

I was loaded, complete with supplies, into Jenkins' van. We drove to Henry's. Arnold hopped out, collected Hugo and deposited him on my lap. We sat in chilly silence while Arnold drove us back to Sea View Cottage.

The Dog stared at me with guilt-laden eyes. He's sorry – but I'm not accepting his apology.

'Hugo must have been frightened with the thunder last night,' Arnold said. 'Best to keep him inside with you when there's a storm on.'

I nodded, looking out of the window to hide my tears. It's not my style to get so emotional. Damn.

August

Saturday 1 August

A bad start to the month: I lost the Dog. Yet again. The infuriating thing is that the Dog didn't even know he was lost. He was missing for hours. Approximately two hours and fifty-five minutes. Result: another body-racking, devastating attack of the tears with the realisation that if I lost the Dog for good, I'd be up the creek without a paddle – camped in a leaky tent on Shelly Beach foreshore, my belongings packed in two Louis Vuitton suitcases.

I decided to make one final survey of Adrian's property before I set off the Shelly Beach alarm, before I announced to the Shelly Beach locals that I'd lost Adrian's dog again, that I was an absolute failure as a dog-sitter.

I found the Dog. He was asleep on a pile of old clothes in a corner of Adrian's shed. I woke him up and marched him inside.

It was time for a seriously serious talk. 'Looking after you is like riding a roller-coaster, Dog. One minute you're here. The next minute you've disappeared.'

The Dog's escape tactics make it very clear he isn't happy with me as his proxy owner.

I called him to sit in front of Adrian's calendar. I tore July from the pages, screwed it into a ball and tossed it into the bin. 'See, it's August. Only five months to go. Unfortunately I'm not leaving until the end of December, so we have to make the best of it. I admit five months sounds longer in Dog time, i.e. about thirty-five months, but it's still not all that long.'

I can understand the Dog wants his old life with Saint Adrian back.

'How do you think I feel? You've still got a life. You live in the same house, get food and water every day, and get taken for walks. How would you like to be me? I don't want my old life back, but it would be nice to think there was another life looming on the horizon.'

The Dog wasn't happy because I'd made him walk up McIntosh Hill – twice. I sympathised. 'I'm having trouble conquering McIntosh Hill too.'

(I'm so regretting cancelling my subscription at Fit and Healthy Gym during my novel-writing year. Couldn't spare the time.)

'I thought you were younger. It's your hole-digging that fooled me.'

The Dog agreed he looks young. And frisky. Adrian has kept him in tip-top condition; however, the Dog's arthritis is playing up. He can walk up McIntosh Hill, but he has trouble coming down.

Message understood.

The Dog thought I looked older than I was. More like sixty-something, nearer Adrian's age. Bloody hell!

He thought it was because of my grumpy attitude. I needed to watch my blood-sugar level. Lighten up a little.

Charming.

We negotiated. Mostly one-sided.

The Dog likes sleeping on Adrian's jacket. He enjoys smelling the leftover scent; it reminds him of happier times. I retrieved said jacket from the shed where I'd tossed it and restored it to its original place – on the back verandah.

Now the Dog can take his morning and afternoon dog-naps on Adrian's smelly jacket. It'll be easy to keep an eye on his whereabouts. All I'll have to do is stick my head out the back door. He'll be there. Sleeping. I have to let a sleeping Dog lie.

Message understood.

The Dog prefers to be called by the name Adrian gave him – Hugo. However, he will answer to Dog. 'Dog' is edgy, as long as it has a capital D. (He'll never answer to Pooch.)

If I try harder to be pleasant, the Dog will try to curtail his quest for adventure. Bloody hell!

That night, musing in front of the fire, we agreed we're caught in one of life's dark patches.

The Dog believes I'm at a crossroads and there's no discerning scent to set me on the right road. I've dug the deepest hole for myself, and it's a tricky one to get out of. It's probably my fault for locking myself in an attic for a year or so to write a failed novel, not looking for a 'proper' job after I was made redundant.

Evidently I'm bogged down in moribund self-pity when I should be concentrating on nitty-gritty survival. For example: where is my next bone coming from?

I crossed off the first day of August on the calendar and noted August's featured recipe – ham on the bone soup. I decided to go the whole hog and cheer the Dog up. I promised him I'd cook the soup and he could have the bone.

He was glad. Adrian always cooked ham on the bone soup and gave him the bone. The Dog loves the bone.

Sunday 2 August

Cantankerous Dog. After I shifted furniture so his bed can fit back in Bedroom Two, the Dog decided to sleep in the living room. He dragged Adrian's old jacket through the pet door and made a smelly nest.

84

To cut the Dog some slack, the noises in the ceiling of Bedroom Two are probably upsetting him. I should have taken his lead and slept on Adrian's couch in the living room. Instead I spent the night composing an attention-getting email in my mind. Couldn't wait to type it and send it off.

To: Adrian <bookstreet@network.com.au>
From: Gina <piececake@email.com.au>
Subject: Rattus rattus
Hi Adrian,
Your house is infested by a plague of rats! Common garden-variety classification – rattus rattus. What do you want me to do? Do you want me to use poison, traps or call in the pest exterminator? Will I find pest exterminator listed under P for Pest or E for Exterminator in your manual?
Let me know as soon as possible. So far I've coped well with the life you've left me – but cannot get adequate rest while hordes of rats continue to use my bed as their playground.
Gina

I did a last edit and remembered advice I'd given my staff in a former life: 'The immediacy of email can lead people to abandon judgement. Give important emails twenty-four hours before you send them. Watch your word choices.'
I decided to reword my email. I can't afford to be evicted.

To: Adrian <bookstreet@network.com.au>
From: Gina <piececake@email.com.au>
Subject: Mice
Hi Adrian,
Your house is overrun by a family of mice. How do you want me to handle this problem?

85

A. Get poison

B. Buy traps

C. Call in the pest exterminator

Gina

P.S. I'll see if I can assist Alf with his 'colour' problem tomorrow.

To: Gina < piececake@email.com.au>

From: Adrian <bookstreet@network.com.au>

Re: Mice

Keep the Sometime Cat in at night!

Check the boxes of tiles at Piece of Cake. The paint charts are packed in one.

Adrian

The Dog and I visited Bossy Child and her mum, Joan. We needed to solve Adrian's cryptic email re: mice. No way did Bossy Child, Joan or baby brother Sam empathise with my intense dislike of mice. They are avid mice-lovers. Standing at the door of Bossy Child's bedroom I viewed her cage of white mice.

'You hate mice?'

'Travelling diseases on four legs.'

'Cute white mice with petal-soft pink noses?'

'Yes!'

'You're scared of one little mouse!'

'When it wakes me in the middle of the night and uses my bed as a major highway – yes!'

I moved the conversation on. Bossy Child knows I do not appreciate tales of smuggling pet mice to school under T-shirts. Gross.

Over a cup of tea the mystery of the Sometime Cat was solved. It's the mangy ginger cat that hung around when I moved in. The cat I chased away by throwing buckets of water at it.

'You didn't!'

'I did. It was eating birds!'

'It wouldn't!'

I ignored Bossy Child. How was I to know the Sometime Cat was community property? He gets fed and finds accommodation when and wherever he touches base with local cat-lovers – Saint Adrian being a Shelly Beach cat-lover. The Sometime Cat mostly abides with Violet of McIntosh Hill.

'Violet loves cats.'

'Well, I don't.'

Shock and horror.

'And I don't know why!'

We borrowed Sam's stroller so the Dog could have an easier trek to Violet's house. After a little negotiation with Violet I gained a loan of the Sometime Cat to scare off my mouse. Just for a week.

I pushed the Dog in Sam's stroller down McIntosh Hill while the Bossy Child carried the Sometime Cat in his cat basket.

During a which-is-harder argument I delivered my ultimatum. 'And if Mickey Mouse has moved his family in, I'm getting traps!'

'Geen-ahh!'

Monday 3 August

I devoted today to solving Adrian's paint problem for his bookshop cafe and flat. After our walk, the Dog and I called into Piece of Cake and found the colour charts. They were packed in one of the boxes of tiles. Now Alf remembers where he'd seen them!

Adrian's colour selection is stunning, very modern: small Italian tiles of yellow, pink, and turquoise. The walls are to be painted matching shades but Alf will use white for bookshelves and woodwork.

Alf said Antoinette, the young colour consultant in Kingston, sweet-talked Adrian into buying the expensive Italian tiles. And she helped him choose the colour scheme. That'd be right! The colours will work well because the bookshop cafe is huge. Piece of Cake will look zappy – completely out of place with the local environment.

Tomorrow I'm going with Alf to Kingston to buy the paint.

Lee called in to exchange Adrian's books. We talked books and drank coffee; a divine way to spend an afternoon. I did my best to ignore my thumping heart. A ridiculous way for a heart of a barely-50-something female to behave when she's in the company of a male young enough to be her son.

No sign of the mouse or his family. They've obviously moved on to greener pastures thanks to the Sometime Cat.

Tuesday 4 August
Alf suggested he'd drive me to Kingston to buy the paint.

I ventured a query. 'You know the MG in Adrian's shed . . . the one that's up on blocks?'

'Yes.'

'Can you take it off the blocks? Can I drive it?'

'No!'

Evidently the MG is Adrian's pride and joy. Alf decided on a change of plan. I could drive us to Kingston. He'd check my driving in Adrian's Ford. Excuse me? Had he forgotten I'd already driven the Ford to Sea Haven?

No, he hadn't, but he wanted to check how I handled the Ford on a longer drive. 'It's unreliable.'

Tell me about it.

'More cars on the road to Kingston. Driving there is a good test.'

For me, or the Ford? I gave up arguing with Alf. He belongs to the old blokey generation that doesn't trust women drivers, but loves to help them when they get stuck.

Kingston, nearly a two-hour drive, is your average satellite commuter town complete with shopping centre. Alf hates crowds and traffic so we bought the paint, dined on hamburgers in his favourite cafe and hit the road again.

The Ford's sad old engine overheated on the way home. Fortunately Alf knew what to do. I observed closely as he gave me a lesson. We resumed our drive home. I felt relieved as we drove over the hill and Shelly Beach stretched ahead.

'Couldn't get a better view in the world.'

I agreed.

I do miss my Audi. I loved my Audi. I can see I'll need a reliable car in six – no – five months' time. Driving a 1987 Ford is not my idea of automotive bliss.

To: Adrian <bookstreet@network.com.au>
From: Gina <piececake@email.com.au>
Subject: Paint
Paint problem solved. Found paint charts. Went with Alf to Kingston and purchased paint for shop and Crow's Nest Flat. I've forwarded invoice to Sea Haven bank. Antoinette, paint-shop chick, sends you her love.
Gina

Wednesday 5 August
Another damp day – usual August weather for Shelly Beach. The Dog and I visited bubbly Bianca of Scissors salon. I wanted to talk to her about the writers' group. Bianca left a client to come to the counter.

'Do you have any free time?' I whispered. 'I've got one or two queries about Adrian's writers' group.'

She did. Bianca loves a chat. She had a break between appointments in the afternoon at 2ish. The Dog and I arranged to meet her in the picnic area on the foreshore in front of the shop. Bianca likes to escape in the fresh air: 'Get away from the hair-product smells.'

At 2ish, on the dot, the Dog and I returned to the foreshore picnic area armed with a flask of coffee and some chocolate cake. From
the foreshore we watched Bianca lock Scissors and dash across the
road to join us.

I poured Bianca coffee and offered her chocolate cake.

She took a slice. 'I shouldn't. I'm on a diet.'

While she was eating a second slice of cake I ventured into rocky
waters. 'I don't want to tread on toes but . . . I was wondering . . .
should I ask Digby Prentice-Hill if he'd like to be key keeper for the
writers' group?'

Bianca choked on her chocolate cake. 'No way!'

It seems Adrian and Digby are like knights jousting. (Bianca's into
Camelot. Been watching heaps of DVDs about knights and stuff.)

'Wasn't Heath Ledger the coolest Lancelot?'

I know Heath Ledger but I was unaware of his Lancelot role. I
was eager to keep the conversation moving ahead, so I agreed.

'Chocolate cake to die for. Did you make it?'

'Yes.' I promised to give Bianca the recipe.

Bianca chirped on. 'The writers' group and Writefest are Adrian's
ideas. Did Adrian mention Writefest? It's a writers' festival to be held
in Shelly Beach. The whole town can see Digby wishes he'd thought
of it first.'

Writefest? Too much information, Gina. Don't go there.

'So it's best you don't ask Digby to be key keeper while Adrian's
away because that would make him the boss of Adrian's stuff.'

I understood.

'Adrian said you were a very responsible and trustworthy person,
and you'd be happy to fill in wherever needed.'

Thank you, Adrian.

'Most out-of-towners come to Shelly Beach to freefall. Violet says
they need to escape stuff. Are you escaping?'

'You could say that. A bad marriage.'

Bianca oozed sympathy. She's had personal stuff to deal with too – the end of her relationship with Josh, smiley Shelly Beach teacher, writers' group member and stand-in convener for the Shelly Beach Book Club.

'We were engaged but Josh dallied.' (Dallied is Bianca's word of the week.) 'And then Josh hooked up with Crystal.'

'Crystal?'

'My sister. Crystal left town ten months ago. Josh still isn't dating anyone, but I've decided to move on. I've set myself a goal. I'm saving for a flight to New York or London where I'll become a leading hair stylist. Build my career. Do you have a goal?'

Do I have a goal? In another life I've had mission statements, strategic priorities and key performance indicators. Do they equate to a goal?

I looked at Bianca. 'Well, I had a goal. Thinking of getting a new one.'

Bianca understood. It's tricky deciding on a goal and then formulating an action plan so you can achieve it.

Thursday 6 August

When we arrived home from school Bossy Child raced to the computer to see if there were any emails from Adrian. The inbox was empty.

'How long have you known Adrian?'

'Not long.'

'How long is "not long"?'

'I met him once – twice – three times, counting the day I moved in here.'

'Is that all? We've known him ever since he came to live here. Dad and Adrian were friends. They used to go fishing together. That was before Dad got cancer.'

What do you say to comfort a child whose father died recently of cancer? 'Let's cook dessert.' And we did: creamy rice pudding and rhubarb fool using rhubarb from Adrian's garden.

When Joan rang, the Dog and I walked Bossy Child next door. The Dog and I were happy to escape the chilly night air and return to our fire. We watched the flickering flames and listened to the rain falling on Adrian's roof.

'The first meeting with your owner was serendipitous, Dog.'

The Dog's eyes glazed over at the mention of Adrian.

'Your owner offered me my escape to Shelly Beach at our second meeting. I was still camping at Eva's flat. It was still cramped and uncomfortable. Dominic, her boyfriend, was staying over, and I remember getting up to avoid Eva and Dominic's coupling noises seeping through the study walls. I'd taken my breakfast onto Eva's expensive bay-view balcony and was attempting to trap a pigeon with toast crumbs when my mobile rang.

'It was your owner asking me if I could see him from the balcony.

'I dodged past the potted palms. Adrian was in the street below: a tall, bearded man holding a mobile phone. He waved his available arm like a dangly scarecrow. I clutched my bathrobe and gave a short wave back.

'He wanted to meet me for coffee. He had a proposition.

'I said I'd meet him in thirty minutes – but did it in fifteen. I took five minutes to shower and dress, ten minutes to put on my make-up. I left a post-it note on the bench for Eva: *Gone for a walk – Gina*.

'In the street, we exchanged a clumsy handshake. Adrian drove us to a bayside cafe that was comfortingly noisy with Saturday breakfast diners.

'As soon as we were served coffee, Adrian delivered his proposition. Would I like to be a house-slash-dog-sitter? He was heading overseas for six months to look after his daughter's children while she had treatment for cancer. After hearing my story at Julia's two days before, Adrian thought it could be the perfect solution for both of us.

Evidently house-slash-dog-sitters are hard to find for out-of-the-way locations.

'Adrian showed me photographs of you, this cottage and Shelly Beach. I could have a rent-free and bill-free contract. All the house-sitter had to do was to take the bills to the Sea Haven bank.

'And the house-sitter was welcome to use his old Ford until it died. He said he planned to buy a new car when he returned.

'Your owner gave me a two-day deadline to reply. Questions were darting through my brain. Did I want to live at Shelly Beach for the next six months or become a Mary Poppins nanny? Maybe even a Nurse Matilda?

'I returned to Eva's apartment two hours later.

'After the contract for my novel had been cancelled, I'd decided to get my act together again. My diary was crowded with appointments for massages, facials, and hair and nail treatments to transform me into an in-control chic-corporate job applicant once more.

'Now, due to my reduced financial position, I'd had to cancel these appointments. One look at my cancelled list and I'd made my decision.

'I rang Adrian and told him I'd look after his house and dog – not imagining his dog would be so difficult to look after.'

The Dog ignored this comment.

'Next I rang my daughter Julia and her husband Simon, and told them of my decision. Julia and Simon understood. And that's the story of how I met your owner for the second time and ended up at Shelly Beach.'

The Dog was asleep.

Friday 7 August
My carnivorous cravings are unquenchable. I was so tired of eating nothing but eggs and vegetables from Adrian's garden. To hell with the budget! It was blowing a gale but I was determined to make a flying visit to Rupert's Butchery to buy some steak.

The Dog didn't want to venture outside. He hates walking in the wind and the rain.

'You can stay home as long as you promise not to run off.'

The Dog promised – dog's honour – not to escape. I believed him.

Gale-force winds and driving rain had reduced the bay to a washing-machine swirl of white-capped waves. I burst into Rupert's Butchery anticipating an oasis of warmth and shelter and was brought to a sudden halt. The little shop was crowded. There were four customers including myself, and Harold's mum (she comes in every Friday to make her world-famous sausages).

'Like a cup of tea, dear? I'm just about to make one.'

I nodded and accepted her offer.

'You've met Digby?'

I nodded and smiled.

'He's just arrived back from Sydney. He's been a star at a huge conference at the university. And you know Henry Shepherd?'

Of course I'd met Henry, owner of fluffy poodle Sally. Another smile, another warm handshake. 'And you know Lee Wang?'

Yes, I knew Lee. He'd been a regular in my dreams.

Harold's mum vanished through a hidden door at the back of the shop and Digby prepared to deliver a charm-blitz.

'We were talking about last week's writers' group meeting. I'm encouraging Henry and Harold to join the group. I was telling them what a brilliant job you did convening the first meeting.'

I smiled. Harold's mum had reappeared with a tray with a pot of tea, milk, sugar and four cups and saucers. I accepted my cup of tea.

'If you don't mind, dear, I have to get on with the sausages. Playing bridge this afternoon.' Harold's mum disappeared again.

Digby continued with his charm-blitz. 'Adrian was relieved to find someone reliable to look after Hugo and his cottage. He mentioned he'd caught you just as you were starting long-service leave.'

Thank you, Adrian, for the white lie. I smiled, sipped my tea and prepared for more charm.

'I can't recall what field Adrian said you worked in? Journalism? Librarianship?'

Without thinking I replied, 'Librarianship.' Skipped the 'unsuccessful novelist' title. (And didn't mention I'd been an IT communications manager – before being made redundant. If I drew a graph of my career it would show an uninterrupted red line rising upwards through the seventies, eighties and nineties. The noughties would show the red line unravelling, ending in a tidy coil at the bottom of the graph.)

Lee was watching me with his intense brown eyes.

Digby was still digging for information. 'Work anywhere interesting?'

'Mainly in the corporate sector. My field was information systems. I've been working with local libraries lately. Taking a break to decide what to do next.'

I gave Digby a cool gaze as I let the (white) lies flow easily from my lips. (I had been taking the Storytime Activities Program every Wednesday at my former local library for the six months before I moved to Shelly Beach: my weekly escape from the attic.)

Digby was satisfied with his information-gathering and moved on. 'I'm transcribing Henry's journals at the moment. They make awesome reading. A brilliant social history of our small town.'

I smiled, and promised Henry Shepherd I'd call and check out his journals sometime.

Digby paid for his meticulously wrapped parcel of sausages.

'Would you like a lift home?'

I could see Digby's comfortable Mercedes parked outside the butchery.

'No, thank you. I enjoy the exercise. I love walking along the beach when it's windy and rainy.' Another (white) lie. 'Blows the cobwebs away.'

Besides, there was the prospect of a short walk along the beach with Lee. Digby left me to 'brave the elements'.

Lee collected the order for Rosa's and I paid for my steak, and bones for the Dog.

As we battled our way along Beach Road, Lee shouted novel-talk above the sound of the wind and pounding waves. He left me at Rosa's. He had to start his shift.

The Dog gave me a waggy-tail greeting at Sea View Cottage. I explained the steak was for me; the bones were for him. He approves of me eating meat. At least we have something in common – we're both carnivores.

I watched the Dog use his sharp little teeth to gnaw shreds of flesh and gristle from his bone. 'If you were a lion, Dog, I'd have to feed you with meat tied to a stick. A long stick.'

Saturday 8 August

I fed the dog, fed the Girls, fed the doves, cleaned the henhouse, walked the Dog, cleaned Adrian's house, did my laundry, weeded Adrian's vegetable garden and helped the Dog fill in his holes. Immersing myself in routines and rituals is comforting.

I've not told the Dog but I'm actually enjoying the weather. 'I haven't been exposed to weather for years, Dog. Or the sky. There's one thing you can say about Shelly Beach: it has huge amounts of sky. You don't see much sky in the city.'

The Dog's not interested in sky. He's more interested in earth – moving it.

Late in the afternoon the Dog scrambled through his pet door from who knows where. I shooed him outside and rang Bossy Child. 'The Dog has a problem. Can you call in sometime?'

In five minutes flat Bossy Child appeared. I didn't need to explain the Dog's problem. We quickly opened windows and held our noses.

'He's found a dead animal or bird at the beach and he's been

96

rolling in it. Probably a pelican. He loves dead pelicans. It's your fault, Gina. You can't let him go to the beach on his own.'

I refused to carry guilt for a Houdini dog.

'You'll have to bath him, Gina.'

'I don't know how to bath a dog!'

'You can't bath a dog?'

'No!'

'Did you look in Adrian's manual?'

'Yes. Under D for Dog and B for Bath. No entries.'

Bossy Child gave me a rolled-eye look. She located Adrian's manual and opened it at H for Hugo. I read the step-by-step instructions for bathing a dog, and noted the last sentence: *Keep Hugo inside for several hours after bathing until he is acclimatised to his new smell. He has a tendency to run off to Henry Shepherd's.*

Bossy Child was called home and I was left with my mission. 'You have to have a bath, Dog. Then you have to be kept to quarters until you dry out.'

Obviously the Dog had checked the meaning of the word 'bath' in his canine dictionary. He went and hid under the couch.

'You'll have to come out eventually.'

I sat and waited for the Dog like a cat outside a mouse-hole.

Sunday 9 August

Knocking on the front door woke us. I pulled back the bedroom drapes. The green-friendly Daphne Schwarz, valued SBWG member, was standing on the verandah. I opened the door, holding a blanket around me, and gave her a pasted-on smile.

She propped a bike against the wall. 'Do you mind if I come in? You look like you need a cup of Adrian's strong coffee.'

I opened the door and watched as Daphne fussed around making coffee in Adrian's kitchen.

I checked the kitchen clock – 8 a.m. Bloody hell!

'I'm short on time. Want to catch the 9 a.m. church service. I thought you'd like to borrow my bicycle while you're staying here. I know Adrian hasn't got one.'

Smile, Gina! Daphne meant well. Through the window I could see a bicycle propped against the wall; a helmet was dangling from the handlebars.

'I've bought myself a new-model bicycle and a helmet. My old helmet should fit you.'

I sipped the coffee she handed me and smiled a thank you.

'Cycling will help to get the weight off!'

I gave another tight smile.

'Make sure you garage the bicycle. The salt air rusts metal.'

I nodded.

'When Lee comes tomorrow, go cycling with him. Get him to show you some easy bicycle tracks. Cycled much?'

'A long time ago.'

'Won't take you long to learn again. Make sure you tell Lee you're just a beginner.'

Daphne finished her coffee, zipped up her jacket and was off.

The Dog came outside to help me check out Daphne's bike. I confessed to the Dog, 'I haven't ridden a bike in decades.'

The Dog thinks riding a bike is as easy as digging a hole. Once you've learnt how you never forget.

I put in a half-hour of wobbly rides up and down Sea Spray Street, the Dog following a safe distance behind. He wasn't impressed with the idea of running beside me on his lead when I go for longer rides. However, if I had a basket on the bike, the Dog would be happy to ride in it, channelling Toto in *The Wizard of Oz*.

Monday 10 August
Lee called in and we cycled around the Shelly Beach locality. Lee chose a flat route. We left cycling along the back-beach cliff tops

for another time – when I'm more confident. Lee left after coffee, cake, and pleasant book-talk. He wanted to get back to his novel: 'It's progressing well!'

The Dog and I decided to visit Shelly Beach's celebrated author, Bill Kruger. We had to collect handouts to be photocopied for the next writers' group meeting.

Bill wasn't in. Deb, Bill's wife, introduced herself. She gave us the handouts to be copied and invited us in for the customary Shelly Beach cup of tea and cake, water and a biscuit for the Dog.

'Hunter's sleeping.'

The Dog was relieved. Hunter is Bill and Deb's two-year-old son. The Dog's definitely not keen on small humans.

Deb, an attractive young mum, was ready for a chat. 'Bill's uptown. He had to talk to the marketing and publicity people at his publisher's. Bill hated the marketing and publicity stuff that came with his first book.

'Siobhan, Bill's editor, is a lovely person. Very warm and nurturing. Siobhan said I had to persuade Bill to let go. His book was ready for publishing.'

Deb thought she heard young Hunter stirring and left the room.

I sipped my tea and checked the Dog. He was sitting under Deb's chair. Obviously he's still sulking over the bath incident. I pulled him out and plonked him on my knee.

'Once I had a caring editor. An editor who lived in cyberspace – we never met. I wonder how an editor feels about a novel (one they've spent hours working on) when it loses its legs? How do they feel as they parcel up the edited, ready-for-publishing manuscript and Express Post it back to its author?'

The Dog was pleased when Deb returned to the room and continued with more Bill novel-talk. 'After the final edit of Bill's novel, Siobhan suggested I take Bill on a holiday to clear his mind, but we didn't have the money. Getting the grant to tutor the writers' group has been a godsend. We're so grateful to Adrian. Preparing the how-to-write stuff for the group has taken Bill's mind off his novel. He did seven rewrites and still wasn't happy.'

Deb poured me another cup of tea and I oozed sympathy. Bloody hell – seven rewrites!

'Violet says Bill's like lots of authors. They don't want to let go of their novel. Violet copyedits Bill's novels. Her father owned a printing company and she learnt to copyedit when she was a little girl. Her father made her use a ruler under each line, working up from the bottom of each page to find mistakes. Violet said it was tough, but it's made her a brilliant speller. And she knows her grammar and punctuation backwards.'

I took note of Violet's hidden talents and experience.

'Violet says she can see Bill standing at a bookshop register, and before he allows a customer to buy his novel he'll change the comma on page 231 to a semicolon.'

Just then young Hunter woke up. The Dog and I decided it was time to leave.

We chatted on the way home. 'I guess if you were a cyberspace editor, Dog, and you needed money for food, rent and bills . . . you'd move on. You'd keep editing and editing whether novels get published or not.'

The Dog had no desire to be a cyberspace editor. In fact he hadn't a clue what I was talking about.

Tuesday 11 August

I'm in agony. I can't believe you use so many muscles when you take one short bike ride. After the Dog and I returned from our walk today, there was a message on Adrian's answering machine. It was Clare. I listened with trepidation while I replayed her bubbly message.

Hi, Gina, it's Clare. Hope you're out and about enjoying this gorgeous chilly morning. Eva, Hester, and self are planning to visit next Saturday. Staying the night, returning late Sunday. Have you room in the inn? We'll bring food and grog. Looking forward to seeing you then – bye.

Bloody hell!

'What do you think, Dog? Can I reply I've got pneumonia? Will ring and arrange another visit when I'm on my feet? Or can I use my standard do-nothing-and-hope-it-will-go-away strategy?

'I hate my friends having to feel obligated to look after poor old Gina, who's in a big hole and struggling to get out.'

The Dog got the 'big hole' metaphor.

By the time the Dog decided on the strategy I should take, Clare had phoned again, and I'd agreed to my friends' visit. Later I found a follow-up message on Adrian's answering machine.

Hi, Gina, it's Clare. We've booked in at Sea Haven Resort instead, but we'll see you on Saturday. Can't wait! See you then.

My comfort-loving friends must have agreed that Sea View Cottage (minus a sea view, plus a lone dodgy bathroom) – and the prospect of tossing coins to see who slept on Adrian's lumpy couch – equals minus one-star accommodation.

Later that night the Dog and I were mulling over stuff in front of the fire. He agreed Clare sounded her usual bubbly self. The Dog thought the sooner I saw her the better. I'm guessing (relying on the fact) that James has not told her about his dodgy proposition.

Bottom line: who cares? Would my world crumble if Clare never spoke to me again?

The Dog thought it highly unlikely.

Wednesday 12 August

Pandora rang and invited me to have a meal with her and Bianca at Rosa's pub before the writers' group meeting tonight. 'We'll help you set up afterwards.'

I accepted her invitation. The Dog promised faithfully he'd stay home. He didn't. He gatecrashed the meeting. When we arrived at the community hall, he was sitting at the door wearing his lost-dog please-take-me look. I didn't ask if he'd been following me all evening. Waste of energy, Gina. Everyone made a huge fuss of him – as usual. He kept giving me his I-told-you-so look.

While Pandora, Bianca and I set up the hall, arranged the cups and saucers and filled the urn for supper, docile writers wandered in and talked about the weather. There was very little talk about writing.

Bill was late again. He lost his car keys. Hunter had hidden them: 'He's into keys at the moment.'

We all understood. Then we launched into a friendly let's-go-round-the-circle exercise. Members shared their ten-word, fifty-word and hundred-word pitches about their novels in or out of progress.

Pandora and I passed on the exercise. Pandora is aiming to write unconnected pieces, and I'm not writing at all. Just opening and shutting the hall and preparing the supper, etc. etc. etc.

Digby did his ten-minute-plus wordwise burst on dangling participles. Bloody hell!

Bianca had no idea what Digby was on about, and she was too scared to ask. I promised to call at Scissors tomorrow with a helpful explanation. 'I'm client-free about 5ish,' she whispered.

Bill, our tutor with the nervous smile and trembling hands, opened his comforting folder containing inspiring how-to tips and tricks. When Bill talks about writing he lights up. He discussed character-driven plots until supper.

The community hall was transformed into a war zone after supper. Violet shared her three-page section from chapter five of her whodunnit, *The Compost Bin Murder,* and an eyeball-to-eyeball battle took place between Violet and Digby.

'Any child can write a standard detective novel,' was Digby's first tactless comment to Violet after she finished her reading. 'Closed-country-house detective novels are out. Crime thrillers with a forensic-scientist sleuth or police procedurals are in.'

Violet defended her writing with amazing tenacity. She quoted astonishing sales figures for Agatha Christie, 'an expert in writing closed-country-house crime fiction. And she's still selling – even though she died years ago!'

Violet gave Digby a final look that would have made lesser mortals wither and die. She gathered up her whodunnit featuring the dashing Red Blaze and stomped out of the hall.

Members of the Shelly Beach Writers' Group sat in frozen silence; too terrified to say a thing. Too terrified to move a centimetre.

Our tactful tutor carefully picked up the pieces of his shattered workshop and talked about the characters in his latest novel. Evidently his characters arrive fully developed. Complete with a personality, attitude, way of speaking, seeing, hearing, etc. Thank you, Bill!

Bill did admit that some authors have to work very hard on their characters until they are fully developed. He handed out the writing tasks I'd photocopied – our homework for the next meeting. Apparently Shelly Beach writers should be able to come up with well-rounded characters by next meeting.

Bill closed the meeting early. Subdued members trickled out of the hall. Daphne whispered to Pandora, Bianca and self, 'Back to my place for a nightcap. Hot chocolate or something stronger?'

Bianca didn't accept Daphne's offer as she had to be up early: 'Heaps of waxing appointments and massages at Sea Haven Resort.'

Pandora, the Dog and I voted for 'something stronger'. I promised to give Bianca the goss tomorrow.

Sitting in Daphne's comfortable home, warmed by a blazing fire, we relaxed. Daphne's orange and poppyseed cake and parsnip wine, served by hubby Charles, worked their magic on us.

'I'll have a word with Digby,' Daphne promised. 'Charles and I have known him for years.'

Charles appeared with more cake and wine. He nodded. 'We met on holidays at Shelly Beach before we moved here. I'm sure Digby will apologise to Violet before the next meeting.'

Pandora whispered, 'Don't hold your breath.'

Daphne ignored Pandora. 'Digby's getting back to his former self now. It's taken him a while to move on after losing Annette so suddenly. I thought the meeting went swimmingly, Gina – in spite of the small fracas. Don't fret. We'll sort it out! We'll get some by-laws up and running. Everything will be fine.'

Back home I voiced my worries to the Dog. 'There's that comforting word again, Dog – *fine*. Why don't I feel comforted?

'I can see Adrian's writers disappearing into an Agatha Christie-style *And Then There Were None* group. The keeper's key will be the only thing remaining when Adrian returns in the summer.'

The Dog's not fussed as long as Adrian comes back.

Thursday 13 August
As soon as Bossy Child arrived she logged onto the computer to check the email. 'Adrian's sent you an email, Gina. He wants to know how the writers' group meeting went.'

To: Adrian <bookstreet@network.com.au>
From: Gina <piececake@email.com.au>
Subject: Second writers' group meeting
Pandora and Bianca helped me open, set up supper and shut
the hall. All members were present and correct last night. Violet
is threatening to leave the group unless Digby apologises for his
comments during the workshop session.

The members have a wild array of novels in progress or to be started. A jelly-bean mix of popular genre, to wit:

- Bianca: romantic, sexy chick lit.
- Lee: blockbuster crime fiction. Murder and vice in the Hong Kong kitchen of a five-star hotel.
- Digby: psycho thriller set in academia.
- Daphne: historical romance (probably Regency). Still to do research.
- Violet : Agatha Christie-type whodunnit. (Already written six novels! Starting on her seventh!)
- Josh: young-adult fantasy/science fiction. He had an idea for a book about a young wizard going to a boarding school but it's already been taken. Joke!
- Pandora: ideas still banging around in her head. She's happy to write unrelated pieces and see what she gets.
- Me: restated my position. Not writing a novel.

Bill talked about character-driven narratives and gave out writing tasks for next meeting.

Gina

To: Gina <piececake@email.com.au>
From: Adrian <bookstreet@network.com.au>
Re: Second writers' group meeting
Well done! Interesting meeting. Would like to have been a fly on the wall.

Adrian

Friday 14 August

Another ordinary day. I was preparing for an early night, tucked up in bed with a good book from Adrian's bookshelf, when car lights in the drive sent me into panic mode. It was Bianca.

'Thank God, Dog, it isn't Smart James again.'

(The Dog says I have to get used to the idea that locals never give you prior warning of their visits.) I opened the door and invited Bianca inside.

'Sorry to bother you, Gina. Can I have the recipe for your scrummy chocolate cake? It's Mum's birthday next week and I want to bake it for her.'

'Right!' I breathed a sigh of relief. No drama. I could do this. 'Would you like coffee, tea? Have you eaten? How about an omelette?'

'That sounds brilliant.'

I put the kettle on, added a log to the dying fire and whipped up an omelette using Adrian's Girls' eggs.

'This is so good. Just finished my last client. Friday's late-night opening. I'm exhausted but that's okay. Scissors is doing well. Only been going six months. I'm gathering a good book of clients. It's tough running your own business.'

I agreed. I found a pencil and paper for Bianca to take down my recipe. By the time we got to the method I realised Bianca was clueless in the cookery department.

She looked at me with her doe eyes. 'Could you make it for me? I'll style your hair in exchange. You could get a rock-chick look.'

The Dog raised one hairy eyebrow. I ignored him, and ran my hands through my out-of-control hair. 'Right. Deal done.'

I took down details. 'When's your mother's birthday?'

'Next Wednesday – the nineteenth'.

I marked the date on my crowded calendar. 'How many people will be at the party?'

'About twelve.'

'I'll make two cakes. That should do it.'

Bianca looked relieved and happy. We talked about the common practice of dumping. Evidently one of Bianca's friends was dumped by email. Another by mobile phone.

'Was yours a royal dumping?' Bianca asked.

'You could say that. It was very sudden.'

'Were you totally heartbroken? Are you still in love with your husband?'

'No. I was planning to be the dumper – not the dumpee. Kenneth beat me to it.'

'When I broke up with Josh it was monumental. Like a knife slicing through your guts, leaving you raw and exposed to every zephyr. I expected Josh to get engaged to Crystal at any moment – but he didn't. Crystal left soon after. I've vowed never to speak to my sister again.'

As you do when your only sister gets it on with your fiancé.

'My stomach still somersaults a little when I see Josh. Does yours?'

'No. And I haven't taken an indigestion tablet for weeks. My digestive system has recovered well.'

'I had zero sleep for weeks after it happened. How about you?'

'I'm sleeping well now.' And I am – apart from the odd mouse incident and sexy dream featuring a chef young enough to be my son.

'Mum says time heals all wounds. You made a cool move coming to Shelly Beach. This is a brilliant place to chill out.'

I nodded.

'You need to find new things to do – take your mind off old stuff. That's why I started my own business.'

I nodded.

'Pandora says nothing heals like a new love – but I haven't found one yet. Neither has Josh.' (Pause.) 'Lee Wang is pretty hot, isn't he?'

'Haven't noticed.' (Lie.)

'It's his voice. It's so seductive.' (Seductive is Bianca's word of the week.) 'And his Hong Kong accent. And his great body. He works out with the Shelly Beach lifesavers.'

No comment.

Bianca is an excellent judge of young men's bodies. She's had the good fortune to grow up with a surfeit of young, tanned, muscular males surrounding her during her short life in Shelly Beach.

She finished her omelette. 'Thank you, Gina, you're a great cook. Have to go now. I open Scissors early on Saturdays. When you drop the cakes in next Wednesday I'll make an appointment to do your hair.'

I watched as the zappy young businesswoman backed her car out of Adrian's drive and roared up Sea Spray Street.

'I wonder how many chocolate cakes will be needed to get you a rock-dog look, Dog?'

The Dog crept into his hidey place under the couch. I went to bed thinking about Lee Wang surrounded by an air of mystery as he jogged along the Shelly Beach sands, visiting Sea View Cottage every Monday to borrow Adrian's novels.

Saturday 15 August
The Dog and I were up bright and early – ready and waiting for my friends' arrival. As soon as Eva, Clare and Hester stepped onto Adrian's verandah I was regaled with flowers and champagne.

'Congratulations, Grandma!'

I felt like I was going to be physically ill.

'You haven't heard?'

'No!'

Clare was beside herself. She had important information to relay. 'You have a grandson. Born on Thursday at 10.23 p.m. A gorgeous baby boy weighing eight pounds two ounces. Julia and Simon haven't decided on a name yet.'

The Dog looked at me. He knew I'd been trying to connect with my daughter again – especially recently. I'd been phoning Julia and Simon practically every day re: the birth of my grandson. Last week I realised my OTT phone calls were driving my nearly-due-to-give-birth daughter and her husband up the wall. I was trying, but how many ways can you ask a pregnant daughter if she's about to give birth?

The Dog said I should listen to my little finger. It tells you when to stop asking questions. (The Dog heard a French backpacker in Rosa's pub say this.)

I ignored the Dog but I trusted my son-in-law. Simon had promised faithfully to ring me as soon as Julia went into labour.

Bloody hell! Somehow I'd missed his call.

Clare connected with my stressed body language. She actually looked flustered. 'Simon said he'd emailed you when he couldn't get through on the phone.'

Emailed me? Of course. If your mother-in-law ignores phone messages, you text or email to let her know her daughter's about to give birth. 'But Simon doesn't know Adrian's email address.'

Clare stared at me. 'I gave it to him. I rang last week and that child you mind gave it to me.'

Damn!

We moved to Adrian's desk in the bedroom and opened the inbox on the computer. There was an email from Simon sent early Friday morning. It immediately bounced into a Disney-coloured, all-singing, all-dancing birth announcement.

Bloody hell! My stomach was a churning mess. I had to go to the city. I must visit my unnamed grandson. I must visit my daughter.

I stowed the thought of a city expedition to the back of my mind and concentrated on my one-day-at-a-time survival strategy. Somehow I would get through this day.

Amazingly the rest of the day passed minus stress. Could there be anything less stressful than finding out your one and only daughter gave birth to your grandchild two days ago, without you knowing? I'd missed the exact moment, time and date of my grandson's birth.

I cooked up a storm for my friends. We (except Clare who was the nominated driver) spent the night drinking far too much. I caught up with the latest meaningless have-you-heard goss.

It was after midnight when I waved goodbye to my friends. Clare reversed Hester's Merc very carefully in Adrian's driveway. She was driving them to Sea Haven Resort – five-star paradise.

I took deep breaths. My shoulders sank to their normal position. The Dog and I stood silently on Adrian's verandah inhaling the soothing, salty night air. No stars tonight.

I fired questions at the Dog when we were back in front of the fire. 'What do you think, Dog? Will my grandson be named Kenneth Junior? Will I bump into Kenneth and Clever Angela when I visit?'

The Dog had no idea. I poured myself a glass of one of Adrian's reds. I wrote the wine label in my notebook so I could replace it.

Sunday 16 August

Clare arranged for us to meet for breakfast at Rosa's pub. It was a revolting day as usual – gale-force winds and choppy waves on the bay. After breakfast we walked against the wind along Beach Road to Piece of Cake.

At Clare's insistence we stopped and took refuge there. I gave my friends a guided tour. They looked suitably impressed (I don't think they were faking it). Piece of Cake is shaping up well. No doubt it will fulfil Adrian's sea-change dream and become an out-of-the-way, jazzy watering hole for upmarket tourists.

Clare had added funds to my bank account, and was thrilled with the transactions she'd made. She had managed to sell my designer clothes with astonishing results. 'Designer vintage evening wear is hot. Some pieces are still being held, Gina. You'll get cash on sale.'

Hester was not so lucky with queries about (my) ownership of the original artworks that had been housed at Montpellier Place. She'd contacted Julia. 'They are part of the firm's assets, Gina. They're being sold as Laurel-Scott Corporation assets.'

110

Damn! Thoughtful Hester gave me a framed Clarice Beckett print – blurry car headlights in a foggy night. I showed dutiful appreciation of the print but I won't hang it. I'll learn to live with the loss of my Clarice Beckett original.

Later that afternoon, Clare and I were standing on Adrian's verandah, watching Eva directing Hester to reverse her Merc.

'I was reading an article about dogs at the doctor's last week, Gina. You're wasting your time talking to that dog. He doesn't understand a thing you're saying to him except "food" and his name. The rest is just "blah, blah, blah".'

I smiled and air-kissed Clare as she got ready to leave. The Dog and I watched my friends' one-car contingent of goodwill depart.

In the quiet and peace of a Shelly Beach evening I confided in the Dog: 'I've felt sick and guilty and terrified the whole weekend. Sick and guilty for not knowing when my grandson was born. Terrified in case Clare announced James had betrayed her – and she knew he'd tried it on with me.

'I should be delighted at the thought of meeting my new grandson, but I don't want to bump into Kenneth and Clever Angela when I visit Julia and baby.'

The Dog thought I needed to move on.

'I'm moving on – but I'm not ready for a Kenneth-slash-Clever-Angela meeting yet.'

The Dog thought it was unlikely I'd meet Kenneth and Clever Angela. They'd want to avoid a meeting too.

'Clare was her usual irritatingly bubbly self. She didn't mention James. I'm assuming everything is fine.'

The Dog thinks I overuse the four-letter word – *fine*. The word that means so little and yet so much.

'If I were a bear I'd hibernate in a cave, Dog. Instead, this young grandmother has to set out on a perilous journey to meet her grandson.'

The Dog doesn't know a thing about bears or hibernating. He

offered me little sympathy. And grandmothers (young or old) do not register on his radar. He can't even remember having a mother. He gave me his abandoned-pup look.

We ignored Clare's comments suggesting that a dog doesn't understand what a dog-sitter is talking about. The Dog understands perfectly.

I took a shower until the warm water ran out, followed by a sleeping pill. Tomorrow I'll organise a trip to the city to meet my new grandson and try to build a bridge between my daughter and me.

Monday 17 August

Lee called in early; he was on his way to the dentist in Kingston. I made coffee and brought him up to speed with the weekend happenings. I told him I'd missed the birth of my grandson and that I was going uptown to see the new baby and my daughter soon.

Lee's a very perceptive young man. Not a mention of my new young-grandmother status.

'Are you upset about missing the birth?'

Bloody hell, yes! I'm upset! Laden with guilt. Stressed to the hilt. But I'm not stepping over our friendship boundary that gives us a permit to discuss books, food, music, wine, Lee's novel – and nothing else. Lee doesn't need to see any baggage I carry.

I sidestepped the question; segued into talk about Lee's novel. Lee is introducing an antsy, secondary female character to sex up his storyline. We talked disconcerting sexy novel-writing talk until it was time for Lee to catch the bus to Kingston.

I mentally prepared an excited grandmother spiel, then phoned Simon. I needed to know the whereabouts of Julia and grandson. Were they in hospital or at home?

I struck lucky. Simon answered his phone. I had actual voice-to-voice contact with my son-in-law. He graciously accepted my belated congratulations.

'Julia and the baby are doing reasonably well. Yes, they're still in the hospital – they'll be staying there for a few more days.'

I murmured appropriate agreeable sounds. Evidently The Parks is an excellent private hospital. Simon's able to dine with Julia and his son in their room each night, with a 'first-class menu'.

'I'm glad to hear it. Did Julia have a difficult birth? Were you there?'

'She had a very difficult birth. Unfortunately I couldn't be with her. I was interstate on business. But she's recovering, getting stronger every day. Our son is doing very well.'

More guilt. I swallowed and resumed our conversation. 'That's good to hear. I'd like to visit Julia and the baby tomorrow – if that's suitable?'

'Of course it's suitable, Gina. You're our son's grandmother. Julia would be delighted to see you.'

I pushed the guilt away. I avoided asking the name of my grandson. That can wait until tomorrow.

Simon gave me directions to the hospital.

Alf helped me plan my travel arrangements to the city and back to Shelly Beach. 'Bus travels from Shelly Beach to Kingston three times a day. A two-hour journey each way. The early morning bus connects with the commuter train at Kingston. It's a two-hour train trip to the city.'

'Right!' No wonder Shelly Beach is a backwater. No other way to get here except by Cobb & Co coach.

I allowed myself a window of two hours to get to the hospital, say hello to Julia and the baby, then race back to the station to catch the train to Kingston to connect with the last bus to Shelly Beach.

Alf's comment on my plans: 'A bit dodgy. Connection depends on which bus driver is on duty. If it's Tom or Alec, they hang around and wait for the city train. If it's Mike, and he's in a bad mood, he leaves on time. Doesn't care if the city train has arrived or not.'

Bloody hell! I hated the thought of being stranded in Kingston late at night; hunting for overnight accommodation that could blow my budget.

I suggested to Alf that I'd drive Adrian's Ford and park in Kingston. 'Then I only have to worry about the train. The train service is reliable.'

Alf shook his head. He doesn't have enormous confidence in the Ford. We reached a compromise. I'll take my mobile phone. Alf will keep working at Piece of Cake until I'm safely home: 'Plenty of jobs to finish there.'

If the Ford breaks down I'll ring, and he'll pick me up. Done deal.

I carefully transcribed my travel arrangements into my notebook. It reminded me of the complicated travel plans I'd coordinated for Kenneth during the early years of our marriage. Travel plans to minimise costs and maximise contracts when he was pitching deals overseas. Later, perky personal assistants took over my duties while I focused on climbing my way up the career ladder.

I decided to wear my Armani trench coat plus chic scarf to maintain an upmarket young-grandmother image. Heaven forbid I should startle Simon's parents or Julia's serious friends by turning up looking like a free-spirited, gone-native grandmother.

The Dog wasn't happy. He'd prefer to be at home rather than hang round Piece of Cake with Alf.

'It's not an option, Dog.'

Tuesday 18 August

I woke at an ungodly hour, took the disgruntled Dog down to Alf and drove to Kingston. I managed to find a park in Alf's secret vandal-avoidance parking spot, and connected with the commuter train.

Dressed in designer armour and ready to fight city dragons, I melted into the commuter crowd.

I hit the city running, and kept running until I reached the hospital – or at least I jogged (fast walked). I remembered my escalator-passenger protocol and kept to the correct side. I sped past coffee shops and department stores – my secret time-filling places during those last months when I was procrastinating about when I would leave Kenneth.

I stopped at a florist's, took a long time deciding between pink roses and exotic lilies for Julia, and was talked into buying a fluffy bear as well by the caring sales assistant. I'd think of a more appropriate and significant grandmother gift when I'd checked out the gifts from my grandson's other grandparents.

At the hospital reception I asked for directions to Julia and the baby. I took time to freshen up in the ladies room. I renewed my lipstick, adjusted my chic scarf and calmed my pounding heart. Then I set off to Julia's room.

Julia was like a queen entertaining at court, a baby cot containing my new grandson beside her. Her hospital room resembled a star's dressing-room. My pink roses vanished into the background of floral tributes.

Simon and Simon's parents were present plus another group of friends, some of whom I vaguely remembered meeting. My grandson was placed in my arms. Warm, soft baby Barnaby. Not Kenneth Junior! Thank you, God.

Obligatory photos were taken: Julia's mother (the dumped younger grandmother) holding Barnaby . . . Barnaby's parents and Julia's mother (the dumped younger grandmother) holding Barnaby . . . Simon's parents (respectable older grandparents) and Julia's mother (the dumped younger grandmother) holding Barnaby.

Cameras were swapped. We went through a repeat performance – to fill Barnaby's digital or print album. Thank God the video camera was missing.

I loved holding this gorgeous pudgy baby – my grandson. I inhaled his magic baby smell. His tiny fingers clung to my finger.

Julia smiled at me. I smiled back at her as I handed my grandson to her. I felt at ease with my daughter for the first time in years.

I kissed Barnaby and Julia goodbye. I gave Julia another hug; I felt her cling to me, and I clung to my daughter.

Then I excused myself: 'I have to catch the commuter train to Kingston.'

Everyone understood. It passed unsaid that Julia's mother (the younger grandmother) was jobless, dumped (passed over for a PA) and had been evicted from her fancy home. In desperation she'd taken a position as house-sitter and dog-sitter on the Peninsula.

I smiled and left.

I raced (well, fast walked) past time-filling stores and coffee shops. I jumped aboard the Kingston commuter train just as the doors were closing. I managed to locate Adrian's Ford, pristine and unvandalised in Alf's secret parking spot, and drove home to Shelly Beach.

Fortunately Adrian's Ford performed valiantly, although I froze due to the broken heating system. Alf and the Dog were waiting for me when I pulled up outside Piece of Cake.

I collected the I'm-not-speaking-to-you Dog. I refused Alf's kind offer of a cup of tea. 'Thank you, Alf, but I'm exhausted.'

Alf understood.

'Mission accomplished, Dog. Thankfully I've avoided seeing Kenneth and Clever Angela. I'll have to see them sometime. Maybe never, with a bit of luck. It was wonderful to see my daughter and new grandson. I've coped well but it's good to be back in Shelly Beach.'

The Dog ignored me. I poured myself a glass of one of Adrian's reds. It was late but I lit the fire. I couldn't go to sleep yet. Too much stuff buzzing round in my head.

'What do you think, Dog? Was that a one-plank visit with my daughter? Is it the start of a new bridge between us?'

The Dog says one plank only bridges a very trickly stream. I'll need to find a lot more planks to make a respectable bridge.

I ignored the Dog. He knows nothing of bridges. He even hates walking out on Shelly Beach pier and has to be carried.

'Did my diplomatic son-in-law Simon arrange for his parents – the respectable older grandparents – to be present for a group photo? Did Simon advise Grandpa Kenneth to avoid the hospital when I visited? Will Simon's parents have to make another trip to hospital for a group photo with Grandpa Kenneth and his pseudo-grandma partner?

'Is it politically correct for Grandpa Kenneth and his new much, much younger partner – young enough to be his daughter – to be in a group photo with my baby grandson?

'What if the new much, much younger partner leaves Grandpa Kenneth because he's old and boring? Will Julia and Simon remove the photograph of Grandpa Kenneth and the pseudo-grandma from Barnaby's photo album?'

The Dog was pretending to be asleep. Obviously he hasn't got a clue about baby photo album protocol.

Wednesday 19 August

I'm in mourning for my recipe book collection. And my fancy cake tins. Where would they be? In Clare's garage? Maybe they're in Hester's shed on her farm?

I remember announcing I didn't want them when I left Montpellier Place but I know my friends ignored me, and judiciously packed them and a few other things to store at their homes.

When the Dog and I decided to race down to Jenkins' to buy the ingredients I needed to make Bianca's cakes, a miracle occurred. Tucked away in Jenkins' Ali Baba's cave of extraordinary products, Arnold unearthed three cake tins. When they surfaced, the Jenkins family beamed at my ecstatic show of joy.

I called at Rosa's pub to borrow Lee's cake-decorating tools. The Dog watched while, back at Sea View Cottage, I cooked two professional-looking chocolate cakes.

'Precision is the secret of baking, Dog.'

The Dog wasn't impressed. He's only eaten the vitamin-packed pellets I dispense for his breakfast and dinner.

'I enjoy cooking, Dog. I'm a good cook. I honed my skills in the early days of my marriage when Martha was caring for my baby daughter and managing our home. I did the entertaining stuff that was necessary to oil Kenneth's business deals when I came home from work.'

The Dog watched while I expertly frosted the cakes. 'I also enjoyed cooking on Martha's days off.'

I refused to give the Dog the basin or spoon to lick. 'You're putting on weight. As a dog-sitter it's my duty to keep a dog the same weight he was when I started dog-sitting.'

The Dog said it was his furry winter coat that made him look fatter. He went to dig precision-driven holes in Adrian's vegetable garden.

By five I'd deposited two classy-looking birthday cakes at Scissors. Bianca booked me in for 'the works' on Friday. A satisfying outcome all round.

I decided to dine at Rosa's pub. I was comfortable with solitary dinners-for-one. The Dog said he was happy to stay at home.

The Jenkins family was at Rosa's, and greeted me like a long-lost friend. Henry Shepherd and Digby were at another table. Pandora and Daphne signalled for me to join them. No solitary dinner-for-one at Shelly Beach.

Daphne once again advised me on the 'hot happenings' at Shelly Beach: 'Football, surfing, fishing, walking, archery. Then there's crafts, painting and patchworking. And green activities. Henry Shepherd and I organise the green activities. Everyone helps with the pelican and seal surveys.'

I smiled. 'I'm thinking about joining one or other of the groups, Daphne.' (Lie.) 'I'll get back to you.'

Daphne's husband Charles joined our table. He gave Daphne the car keys and Daphne left for her life-drawing class: 'My turn to model.'

Charles had been at a camera club meeting. 'Just yell when you're ready to join, Gina.'

I smiled my thank you. 'I'm still settling in, Charles. Things have been very hectic.'

He understood.

Back home I made a fire. 'Firewood's getting low, Dog. Remind me to ask Alf where I can order another load.'

Gazing into the flames, the Dog and I reminisced. 'You know, don't you, Dog, that I'm a failed writer? I spent a year writing that novel. Like a dream, it was picked up by the first publisher I sent it to. I spent three months working on it with my diplomatic editor.

'Then a new CEO drove into my publisher's on his chariot. The company had been taken over, and its bottom line was not looking good. Budget cuts were necessary. Lists were cut. My contract was terminated by email.'

The Dog was doing his one-eye shut, the other eye half-open trick. Infuriating! You couldn't tell if he's asleep or listening.

'I was allowed to keep my advance.'

No comment.

'I could start writing another novel.'

Still no comment.

'Adrian's been writing a novel.'

The Dog knows I know Adrian's been writing a novel because I'd discovered the folder labeled *Novel* on Adrian's computer.

'I haven't opened it. Been tempted. But I haven't read a single page of any of the seven chapters – or the synopsis, or the chapter outlines.'

The Dog knows this is not true.

'The year I spent in the attic writing was also the year when

Martha, my perfect mother-in-law, moved out. Martha had lived with us since Julia was born – yes, for years. One morning she came down to breakfast and announced, 'I'm leaving at the end of this week.' And she did. She left to marry an ageing count. Went to live with him in his Tuscan villa.

'After Martha finally left to live with her ageing count, I had a huge attack of the guilts. I realised I hardly knew my daughter. I'd been too busy pursuing a career. I wanted to spend more time with Julia, but it was too late. She didn't need her mother; she was a grown woman with a partner and a career as the Laurel-Scott Corporation's accountant.

'Suddenly huge changes were happening at my workplace. I was involved in deciding staff cuts across my department. Then it was my turn to accept redundancy . . . but with a very generous payout.'

The Dog was snoring. I woke him with a loud 'SO . . . after I was retrenched, I decided to keep on the cleaning company, the pool person and the garden girl. I continued to take Kenneth's shirts to the laundry, his suits to the drycleaner's. I cooked the occasional gourmet meal, met with friends for the occasional lunch and wrote my novel.'

The Dog's seen my ready-to-go, edited but contract-cancelled novel still in its Express Post package on Adrian's desk.

'Kenneth has probably found the novel on my laptop. He's probably trashed the file by now.

'If Kenneth tried to steal my novel I could sue him – but that would be a useless operation because he hasn't any money.

'Besides, I've backed up my novel. I brought it to Shelly Beach with me in its structural and copy-edited, ready-to-be-published digital format.'

The Dog was totally nonplussed by me, a failed novelist, still hanging on to her novel tucked away on an electronic device.

'Change of subject, Dog. Has Adrian read any bits of his novel to you?'

The Dog gave me his snarly smile that reveals his sharp little teeth.

'I'm just mentioning it in passing. I was wondering if Adrian's novel has a theme? How far is he into it? I bet he's writing a literary novel.'

The Dog pretended to doze off. I know he knows I've read Adrian's just-started novel.

'Dogs are supposed to be a human's best friend. They're supposed to comfort and support their owners. If their original owner isn't around, they're supposed to transfer affection and loyalty to the stand-in owner; comfort her when she's depressed, thinking about wasting a year of her life writing a tragic go-nowhere novel.'

The Dog left through his pet door for guard-dog duty. He thought he'd heard a fox.

Thursday 20 August

A rain-free day. Clear blue skies, a squadron of pelicans flying overhead and the smell of the sea in the air. I located an efficient chainsaw in Adrian's shed. The Dog and I spent a productive day in the garden.

The Dog divided his time between digging holes and rounding up the Girls. I did some pruning. Then we harvested Adrian's citrus mini orchard: medium cumquat and grapefruit crops, a huge crop of lemons.

I decorated the house with multiple bowls of glistening lemons before we raced off to collect Bossy Child from school.

When we arrived home, Bossy Child went to lock the Girls up for the night. 'Geen-ahh!' Her scream reached us in the kitchen.

'It's your fault, Dog. You forgot to fill your holes in.'

Bossy Child burst into the kitchen. 'You've wrecked Adrian's garden. He'll never be able to enter it in Shelly Beach's garden competition.'

Bloody hell!

Bossy Child stared at the baskets of cumquats and grapefruits on the kitchen table. 'You've picked the fruit from Adrian's trees?'

'Yes.'

Bossy Child walked into the living room. 'You've picked the lemons too!'

'Yes. My aunt Abby used to say, "When life tosses you lemons, make lemonade." I'm going to make lemonade.'

'Why didn't you check F for Fruit in Adrian's manual?'

Why not, indeed?

Bossy Child gave me a rolled-eye look. 'Adrian never picks his own fruit. He lets people come in and pick it whenever they want to. He belongs to the Shelly Beach Locavores Club.'

'Excuse me?'

'Shelly Beach locavores share the vegetables and fruit they grow. Mum and I don't grow much stuff but we get heaps given to us.'

'Right.'

'Now Mum will have to organise a marmalade working bee for all that fruit. And she's under the pump at the moment.'

'Excuse me?'

Rolled-eye look from the Bossy Child. 'It's tax time!'

Of course a single mum with two children who works in an accounting business would be under the pump at tax time.

'The money from the working bee will probably go to the Save Shelly Beach Foreshore fund. You'll have to help, Gina.'

I nodded a guilty acceptance.

I received a rolled-eye look plus a cross-eyed one from Bossy Child.

'I wouldn't keep doing that. Your eyes will stick together if you're not careful.'

I dished up a gourmet dinner of chicken marengo and black forest chocolate cake to take Bossy Child's mind off Adrian's trimmed and tidied garden, which hopefully will grow bigger and better by spring.

The Dog refused to take any responsibility for my garden

landscaping. But he said not to worry – Digby always wins Shelly Beach's garden competition. Digby's gardener does a brilliant job.

A marmalade working bee will probably be a highlight of my week.

Friday 21 August

We visited Piece of Cake, had morning tea with Alf and admired his handiwork. Adrian's newly painted bookshop cafe and Crow's Nest Flat look brilliant.

Alf wants me to email Adrian. 'I'm a cat's whisker away from finishing the shop and flat. I want to start work on the bungalows. Can't because boxes of books are in every room.'

To: Adrian <bookstreet@network.com.au>
From: Gina <piececake@email.com.au>
Subject: Shelving books
Alf's finished painting Piece of Cake and Crow's Nest Flat. They're looking good. He's organised for the floor-polishing guy to come. He wants to start work on the bungalows but he needs to move the boxes of books. Are you happy if I shelve the books in Piece of Cake?
Gina

To: Gina <piececake@email.com.au>
From: Adrian <bookstreet@network.com.au>
Re: Shelving books
Go ahead with the shelving. A plan is on the bathroom ledge in Crow's Nest Flat (where the tiles were stored). Locate the current hourly rates of pay for a librarian. Send me your invoice when you've finished.
Adrian

'Sometimes, Dog, your owner can be extremely annoying, but I could do with the cash flow. And I know how to shelve books. A basic library degree acquired long ago is still useful sometimes. I'll dig Dewey numbers up from the deep dark recesses of my brain.'

The Dog was smug. He always remembers the precise locations of his buried bones.

Saturday 22 August

What do you do on a wet and windy Saturday morning in Shelly Beach? Big decision time.

Finally the Dog and I decided to walk along the beach track edged with its gnarled tea-trees. Between gaps in the foliage we could see the white-capped waves on the bay. If we'd gone to the back beach we might have met Lee, but the Dog hates the crashing waves that could capture a little dog and sweep it out to sea.

However, we did meet kind old Henry Shepherd and fluffy poodle Sally. 'Come back for a cuppa. I'd like to show you my journals.'

The Dog is besotted with Sally. He ignored the ready excuse I whispered in his ear, so I had to accept Henry's invitation. If I said, 'Walking to Henry's equals walking up McIntosh Hill ten times,' the Dog would still want to go play with Sally.

Henry is incredibly friendly and chatty, and you can't help but be friendly and chatty back. It's like playing tennis. Someone hits the ball to you, and you hit the ball back. Henry had managed to tell me his life story by the time we arrived at his house.

He doesn't live far from the Shelly Beach foreshore. 'My sheep farm is further inland. I left the farm when Hilda, my wife, died last year; moved into Shelly Beach to be near our daughter Carol and her family. My son and his family are working the farm – breeding high-quality merinos for the international market.'

As we approached Henry's home, we noticed smoke curling from his chimney. He was pleased. 'Digby's here. I leave a key. Digby works on my journals whenever he has the time.'

Digby, wearing a chef's apron, opened the door. He greeted me with a big hug. 'You will stay,' he said, setting another place for lunch. 'I've made beef and mushroom pie – Henry's favourite!'

Of course the Dog and I accepted Digby's invitation. The Dog loves beef and mushroom pie.

Henry's well-worn journals were stacked on the floor. 'They span over sixty years. 'I started writing on my twenty-first birthday. I've kept a journal for each year of my life since then.'

I was impressed.

Henry showed me one of his journal entries. 'I wrote very little on some days.' I read the entry in his beautiful handwriting: *Sheared from dawn to dusk.*

No wonder.

Digby entered the room and untied his chef's apron to join us. 'Henry writes brilliantly. His journals give a unique glimpse into Shelly Beach local history. I'm sorting them thematically – war years, entries connected with his farm, the wool industry and his family – but I'm not sure whether a chronological structure would work better. What do you think, Gina?'

I offered one or two suggestions as I looked through the journals. We lingered over wine and coffee. The Dog and I were persuaded to stay for the rest of the afternoon to help Henry and Digby sort photographs.

When we left, Digby gave me a warm – very warm – handshake and an invitation to help him sort Henry's journals. 'Visit me at the castle.'

I accepted. 'Why not, Dog? The man is charming – and intelligent.'

The Dog thought I'd gone man-crazy. I ignored this and chatted to him as we walked home. 'Keeping a journal for sixty years constitutes an heroic writing effort. Writing an entry a day is hard work. I wonder if Henry Shepherd skipped days?'

The Dog wasn't interested; he just wanted to get home quickly. I checked the email when we arrived home.

To: Gina <piececake@email.com.au>
From: Adrian <bookstreet@network.com.au>
Re: Shelving books
When do you plan on starting the shelving?
Adrian

Bloody hell!

Sunday 23 August

An exciting day spent in the marmalade production business at Bossy Child's place – penance for picking Adrian's fruit. Daphne, Pandora and Violet were also part of the tight little marmalade-making team.

Digby called in to leave his deceased wife's recipe and donate extra fruit. (Annette, wife no. 2, made perfect jam.)

I was given the sticking-labels-on-jars test and passed. While I was performing the task, Violet delivered a warning: 'Digby can charm a tree off a mountain, Gina.'

She thinks I'm an excellent target for Digby. Hello?

'You're in the perfect age bracket. He feels comfortable with fifty-something women. Not too challenging! You've a good head on your shoulders, too – he likes intelligent women – and you've a good pair of legs.'

Thank you, Violet!

'Digby's a sweet-talker,' she added, carefully pouring the golden marmalade into jars.

Pandora whispered, 'A romantic bullshitter. But fun!'

I'm leaning towards Pandora's personality summary of Digby.

Everyone was marmaladed out by 5 so we decided to go to Rosa's pub.

Pandora rang and booked a table. 'We got the last table. The pub's doing great business. Rosa's giving Lee carte blanche with the specials.'

The Dog looked exhausted. 'If you've done any earth-moving work in Bossy Child's garden, you'll be in big trouble. And I'm not bailing you out.'

I'll have to do something about the Dog's hole-digging obsession soon.

Monday 24 – Tuesday 25 August

I walked into the living room on Tuesday morning and surveyed the frazzled room.

The Dog gave me his hairy raised-eyebrow look.

'I know. I know. The room's messy. Haven't you ever had a good time and left stuff to do for the morning?'

No comment from the Dog. He was staring at the empty dog food packet I held over his bowl.

'How would you like some delicious leftover Thai curry?'

The Dog gobbled the curry and retired to sulk in front of the dead embers in the fireplace. I knew I'd get the blame if he got indigestion.

'Don't give me your shocked-dog look. I bet you've been witness to Adrian having sex with his email girlfriend Leonda. No. I bet he locked you out of the house.'

The Dog ignored me and vanished through his pet door.

I grabbed a cup of coffee and followed him into the garden, shouting, 'Don't you dare put one paw outside this garden!'

I gathered my robe around me and dashed back inside.

Considering it's not Friday the thirteenth, maybe I'll strike it lucky and Shelly Beach locals will miss the fact that Lee spent the night here. Then again, considering Shelly Beach locals talk about what you do before you've done it, it'll be highly unlikely.

I blame Violet – and the weather. Violet asked Lee to order a dozen bottles of 'oaky' chardonnay from Antonio's Winery, and I needed to order replacement wine for Adrian's cellar. Lee and I decided to cycle to the winery, place the orders, and cycle back. Pleasant stuff to do on a pleasant day.

Then the weather took a turn on the way home and we were caught in a downpour.

Back at Sea View Cottage we changed out of our sodden clothes and took hot – correction – lukewarm showers. I showered first and changed into my expensive cashmere dressing-gown bought with funds from a former life.

Then it was Lee's turn to shower. I knocked on the door with a towel. He didn't hear me so I ventured into the bathroom – obviously trying not to look. He grabbed the towel – and me. And that was the beginning of the most delicious sex I can remember in a long, long time.

We actually had sex on most surfaces of Adrian's cottage. Against the kitchen wall, on the kitchen table, on the worn mat in front of the fire and in the two bedrooms. (I can't believe I've done this.)

At some stage of the night we stopped to light the fire to dry Lee's clothes, and we heated the Thai curry he'd brought with him.

I remember later in the night opening a bottle of Adrian's red as we talked about our lives.

Then we cleared the kitchen table. (That was when we had sex on the kitchen table. Never done *that* before.)

Tearing myself from my memories, I checked the back yard. The Dog was digging holes like a demented road worker. I called him inside.

The Dog was annoyed at my whimpering: a combination of guilt – having a one-night stand with a young man I've known for a very short time – and pleasure. Pleasure at remembering the best sex I'd ever had. Incomparable with Kenneth's sex-by-numbers.

'Now I know why Kenneth kept having affairs. He'd run out of numbers and had to start back at one again!'

The Dog ignored my comment. I ignored the Dog. I went back to bed and dreamt of the insanely good-looking Lee Wang, who'd left me feeling like a million dollars.

The Dog sniffed me out hours later. I was standing naked in front of Adrian's patchy bathroom mirror in the minus one-star bathroom. It was freezing but I made myself stand and stare at 'the' body.

The cuddly layers that had developed during my writing-in-the-attic year had disappeared. My body had changed like a caterpillar's in a cocoon and I'd hardly noticed. My comfort-sized clothing had just become more comfortable.

The Dog was hungry.

'Sorry, there's no dog food. How do you feel about porridge? Bears love porridge.'

I noted Lee had left the novels he'd selected from Adrian's bookshelves and his indie CDs on the side table.

'These are good signs, Dog. He'll be back.'

That night I slept the sleep of a contented woman.

Wednesday 26 August

The thought of meeting Lee at tonight's writers' group meeting was making me feel queasy in the stomach. I didn't want a one-night stand to create unpleasant ripples that could affect Adrian's writers' group.

If Lee was in a relationship with someone else I wouldn't feel good. I knew Kenneth had multiple affairs but I never felt the need to keep up with him. Not that I didn't have the opportunities. I had my fair share of propositions – especially from colleagues. But I was always careful not to mix work with play.

I watched the Dog from the kitchen window. His neurotic hole-digging was not conducive to problem-solving. Anyway, considering I didn't have a legitimate job, I could classify convening Adrian's writers' group as 'work' and maybe an ongoing relationship with Lee as 'play'. Therefore I'd broken one of my basic rules and mixed work and play. Bloody hell!

What would I say to Lee? Maybe he wouldn't come to the meeting. Maybe, in Bianca language, he will have slipped away 'like a phantom disappearing into the sea mist'.

I called the Dog inside for his breakfast. Porridge again. The Dog was not impressed with Three Bears' food. He watched while I wrote *dog food* on my To Do list.

The Dog thought I'd crossed the line. He said it's a given that sexual chemistry is everywhere, and lovers come and go. But he prefers to have a good friend to play with at the beach or on the foreshore. Friends are superior to lovers. Friends can hang around for a long time – although sometimes they end up on death row in a lost dogs' home.

The Dog was heaping on the guilts. He'd finished his breakfast and was staring at me with his little eyes.

'I know I shouldn't have had sex with Lee. I should have kept our relationship on a friends-only basis. But I'm ignoring your insinuation that Lee is too young for me.'

The Dog pattered across the living room and out the front door. I followed him on to the verandah and watched him doing his early-morning guard-dog duty.

'You can't talk. You're a hundred dog-years older than Sally.'

The Dog turned and gave me his snarly smile. His sharp little teeth glistened. The Dog hates it when I use hyperbole.

We prepared for the writers' group meeting in silence.

Digby was waiting when the Dog and I arrived to open the community hall.

'Sorry I stuffed up the last meeting. I've sorted the issues with Violet. I've apologised to her and Bill Kruger. The food and grog is my apology to members for making things uncomfortable.'

I helped Digby unload his car packed with excellent food from the Sea Haven caterers, plus a box of grog. Well done, Digby! When Digby does sorry he does it with style.

Pandora and Bianca arrived soon after. We set out welcoming tea and coffee and Digby's swanky banquet.

Our small group of writers lit up like Christmas trees when they entered the hall and saw the tables set with food and grog.

Digby went OTT with his apology but it was an excellent beginning to the meeting. 'I was a bit under the weather last meeting. I need to get myself grounded. It's difficult when you've worked in the academic arena. Strong criticism slips out easily.'

We understood.

I must remember to compliment Daphne on the success of her damage-control exercise. I'm assuming Digby reads people well; he decides which battles to fight and which battles to yield. Obviously he's not interested in making things hard for himself in Shelly Beach.

Lee arrived late. He sent me a smile across the room and my heart started thumping at a ridiculous rate. During the evening he managed to discreetly but significantly brush up against my body. I breathed a sigh of relief. These were good signs. It looks like Monday assignations will still be on – but we'll need to sort out some rules.

Daphne introduced the draft copy of our Shelly Beach Writers' Group by-laws. Cooperative writers agreed with the by-laws and got down to the writerly business of sharing character profiles.

Violet was very happy with her two-dimensional seventy-year-old sleuth, Red Blaze. 'I've got no intention of rounding him out,' she snapped.

Violet focused her steely eyes on Digby. 'I'm not into writing three-dimensional characters. Red Blaze, my main character, is a trouble-shooting engineer. He flies all over the world to solve big engine problems. Wherever Red Blaze lands there's a crime to solve.'

She continued to stare at Digby, daring him to make a comment. Digby nodded, and gave a slight smile of agreement. We breathed a sigh of relief and continued with our sharing.

Bianca's new word of the week is 'protagonist'. Digby gave it to her when he called into Scissors for a haircut and a beard trim. Bianca has based her two protagonists on Josh and herself – 'A bit like Romeo and Juliet, only we're still alive.'

After supper and more of Digby's excellent wine, Bill chatted on about point of view and dialogue using notes from his beautifully organised folder of how-to-write-a-novel info.

Pandora and I are sure that nothing will prevent our conscientious tutor from delivering his planned novel-writing sessions. Shelly Beach Writers' Group members will receive the full quota of Kingston-grant-funded lifelong literary learning – even if we don't want to write another novel!

Thursday 27 August
Bossy Child was checking Adrian's email. 'You've got mail, Gina! Adrian wants to know how the writers' group meeting went. And he's asking about Hugo. Do you want to tell him that Hugo's been digging holes nonstop since he left? Hugo never dug one single hole in the garden when Adrian was here.'

I yelled back, 'No!'

I looked at the Dog. 'Traitor! You told me you were allowed to dig holes.'

While we ate dessert, Bossy Child delivered canine advice. 'You'll have to talk to Violet about Hugo's hole-digging. She knows heaps of stuff about cats and dogs. Why they do stuff. Things like that.'

'Right.'

'If Violet can't help you could go to the Sea Haven vet. He might know how to stop Hugo digging holes.'

'I'm emailing Adrian about the meeting.'

Bossy Child was concentrating on her chocolate mousse. She signalled her approval.

To: Adrian <bookstreet@network.com.au>
From: Gina <piececake@email.com.au>
Subject: Writers' group
Looks like your writers' group is still viable. Digby undertook an excellent damage-control exercise. Now Violet's happy to stay in the group. You'll be pleased to know your Shelly Beach Writers' Group has a set of by-laws. Bill gave handouts re: viewpoint and dialogue plus a writing task for next meeting.

How do you feel about a Shelly Beach writers' publication to flog at your Writefest next year? Working title: *Just Write! How to Write a Novel and Get Published: An A–Z Guide*. Daphne and Digby are confident they can raise local funds for a small print-run. Digby's happy to include his wordwise stuff. Bill's okay about us including his handouts as long as he can use them again.

Hugo is well. He says, 'Woof! Woof!'
Gina

To: Gina <piececake@email.com.au>
From: Adrian <bookstreet@network.com.au>
Re: Writers' group
Glad to hear writer's group and Hugo are thriving. I like the idea of the publication. Tell Daphne to contact Antonio's Winery. Antonio will probably come good with some funds if we give him a full-page ad for free.
Adrian

Friday 28 August
Still raining. Knowing it's the wettest winter on record for Shelly Beach is no comfort. The Dog and I decided to spend the day

shelving books at Piece of Cake. With the heating on, Piece of Cake was a pleasant place to work.

Boxes of books covered most of the newly polished floorboards. The Dog sniffed out Adrian's meticulously labelled layout for the shelving plus stylish signage in jelly-bean-coloured lettering. We chose a box of books and started shelving.

Adrian's specialising in murder and mystery fiction and non-fiction titles on writing.

I shelved, in alphabetical order by author's surname, the murder and mystery fiction. My long-neglected librarian's heart stirred as I checked shelf after shelf – each book in its designated place. Shelving the non-fiction was messier. Some serious Dewey order was definitely needed.

'Mastering the Dewey decimal system in my student days has come into its own, Dog.'

The Dog wasn't interested. He was bored with shelving.

We finished by the time the rain stopped. I just had time to buy my weekly allowance of Harold's happy organic steak.

Harold of Rupert's Butchery was ready for a chat. 'Can you mind the shop while I slip out the back to make us tea?'

Of course I could. When Harold returned we opened with writers' talk. 'I've a novel on the go – but I don't think I'm ready to join your group yet.'

'Right. Maybe when Adrian comes back?'

'No offence to you, Gina.'

'None taken.'

'I've heard you're doing a brilliant job to help the group run smoothly.'

'It's not difficult: photocopying, opening and shutting the hall, doing the supper deal.'

'Word is you're so cool you could land a 627 on a golf course.'

I smiled a thank you.

Harold counted on his fingers. 'I'm secretary for the local footy, fishing, bird observer and Shelly Beach Lifesavers clubs. Keeps me busy writing the minutes.'

'Writing minutes is valiant work, Harold.'

'What I'm planning to do is shut the butchery for a couple of months next year. Go backpacking through Europe with my friend Gary. Get some material for my novel. I've already sorted out a temp butcher. He's keen to look after the butchery while Gary and I are away.'

'Sounds like a brilliant plan, Harold.'

'But Mum won't hear of anyone taking over the shop – even for a few months. She thinks they'll steal our sausage recipe. And I haven't told her about Gary. Or our plans. Do you have any idea how I could broach the subject with her?'

Bloody hell! Gary? I started to understand Harold's problem. 'I don't know, Harold. I hardly know your mother. But it sounds like you have to talk to her.'

'I've tried, but she won't listen.'

'Right. If you haven't had any success by the time I leave Shelly Beach, I'll have a chat to her, if you like. There'll be plenty of time to get passports and book flights.'

Harold smiled his thanks as he wrapped my steak and a bone for the Dog.

At home I pondered the wisdom of disclosing relationships and giving the Dog a bone.

'I'm not sure a bone is the best thing for you, Dog. Perhaps I'll save it until we go to the beach. You can bury it in the sand like a pirate burying his treasure.'

The Dog gave me his lost-pup look.

I relented and gave him the bone. 'Think creatively. Bury it in Bossy Child's garden. Not in the herb garden. Up near the compost bin behind the shed. That's a lovely place to bury a bone.'

The Dog went off on his bone-burying mission and I sent an email to Adrian.

To: Adrian <bookstreet@network.com.au>
From: Gina <piececake@email.com.au>
Subject: Shelving books

Completed shelving. Could have done it quicker except for constant interruptions from locals who've been drinking all your tea and coffee, and eating Alf's biscuits. We still have about twenty boxes of assorted paperbacks left (definitely not M and M or how-to-write titles).

What do you want me to do with them? Alf refuses to store them in the bungalows again – he wants to start on the renovations as soon as possible.

I'm guessing you want to keep Crow's Nest Flat clear to receive furniture and summer residents.

Gina

P.S. I've shelved non-fiction titles under Dewey numbers.

To: Gina <piececake@email.com.au>
From: Adrian <bookstreet@network.com.au>
Re: Shelving books

Thank you, Gina. Send me your invoice for shelving. Planned to donate spare boxes of books to sell at a future fundraising event. When you go to the action committee meeting at the pub, tell Rosa about the spare boxes of books. She'll store them in one of the pub's sheds.

I'd ordered wooden slat blinds for the shop windows. The shop faces north and will get a lot of sun in summer. Can you locate the order and get it moving? Alf will give you the address of the retailer in Kingston. Select some window coverings for your bedroom. I've heard Lee helped you remove the old ones and helps you hang sheets when he visits.

Adrian

Bloody hell, Adrian!

And I was sure there wasn't a clause about attending an action committee meeting in my contract.

The Dog disagreed.

Saturday 29 August

'Two days before Lee visits us again, Dog.'

The Dog was so over my mantra – 'young enough to be my son'. I promised I wouldn't repeat it again.

'You like Lee visiting us. He always brings treats for you.'

The Dog ignored me. He was more interested in driving with Bossy Child and me to Kingston in Adrian's Ford. Before we left we called in at Piece of Cake to check the measurements for the blinds.

'Wow!' Bossy Child's face lit up as she stood in the middle of Adrian's bookshop cafe. Light streamed through the shop front onto the polished pine floors. The shelves (with jelly-bean-coloured lettering), filled with Adrian's secondhand books, surrounded us on three sides.

I admit Adrian's bookshop cafe is looking good. The renovations have taken in what was once the baker's shop, plus the huge area that was the actual bakery.

'It's going to be awesome.'

True.

Bossy Child found a container of small blackboards (framed in jelly-bean colours) and a box of chalk. She read Adrian's attached note: *Use for menu, literary and writers' quotes.*

Bossy Child held a blank blackboard against the wall of the cafe area and read the quote that was attached on a piece of paper: *Outside of a dog, a book is a man's best friend. Inside a dog it's too dark to read. Attributed to Groucho Marx.*

The Dog was not amused.

'Adrian's thought of everything, hasn't he?'

'He has.'

We completed the measuring for the blinds and drove to Kingston.

After we delivered Adrian's order, we stopped at the library. I borrowed a bunch of books on dogs, and ignored a title called *Healthy, Sexy Workouts*.

We called in at Violet's on our way back home, hoping she'd have a solution to the Dog's hole-digging fetish.

'Give him a ball. He used to play fetch with Adrian. It's safer and won't destroy Adrian's garden.'

Guilt about the garden must have flashed across my face.

'Plants grow back, Gina. Hopefully by the time Adrian returns.'

Then Violet tried a nifty segue, her writer's antennae up in their constant search for whodunnit plotlines. 'Mysterious young man, Lee Wang. He's probably hiding an interesting back story.'

I ignored Violet's conversation starter. While we ate sardine sandwiches and sultana cake, and drank tea, Violet counselled me on pets – not young lovers.

'Cats get attached to houses, not people, and are more calculating than dogs. Dogs get attached to an owner, and they feel tension and sadness when the owner leaves.'

I'm ignoring how a dog might feel if its substitute owner has wild sex in its territory.

We walked home, and after Bossy Child left, the Dog and I had a serious talk. 'You have to stop digging holes. I refuse to feel guilty because you're worrying about what I'm worrying about. Adrian will be home soon, and he'll be really angry if you keep digging up his garden. You've got nothing to worry about, trust me. You don't have to stress about getting back into the workforce or the age issue in your relationship with a younger man. You life is all sweetness and bones.'

The Dog gave me his raised-eyebrow look.

Sunday 30 August

I made an SOS phone call to Bossy Child. 'You'd better come over. The Dog's acting very weird!'

Bossy Child appeared later in the morning. 'I couldn't come earlier. Had to tidy my room.'

'Right. Look.'

We watched the Dog scraping his rear end along the verandah. Not a pretty sight.

'He's got a blocked anal gland again.'

'Bloody hell! What do I do about it?'

'You're swearing, Gina. Hugo's had this before. Adrian fixed it himself. You get a bowl of disinfectant and cotton wool and you just squeeze —'

'Don't go there! I'm not doing that!'

'Well, ring the vet tomorrow.'

'Tomorrow? Not today?'

'You'll have to pay extra for out-of-hours surgery. Tomorrow will be fine. It's not life-threatening.'

'Right.'

'Mum wants to know if you'd like to come to lunch. She's cooking on the barbecue.'

I looked at the Dog. I didn't want to spend a miserable day with a miserable dog. 'Excellent idea. We'll come.'

'You'd better carry Hugo.'

I went to find a blanket for one sad and sore dog.

Monday 31 August

All day I went over one question in my mind. Would Lee call in today?

Comforting answer. Monday is his day off. Lee always calls on Mondays to exchange Adrian's books. If not I'd meet him at book club tonight.

The Dog was miserable but he ate his breakfast. This was a good sign. I made an appointment to take him to the vet's clinic this afternoon.

'You'll feel better after you've been to the vet, Dog.'

Violet called in just as we were leaving. 'Book club's cancelled tonight. Most of Shelly Beach is down with the flu.'

'That's a shame. Hope everyone feels better soon. Sorry, Violet, can't stop to make coffee. I have to drive the Dog to the vet's in Sea Haven,' I whispered so as not to upset the Dog. 'The vet said he'd keep the Dog in overnight. He'll operate if necessary. Terri thinks the Dog has a blocked anal gland.'

Violet checked the Dog, much to his embarrassment, and confirmed Bossy Child's diagnosis.

I carried the Dog out to the car. 'Now that book club is cancelled, do you think Lee will use this as a perfect excuse to avoid coming here?'

The Dog was too uncomfortable to concentrate on my romantic problems.

I apologised.

The 'Hi, I'm Lyn' receptionist presided at the desk of the Sea Haven Veterinary Clinic. I delicately mentioned the subject of pricing and flinched as she gave me the cost of one small operation for one small dog.

I whispered about Adrian's arrangement to pay the Dog's veterinary bills. Hi-I'm-Lyn checked the books and announced in her megaphone voice so all waiting-room clients and their owners could hear, 'Yes – that's correct. The owner has left arrangements with the bank. He will pay for his dog's care.'

I gave a thin smile to Hi-I'm-Lyn, who obviously had never had a money worry in her life. The vet was probably her husband, they were making a mint and they'd just inherited a fortune from an elderly aunt they never knew.

Back home, guilt and worry at leaving the Dog there swept over me. My jobless, homeless and cashless position on this planet kept playing in my mind like a television soapie episode.

Fortunately Lee arrived and shut down the soapie. He was laden with Adrian's books and ingredients to cook a seafood pasta. Once he'd put all that down, he wrapped his arms around me and kissed me slowly on the lips.

I disentangled myself. 'We should sort things out before this goes any further.'

'Right.' Lee made coffee and we sat down at Adrian's kitchen table.

'I have some questions I need to ask. Do you have a current girlfriend?'

'No.'

'Lover?'

'No.'

'Partner?'

'No.'

'Wife?'

'No.'

'No relationship of any kind?'

'No.'

'Good. I'm free too.' I breathed a sigh of relief.

Lee gave me a kiss on the cheek. 'I'll start dinner.'

'Right.'

Unspoken rules were set. I made a mental note to tell the Dog what was happening when he returned tomorrow.

Lee pulled an indie band's album from his backpack and put it on. He opened a bottle of Adrian's red and poured two glasses. He left the wine on the table as he took me in his arms. Hallelujah for Mondays!

I woke the next morning to find a little pile of hi-tech paper devices on my bedside table. Lee had made me small triangular card-board wedges to stop the shake, rattle and roll of Adrian's windows.

To: Adrian <bookstreet@network.com.au>
From: Gina <piececake@email.com.au>
Subject: Blinds and blocked anal gland
I've taken Hugo to the vet. He needed to get an anal gland cleared. He's staying overnight. The vet said to say hello and to tell you that it wasn't a serious problem.

I found the order for your slat blinds and have actioned it. You're right. The books will need protection from the afternoon sun . . . if Shelly Beach ever sees the sun again.

No need to worry about curtains for Sea View Cottage. I bought material in Kingston. Borrowed a sewing machine and made them. I plan on taking them with me when I move.

Your chef friend, Lee Wang, is still borrowing your books. Hope this is okay.
Gina

To: Gina <piececake@email.com.au>
From: Adrian <bookstreet@network.com.au>
Re: Blinds and blocked anal gland
Make sure the bills for Hugo's treatment and the blinds are invoiced to my account.

I'm happy Lee's still borrowing books.
Adrian

September

Tuesday 1 September

The Hi-I'm-Lyn receptionist left a message on Adrian's answering machine: 'The operation was successful. You may collect Adrian Fraser's dog.'

I drove to the Sea Haven Veterinary Clinic to pick up the sad Dog, complete with a plastic-bucket collar to stop him licking his rear end. Said rear end is shaved and looks very tender. Ouch!

The vet assured me the Dog was fine. There's that word again – fine. 'Keep Hugo away from water. He must wear his collar. Bring him back in a week for a check-up.'

I smiled a thank you and carried the Dog out to the reception desk. I whispered to Hi-I'm-Lyn, 'The owner is settling the bill.'

'Yes, thank you, Ms Laurel. We're aware that you won't be paying.'

A fresh collection of waiting-room clients – animals and humans – stared anywhere but at me. Everyone now knows I don't pay the Dog's vet bills.

Do I care? Yes, I do care. But reality check: if I paid the Dog's vet bill it would put a large dent in my carefully managed cash reserves.

When we arrived home there was a message from Clare on Adrian's answering machine.

Hi, Gina – it's Clare. A dull rainy day here in town. It's probably the same at Shelly Beach.

James' company has organised a family golf tournament at Sea Haven Resort next weekend. James is partnering some person in his office, and I said I'd rather spend Saturday with you.

Hope this fits your schedule. If I don't hear from you by Thursday I'll take it that it's okay. Hope you're well, and see you soon.

Bloody hell. 'It doesn't fit my schedule, Clare!'

The Dog woke from his anaesthetic-recovery snooze and gave me his invalid-dog look. I apologised for shouting and told him to prepare for a visit from Clare on the weekend.

Bianca dashed in during her lunch break. She'd heard the Dog was sick, plus she had vital information to give me. 'I forgot to tell you, Gina. There's an action committee meeting tonight. You have to come. Adrian left his proxy vote for you.'

Bloody hell! 'I can't come. I can't leave the Dog. He's recovering from surgery.'

'Mum said she'd come and sit with Hugo. The action committee meets at Rosa's. You'll know just about everyone. We have a meal before and the meeting is usually held in Rosa's back room. No one is allowed to play billiards on action committee nights.'

'Right.'

'You'll be there, Gina?'

'Yes, I'll be there.' Bloody hell, Adrian – more fine print I missed in my contract?

'Remember you have to vote no.'

'Let me get this straight. I vote no. Why?'

'Digby's trying to get Adrian's Writefest cancelled.'

'And remind me what Writefest is?'

Bianca looked at me and spoke slowly. 'It's a two-day writers' festival, remember? Adrian was going to hold it this coming summer, but he had to go to England.'

'And Digby . . . ?'

'Digby wants Writefest cancelled.'

'And Adrian . . . ?'

'Adrian wants his Writefest moved to winter next year. Then he can run it when he comes home.'

'Right!' Power play and politics in Shelly Beach. 'So we vote no to cancelling Writefest, but yes to moving it to winter?'

Bianca looked happy. 'Yep, you got it.'

'As soon as your mother relieves me from Dog duty I promise I'll be there.'

'Cool. I have to go. I've got a client booked for a facial. Daphne's calling in to lend me a book on how to write chick lit.'

'Excellent.'

I watched Bianca drive away. 'I hope I don't stuff up at the meeting, Dog.'

The Dog didn't care. He wobbled off to rest in his basket in the bedroom.

Bossy Child called in after school. She went to the bedroom to check on the invalid Dog.

I called after her, 'Doesn't he look cute in his collar?'

'He's not wearing a collar, Gina.'

Bloody hell. Sneaky Dog. We found the collar under the bed.

'You have to keep this collar on, Dog. It's for your own good.'

I put Bossy Child and her mother on emergency call, 'in case Bianca's mum has a problem with the Dog'.

'Can I email Adrian and tell him Hugo's doing well?'

146

'Yes. Don't tell him about the missing collar. Tell him I'll email after the action committee meeting.'

Wednesday 2 September

To: Adrian <bookstreet@network.com.au>
From: Gina <piececake@email.com.au>
Subject: Action committee

I attended the Shelly Beach Action Committee meeting last night and placed your proxy vote. Bianca asked me to keep you up to date. She hasn't time to scratch herself what with working frantically to save for flight to US to land job with international hairdressing salon.

Ten members present: Bianca, Digby, Rosa, Daphne, Charles, Harold, Pandora, Josh, Alf and Beryl, plus the Kingston Council guy and me (your proxy voter). Your Writefest has not been cancelled – just moved on the calendar. Now it's official. The Shelly Beach Winter Writefest is to be held over two days sometime in July or August next year. Moved Bianca. Seconded Rosa. Voted in favour 11–1.

Digby offered to take over the organisation of Writefest, but members are happy to wait until you return. Rosa's happy too. She's planning to advertise two-day getaways to coincide with your festival.

There were complaints directed to the council guy. Bianca says you know about the issues re: the foreshore band pavilion, toilets and bus shelter, which are slowly falling apart. The council guy told us Shelly Beach was second on the infrastructure list. Sea Haven's kids' playground is top. Council guy left after giving us a 'feel grateful we live at Shelly Beach' pep talk.

The committee voted to go ahead with three fundraising events to raise cash to operate the Winter Writefest. It'll hold a trivia quiz, speed-dating night and collectors' fair. Digby's in charge of the collectors' fair.

Rosa pushed to get these events through before the end of the year. Bianca says Rosa just wants the custom for her pub, but everyone agrees Shelly Beach needs sparking up. Dead as a dodo at the moment. Hugo says, 'Woof! Woof!'
Gina
P.S. Rosa's happy to store your books in her shed until you hold Writefest – or until whenever.

To: Gina <piececake@email.com.au>
From: Adrian <bookstreet@network.com.au>
Re: Action committee
I'm glad Hugo's recovery is progressing well. Thanks for your help at the action committee. Tell Bianca I appreciate her support.
Adrian

Thursday 3 September

Flipping through Sweet-Scary Tutor's textbook, I read another of her writing tips: *When you write in your journal about the small things in your life, it can be a trigger for elements in your novel.*

I'm missing one sock. One finest quality pure-wool black sock. This tragic loss has turned into a nagging problem that won't go away. Could my missing sock be a trigger for an element in a novel – if I were ever to write another novel?

The Dog is not fit for a sock hunt. Last week all I had to do was dangle a sock under the Dog's nose and in a few seconds he would return with sock no. 2. Not this week.

'Can you remember Bossy Child's mum, Joan, saying she'd help me work out a survival budget? Do you remember? We were chatting outside. Pandora says Joan —'

I broke off while the Dog attempted to scratch himself but failed because of his bucket collar.

I continued, 'Joan has a brilliant reputation among the Shelly

Beach community because of her accounting skills. I bet she advised Adrian on a financial strategy for his sea-change plan.'

The Dog couldn't recall. He wouldn't recall.

Bossy Child arrived at Sea View Cottage after school. Violet collected her today. The Dog won't venture out in public wearing his collar.

There was little sympathy from Bossy Child when I explained my sock challenge. 'One of my socks has gone missing. I know the Dog has hidden it, and he won't hunt for it.'

I ignored her cross-eyed look as she said, 'Move on, Gina.'

I can't move on. The missing sock belongs to five and a half imported wool pairs with stay-up tops: socks that look satisfyingly stylish when glimpsed beneath basic black pants or jeans.

'The Dog might have forgotten where he hid it. He's probably buried it in one of his holes. Which hole? That's the question.'

A rolled-eye look from Bossy Child.

Bossy Child couldn't appreciate the implications of the missing sock – one that completes six pairs of outrageously expensive socks purchased using Kenneth's soon to-be-cancelled credit card. According to my cunning estimation, with gentle hand-washing, the six pairs would last for five years. Or longer.

One missing sock has illuminated my mindset in regards to money. It's blown my avoidance survival technique: 'Don't think about tomorrow – or four months down the track.'

Now that I'm down to five pairs of black socks, it's time for a reality check. My contract, involving a rent-free cottage with all bills paid, plus free vegetables, fruit and eggs, as well as the use of a crappy Ford, is not going to last forever. I need a budget. I would like a car. Anything on four wheels that's a step up from Adrian's Ford.

I collected my current bank record and financial papers. Time for action.

'Remind me to give these papers to your mother when we see her tonight.'

Bossy Child agreed.

'Do you think a month's worth of dinners is enough to thank her for helping me sort out stuff?'

'She's always under the pump.'

'I understand that.'

'I'll let you know, but I'd say that'd be fine.'

'Right.'

'I'll tell you what we like to eat. And once a week you could cook a roast and invite us to eat here. We wouldn't stay long. Mum likes to get home and organised for the next day.'

'On top of the night I look after you?'

Bossy Child stared righteously at me. 'Yes.'

'Right.'

We watched the Dog while he noisily slurped leftover stew.

'Hugo's looking better.'

I agreed.

'Can I tell Adrian?'

'Go ahead.'

Bossy Child returned from the computer. 'Your friends want to know if you'd like them to do a CV for you.'

Bloody hell! I raced to the computer and read Eva's email. Eva and Hester have been gently nagging me to get a CV assembled in order to attack the four-letter word – *work*.

To: Eva<eva@slick-promotions.com>
From: Gina <piececake@email.com.au>
Re: Work
Hello Eva,
Yes, I'll be forever grateful if you and Hester can start writing (creating) my CV. I need a job.
OXOXOXO
Gina

Friday 4 September

The Dog and I waited for a reasonable time – after dinner when the children were well settled – before we visited Bossy Child's accountant mum and gained her verdict on my pathetic financial position.

'I can't believe I was so stupid, Joan. I had an A-list career. I managed big-time projects and budgets for my department.

'I poured cash into building Montpellier Place and Kenneth's companies over the years. I can't believe I allowed Kenneth to mix our personal monies with the Laurel-Scott Corporation!'

No diplomatic comment from Joan. She went to check on her children and make coffee.

When she returned I continued my sorry saga. 'And then there was my final stupidity. Investing my redundancy payout in the Laurel-Scott Corporation.'

'Your case is not uncommon, Gina. I've known women in total control of their careers, but who make a mess of their private lives. You've been derailed. You'll get back on track. Your financial situation isn't totally desperate. But I'd advise you to start looking for a job – soon. You'll need a regular income before you can take a lease on a rental property and purchase a car.'

Sam woke up and started crying.

'Sorry, Gina. I'll get back to you later.'

And I was dismissed by my friendly neighbour, aka Competent Accountant.

Back at home I watched the Dog try to exit through his pet door. Wrong move. He got stuck. I retrieved him and straightened his collar. Tough times for a small dog with a big bucket collar.

'Compared to Joan, my problems rate as zero.'

The Dog agreed.

I sat the Dog in front of Adrian's calendar and performed our tear-and-destroy monthly ritual. I ripped August into confetti pieces.

September, with its photo of cute spring lambs frolicking in a daisy-dotted green meadow, didn't impress the Dog.

Another reality check: 'Only four months until your owner returns, Dog.'

The phone rang, and without waiting for the answering machine I picked up. It was Clare. 'Hi, Gina. Just confirming my visit tomorrow. I've been to visit Julia and your grandson. He's adorable!'

I held the phone away and took a deep breath. My exhalation blew into the Dog's bucket collar. He stared at me.

'Sorry about the garlic breath,' I mouthed. 'It's Clare!' The Dog understood.

'Have you visited Julia and little Barney lately?' Clare asked.

I whispered to the Dog, 'She knows perfectly well I haven't been to see my daughter or grandson recently.' And to Clare: 'No. I'm planning a visit soon.' (Lie.)

I've wanted to visit Julia and Barney again, but limited transportation is a huge problem. However, I've been trying hard – very hard. I've been doing the grandmother thing, ringing religiously to chat with Julia about her health and my grandson. They're doing well. But I needed to visit. I wanted to hold my gorgeous grandson in my arms once more. Before he grew up and left home.

The Dog understood. We tuned in to Clare again.

'Julia and the baby are doing beautifully. Nanny Anny is a gem!' Clare exited our conversation with the excuse she uses when she has someone more important to see, or something more important to do. 'Someone's at the door. I'll see you tomorrow, Gina.'

'What do you think, Dog? Is my grandson Barnaby to be called Barny with a Y? Or is it Barnie I-E or Barney E-Y?'

The Dog was asleep. He won't be happy when I tell him I'm leaving him to visit my daughter and grandson in the city.

Saturday 5 September

Bright and early a limo came to a halt in Adrian's drive. James' driver deposited Clare at Sea View Cottage. No sign of James. Clare was her chatty self. Assumption: James must be keeping quiet.

'OhmaGod, Gina! Look at your hair! Who's your colourist?'

According to Bianca my appearance has been transformed with an edgy, textured cut and colour. Bianca has promised to redo the colour if I get sick of it. The Dog likes it. He doesn't think it looks too red.

'Bianca. She's Shelly Beach's resident hairstylist. I exchanged two cakes for a shampoo, cut and colour.'

'OhmaGod, Gina! Two cakes?'

'Bianca freezes them. Has them when she has friends over for a meal.'

I ignored the Dog's why-are-you-explaining-to-Clare look.

'How clever. You're bartering! Maybe three chocolate cakes will equal a manicure and a pedicure? By the way, I'm dying for a hit of caffeine, Gina.'

I took deep breaths and brewed Adrian's coffee.

Clare's attention was directed to the Dog. 'What have you done to the dog, Gina?'

The Dog looked daggers at Clare.

'He had a blocked anal gland. He's been to the vet. He can take the bucket collar off in a few days.'

'OhmaGod!'

Over coffee Clare filled me in on the latest goss she believed I needed to hear to maintain a connection with my former life.

'Do you remember Ian and Abby Trent?'

'Vaguely.'

'They lived four doors up from you in Montpellier Place. Abby was a brand consultant. Ian was in marketing. You met them at our place. When I held my 1950s cocktail party to raise funds for the hospital.'

'Right.'

'Well, they've split up.'

'And . . .?'

'They've been fighting over custody of their poodle, Jean-Paul. Abby's had custody of Jean-Paul but Ian walks the dog every second Sunday. Jean-Paul's in a terribly anxious state: his fur is coming out in chunks. He's ripped their original Eames chair to pieces. Abby's taking him to a canine behavioural therapist.'

The Dog went to hide under the couch but his collar stuck. I released him and carried him to his nest in the bedroom.

When I returned Clare continued. 'The canine therapist says if couples thinking of breaking up have pets, they should put differences aside.'

Petless Clare prattled on with no comment from me. 'I read an article at my hairstylist's. It said family pets have a value way beyond their market value.'

The Dog would be pleased to hear this.

'Just as well you and Kenneth didn't have a pet. I don't suppose Kenneth would have kept it. Depends if pets are allowed in Angela's apartment. You and Kenneth could have had a pet custody battle on your hands.'

I gave Clare a very tight smile. 'Thankfully that hasn't happened, Clare.'

Somehow I time-filled Saturday with Clare. I took the Dog next door and placed him in Bossy Child's care while we lunched at Rosa's pub.

Clare made her usual tortuous menu requests. 'No salad dressing. I'll have low-fat yoghurt instead of mayonnaise – and hold the French fries.'

During the meal Clare continued with her confected goss. 'Do you remember Jasmine?'

'Not really.'

'Jasmine and Ewen who lived in the Grove? She was CEO at a bank.'

'Vaguely.'

'She's made a complete life-course correction.'

'Excuse me?'

'She left Ewen. Resigned from her job. Bought a villa in Normandy. Or is it Brittany? Anyway, she plans to renovate. She's going to write a coffee-table book about renovating. She's already got a contract and an advance. She's been having an affair with the commissioning editor of a publishing company – Tom something or other. He's going to live with her in Normandy. Or is it Brittany? Anyway, he's going to do the photos for the book.'

I made a note to tell Pandora how she could kick-start her writing career. Somehow, though, a coffee-table book about renovating in Shelly Beach doesn't have the same 'must buy' feel as renovating in Normandy – or Brittany.

Then came Clare's sugar-coated reality hit. 'Jasmine's situation is similar to yours, Gina. Except Jasmine's in control of her life. I'll order the coffee. Low-fat milk?'

'Thank you, Clare.' I watched as she failed to negotiate low-fat soy milk when she placed her order at the bar.

Lee, looking insanely handsome and cool in his slick chef's uniform, brought the coffee to our table. 'Just finishing my shift, Gina. I'll call tomorrow to exchange Adrian's books.'

Lee rested his hand on my shoulder as I introduced him to Clare. My heart was thumping. I couldn't stop a Cheshire-cat grin from escaping as Lee effortlessly exchanged foody chit-chat with Clare. When he left I concentrated on stirring my coffee, and ignored Clare's raised eyebrow.

On the way home Clare insisted I give her another inspection of Piece of Cake. Alf had found the tables and chairs stored in Adrian's shed and moved them into the cafe area. Piece of Cake was looking good.

Clare gave Adrian's bookshop cafe her real estate seal of approval. 'It's charming, Gina. Once Adrian gets this place up and running it'll become a seaside icon. Each chair is a different colour! And a different design! How clever!'

True. I've wondered how Adrian dreamed up this nifty decorating trick. Has it been a lifelong goal – collecting and painting odd chairs different colours?

Clare took shots with her new digital camera. 'It's foolproof, Gina. A present from James! Hugely expensive.'

Kind, compensating James.

'I can send these photos to Adrian if you give me his email address.'

'I've already sent Adrian photos.' (Lie.) No way was I allowing Clare access to Adrian – a lever into my new life. Such as it is!

Before she left Clare handed me a substantial wad of cash from the sale of clothes from my former life. Hallelujah for a niche market for my high-end, worn-only-once designer outfits. I accepted the cash with grace. Beggars can't be choosers.

Thankfully the company's limo pulled up at Adrian's at 5. James' driver skilfully backed out from the driveway. No problem – he'd done it before. Clare, ensconced in the back seat, gave me a mock royal wave. I took huge gulps of salt air and lowered my shoulders from their up-near-my-ears position. I called the Dog from his resting place in the bedroom.

'We've survived, Dog. What do you think? Should I tell Clare that James hit on me? To tell? Or not to tell?'

The Dog is going to think about my questions. It was chilly so I lit a fire. We gazed at the flickering flames and contemplated infidelity – an eternal theme for writers of novels.

Clare had left these standard weekend hamper of holiday goodies. I read the label on the cane basket handle: *With compliments of Sunny Hill Larder Tailored Hamper Service.*

Whenever we had a girls' weekend away we'd rely on Clare to produce one of these hampers. The Dog watched while I unpacked jars of olives, artichokes, bottles of extra virgin olive oil, balsamic vinegar, pasta, jars of pasta sauce, Parmesan cheese and a cloth-wrapped cheddar.

I read a carefully labelled package: *Irresistible snacks to nibble by the fire or on a sun-filled balcony*. The Dog watched in amazement as I kept producing item after item from the *Wind in the Willows*-style picnic basket. 'Clare's gone over the top this time, Dog.'

I placed a packet of coffee beans, a grinder, a percolator, assorted quality teas, a tea pot and a strainer on Adrian's kitchen table. Six bottles of wine – chardonnay and pinot noir – plus a six-pack of premier lager and six wine glasses appeared like magic from the hamper.

The Dog was particularly interested in the grain-fed steak in its vacuum-sealed packaging. Packets of assorted dark-chocolate wafers and dried fruit and nuts were the last items at the bottom of the basket.

We read Clare's enclosed card:

Enjoy, Gina.
Don't forget to buy fresh salad ingredients, eggs and bread from your local suppliers.
Love Clare

'There you go, Dog. Food and sustenance from Lady Bountiful for her poor, starving friend.'

The Dog was impressed by the food that appeared from the hamper, but unimpressed by my reluctant acceptance of said food and sustenance.

'I hate being on the receiving end of Clare's good deeds! Clare is an infuriating friend. You know she was the last addition to our group.

Eva, Hester and I have been a tight-knit team since university. Eva and Hester don't do over-the-top stuff. They help when it counts.'

The Dog doesn't understand the complexity of human friendships. If he meets a friendly dog, all good. If he meets an unfriendly dog, he heads in the opposite direction.

Sunday 6 September

I'd spent the entire morning searching the garden for Houdini Dog's bucket collar. He'd wriggled out of it again. I found it, repaired it and attached it to the Dog. He slunk off to sulk in the bathroom.

The remainder of this exciting Sunday was taken up with a visit from the Sometime Cat. The Dog and I agree he's the ugliest cat we've ever seen but he has presence.

We fed the Sometime Cat and watched him pad off, all skin and bones, to make another Shelly Beach house call.

Monday 7 September

The Dog pattered into the bedroom and woke me. I looked at the clock – exactly time for breakfast. He was definitely on the mend.

I watched the Dog eat then refastened his bucket collar. 'If you behave and keep your collar on, the vet will take it off on Wednesday. You'll never have to wear it again.'

The Dog dislikes the word 'behave'. He started towards his pet door, remembered it was a no-go for the moment, reversed and walked decorously out the kitchen door. I picked up my coffee and followed him into the garden.

Adrian's garden was filled with damp spring smells. The doves' cooing was deafening.

'Last night I decided I have to go to the city again to visit my daughter and my grandson.'

No comment.

'I can't go today. Lee's visiting this afternoon. I've decided to bite

158

the bullet and go tomorrow. I'll need a stopover, because eight hours' travelling in one day leaves me very little quality time with Julia and Barney.'

The Dog thought I'd overestimated the travelling time and a stop-over would not be necessary.

'Two hours on the bus to Kingston, two hours on the train to the city, multiplied by two equals eight hours.'

Now the Dog was having trouble with my 'bite the bullet' idiom. And he definitely didn't understand the concept of quality time.

'I plan to return in time to take you to the vet's on Wednesday afternoon, and open the hall for the writers' group meeting.'

The Dog gave me his sad invalid-dog look. He listened while I phoned Julia. She opened with the standard excuse she uses to cut short any conversation with me in case it ventures into murky waters: 'I have to be at a meeting in five minutes, Gina. Yes, tomorrow fits my schedule. I'll be working from home. I'm only working a four-day week.'

I put the phone down. 'I think my daughter has gone back to work too early.'

The Dog gave me a don't-go-there look. The Dog knows I went back to work six weeks after Julia was born.

'Tomorrow's perfect, Dog. Now to arrange a low-cost stopover.'

I phoned Eva on her work number. 'Do you have a one-night vacancy for tomorrow night?'

I could hear papers rustling in the background. I got the message. This had to be a short, sharp call. Eva was busy. In a former life I was constantly busy. I loved the bustle of business.

'Yep, no problem. Dominic's not around. Visiting his mother.'

'And can you drop me at the station in the morning on your way to work? I have to be back in Shelly Beach by late afternoon.'

'No problem, Gina. Just as well you're coming here. There's some news you need to hear and it's best delivered face-to-face.'

I could hear voices in the background. I quickly concluded our call.

'Eva's a true friend, Dog. She was in a meeting but she still answered her mobile when my name came on the screen.'

Gentle rain started to fall. We decided to move inside. 'I never imagined Dominic as a dutiful son, Dog, but his absence will give Eva and I more time to catch up. And I'm not thinking about news that is best delivered face-to-face.'

The Dog gave me another sad invalid-dog look.

'I know. I have to find someone to look after you.'

I resurrected my PR skills and did some high-level negotiating. I phoned Alf, who was working at Piece of Cake. Alf and wife Beryl can dog-sit on Tuesday and Wednesday – but not Tuesday night. 'Tuesday night is our bridge night. No dogs allowed. Someone's dog – can't remember whose – bit Beryl on the ankle the Tuesday before last. Nasty bite. She had to get a tetanus injection.'

'Right.' The Dog and I visited Bossy Child and her mum. The Dog's collar stopped him sitting in his cute-dog pose with his head on the side, but they still made an unbelievable fuss of him. 'We'd love to look after Hugo on Tuesday night. I'll take him to Alf at Piece of Cake in the morning before I drop off the kids and go to work.'

Thank you, Joan.

'There you go, Dog. I'll pick you up from Piece of Cake on Wednesday afternoon and take you to the vet.'

The Dog was not happy with his complicated dog-sitting arrangements.

'It's the best I can do. I have to visit my daughter and see my grandson again. You'd feel the same if you had a pup and your pup had pups. You'd want to see them. Then we'll go to the vet's and he'll remove your bucket collar. And then we'll go to the writers' group meeting. You like going to that meeting.'

The Dog was unimpressed with the spin I was putting on my absence.

Lee arrived and made coffee. 'I can't stay tonight. I need an early start tomorrow. I'm going to the city for more dental treatment. A friend is driving me.'

I understood. I thought about asking if there was room for another body in Lee's friend's car – but I let it go. I don't want to step over the boundaries we've established.

I commiserated with Lee over his dental issues. These sorts of things rate high on life's priorities. I didn't want to go near dental issues. All I needed now was a root-canal treatment and my cashflow would be blown to smithereens.

Over coffee we talked about the complicated plot Lee is writing for his novel. Lee works out ideas for his plot and characters in his head while he's prepping in the kitchen. He writes them up when he gets home.

I'm in awe of Lee's writing routine. He wakes at 5, goes for a five-kilometre run before breakfast, eats breakfast then sits down at his computer and writes for two hours before he starts work at the pub. He writes for hours in the evening as well.

'This novel is really getting to me.'

I can see that. Lee left copies of chapters ten, eleven and twelve with me. I promised to give them out to members on Wednesday whether he came or not.

'I'm not sure I can get back from the city in time for the meeting. Written feedback on the chapters will be fine. I need to know how my cliffhangers are working.'

Later that night I checked Alf's instructions for bus and train connections to and from the city. 'I have to catch the 8 a.m. train from the city on Wednesday morning in order to be back in time to take you to your medical appointment, Dog.'

No comment.

The Dog watched me while I collected Bill's handouts for the meeting. I picked the Dog up and put him on my knee while I counted the copies. The Dog's right. His bucket collar is very unfriendly.

'The handouts are all about plotting, Dog. Lee's got a brilliant plot. Lots of twists and turns and dead ends. And he writes an outline for each chapter. If I were to write another novel I'd write chapter outlines. And I'd concentrate on character development so I'd have characters still standing by the last page. Did you know that Ian Fleming, the guy who wrote the James Bond books, advises writers to use four-letter names for their characters because that will be the name you type the most?'

The Dog wasn't at all interested in engaging in a writerly conversation.

I thought back to the phone conversation I'd had with Eva. What did Eva have to tell me that she couldn't say over the phone or in an email? What news is best told to a friend face-to-face?

'What do you think, Dog? Is it a cliffhanger?'

The Dog gave me his snarly smile. His little teeth gleamed. If I'm not back in time to get him to the vet I'm in serious, serious trouble.

Tuesday 8 September

I packed my overnight Mary Poppins bag with great care. It contained a handmade baby rug bought from the Sea Haven market, public transport timetables, a mobile phone, water bottle, sandwich, book, torch, change of underwear and toiletries. I was prepared for battle.

Alf called to collect the Dog and dropped me at the bus stop, which was a sweet thing to do. He'd filled me in on Shelly Beach bus protocol. A boarding passenger says hello to the seated passengers. Passengers wave goodbye to fellow passengers and thank the driver when they alight from the bus. And Shelly Beach passengers like to sit in their regular seats.

After the prescribed hello after boarding, I made three attempts to find a seat only to be met with, 'Sorry, this is saved. My friend is getting on later.' I finally found a seat beside a Shelly Beach sea-change commuter who related her potted life story to me in one paragraph of 108 words. She's learnt it's easier to disclose relevant information in one paragraph. If you don't, relevant information is extracted, sentence by sentence, word by word.

She and (twenty years older) husband have bought a farmhouse and land at Shelly Beach. Husband is retired; he lives at Shelly Beach full-time. She's a senior insurance broker. Works from home on Mondays. Commutes to the city on Tuesday – returns Friday night. Shares a city flat with her daughter and uses the firm's car when she's in the city.

My Shelly Beach sea-change commuter finds public transport enhances her life. There's time to read on the bus, and she uses her laptop on the train to get ahead of things before she arrives at work.

I watched my in-control commuter fossick in her briefcase. She extracted a bulky airport novel and opened it at the bookmarked page.

I fossicked in my Mary Poppins bag for one of Adrian's literary novels. I fake-read while gazing at the blue sea from my window as the bus hugged the coastline. On the train I continued to fake-read to ward off talkative strangers. I observed my Shelly Beach commuter at the other end of the carriage. The airport novel had been stowed away. She was talking on her mobile, her laptop at the ready, and she had a takeaway coffee.

I noticed several other commuters using their mobiles and laptops, diligently working on their way to work.

I made a mental note: buy coffee from the station kiosk before boarding the train next time.

I had no trouble connecting with a bus to Julia's. Barney with an E-Y was cute but fretful. Mother and grandmother teamed to jiggle and rock him to sleep. Barney probably misses competent Nanny Anny – Tuesday's her day off.

Julia filled me in on news when we took a much-needed tea break. Her new business was running smoothly and Nanny Anny was a dream. The final assets of the Laurel-Scott Corporation were being processed, and there might be more papers to sign.

Julia sighed suddenly and looked away. 'There's no other way to say this, Gina. Kenneth wants to fudge dates.'

I gave Julia my practised blank stare. 'Fudge dates?' I stirred my tea. What was Julia's cunning old dad up to now?

'With the divorce. He wants to backdate the day you left him.'

I stirred my tea. 'A quick divorce?'

Julia looked embarrassed. 'Yes.'

I put my tea down. Why would Kenneth want a quick divorce? Probably because a new company would be easier to set up if he used his wife's name. His *new* wife's name.

I had a ridiculous desire to laugh. The day I left Kenneth? Don't laugh, Gina. Don't laugh. Deep breathing, Gina.

It was not the way I planned my marriage to end. I planned Kenneth and I would make a jointly executed decision to separate. We'd send out joint emails. Give our news to our daughter and small group of friends. I'd even chosen the words with cherry-picking care.

This is a mutual decision following a process of long and careful consideration. After a great deal of thought we have decided to separate. We do not intend to comment any further. Gina and Kenneth.

I smiled at Julia. 'I'm happy for your father to get the legal stuff for our divorce happening as soon as possible. Our sick and sad marriage is well and truly over. I'm moving on.'

Julia looked distressed. I rubbed her back. She's realising that her father is mean asking her to be the go-between – leaving the messy stuff to her.

I watched Julia leave the room, and return with papers marked with the usual 'sign here' tags.

I signed at the appropriate places. Barney was stirring. 'I'll take my grandson for a walk so you can have a rest.'

I could see a look of relief flit over Julia's face. She was exhausted. Maybe as a helpful grandma I could rebuild our relationship? I took Barney in my arms. His podgy fingers grabbed my naked ring finger. I'm going to like being a helpful grandma.

Barney and I set off on our allotted two-hour-maximum walk. Julia drew me a map showing the nearest park and coffee shop. She made up a bottle for Barney, 'just in case!' She's not breastfeeding. 'It didn't work out. Can you change a nappy?'

'Of course I can.' I hadn't changed a nappy for decades.

I made consoling noises to the exhausted mum and escaped with my gorgeous baby grandson in his Ferrari-designed pram.

Out of range I stopped and had a go with a disposable nappy from Barney's emergency bag. Simple. Like covering a book. Apply cover to surface and fasten.

It was a pleasant day. There were patches of spring sunshine. Barney and I had a happy time. It's amazing how new babies can attract so much doting attention from total strangers. But Barney is an astonishingly beautiful baby.

Two hours later I returned Barney to his mum and received a grateful hug.

Travelling to Eva's in the bus that afternoon, I smiled at one or two fellow passengers. I felt smooth and caramelly from being in Barney's company. My Mary Poppins bag was lighter. Julia had loved Barney's handmade rug. And all things considered, I actually felt quite good about getting a quickie divorce.

Eva had arranged for Hester to meet us for dinner later that evening. Unfortunately (fortunately) Clare couldn't make it. I'm so over Clare's Q&A sessions re: my survival at Shelly Beach.

Eva greeted me at the door wearing sexy leopard-skin underwear and not much else. 'I just need a moment to shower.'

I sat on Eva's balcony watching the city lights. She joined me soon after. I don't know how she can look so good after working the hours she does.

She handed me a glass of wine. 'You're getting sex, aren't you?'

'Excuse me?'

'It's written all over you. You're positively glowing.'

Silence.

'Come on, tell me about him. Trust me. I won't tell anyone.'

I trusted Eva. Of course I trusted Eva. She knows I have enough confidential goss about her and the men in her life to fill every celebrity magazine for a year.

'It's nothing serious. Lee's the chef at Rosa's.'

'The drop-dead gorgeous Asian guy? The one with the ponytail?'

I nodded and ignored Eva's war dance as she pranced round the room, arms punching the air. 'Yes! Yes! Yes!'

This was followed by a puffed, back-to-earth, 'Good for you, Gina. Finish your wine – Hester will be waiting for us at the restaurant.'

During dinner Hester and Eva divulged the latest Kenneth news. High-priority news they felt I should know – news I agreed I needed to know and that was best told face-to-face.

'Kenneth's going to marry Angela. Soon.'

There it was: Kenneth was not only getting a divorce; he was getting married again. Kenneth had had affairs with his young PAs, but he'd never wanted to marry one before.

Kenneth was marrying Clever Angela. Angela Vereska, whose father was *the* Paul Vereska, prominent businessman. Kenneth had hit the jackpot this time. Father-in-law-to-be was a VIP; a charismatic contributor to business and civic life. A very smooth operator.

And Angela was marrying a man old enough to be her father. I guessed she'd taken this into account. My Shelly Beach sea-change commuter seemed happy being married to a man twenty years older than she was.

'How do you feel?' My concerned friends waited for my reply.

'It's not the way I planned to get a divorce from Kenneth.'

Hester and Eva waited while I collected my thoughts.

'Kenneth pulled the plug before I did.' I should have guessed when I signed the divorce papers that Kenneth had a plan. It looked like he'd managed to pull himself out of a quagmire. Would he be able to resurrect his career? He'd done it before. Kenneth may have planned his relationship with Angela while thinking of her father's valuable network connections.

I looked at my friends' concerned faces. 'I feel relieved. Really, I do. Never again will I have to be involved in Kenneth's calculated schemes. It feels good.'

Once or twice during the night I caught Eva smirking at me.

'Don't even go there!' I mouthed subtly. And she didn't. I gave Eva permission to tell Hester about Lee. Later.

The bill was alarming but I didn't quibble when Hester and Eva covered it. I'd paid for some very expensive celebratory wine. Wine to celebrate my divorce – without the email ending.

Wednesday 9 September

The next morning Eva dropped me at the station on her way to work. The trek back to Shelly Beach was painless. I felt pleased with myself. I'd travelled on multiple buses and trains without ending up stranded like a cow on a rooftop in a flood.

Back at Sea View Cottage I dumped my Mary Poppins bag, drove the short distance to Piece of Cake, collected and deposited the Dog in Adrian's Ford and set off for the vet's. The Dog now has a clean bill of health and his bucket collar has vanished.

I repeated the vet's warning on the way home. 'If you start licking your rear end the collar will have to go back on again, Dog.'

We just had time to grab a toasted sandwich and a bone before it was time to open the hall for the writers' group meeting.

'Please take note, Dog. I'm meeting my contractual obligations by convening yet another Shelly Beach Writers' Group meeting.' We checked the calendar. 'It's the fourth one, too.'

The Dog watched while I put a careful cross through the ninth of September.

While we were eating I filled the Dog in with my just-learnt Kenneth news.

The Dog thought it was time I got my train back on track.

I don't think the Dog has ever seen a train, much less one off its track.

The Dog said underestimating humans and dogs – what they've done in the past, are doing in the present, and can do in the future – is one of life's great mistakes.

He never underestimates the bite-power of a small dog.

As a woman in the know, I agreed.

To: Adrian <bookstreet@network.com.au>
From: Gina <piececake@email.com.au>
Subject: Writers' group
Hi Adrian,
Hugo and I did the opening and shutting for your writers' group
and served faultless welcoming tea and coffee. Full quota of
members except for Lee Wang. He's staying in the city to have
dental treatment.

Daphne talked about doing research for her historical
novel – gave us a *Tips for writing historical novels* handout. (Outside
the literary interests of Digby, Bill and Josh – but they were polite
and listened.) Our tree-hugging activist has decided to set her
romance in the Regency period. Loves the costumes, banter, sword
duels, etc. etc.

Bill talked about planning and plotting and gave us a handout (I've kept a copy). Bill's big on handouts, which is comforting. Bianca went home to plot-point her plot. She jailed her antagonist in chapter three. Now she thinks she'd prefer to jail him in chapter six or seven. Her novel was getting very dull without an antagonist – although she's loving writing the sexy bits between her hero and heroine.

Next meeting Josh's bringing his plot chart and workshopping his sci fi/fantasy novel.

Your dog now has a clean bill of health. He's revelling in his bucket-collarless state.

Gina

Thursday 10 September

When Bossy Child arrived from school she raced to the computer. Screams came from Bedroom Two. 'You've got a job offer, Gina!' She raced out and handed me an email printout.

To: Gina <piececake@email.com.au>
From: Hester <hester@bizevents.com.au>
Subject: Job offer
Hi Gina,
I'm running a conference at the Hyatt soon. I'd employed Eva's Dominic to be Boy Friday but he's landed a better job. Would you like to be Girl Friday? Starting Monday 14, finishing Friday 18. 24/7. Above union rates of pay! Free board and lodging at hotel.
Love Hester

'I can't do it!'

'Geen-ah!'

'Who'll look after the Dog? And you? Who'll feed Adrian's chick-ens? And the fish? And the doves?'

169

'Henry Shepherd can look after Hugo. Hugo will love being with Sally. I can walk to Bianca's and hang out at Scissors until Mum gets home. And I can feed Adrian's chickens and the fish and the doves every day.'

Before I could stop her, Bossy Child rang Bianca at Scissors.

'That's fixed. I can hang out with Bianca until Mum gets home.' I continued watching while Bossy Child dialled Henry Shepherd's number.

'It's settled, Gina. Hugo can stay with Henry for the five days.'

Already I'm disposable. 'I can't go. I've got nothing to wear. It's an upmarket job. I have to at least look like an upmarket employee!'

'Daphne will find something for you to wear in the charity shop.'

I could hear Clare's 'OhmaGod!' echoing in my head. *You didn't get those clothes from a charity shop, Gina?*

Bossy Child left with a reminder. 'We'll pick you up at 5 o'clock on Saturday night to go to the Spring Wing Ding at Pandora's.'

The Dog and I have ungraciously accepted an invitation to attend the Spring Wing Ding. How could we refuse? Everyone goes. The gold coin donation goes to the Lost Dogs' Shelter. The Dog gave me his dog-on-death-row look.

'I know the Lost Dogs' Shelter was where Adrian found you.'

Joan rang and the Dog and I deposited Bossy Child back home.

Friday 11 September

At 9 o'clock this morning the Dog and I drove to Daphne's charity shop in Sea Haven.

Bianca was waiting. Her mission: to find quality armour for me to survive five days in the corporate world.

I moaned, 'I hate buying clothes.'

My stylists ignored me. Daphne and Bianca, like true hunters and gatherers, set to work among the colour-coordinated racks of preloved clothes.

'Daphne's been a fashion stylist for a department store,' Bianca whispered.

'After or before she was a tree-sitter?'

'After, I think.'

I surveyed the sixties, seventies, and eighties retro outfits. Fortunately the smell of the former wearers of said preloved garments didn't linger. Daphne's secret: the liberal use of room freshener.

'I've kept aside some edgy suits for you to try on, Gina. And some little tops just shouting pizzazz.'

'Thank you, Daphne.' I pasted on a smile and refused to think of the previous wearers of edgy suits and little tops just shouting pizzazz.

I barely recognised the resized body in the fitting-room mirror: hardly a new and shiny body, but a different body.

'You've lost heaps of weight, Gina.'

'It's the dog-walking. And sensible food.'

I looked at my new BFs discussing my wellbeing and fitness. In a weird sort of way it was comforting.

Not long after I emerged from Daphne's emporium with a respectable selection of armour – at a very respectable cost.

'I'll come round tonight and lend you some of my bling!' Bianca raced off to Scissors to meet her 11 o'clock client.

That night she arrived as promised and coordinated some jewellery with my new look. 'You'll look cool, Gina!'

She booked me in at Scissors tomorrow for a shampoo, trim, colour with two-toned highlights and blow-wave in exchange for delivery of three casseroles and two chocolate mud cakes when I return from the conference.

'I love this bartering thing, Gina. Most of my cooking starts with or includes toast.'

I understood.

My Prada handbag and Armani trench coat from a former life received a five-star commendation from Bianca. But not my shoes. 'Don't you have higher heels?'

'No.'

Saturday 12 September

Bossy Child called after lunch to check on the Dog, my new wardrobe and hairstyle.

'Gina, you'd better come and see this,' she called in a strangled voice from Adrian's back verandah.

I went to check the reason for Bossy Child's panic. We raced back inside and emailed Adrian.

To: Adrian <bookstreet@network.com.au>
From: Gina <piececake@email.com.au>
Subject: Dead cat
Hi Adrian,
The Sometime Cat has turned up dead on your back verandah.
     What should I do?
Gina

To: Gina <piececake@email.com.au>
From: Adrian <bookstreet@network.com.au>
Re: Dead cat
Hi Gina,
Bury it. And tell Violet.
Adrian

Bossy Child was in control. Obviously nothing was going to stop us attending the Spring Wing Ding. 'I'll tell Mum. Have you got anything I can wrap the Sometime Cat in? We'll leave him in the shed and we can have a funeral tomorrow. You can talk to Mum about the funeral at the Spring Wing Ding. Don't be late, though. We're picking you up at 5, remember?'

After gently placing the Sometime Cat's Egyptian-mummy body in its temporary resting place in Adrian's shed, Bossy Child raced home to tell her mother about the latest catastrophe involving the house-sitter next door.

The Dog wasn't interested in attending the Spring Wing Ding; he's definitely not a party animal. I sympathised. 'I know you hate loud noises. But I do not trust you alone at home, Dog – especially with a dead cat in the shed. You can sleep in Pandora's laundry. We'll come home early. I promise.'

Bossy Child was right. The Spring Wing Ding is a highlight on the Shelly Beach social calendar. Every available Shelly Beach local was gathered at Pandora's. I settled the Dog in her laundry and stepped back into the party.

Josh's band, Ellipsis, was set up in the living room, belting out a mix of music magnified at incredible decibels of sound. Alf and Beryl were executing a mean jive. Bossy Child bopped with Sam. Non-dancing locals shouted weather-speak to each other above the music.

Fortunately I'd checked Adrian's manual under S for Spring Wing Ding. I handed over a dozen bottles of Adrian's red wine dutifully labelled *For the Spring Wing Ding Auction*.

Daphne's hubby Charles, aka the auctioneer, was a bit stressed. 'Not sure whether we'll auction them by the bottle – or the dozen? The important question is which will bring in the best return?'

I left Charles with his fiscal problem and slipped between groups using my practised line as an exit when required. 'Sorry. Must go. I'm helping Pandora with the supper.' (Lie.)

When Lee arrived I dredged up steps I'd learnt at university to match his energetic jive (learnt in a Hong Kong dance school).

Then his mobile rang and he was called back to Rosa's: an emergency in the kitchen. Mice trouble.

Daphne found me regaining my breath. She whispered, 'Bianca needs you.'

Bianca was sobbing her heart out in Pandora's pantry. 'Don't look at me. I know I look like one of Adrian's doves caught in a tsunami.'

I allowed Bianca's simile to pass.

'It's Josh. He's playing all of my favourite covers.'

Another flood of tears.

'And he's painting new stuff on his van each week. Digby says they're quotes.'

I offered tissues.

'This week it's about revenge: *Revenge is like swallowing poison and watching the other person die.* Does that come from Shakespeare?'

'Not that I can recall.'

'Does Josh mean I'm full of vengeance because of what happened with Crystal?'

Bianca burst into another torrent of tears. Coping with sibling rivalry is difficult.

'We were so happy. Josh gave me a gorgeous ring. We planned to get married last school holidays. Crystal always wants what I have.' More tears and more tissues. 'I'm guessing Crystal instigated everything.' (Instigated is Bianca's word of the week.) 'I still haven't returned the ring. Mum keeps reminding me that it's under her bed. I know it's the honest thing to do . . . return the ring . . . but I did like being engaged.'

Bianca blew her nose loudly. 'I have to focus on my goal to be an international hair stylist.'

I understood. 'Why don't we drive back to Adrian's? I'll make supper.'

Bianca was happy with this plan. The Dog was ecstatic. I told Joan we were getting a lift home.

174

Once there, I lit a fire. It wasn't cold but the fire was comforting. Bianca and I drank hot chocolate and ate ice-cream smothered with chocolate fudge sauce. I promised to give Bianca my chocolate-fudge sauce recipe.

'I'm tired of being heartbroken,' Bianca confessed. 'What I'd like to do is find a really good male friend. Have an uncomplicated friendship with no strings attached. No sex.'

'Right.'

'I haven't even felt like having a just-right-for-now date. And I could. Practically all the Seagulls are keen to date me.' (The Seagulls are the football team who split into Shelly Beach Cricket and Lifesavers clubs in summer.)

I don't doubt that.

'What about you, Gina? Have you thought of starting a just-right-for-now relationship?'

'Excuse me?'

'You know – when you go out with someone . . . have an uncomplicated relationship you know won't last forever.'

'No, I haven't.' (I'm ignoring the sex-with-Lee relationship.) But if Adrian-with-the-friendly-eyes was around I'd be happy to have an uncomplicated relationship with him. Friendship. And Digby's great company.

I stopped fantasising about the men in my life and persuaded my strong, sexy friend Bianca to stay the night and sleep in Bedroom One.

The Dog and I sat in front of the fire until it burnt itself out. He agreed with me that life gets very messy at times. No matter what age you are.

I agreed with the Dog that the trick is to pull your head out of the sand, look at your mess and do something about it. Then you feel better. You can start again. Maybe get your head stuck in the sand again?

The Dog decided to end our discussion on sand. He knows I get furious when he forgets to wipe his paws on the mat before he enters Adrian's house.

Sand is definitely a bone of contention between us. I hate the crunchy sound of it under your shoes when you walk on Adrian's floorboards. Worse still – picking up sand on the soles of your bare feet when you walk around the bedroom.

And we didn't go near the subject of a certain dog who collects sand in his fur and deposits it on a substitute owner's bed when said dog is sneaking an afternoon snooze.

As a woman who's finally pulled her head out of the sand, and who's finally doing something about her messy life, the Dog thought I should have a more tolerant attitude to sand.

I ignored the Dog.

Sunday 13 September

Bossy Child, little brother Sam and mum Joan came to help dig a grave for the Sometime Cat. Bianca decided to stay while we held a small, private burial service.

Joan provided angel cakes for the wake.

I plan to call on Violet and tell her the sad news when I come back from the conference. (Bossy Child doesn't want to tell Violet, which is fair enough. The Sometime Cat did pass away on my temporary premises.)

Lee cycled around after his evening shift – compensation for missing tomorrow's assignation. He produced gifts he'd brought back from the city last week: coffee, packets of herbs for Adrian's store cupboard, cheese, chocolates, perfume, a bottle of brut, a Hermès scarf and two Hitchcock DVDs. He'd also brought his portable DVD player.

We spent the evening watching movies. Lee knows I love Hitchcock. Was this a calculated move? Watching a movie takes away the need for conversation – meaningful conversation. Lee was very intro-spective. He hardly spoke the entire evening. My sensory antennae were up. At least Lee hadn't arrived bearing sparkly compensatory gifts.

He gave me a slow, lingering kiss when he left. I watched the lights on his bike disappear as he cycled up Sea Spray Road, his backpack loaded with his DVD player and the DVDs he'd borrowed.

'What do you think, Dog? Have I become a hobby that has passed its use-by date? Is our affair coming to an end after just a few weeks? Is it time for both of us to move on?'

The Dog yawned. He wasn't interested in the relationship stuff humans get entangled in. He knew one thing for sure, though: I'd blown any opportunity of a platonic relationship with an interesting male companion.

The Dog and I stayed up and discussed the wordless scenes Hitchcock uses to build up tension. Major plot points are revealed through small, barely noticeable details, such as a dirty smudge on a shoe or a sliver of light sneaking out from a blind.

We both agreed that *Rear Window* is our favourite Hitchcock movie. *The Birds* is at the bottom of our list. The Dog thinks that the plot, i.e. birds turning feral and attacking the residents of a small seaside town, is a little too close for comfort. Pelicans going wild and dive-bombing small dogs are the stuff of nightmares.

I waited while the Dog played his sniffer-dog role around Adrian's garden. The Dog thought there was a renegade possum lurking out there. Definitely not a fox.

I checked his paws for signs of grave-digging. All clear. Playing fetch is no doubt a more appealing dog hobby than digging. But I need to teach the Dog to throw his own ball.

'Will you still like me when I return next Saturday, Dog?'

Of course he will. I haven't organised anyone else to feed him on Saturday.

Monday 14 September

Camouflaged in my Armani trench coat I conquered transport for the masses – now being one of the masses. I dragged Pandora's classy flight-stewardess luggage-on-wheels behind me.

It was only a five-minute walk from the station to the Hyatt Hotel but I hired a taxi to create a fitting entrance. No-imagination taxi driver was amazed at his one-minute fare. The doorman helped me out of the taxi and took control of Pandora's luggage. I pasted on a smile and practised d-e-e-e-p breathing.

Hester was generous to offer her out-of-date friend work. Hester's cool appraisal of my gear proved that my Shelly Beach stylists and choice of preloved clothes were successful. I wondered if cool, calm Hester had a Plan B in case I popped up looking like an out-of-town freak? Would she have paid me in kind – appropriate gear instead of wages?

My Girl (Woman) Friday role consists of small tasks to keep the conference ticking over smoothly: endless smiles, refreshing cups of coffee and water, and mints. My mission: to ensure Hester's reputation for running meticulously detailed events remains intact.

My how-can-I-help-you role also consists of photocopying and compiling presenters' papers for participants. My basic knowledge of electronic equipment has returned. Like knowing how to ride a bike, it had just slipped into a microspace in my brain.

Hester explained that my major challenge (translated: problem) was to cope with the wants of Jeremy Harvey. He's an international speaker who's being paid a gigantic salary he does not deserve. He has multiple issues with the conference, from the quality of the paper for his handouts to the lack of a complimentary fruit bowl and an inadequate number of fluffy towels in his room.

Using my pasted-on smile and mustering the most fawning of services, I had no problem providing a solution to my major challenge.

Hester had negotiated accommodation for us at the Hyatt as part of the conference deal. 'It's more convenient when you need to be on call for conference members.'

At the end of Day One, I can't describe how much I appreciated the guilt-free, endless hot shower and the leak-proof bedroom ceiling. I was extremely happy with my fluffy towel allotment. I rang Henry to check how things were going. I had a short conversation with the Dog and told him to behave himself. Four days to go.

Tuesday 15 September
Hester likes early starts, but I'm far from enamoured with my 5.30 wake-up call.

The conference is not arduous work. You could even call it enjoyable, considering I haven't undertaken 'work' for a year or more. As a customer service facilitator I'm not responsible for the organisation of the conference or the delivery of a mesmerising PowerPoint presentation.

There were a few challenges (problems) today, and it was only Day Two. From memory, Day Four is usually the day from hell. On Day Four attendees get tired, bored, sexed up, and fed up. They want out.

The after-dinner sessions went well. Hester and I had complimentary hibiscus-juice cocktails in the hotel bar afterwards. Earlier that evening I'd taken pain-in-the-butt international speaker to the airport and tipped him into a plane. I was in the process of tearing his business card (including personal number in case I ever touched down in LA) into tiny, tiny, tiny fragments.

Hester was relaxed and happy. 'Excellent number of participants, considering the economic climate.'

I agreed.

Then Hester segued with mind-jolting news. 'Last week I texted Paul – *I WANT A DIVORCE!*'

Bloody hell! I stared at my calm, always-in-control friend. What on earth had Paul done to deserve such a brutal end to a twenty-year marriage?

'Our marriage has been going through a meltdown. Didn't you realise, Gina?'

'Sorry. No.' (I didn't add that from my experience, the only people who know what's going on in a marriage are the people in it.) 'I've been concentrating on surviving at Shelly Beach.'

Hester accepted my explanation.

'We probably could have got counselling and moved on if I hadn't discovered the birth certificate.'

Birth certificate? Should I have known about the birth certificate?

'We'd been cleaning up the farm a little while ago. Getting it ready to sell.'

I nodded. I'd heard about this. Paul and Hester were selling their hobby farm. They were tired of their part-time tree-change. Too much work for a time-poor couple.

'I found a box of papers in the shed: letters and Rob's birth certificate.' When Hester and Paul first met, Paul had come as a package deal, complete with Rob, his three-year-old son. 'I didn't bother to read the letters – they were from Carol, Paul's first wife.' (Rob's mother.) 'The birth certificate for Rob was the killer document. It named a Thomas Simpson as Rob's father. Paul's not Rob's biological father.'

I struggled to get my head around this new info. 'Paul's not Rob's father?'

'No. Paul can't have children! He's lied to me since the day we met. He's sterile! If he had told me he was sterile I could have resigned myself to the fact that motherhood was unattainable. Maybe we could have adopted? Used a sperm donor? IVF? But I thought it was me!'

My stomach turned over. A betrayal. A huge lie. A monstrous twenty-year-old lie. I'd known Hester's marriage in the early years was shadowed by the fact she couldn't conceive. After several years of trying, Hester being Hester, she decided she'd live with the pain of being childless. She moved on. She had her career. And of course she had Rob: a ready-made son, whom she'd grown to love dearly.

Hester searched in her handbag for more complimentary drink tokens. I ordered a Scotch.

I've long envied Hester's relationship with Rob. She's an excellent stepmum. She and Rob are bonded as though biological mother and son.

'It can't change how you and Rob feel about each other.'

'Of course it won't!'

Stupid comment, Gina.

'But I won't be married to a partner who's lied to me for years.'

I reached for Hester's hand. She shook me off. 'Don't worry. I'm over it. It's finished. At least we're being civilised about the divorce and settlement.'

I looked at my in-control friend. Amazingly, Hester's divorce and settlement seemed to be working for her.

Hester changed the subject again. 'Conference is going well. You're doing an excellent job, Gina.'

When I returned to my room it was too late to ring Henry and check on the Dog. There were no messages, so I presumed the Dog was happy and having fun with his poodle friend Sally.

I couldn't get to sleep. I tossed and turned for hours thinking about my friend's marriage suddenly going down in flames. Or more like a firecracker that's been snuffed out before it explodes. At least Hester didn't have her head stuck in the sand. She'd accepted her marriage was a no-go and she was doing something about it . . . unlike people who keep marriages on barely-simmer for years.

Wednesday 16 September

Woken by another 5.30 wake-up call – but I enjoyed a long, hot shower and room-service breakfast.

My feet are killing me. I'm so glad I refused Bianca's loan of her latest charity shop coup – Jimmy Choo shoes with thirteen-centimetre heels.

Edgy suits and tops with pizzazz are working. When I'm not at the meet-and-greet, let-me-solve-your-challenge desk, and minus my name tag, I melt into the conference crowd with anonymity.

I missed session one on Day Three because I slipped out to ring the Dog. He was doing fine. He wasn't missing me at all. I then phoned Daphne. I had the guilts. 'Can you please email Adrian? Tell him I'm working at a conference. Assure him that the Dog is happy and safe at Henry Shepherd's.'

'Not a problem. I've already emailed him.'

Bloody hell!

I returned in time to sit at the back of the room and soak up information from session two. Will I adopt a long-term goal? Will a long-term goal provide a pathway to my future success in these tough times?

After catching session three I'm now into 'thin slicing'. We apparently make intuitive decisions based on thin slices of information. The trick is to consider a few variables and discard other details. Way to go!

I missed the after-dinner session four. I was busy, busy, busy arranging emergency travel home for a participant.

I oozed empathy. 'So upsetting and inconvenient when your pet dies.' (If the Dog lets anything happen to himself while I'm away he's in serious trouble.)

I also arranged an emergency flight home and oozed empathy for a second participant. 'I understand. So upsetting when your wife walks out on you when you're at a work conference.'

Hester was fluffing around till very late so I went to my room. I ordered a room-service club sandwich and ate my way through the surprise complimentary fruit basket. (I'm pretty sure I received pain-in-butt international speaker's fruit basket.)

I watched a necklace of car lights threading their way in and out of the city (Bianca language) as I chatted on the phone to Bossy Child, Pandora, Bianca and the Dog.

Thursday 17 September
Day Four of the conference was fine until about 5 in the afternoon. I'd excused myself from the noisy, fun-for-all drinks session to work at the meet-and-greet desk preparing complimentary product bags for Day Five. I had to make sure each participant had an authentic attendance certificate to take home – essential CV memorabilia and professional development evidence for bosses and company boards in atrocious economic times.

I was ready to limp back to my room and soak in a hot bath when the lift doors opened and Lee emerged. A Lee I'd never seen before. A cool, immaculately groomed, young-enough-to-be-my-son Lee in a very expensive suit.

Bloody hell!

'Are you free for dinner, Gina? I've important stuff to tell you.'

With a thumping heart I headed to the hotel bar and located Hester in the drinks crowd. She waved me off. Hester was firing!

I grabbed my coat and bag, and we left. We took the lift down to the basement car park to Lee's car: a dazzling red Porsche Cayenne.

'A gift from my parents.'

Hello? For a guy who's been riding a bicycle around Shelly Beach this was a huge jump up the transport ladder.

'Right. You have very generous parents, Lee.'

Lee opened the passenger-seat door of the car and I slid onto the leather upholstery.

'They are. Both my parents are surgeons. They live in Hong Kong.'

'Right.'

Lee paused before starting the Porsche. 'I completed four years

183

of medicine in Hong Kong. Decided not to do my final year. Came to Australia to stay with relatives instead.'

'Right . . . and?'

'Then the chef stuff followed – which you already know about.'

'Right!'

'I've got some really great news: my parents are giving me the deposit to buy a noodle bar in Nelson's Lane. Do you know Nelson's Lane?'

'The trendy one with all the restaurants?'

'That's it.'

I sat stunned, enveloped in the luxurious interior of Lee's Porsche, while Lee concentrated on driving in the city traffic. He parked at the rear of his soon-to-be restaurant. He was excited. 'The noodle bar comes complete with a warehouse-conversion apartment above. The refit is nearly done.'

He let us in via the rear entrance and walked me through his cool soon-to-be noodle bar and upstairs to his apartment. It was brilliant – as are all warehouse-conversion apartments built above noodle bars when no expense has been spared.

'We've crunched the numbers and are pretty confident we can make this work. The noodle bar has excellent commercial potential for a chef-owner and a small staff.'

'I'm sure it has.'

We spent the rest of the evening talking, talking, talking. We started in the apartment and then moved from bar to bar. Sometimes for variety, sometimes because owners pulled the pin on us and closed shop.

Lee left me at the Hyatt at 4 in the morning. I didn't bother going to bed. One and a half hours and I had to get up again. Bloody hell! I made myself a cup of earl grey tea and watched the fading city lights.

Lee is leaving Shelly Beach. Next week. I understood. I'm really happy he's picking up his life again. I'm happy he's accepted his parents' assistance although I shuddered at the thought of ever meet-ing said parents. A nightmare idea.

I looked at the key in the palm of my hand. It was a key to Lee's new apartment. I hoped he had duplicates. He'd need them for all the young women he'd meet. We've had a great time. The sex has been fantastic. Lee's made me feel so good – but I don't love him. And I'm sure he doesn't love me.

I opened my hand and dangled the key above the bathroom waste bin. But I couldn't do it. Not just yet.

I turned on the shower. Thank heaven for guilt-free endless hot water.

Friday 18 September

I made a quick phone call to Henry this morning before I fronted up for duty. The Dog was fine. I applied make-up, put on my armour, and pasted on a smile to do a flight-stewardess farewell to confer-ence participants.

Hester was on a high. No mention of my late – early morn-ing – return. The conference has been a great success. I agreed with Hester that Day Three, session one (speed networking) was a stand-out on the tick-the-boxes evaluation sheets.

Judging by the elevator pitches I'd overhead, all conference attendees were now able to capitalise on a two-minute opportunity. Two minutes, or until the elevator stops, is all you need to communi-cate your value to others.

Hester complimented me on my 'soft skills' – communicating, managing feedback and soothing disgruntled participants.

'You'll obviously need more product and technology training in the area you decide to work in, Gina. But you have excellent employee potential – in spite of your obvious lack of currency.'

I thanked Hester and left. Bloody hell! Sometimes she can be too objective.

This time I decided to walk the five minutes to the station. I dragged Pandora's flight-stewardess luggage behind me like a turtle dragging its shell. I wondered whether my in-control friend Hester might strike a few potholes in her determination to maintain an objective balance – at work and in her home life.

Digby was waiting for me when I got off the train. He'd been in Kingston to pick up some books and waited on the off-chance I was on the late afternoon train.

Hallelujah! For once I didn't care who told who what. I sat beside Digby in comfortable silence as his Merc lapped up the miles on the drive back to Shelly Beach.

'Do you feel like a meal at Rosa's tonight?' Digby asked.

'No, thank you. I'm exhausted. But I'd love a rain check, if that's okay?'

Of course it was. If I can convert Digby into a friend . . . he'll make a good friend.

I left my luggage in Adrian's living room and stood on the verandah taking huge gulps of Shelly Beach salt air. Then I rang Henry to tell him I was home and was coming to collect the Dog.

Saturday 19 September

A dull overcast day, a perfect excuse for a stay-in-bed day. Eventually I gave in to the Dog's pleading look and took him for a walk along the beach in the drizzly spring rain.

The gentle sloshing of the waves on the sand helped to blank out the leftover hum of conference rooms and full-on business types: males in designer suits and pastel shirts with toned ties; females in short skirts, long legs sheathed in stockings – stilt-walking on absurdly high heels.

I explained to the Dog that if I didn't smile for a few days it wasn't an indication that I didn't like him any more. I'd run out of smiles. I'd used too many at the conference. He understood.

The Dog watched while I deposited hotel bathroom micro-products on the shelf in Adrian's bathroom. He was unsure of my ethics in obtaining hotel products.

'It's not stealing! They give you a new set each day if you hide any you haven't used the day before.'

The Dog was still puzzled.

'It's as though Adrian sent you to a kennel for a week's stay and they gave you a supply of bones each day. You'd bury what you didn't eat and bring them home with you. They'd be included in your bill.'

The Dog continued to watch me stack my booty in Adrian's minus one-star bathroom.

'They're good-quality products. I can't afford to buy stuff like this with my cashflow problems.'

The Dog followed me to the kitchen where I deposited tea-bags and individual packets of coffee and sugar into Adrian's store cupboard.

At the bottom of Pandora's flight-stewardess luggage, I found a draft copy of my CV. A work-in-progress that my friends Hester and Eva are writing (creating) for me. A CV that reads like a novel.

I fully appreciated the importance of the active language they'd used. I was impressed with the sentences that started with strong words such as 'designed', 'implemented', 'delivered' and 'initiated'. Eva had added questions in red.

Can you see where we've omitted or disguised your lack of recent experience?

Yes!

Could you talk about your lack of currency in an interview?

Admit wasting a year of my life writing a go-nowhere novel? No!

Can you enrol at a college or find some volunteer work at Shelly Beach to update your IT skills?

'They have to be joking, Dog!'

Hester and Eva would like to omit 'children's' and 'volunteer' in

187

relation to my experience running storytime activities and holiday workshops at the local library.

'Hello! Challenge there, Dog.'

The Dog agreed that 'children's workshops' do differ from 'adult workshops', and 'volunteer' equals unpaid work.

'I know the implication is that you may not have gained said employment if the library had had to pay for your services. Then again, Dog, maybe adults like to conclude workshops with a gingerbread-man puppet on a popsicle stick.'

The Dog was not enthused by my cynical attitude towards obtaining a job or my lack of appreciation of friends who were working hard to produce a respectable job-getting CV for me.

I ignored the Dog.

I went to bed early and took a sleeping pill. I refused to dream of Lee. Instead I dreamt I had a job as a vet in a zoo. I had to fit a bucket collar on an elephant – and it wasn't easy.

Sunday 20 September

I had more than one well-meaning visitor during the afternoon. All came bearing cakes. They gave me sympathetic hugs and cheek kisses and left hurriedly.

'Okay, Dog. Time for a walk. I've a strong suspicion locals are bringing me complimentary comfort food because they imagine I'm devastated now that Lee is leaving town. I guess they know I've been having it off with a chef young enough to be my son.'

The Dog couldn't care less about my love-life but he *was* interested in a walk. However, Bossy Child's visit put a stop to our escape. She needed help with her school project, and like Red Riding Hood she came complete with a basket of muffins.

Red Riding Hood was open-mouthed when she saw my collection of cakes on the kitchen table.

'You can take the cakes and your muffins home. No – leave two muffins. If you don't take the cakes, I'll give them to the Girls. Bloody locals being kind and thoughtful!'

'You're so mean, Gina.'

'I like being mean.'

'Everyone's being nice to you because they've heard Lee's leaving Shelly Beach. They think you'll be sad and lonely and will need cheering up.'

'Bloody hell!'

Bossy Child gave me her cross-eyed look. 'Everyone knows you've been dating Lee, Gina!'

'What do you know about dating?'

'Dating is when you go out and have coffee or eat food with someone. Except you couldn't go out and drink coffee or eat at the pub with Lee – so he came here.'

Silence while Bossy Child thought about adding more to her definition of dating.

'If you had coffee or dinner with Lee at the pub, it'd be like Bianca coming to school and eating sandwiches in the playground with Josh. Or Josh going to Scissors and having a cup of tea and biscuits while Bianca cuts someone's hair.'

'Right.' I stared at Bossy Child and she stared back at me.

I knelt down on the floor and yelled through the pet door. 'You can dig up my crocodile-skin shoe, Dog. I know you buried it this morning.'

I looked at Bossy Child. I'd promised to help with her homework. 'Let's get started on your essay. I suggest you choose sharks. I can tell you heaps of stuff from personal experience about sharks.'

Rolled-eyed look from Bossy Child.

Monday 21 September
Bossy Child called after school for help padding out her essay, but she refused my excellent suggestions.

'I'll finish it at home, Gina.'

We made hot chocolate and took it outside to enjoy the spring sunshine on Adrian's verandah.

Bloody hell! The Sometime Cat had turned up again! Very dead and very smelly!

'It's karma, Gina. You should have told Violet that the Sometime Cat had died before you went away to the conference.'

I ignored the Bossy Child.

Then more tragedy. We discovered Gretel dead in the henhouse. Like she couldn't have died last week when I was at the conference! We rescued her body from her two best friends who were attempting to peck her to death – not realising that she was already dead.

Bossy Child and I decided it would be safer to bury the animals in her garden, considering the Dog's renewed confidence in his digging ability. We buried Gretel and reburied the Sometime Cat under Bossy Child's peach tree. After quick but sentimental ceremonies, Bossy Child, the Dog and I prepared for a trek up McIntosh Hill to Violet's.

Bossy Child was acting as my Jiminy Cricket conscience. 'You have to tell Violet straightaway that the Sometime Cat is dead. Confessing to stuff makes you feel better.'

'Right.' I obviously didn't need to confess about my love life. Every Shelly Beach local was aware of it. I wondered if Lee used our short affair in his novel? Was his main female character older than his hero? I decided to save these writerly questions for the Dog to answer later.

Violet was working on her novel when we arrived. She made us wait while she finished a paragraph: 'An idea left in mid-paragraph vanishes quickly.'

True.

I explained the sad demise of the Sometime Cat.

Violet wasn't upset! 'The Sometime Cat was diagnosed with cancer six months ago. I didn't expect him to live much longer. He's had

190

a happy life. I hadn't seen him for a few days and figured he'd gone to the Great Cat Basket in the sky.'

Bossy Child smiled her I-told-you-so smile.

Violet made a pot of tea and cut slices of her award-winning cherry cake.

I signalled for Bossy Child to refuse a second slice of cherry cake. 'Have to get home, Violet, to lock up Adrian's chickens.'

We hurried outside and untied the Dog.

On the way home an irritable Bossy Child – 'You could have waited, Gina, while I had a second slice of cake' – discussed my use of white lies.

'You told Violet that the Sometime Cat died last night and we buried him this morning. He died last week, Gina. We buried him last week. We *reburied* him this morning.'

'I thought it would upset Violet if she knew the Sometime Cat's grave had been interfered with.'

'You lied, Gina.'

'A friendly white lie.' I refuse to carry irrational guilt over a dead cat or a young lover. 'Have you forgotten I used my pashmina to mummify the Sometime Cat?'

'No. But you still lied about the date the Sometime Cat died.'

I ignored Bossy Child. The Dog understood about white lies. In order to resurrect a career they can be necessary. And he's promised not to do any grave-digging in Bossy Child's garden – especially under her peach tree.

I wrote a Post-it note before I went to bed: *Transfer the Sometime Cat's headstone to his new grave in Bossy Child's garden.*

To: Adrian <bookstreet@network.com.au>
From: Gina <piececake@email.com.au>
Subject: Tragedy
Hi Adrian,

Sad news. One of your Girls – Gretel – literally dropped off her perch either last night or this morning. We laid her to rest in Terri's garden beside the Sometime Cat's second resting place – away from Hugo's grave-digging. Do you want me to buy another chicken or will you wait until you come home?

Alf wants to know if you want the furniture for Crow's Nest Flat delivered before the plumber plumbs the bathrooms? Alf's done all the work he can do in the flat.

Gina

To: Gina <piececake@email.com.au>
From: Adrian <bookstreet@network.com.au>
Re: Tragedy

Hi Gina,

Don't worry about replacing Gretel. Tell Alf to organise Swinton's to deliver furniture for Crow's Nest. Swinton's are also holding a stove for Piece of Cake. They can deliver that at the same time.

I'm ignoring the Sometime Cat's resurrection.

Would you mind attending the action committee meeting tonight? We have to get the date of Writefest changed again. I've realised winter is impossible. I'm trying to get international authors to visit. No hope unless Writefest is held in spring or summer next year, and we know summer's problematic. Go for spring!

How are fundraising activities going? I'll need cash to fund international author/s' visit/s.

Heard you did brilliantly at your conference. Well done!

Adrian

'Bloody hell, Dog! I was banking on an early night.'

I rang Pandora and arranged to go to the action committee meeting with her. I quickly showered and changed. I waited on the verandah for Pandora with BYO Dog.

Tuesday 22 September

'It was worth missing an early night and attending the action committee meeting – wasn't it, Dog? Plenty of fireworks!'

The Dog was being sulky. I forgot to buy boring vitamin-packed pellets. Last week, at great expense and effort, I'd carried home tins of Pampered Pet dog food from an exclusive pet shop in the city. I've tried two tins: Tender beef chunks in red wine sauce and chicken in apricot jus. He refuses to eat one mouthful. Wrong: he tasted a mouthful from each can and vomited.

'Cleaning up your mess isn't in my contract, Dog.'

The Dog didn't care. He knew he'd win. I'll buy him boring dog food. I can't afford to let him starve to death before Adrian returns.

Pandora filled me in on the meeting agenda when we drove to Rosa's. 'Shelly Beach locals are launching a public protest. Rosa raised the first call to action. She overheard council plans when workers were talking at the pub. Kingston Council plans to cut down ten hundred-year-old Monterey cypresses on Shelly Beach foreshore to make way for a car park.

'Rosa passed the news on to Digby, Alf and Josh, who were there at the time, and Shelly Beach locals have sprung into action.

'But after all that, Rosa isn't taking any part in the protest. She's raving on about it being bad for business if she passes on bar secrets.'

True.

Rosa was on her soapbox when we arrived. 'I want everyone to be happy at Rosa's. Look at the sea. Look at the sky. Look at the trees. How can we not have those trees?'

Bianca whispered, 'Money's Rosa's bottom line but she gets things started.'

True.

The meeting began quietly. Then came the fireworks. Digby assumed he'd be team leader for the protest. He didn't realise that Daphne assumed she'd be team leader.

Bianca's whispered asides kept Pandora and me up to date with Shelly Beach politics. 'Daphne's a seasoned activist. It's not a good idea to cross her.'

Digby spoke to the meeting with his usual charm. 'Of course I acknowledge Daphne's background. We're aware of the work she's done and continues to do to save the Shelly Beach environment.'

More whispered asides from Bianca: 'Digby has to say this. Daphne's husband Charles is Digby's friend. Charles was a tree-sitter too. But not Digby!'

Daphne replied in a voice iced with venom, 'The only activist experience Digby's had was when he rang the police to break up a student sit-in at his university.'

A deathly pause.

'. . . However, I acknowledge and appreciate Digby's formidable network of contacts. I suggest we work together as a joint command for our protest.'

Digby agreed. The motion to hold a community protest on Sunday was passed. Action committee members sighed with relief.

Bossy Child said, 'If you slit your eyes and make people blur . . . you can imagine what they used to look like. A bit difficult imagining Daphne and Charles living on the top of an old-growth tree.'

True.

To: Adrian <bookstreet@network.com.au>
From: Gina <piececake@email.com.au>
Subject: Action meeting
Hi Adrian,
1. The action committee meeting was mainly taken up with organising a citizen action campaign to save the trees on the foreshore.

Pandora and I are doing the media coverage. Rosa's letting us use her phone, fax and email but we're not to let anyone see us doing it! Did you know Pandora was a high-profile spin doctor in a former life? She's using contacts and pulling favours owed to her so we can get publicity for the Save Our Trees protest.

2. We were able to get your winter Writefest changed to a spring Writefest next year. Fundraising events – the trivia quiz and speed dating – are going ahead next month. Not sure about the collectors' fair. I'd look for a celeb author/s who delight/s in a boot-camp experience and love/s flying economy class.

Gina

Wednesday 23 September

I took the Dog for a walk along the beach. I gave him a hands-on digging-in-the-sand demo. 'Much more fun than digging in a garden, Dog.'

This was the first time Shelly Beach bay had resembled Adrian's photographs. The blue sea glittered in the sunlight. A gentle sea breeze caused small white-capped waves to wash onto a sandbank I never knew existed. Seagulls were clustered in an untidy line at the water's edge gourmandising on fish.

The Dog loves chasing seagulls but isn't convinced it equals gardening as a hobby. He can't decide whether he likes chasing seagulls better than digging holes.

Bloody hell!

At home the Dog watched while I crossed off the fifth Shelly Beach Writers' Group meeting on the calendar. We were feeling pleased with the world when Bianca called to take us to the meeting.

Disaster struck as soon as we arrived at the community hall. Bianca left her novel on top of her car while she was helping me to open the hall door – and the whole manuscript blew away.

Bianca burst into tears. 'I've written at least a hundred pages – maybe more! And I've worked out my viewpoint.'

Opening chapters of chick lit blew along the sand and drifted out to sea. Pages of chick lit were swept up by the wind and distributed along the foreshore. Pages were pinned in trees and stuck in bushes.

'Do you have another hard copy?'

'No! And I didn't number my pages.'

'Bloody hell!'

'The numbering thingy shut down on my computer. I was going to number the pages by hand before the meeting tonight.'

This was a serious writerly problem. As members arrived they joined in the page hunt to find Bianca's lost chapters. 'I can't even remember how many I wrote,' Bianca wailed. 'I've been so busy at Scissors.'

Members oozed sympathy. After an hour, every square metre of the floor and available flat surface of the hall was strewn with pages of Bianca's just-starting-to-sizzle story. 'I was getting the frisson frissoning between my main characters.'

We understood. Tutor and members continued to work tirelessly and generously for a large part of the evening to connect Bianca's broken romance. Result: possibly several pages in the wrong places and a few pages now at sea.

Bill was one hundred per cent understanding. When Hunter was eight months old, he reorganised (chewed, crumpled, vomited on) the final draft of Bill's yet-to-be-published novel. Bill had the file on his computer but he wasn't sure if he'd saved the final draft or only the draft before the final draft. It took Deb and him ages to piece his jigsaw-puzzle plot together again.

Bianca whispered, 'Bill's using the car as his office now. It's safer. Deb's decided to return to teaching in the new year so they can pay rental on a bigger house. Her mum is going to look after Hunter. Deb says that even if you've had one bestselling novel you don't make much money as a writer. She's keeping her fingers crossed for mega sales for Bill's next novel.'

Gallant Digby came to Bianca's rescue. He's going to give her his late wife's laptop which has a 'page-numbering thingy'. I promised to call into Scissors and show Bianca how to set up the computer for her writing and use the 'save' and 'save as' features.

'I know how to use my computer for business, but writing stuff on a computer is so different.'

We all understood.

Time was short due to the fact that members had helped Bianca collect her escaped chick lit. Josh was happy to save his writing for the next meeting's workshop. A few stalwart others shared their plot plans and gained elephant stamps.

I gave out chapters nine, ten and eleven of Lee's novel, plus the synopsis. Members were happy to bring them to the next meeting – complete with constructive comments to post to him.

Bill raced through his segment on setting and gave out his (optional) writing task.

Members left with their writers' minds brimming over with the feel, sound, smell and taste of the community hall, situated on the foreshore in the small seaside town of Shelly Beach.

Thursday 24 September

Bianca called in to check if I wanted a trim or new highlights. 'How about a pedicure? I need more food to freeze. Anything you can serve on rice with a sprinkling of coriander?'

'I'll do the food. You can store up my hair and pedicure credits.'

While I made sandwiches and tea Bianca chatted and I listened.

'Did you know Lee left Shelly Beach this morning?'

'No.' But now I did.

'I saw him drive off when I was opening Scissors. He's left as quietly as he came. Like a knight on horseback, except he was in a car. Rosa wanted to give Lee a send-off at the pub, but he said no. Did you know he has a Porsche? He kept it garaged at Rosa's the whole time he's been working here.'

'No.' (Lie.)

'Absolutely gorgeous car!'

'They are.'

'I think I'll give one to my protagonist . . . or maybe my antagonist?'

Bianca relayed more information as she munched through her salad sandwich. 'Rosa doesn't care too much about losing Lee. Her cousin Lorenzo has just arrived from Naples, and he's a cook and is looking for work. Rosa's going to employ him. She wants to have a full "Italiano" menu at the pub. Bring a Mediterranean touch to Shelly Beach for the summer trade. Rosa wasn't into the Asian fusion thing, although Lee was a fan-*tas*-tic chef.'

Then after another mouthful, 'I posted Adrian a copy of the action committee minutes this morning. Adrian left SSAEs for me. He thinks of everything – doesn't he?'

I nodded. 'He does.'

Bianca had to leave. 'I'm going to Daphne's yoga class. You should join, Gina. Yoga's very relaxing.'

The Dog and I watched Bianca back her car up and zip down Sea Spray Street.

'Does everyone think I'm stressed and uptight?'

The Dog thought I was the most self-obsessed human he's ever known. For a Dog obsessed with hole-digging he's in no position to comment.

I went inside to make a strong cup of coffee. The Dog followed. He wanted a bowl of water.

'I'm going to miss Lee's visits. Our writerly and bookish discussions.'

The Dog stared at me with his beady eyes.

'All right! And. The. Sex.'

The Dog gave me his dog-on-death-row look. He turned and exited through his pet door.

I knelt down and yelled through the door, 'Great sex! Wild sex!

And you'd better return my salmon lizard-skin platform shoe. One of the pair I bought from Daphne's shop last week. I know you took it!'

The pet door flapped shut. I looked at the clock. Damn. I walked – head high, shoulders back, stomach in – slowly out onto Adrian's back verandah to collect the Dog. 'I forgot that it's time to collect Bossy Child from school.'

We decided to walk along Shelly Beach to Bossy Child's school. The bay looked like frosted icing. Millions of tiny crested waves stretched to the horizon line.

'You know, Dog, Lee broke all the assumptions I had about young single men. We had great conversations. We had a no-strings-attached relationship but it wasn't shallow or unsatisfying.'

The Dog liked Lee too. Especially his Thai curries – even though they gave him indigestion.

We took deep breaths of calming sea air and then fast-paced it to the school.

Friday 25 September

I heard the phone ring but I didn't get out of bed to answer it. I put my head under the blankets and went back to sleep. Eventually I gave in to the Dog's persistent nagging about his breakfast and strug-gled out to the kitchen. The red light on Adrian's phone blinked like a nuclear alarm warning. Clare had left a message.

> Hi Gina, it's Clare. Hope you're well. Is it okay if I call next Monday 28 – about 1ish? I've a payment from the sale of your clothes from Silver Heirlooms. If I don't hear from you I'm presuming it's okay. See you soon!

I took my preferred strategy of choice and did absolutely nothing. 'Maybe something more exciting will appear on Clare's radar, Dog.

199

Result: no visit. She'll transfer the Silver Heirlooms money into my bank account and peace and quiet will reign at Shelly Beach.'

The Dog hoped so.

Alf arrived around lunchtime complete with building toolkit. 'I'm going to be working full-time on Adrian's bungalows from now on. Getting them ready so Adrian can rent them for the summer. Hope the noise won't upset you, Gina.'

'It'll be fine, Alf.' What else can a house-sitter say?

I made tea while Alf chatted about this and that. 'Have you heard that Lee has left?'

'Yes I have.' I moved the conversation on. 'Why didn't Adrian ask Henry Shepherd to look after Hugo while he was in the UK? The Dog's very happy staying with Henry and his poodle.'

'Henry's been sick. Had a heart attack earlier this year.'

I looked at Alf with dismay. 'I left the Dog with Henry for five days last week. Two dogs could have been too many.'

'It was okay, Gina. Beryl and I kept an eye on him. We checked every day.'

Of course they had. 'I was going to ask you if you thought it was okay to leave the Dog with Henry for a couple of single nights next month. I'd like to go to the city to visit my daughter and grandson again.'

'No need. We'll look after Hugo. I'll be working here all day any-way, and Beryl can come over and cook dinner. We'll do a sleepover. We're happy to look after Hugo whenever you need us, Gina. We used to do it all the time when Adrian went away.'

Bloody hell! Guilts for nothing. I was relieved. I needed to keep in touch with Julia and Barney.

'Count on us being at the protest on Sunday, Gina. Wouldn't miss the action for quids.'

Alf left to start work on the bungalows. Pandora rang. The Dog and I met her at Rosa's to organise publicity stuff for the protest. Pandora in full flight is something to behold.

Later that night the Dog and I were stargazing on Adrian's back verandah. We discussed Clare and her visit. It loomed like a dreaded school reunion. 'Clare was very pretty when she was young. She had chocolate-box looks and worked as a model. Her face was plastered on billboards.'

The Dog said he knew a dog that was wrenched into the glare of long lenses and flashguns. Her photo was on chocolate boxes and greeting cards. The Dog doesn't fancy being on a chocolate box. On a pet food can, yes – but not a chocolate box.

'Clare's modelling career didn't go far, though. Instead she went into real estate. However, she's worked long and hard over the years to maintain her looks – to become the perfect partner in a perfect marriage for high-achieving husband James. And after James pressured us to admit her to our group, she's worked bloody hard to stay there.

'Clare employs a personal trainer to help with her diet and fitness. Eva says it's fortunate that James is earning good money. The cost of Clare's cosmetics, Botox, dermal fillers and spa treatments would be considerable.'

The Dog ignored my catty comments. He plans to hide from Clare when she visits. He can't understand why humans have friends they don't really like.

The Dog has no understanding of the complicated friendships humans can have.

Saturday 26 – Sunday 27 September

On Saturday the Dog and I spent a mind-numbing day with locals making stuff for the protest – signs, posters and costumes. The Dog joined Bossy Child and her nerdy friends – the gluing-on-eyes-and-whiskers team. After surveying a number of costumes I reluctantly agreed to wear Wilma Wombat's body suit. If I'm caught on TV no one will recognise me. Thus equipped, I joined Pandora's team. Sign-writing I can do.

On Sunday we returned home from the Save Our Trees protest in the afternoon, soaking wet but elated and buzzing with leftover adrenalin. I should have known a catastrophe was looming. There was another message from Clare on Adrian's answering machine but the infuriating bubble was missing from her voice.

> Hi, Gina, it's me, Clare. Looking forward to seeing you tomorrow morning. Bye.

The Dog and I moaned. 'Can't do anything about this, Dog.' We logged onto the internet to send a feel-good email to Adrian.

To: Adrian <bookstreet@network.com.au>
From: Gina <piececake@email.com.au>
Subject: Save Our Trees campaign
Hi Adrian,
Shelly Beach locals brushed up well on TV tonight but don't think we'll make global viewing. Fight-to-the-death average John and Jane Doe citizens were transformed into residents and ratepayers who'd sacrifice anything to save their historic trees from an unthinking, idiotic council decision. Teacher, parents, kids, other locals and dogs carried Save Our Trees propaganda. Unfortunately messages merged into coloured rivulets of nothingness on TV. Pandora says we need to use waterproof paint for future campaigns.
    Daphne did a star interview on pier. Delivered her three-minute practised grab brilliantly! Why destroy ten irreplaceable, historically significant trees to make a car park when you can build a car park behind the Beach Road shopping strip?
Gina

Monday 28 September

Clare arrived at 11ish – on the dot. 'Panting for caffeine, Gina.'

While I made the coffee I could see Clare's finger itching to do the dust test. 'Sacked my last cleaning person. James is overseas so I've let things go to the dogs.'

An unfortunate comment considering the Dog was within earshot.

'Do you mind if I stay the night?'

'Sea View Cottage is not exactly five-star accommodation, Clare. The plumbing's disastrous. Alf is working on the bungalows in the garden. He likes to start work early. It'll be hellishly noisy.'

Clare ignored me and took her Prada overnight bag into Bedroom One.

'Clare's staying the night, Dog.'

The Dog escaped via his pet door into the garden to talk to Alf.

We lunched at Rosa's to escape Alf's hammering and the noise from his chainsaw. Rosa's was buzzing with locals and excitement from our successful protest.

Josh met me at the door. 'Are you coming to the book club tonight, Gina? You friend is welcome too. It's at your next-door neighbour's.'

I frantically whispered our apologies and promised to drop the wine in. No way did I want Clare to be any part of my life at Shelly Beach.

Clare listened wide-eyed over lunch as locals reported their activist news. Everyone was keeping fingers crossed for a positive outcome for our trees.

During our meal Clare gave me the final payment from the sale of my vintage clothes. I accepted it with a gracious smile. I'll need a car very soon. There was no comment, thank God, re: the missing fabulous Asian-fusion menu – or the drop-dead-gorgeous chef.

Clare insisted we eat at the Sea Haven Resort for dinner. 'I'll use James' company account.'

I didn't object. A free dinner is a free dinner – and it would be an excellent time-filler.

When we returned home, I lit a fire to warm the chilly spring air and played one of Adrian's CDs, which I hoped would drown out the bookish frivolity coming from next door.

We were relaxing with a glass of wine when Clare's questioning began. It started subtly: 'How is Hester coping with the divorce?'

'Fine.'

'Do you know why Hester and Paul decided to get a divorce?'

Bloody hell, Clare! 'There was a lot of stuff they hadn't worked through over the years. They decided it was best to separate and move on.'

'James has seen Paul recently. He says they're having a very amicable divorce settlement.'

'Some marriages can end amicably. I'm not surprised Paul and Hester are handling their divorce well. The fact they can both look forward – see a promising future in which they're not married – is a plus.'

'Does Hester know that Paul isn't Rob's biological father?'

I looked at Clare intently. 'She does now.'

'Paul told James that Hester found out from old papers and letters at the farm.'

'Yes, she did.' (What else do you know, Clare?)

'Do you know if Hester read those letters?'

I stared at Clare. She looked desperate. She was in deep trouble. 'What's wrong, Clare?'

'Oh God, Gina. It's a terrible mess! Paul and I had an affair. On and off. For eleven years. The letters were mine.'

Bloody hell! An affair. For eleven years!

Clare started crying. I didn't leave my seat to comfort her. It was like a plot from a romantic novel. The protagonist (or was it the antagonist?) was in the throes of a torrid affair with her best friend's husband that had lasted eleven years. 'Do you love Paul?'

'God, no! I broke it off about two years ago. Paul still wants to continue but he's changed. Our relationship had run its course.' Clare confided, 'Paul's aged so quickly. Put on so much weight.'

'How on earth did you keep seeing each other without anyone finding out over the years?'

'It wasn't easy. At first we met in properties Paul or I were selling. We'd wait until client inspections were over. Sometimes I'd go to Paul's office. When James was overseas, and the kids were older, Paul came to our house. When we both had mobile phones it was easier.'

I stared at Clare. Of course it's easier to meet with a mobile phone. You can arrange things spontaneously but safely.

Clare shrugged. I could see she was reading my body language and was annoyed with my reaction. 'It wasn't like we had a nonstop affair during the eleven years. There were breaks. James has never found out.'

I doubted this. A game-player like James would have smelt something.

'Do you think Hester knows?' Clare asked, the desperate look returning.

'No – she doesn't. She never read the letters. She assumed they were old love letters from Paul's first wife. She was only interested in Rob's birth certificate.'

A look of relief crossed Clare's face. 'Good. Paul's now destroyed the letters. Everything's fine then.'

I looked at Clare. 'It's not fine, Clare.'

'Gina?' Clare looked at me in disbelief.

'I think it's best if you leave, Clare.'

'You want me to leave – now?'

I looked at Clare. Bloody hell! How much had she drunk? Was she fit to drive?

'Stay the night. Go in the morning.'

The Dog and I stayed up and talked. Once you step over relationship boundaries you're in big trouble.

Tuesday 29 September

Clare was up early. I lay in bed and listened to Adrian's lukewarm water trickling out of the shower. I heard Clare's squeals. Good!

Clare was in control mode when I walked into the kitchen. She was dressed in her casual weekend gear, hair and make-up immaculate. The kitchen smelt of coffee and toast. 'Coffee?' she asked.

I nodded. I noticed her Prada overnight bag was packed and standing at the front door.

'Would you like me to cook you an omelette?' Clare asked. 'You've got plenty of eggs.'

I shook my head. Deep breath. 'I don't want to see you again, Clare.'

Clare sipped her coffee. She started to cry. 'OhmaGod, Gina! What will I say to Hester?'

Bloody hell! 'You say nothing to Hester. Nothing. Do you understand?'

'Yes.'

'What will I tell James? And Eva?'

'Tell them I've lost the plot. Tell him we had a huge argument.'

'I never argue with anyone.'

'Right! Tell them you thought my behaviour was totally unacceptable. And you don't want to talk to me for a long time. They'll understand.'

Clare relaxed. No exchange of air kisses. I watched her gather up the Prada bag and stow it in the boot of her Alfa (birthday gift from Smart James). She made one last attempt before the links between us were severed for good.

'What about your citrus trees? Do you want us to bring them down here? They're worth a lot of money.'

I visualised my Tuscan mini citrus trees in their collectable pots, now flourishing on Clare's terrace. Booty from Montpellier Place. 'You and James can keep them, Clare. Donate them to a charity. I never want to see the bloody things again.'

Clare gave a rueful smile.

The Dog and I stood on Adrian's verandah and watched as Clare carefully backed her birthday present out the drive.

'Well, Dog, in a very short time I've had a marriage breakup and a friendship breakup. And I don't want to mend either. Time for a long walk, I think. And don't start complaining. Exercise is good for you.'

Wednesday 30 September

I woke with a life-threatening virus – could be the start of pneumonia – from standing on a pier in the rain for hours while dressed in a leaky Wilma Wombat outfit and holding a sodden Save the Trees placard on high. Maybe my body's immune system is breaking down because it's been overloaded with toxic friend Clare's monumental 'dear diary' confidences.

Digby called in. The Dog showed him to my bedroom where I lay incapacitated in bed. Digby had two bunches of red roses. One for me: a thank you for my help in the Save the Trees protest. The other bunch was for Pandora.

He took one look at me – eyes and nose streaming, bed covered in tissues – and vanished from my room to deliver the second bunch of roses to Pandora.

The Dog was annoyed. Digby left before I had time to mention the monster noises in Adrian's ceiling that are keeping us awake at night.

Pandora called in during the afternoon to see how I was. She wouldn't step past the entrance to the bedroom. 'Don't want to contract your germs, Gina. Have to finish painting the balcony.'

Some friends are pathetic. Just as well I haven't got the plague. Evidently Pandora and I have gained a whole scorecard of brownie points from Shelly Beach locals for our media campaign. Who cares?

Later that day the Sea Haven florist delivered another dozen red roses: from Clare.

I phoned Bianca at Scissors to come and pick up a dozen red roses. Not Digby's.

To: Gina <piececake@email.com.au>
From: Adrian <bookstreet@network.com.au>
Subject: Fundraising
How are fundraising activities going? I need cash to fund
international author/s' visits next spring.
Adrian

To: Adrian <bookstreet@network.com.au>
From: Gina <piececake@email.com.au>
Re: Fundraising
Fundraising events proceeding apace. Probably more news to
report next month. Digby's trying to get the collectors' fair up for
November. He also mentioned he's happy to help with anything.
Would you like some of his celeb author contacts in the UK? I'd
make sure your celeb author/s are happy with tent accommodation
on the foreshore, and budget air travel. And next year will probably
be another wet miserable spring! Maybe beat this year's record.
Definitely not sun-tan weather.

Forgot to tell you how beautiful your garden looked earlier this month. Your fruit trees – apricot, apple, plum, whatever – looked spectacular when they were covered in blossom. The blossom didn't last long. Gale-force winds stripped the trees bare.

Alf is now working on the bungalows. Crow's Nest Flat is already let for the summer – but the plumbing in the bathrooms isn't finished. Alf's planning to have it ready by summer.

I have to go to the city two or three times next month. I've spoken to Alf and Beryl. They'll sleep over at Sea View Cottage on these nights and dog-sit. I hope this is okay with you. I'm quite happy to accept an adjustment in my contract.

Gina

P.S. I have been seriously ill with flu but I'm recovering now.

To: Gina <piececake@email.com.au>
From: Adrian <bookstreet@network.com.au>
Re: Fundraising

Sorry to hear you've been ill.

Thank Digby for his offer of help. Glad to hear Crow's Nest Flat is let. I'll keep it in mind. There'll be no alteration in our contract. If you head to the city to visit daughter and grandson I know Hugo will be in good hands if Alf and Beryl look after him.

Am returning to Australia for week 5–11 October for daughter Tania's wedding. Plan to visit Shelly Beach on weekend 10–11. Flying back to UK Sunday night.

This will in no way interfere with our contract, which will continue until 31 December.

Best wishes,

Adrian

Bloody hell!

October

Thursday 1 October

I sat the Dog in front of the October calendar featuring one lone seagull standing on Shelly Beach, and performed our tear-off-the-last-month-and-burn-it ritual.

'Pay attention, Dog. I've some tricky news to tell you.'

The Dog sat to attention.

'Adrian is coming back next Saturday and Sunday. The tenth and the eleventh.' I circled the dates with a red pen.

The Dog's ears pricked up at the mention of the 'A' word. His little tail started vibrating furiously.

'Don't get excited. He's not staying. Just coming home to snoop around. Arriving next Saturday, leaving on Sunday night. A micro-visit.

'It's your duty to look your best, and demonstrate that you are comfortable with me as a dog-sitter until he returns at Christmas. I need a few months yet to sort out what I'm going to do.'

No comment from the Dog.

'And you'll have to help with some spring cleaning and gardening before he arrives. Typical. You start to get back on track and stuff happens.'

212

No sympathy from the Dog.

'At least my bank balance is looking healthy thanks to the sale of my sundry assets plus the respectable income I earned from Hester's conference.'

The Dog didn't care about my cashflow issues. He was still cranky about being left while I vanished to the city for five days last month. And I don't think he's got his head around Adrian returning even only for a short visit. If the Dog becomes more neurotic after Adrian's visit it's not my fault!

Bossy Child was performing flea leaps when we picked her up. 'Have you heard? Adrian's coming home – but just for the weekend. He's going to his daughter's wedding in the city and then he's coming here.'

'I know. But he's not coming this weekend. Next weekend!' I segued into a more important issue. 'What can I do about the noises in the ceiling?'

'They're possums, Gina. It's possum mating season. Everyone gets possums in Shelly Beach. Some people love possums. They build nesting boxes in their gardens for them. We put apples on the fence at night for our possums.'

'I can't afford to buy apples for possums. And I can't build nesting boxes. Adrian should have built some before he left.'

Bossy Child gave me a rolled-eye look and left to play with the Dog.

During the night the cacophony in Adrian's ceiling started again. The Dog watched while I banged on the ceiling with the broom handle. I'm hoping and praying it's not a family of big black rats picnicking in the ceiling above my bed.

The Dog concurs.

Friday 2 October

We've been awake all night due to the gruesome noises in the ceiling. I lay in bed and watched the birds nest-building from my bedroom window. Adrian's garden is looking lush and springy – a satisfying result from my conscientious pruning.

The Dog ambled in and out of the bedroom. A time-for-breakfast reminder.

To: Adrian <bookstreet@network.com.au>
From: Gina <piececake@email.com.au>
Subject: Dodgy roof
Hi Adrian,
You've got an elephant or possum/s in your roof. (Not thinking rats!) And the ceiling in Bedroom One is looking seriously dodgy. Combination of rain (wettest spring on record) plus elephant or possum pee has made it droop perilously.
   Will you have time to fix elephant or possum problem and your dodgy roof when you are here next weekend or do you want me to action this before your visit?
Gina

To: Gina <piececake@email.com.au>
From: Adrian <bookstreet@network.com.au>
Re: Dodgy roof
Hi Gina,
Ask Alf to repair the ceiling and roof. Tell him to stop working on whatever he's doing. Concentrate on Bedroom One. Do whatever it takes to make the roof and ceiling rainproof.
Adrian

To: Adrian <bookstreet@network.com.au>
From: Gina <piececake@email.com.au>
Subject: Animals
What about the elephant or possum/s? Do you want me to catch it/them before Alf starts work, or can Alf work around it/them?
Gina

To: Gina <piececake@email.com.au>
From: Adrian <bookstreet@network.com.au>
Re: Animals
Ignoring possibility of elephant. Catch possum/s before Alf starts
work. Daphne will be able to help you with borrowing possum
cages. She'll tell you where to release them when you catch them.
Adrian

Saturday 3 October

'Only twelve weeks' free rental remaining and I'm faced with a catch-
a-possum challenge and a micro-visit from your owner, Dog. Where's
the idyllic Shelly Beach life I was promised? Where's the tranquillity
I imagined – living in an enchanted seaside cottage, looking after a
cute little dog . . . with ample time to plan a new life?'

The Dog ignored me.

'In what part of my contract does it say: *Catch possums and
release*?'

The Dog didn't care about my contract – he just wanted the possums caught so he could relax and get a good night's sleep. And I
know he wishes Adrian was coming home for good.

We walked along a shimmering blue Shelly Beach bay to visit the
Dog's favourite shop to buy bones. (I'm thinking burying bones is
preferable to burying shoes.)

In Harold's butchery I caught up with the hot buzz buzzing around
Shelly Beach. Harold's mum has won a seven-day tropical cruise.

'Can you believe it? Mum's leaving on Monday. Can you come
to her farewell dinner party at Digby's tomorrow night? Daphne's
organising it.'

I accepted gracefully.

'I'm telling Mum about Gary before she goes overseas.'

I nodded. I was pretty sure I knew what Harold was going to tell his
mum. And of course Shelly Beach locals would help Harold organise

what could well be his 'coming out' party. Shelly Beach locals know and love Harold. He grew up here. They must know what's going on. And Harold doesn't cause one blip on the Shelly Beach radar.

'You have the kind of calm that trickles over people, Gina. It'll be good to have you at the party when I speak to Mum.'

Daphne came into the butchery at that moment and saved me searching for a suitable reply. The Dog said that under my coat of trickle-calm was a volcano that erupted from time to time.

I ignored the Dog.

'Been trying to catch up with you, Gina.' Daphne looked at Harold. 'Harold's told you our plans for tomorrow night?'

I smiled agreement.

'Good. Now we need twelve of your incredible individual chocolate puddings for the dessert course. You can bring the ingredients and cook in Digby's kitchen. He's got an excellent stove. Sound okay?'

'Right.'

Outside the butchery the Dog reminded me about our possum problem.

I called to Daphne who was making her way home. 'I need to borrow possum cages. Can you help me?'

'Sorry, Gina. Digby borrowed four cages last week. Check with him. He's probably captured and released his possums by now.'

Or else they've moved house to Sea View Cottage. I smiled my thanks.

When we returned home I phoned Digby with my possum-cage request. I received a couldn't-be-nicer reply. 'Heard you're doing the dessert course for Harold's dinner party tomorrow night. Well done. You can take the possum cages home after that. Have you heard the news? Adrian's visiting next weekend.'

'He emailed me.'

'Excellent. See you late afternoon tomorrow. We can have a sherry before you start in the kitchen.'

I gracefully accepted his invitation.

Now I have two problems to worry about. Cooking a *wow!* dessert to sweeten a potential blow-up when a son announces big news at a dinner party, and possum invaders to remove from the roof.

The Dog wants me to concentrate on the possum problem. He knows I can cook hot chocolate puddings.

I took the Little Red Hen mentality on board re: possum capture. 'Capturing possums can't be all that difficult, right, Dog?' I spent some time trawling the internet to find answers to my questions. Where do you position the cages in ceilings? Do possums bite? If they do, is their bite poisonous?

The Dog hadn't a clue. He likes to keep his distance from possums.

Pandora rang late in the afternoon to see if I wanted to eat at Rosa's. 'I'll call by and pick you up about 6.'

It was hardly a heart-jolting invitation, but I needed to stop thinking about Adrian's return, and another night gazing at Adrian's snowy television didn't appeal. I accepted.

Rosa's was jumping with good vibes from Josh's band. News of Adrian's visit next weekend was flying around the pub. Bianca waved at me. She was the lone female sitting at a table of males, talking animatedly to what looked like the Seagulls' football-slash-lifesavers' club. She was doing her best to ignore Josh and his band.

Violet joined us at our table, *avec* cat basket, which she stowed under the table. 'Mehitabel's poorly. I didn't like to leave her at home.' She looked around the packed room. 'The new chef's menu has brought the crowd in.'

Already Lee's food is forgotten.

Violet filled us in with local cuisine history. 'Paddy Murphy owned the pub before Rosa. He cooked a very limited menu: steak, eggs and chips; chops, eggs and chips; sausages, eggs and chips; eggs and chips; or just chips.'

I nodded understandingly. When Violet returned to our table after a mean tango with Henry Shepherd she filled us in with background goss on Adrian and Digby, 'Shelly Beach's jousting knights'.

'Adrian and Digby were Kingston High boys. One was dux of the school, the other head prefect and runner-up in academic studies. They had a healthy rivalry during their university days, but stayed good mates. Shared a house when their academic careers took them to the city. The healthy rivalry turned into open warfare when they competed for faculty positions. Leadership ambitions took flight and clashed badly.'

Pandora and I ordered another gin and tonic for Violet to keep her talking. We two supposedly intelligent women didn't want to admit to enjoying local gossip, but I needed ammunition before Adrian's micro-visit.

Violet continued, 'Way back there was competition over a woman as well. Digby and Adrian have an equal wives' tally. They'll both be looking for third wives. Their last ones died. Annette took that dive from her balcony, and Adrian's wife had cancer.'

I ventured, 'Strange Adrian and Digby have returned to Shelly Beach.'

'Not really. Folks like to return to places where they've been happy and feel comfortable.'

Violet left soon after with poorly Mehitabel. 'We have to get home to Ginger. She's due to have kittens.'

Pandora and I lingered over coffee. I pursued information about Adrian like a vulture picking at a carcass. 'I've always thought Adrian was a sea-changer.'

'No. He'd have kept Shelly Beach at the back of his mind all these years. You won't find many sea-changers at Shelly Beach, Gina. Most of us have ties to the place.'

And that was the end of my information hunt – for the moment. The Dog was waiting up when Pandora drove me home.

'I heard some interesting goss about your owner tonight.'

The Dog wasn't interested. He knows everything he needs to know about Adrian.

Sunday 4 October

I carefully collected all the ingredients to make twelve self-saucing chocolate puddings. I packed a cook's apron I'd found in Adrian's cupboard, and took time deciding what to wear to a possum-cage pick-up with the promise of a pre-dinner glass of sherry with my host, followed by the dinner party.

I decided against something short and flashy, and chose straight-cut jeans, a classic white silk shirt and red ballet flats (Daphne's charity shop must-buys.)

Digby was super-charming. However, I did ask him to stack the possum cages in Adrian's Ford before we had our sherry – just in case I needed to make a quick getaway. If King Arthur aka Digby is really as harmless and pleasant as I think he is, I'm going to kill Pandora and Violet with their 'sweet-talker' warning.

I'd left the Dog in the car. He growled reassuringly and showed his sharp little teeth when Digby stowed the cages in the boot. I picked the Dog up to carry him back over the drawbridge to Digby's castle. He was invited to the dinner party too.

Digby helped carry my cooking stuff to his kitchen and showed me how his oven works. Thank goodness it was new.

When we returned to the entrance hall, late-afternoon sunlight was shafting though the stained-glass windows. The apricot walls were the perfect backdrop for glossy antique furniture resting on polished mahogany floors. I watched hypnotised as Digby slowly poured amber liquid into two exquisite crystal glasses. A magic moment! (Bianca language.)

Digby's castle, his late wife's family home, is stunning. A Victorian homestead set in what was a grazing property.

'Annette, my wife, inherited her family home in the 1990s. We spent every spare moment restoring it to its former glory.'

I took the guided tour as we talked Shelly Beach goss: Harold's dinner party, Adrian's visit and coming events to raise funds for Writefest next year.

(I avoided checking the balcony accessed through the main upstairs bedroom. I don't need to know if petunias are blooming in the flowerbed below, where – according to Violet – Digby's wife met her demise.)

I oohed and aahed over the artwork, antique furniture, glass, china and restored Victorian architectural features until my tour ended in the grand hall. The drawbridge was lowered, the portcullis was down. We could hear voices and cars arriving.

I relinquished my sherry glass. Digby graciously offered to help with the cooking. I refused. Digby went to meet dinner-party helpers and I went to set up the kitchen to cook my *wow!* dessert.

Driving home that evening I discussed the night's success with the Dog. 'It went off swimmingly. Harold's very pleased.'

The Dog was happy Harold was happy. He likes Harold.

'It was brave of him to announce to the guests – even though they no doubt knew the story – that he was gay and proud to be gay, and an excellent idea to do so before my dessert.'

The Dog agreed.

'And it's a good thing Harold's mum is leaving on her cruise on Monday. She was weepy but my dessert worked its magic. It's that moment when you break the crispy outside and the hot chocolate sauce oozes out.'

The Dog agreed.

'Digby's very charismatic. Can you believe I refused his help to put the possum cages in the ceiling? Now you'll have to hold the ladder.'

But the Dog didn't have to. Pandora followed us home. 'Nothing better to do in Shelly Beach at the witching hour.'

220

She held the ladder while I climbed up. She handed the cages to me. I scrambled over Adrian's ceiling, pushing the cages ahead of me. I was looking for the best possum-enticing spots, until my left foot and most of my left leg fell through Adrian's ceiling.

'Pull your leg up slowly!' Pandora shouted from below.

Back on terra firma, Pandora assessed my injured leg and foot.

'Just a few grazes. Nothing to worry about.' Pandora's medical opinion is not comforting.

She left with ominous warnings. 'Better check if you've had a tetanus injection! And when you catch the possums you'll have to release them into the Coastal National Park.'

Bloody hell! Then I guess they'll bushwalk straight back here in a few days' time.

'And you'll have to tell Alf about the ceiling. It looks as if it will collapse at any moment.'

Monday 5 October

As soon as I woke, I gingerly ventured up the ladder and checked Adrian's ceiling. I shone a torch past the giant hole. Two confused possums were curled up in the cages.

Safely back down with the cages, the Dog and I looked at our sad possums. 'Now we have to get them back into the wild.'

The Dog was not impressed. He doesn't want to have anything to do with the possums.

Pandora arrived to check on our progress. 'Shelly Beach isn't exactly jumping at the moment. I'll come with you to help release the possums. I know the Coastal National Park well. Bushwalked all over it.'

We drove to the park that hugs the back beach with two bewildered possums loaded in the back of Adrian's Ford. Releasing them was simple. Once the cages were open the possums were off.

'It's a great feeling when you finally manage to escape. Start again.'

I agreed with Pandora.

Pandora returned my possum cages to Daphne. I went home to organise a visit to my grandson and daughter.

I rang Julia to test the waters. 'I'll be in the city tomorrow.' (White lie, but I could be.) 'Is it a convenient time to visit?'

'Of course it is, Gina. I'm at home tomorrow. Barney and I will look forward to your visit.'

I was buoyed by the positive reception of my request and phoned Eva. 'Any room at the inn? Can I have a stopover tomorrow night?'

'Sure, Gina. And Dominic's away again.'

'Great!'

Another visit to Julia and Barney was inexpensively actioned. The Dog will stay here with Alf while he's working on the bungalows. Beryl will join them at Sea View Cottage for a sleepover.

The Dog was fine with me transferring my dog-sitter responsibilities to Alf and Beryl. He's a dog of habit. He prefers sleeping on the bed in Bedroom Two.

Alf inspected my hole in Adrian's ceiling and promised to repair it while I'm uptown. He and Beryl will sleep in Bedroom One. The Dog flashed me an I-don't-care-you're-leaving-me look. He was glued to Alf's side like a shadow.

I was explaining to the Dog that I'd only be away for one night when the phone rang. It was Daphne. 'Small challenge. We'll have to cancel the writers' group meeting next week. The quilters' club has a long-standing hall booking for their exhibition. Adrian must have forgotten about it. We can hold the meeting this Wednesday – or just wait until our next meeting.'

Bloody hell!

'Do a ring-around, Gina. Start with Bill. If it's okay with Bill, ring the other members. Let me know the outcome tonight.'

'What do you think, Dog? Ten bones to one we'll be able to cancel the sixth writers' group meeting. And it won't be my fault.'

I was wrong. Every member was happy to attend our sixth writers' group meeting this Wednesday.

Tuesday 6 October

Travelling on public transport is still an eye-opening experience for me – a reality-check. Two cheerful women – one old, one young – got on the train at Kingston with me. They smilingly refused my assistance. I watched in awe as they manoeuvred their motorised wheelchairs on to the disabled access ramp at the end of the train compartment. I really have nothing to complain about.

A newly compassionate grandmother arrived at her daughter's house to find a totally stressed-out mother and a screaming baby.

Julia gladly handed Barney to me. 'He hasn't stopped crying all morning. I have to have a shower. And I have some urgent accounts to finish.'

I rocked and jiggled my beautiful bundle of grandson in my arms. I watched his perfect eyelids flutter and finally close. Victory. Barney was asleep.

Julia returned. I passed the precious bundle to her and she placed Barney in his Bugaboo pram.

'Is he teething? Is Barney too young to get teeth?'

I avoided my daughter's question and went to make tea.

I was hardly around when Julia was a baby. I trusted her grandmother to look after her while I worked my way up the career ladder. I loved my career. I thrived on it. I was extremely focused. I thought I knew what was important.

Over tea I ruthlessly set out to query Julia about Adrian's past. I wanted to know more fill-the-gap information. Adrian knows my back story – fair's fair. 'I can't recall what happened when Adrian split up with his first wife – Tania's mother? Did Adrian hook up with someone else? Or did Tania's mother leave Adrian and get together with some other guy?'

Julia filled in the details while she absent-mindedly pushed the sleeping Barney's pram with her foot. 'Tania's mum, Sharon, left Adrian. Tania was upset for her dad. If I remember rightly, her mum said Adrian was boring.'

So Adrian was a member of the boring club too. Welcome, Adrian. 'Then what happened?'

'Sharon and the two girls stayed in the family home. Adrian moved interstate, took a position at a regional university. Tania visited on holidays. I stayed at Adrian's with Tania for several holidays. Don't you remember?'

'No.' I continued my inquiry. 'Didn't he get married again?'

Julia was losing focus. Barney was stirring. I patted Barney while continuing to act like a TV prosecution lawyer. 'Didn't Adrian marry again?'

'I'm not sure.'

Think, daughter. Think!

Barney was awake. Julia picked him up. I waited while she mopped baby sick from her Scanlan and Theodore jumper.

'Yes, maybe he did, because he had a new partner, Pam. He brought her to our graduation ball. Tania and her mum were seriously peeved. Adrian and Pam made a huge spectacle of themselves – tangoing on the dance floor. Weren't you there?'

'No.' I took my bundle of grandson from Julia so she could finish her tea.

'I'm sure you were introduced to Adrian and Pam.'

'Was I?'

'Pam died about seven years ago. Cancer, I think. That's when Adrian resigned from his job as a lecturer at the university, sold up and moved to Shelly Beach.'

End of conversation. Simon arrived home and took Barney. Julia excused herself to change. They were going out for dinner with some overseas clients and had employed an agency babysitter.

'Next time I visit, Simon, I'll be happy to babysit.'

My offer was lost in the babysitter's arrival. Simon handed Barney over so he could check his BlackBerry.

I wrote a Post-it note to self: *Make sure Julia understands I'm happy to babysit Barney anytime.*

I now handle public transport like a veteran. I felt at home in the city crowds. I allowed the correct time to walk to Space – Eva's current fave restaurant.

Clare had a prior engagement and sent her apologies. I breathed a sigh of relief. And Hester couldn't make it – she was interstate on business – but she sent her love and a cheque from the sale of more flotsam and jetsam collected from Montpellier Place.

Eva could hardly wait until we'd ordered before she started questioning me. 'How's your love-life going, Gina?'

'It's not!'

'What happened?'

'Lee left town. He's running a noodle bar in the city.'

'How do you feel?'

'I feel fine. Lee and I both knew our affair – fling – sex between two consenting adults – whatever – was not going anywhere. Actually I've hardly had time to miss him. Life at Shelly Beach is one huge neverending roller-coaster of stuff to do for Adrian.'

'You'll have to find work soon. Hester said you were brilliant at her conference. She's happy to recommend you for any job you decide to take on. So am I.'

'I know. I appreciate your help. I'm joining the job queue soon. Adrian's making a micro-visit from the UK this weekend – after he's left I'll have time to focus on job-hunting.'

'Good.' Eva concentrated on the dessert menu. 'How about a double-chocolate mousse in a sugar-spun toffee cage?'

Thank God Eva's not the kind of friend who goes overboard with advice.

Wednesday 7 October

Eva left me at the station on the way to the gym this morning. I sensed an underlying weariness in my usually high-octane friend.

'Energy meter needs topping up. I've booked a five-day break in Vanuatu. That should do it.'

Eva's probably right. She copes amazingly with her long-haul career and its ever-shifting goals.

Safe on the bus to Shelly Beach, I checked the note that accompanied Hester's cheque: *There are still a few more pieces to sell, Gina. I'm waiting on valuations. Thinking we'll use eBay.*

Alf was repairing my hole in the ceiling when I arrived home. 'Lucky you didn't pull Adrian's whole ceiling down, Gina.'

I whispered to the Dog, 'Lucky Adrian didn't arrive next weekend with a dog-sitter's corpse rotting in his roof.'

The Dog hates me saying stuff about Adrian.

We just had time for a quick snack before we raced to open the hall for the sixth Shelly Beach Writers' Group meeting.

Bianca met us. She was buzzing – a combination of nervous excitement and student guilt. 'I've written too much! Does it matter?'

'How much too much?'

Bill said to write a hundred words. I've written 503!'

'I'm sure it won't bother Bill.' (Members who aren't avid fans of chick lit might not like it.)

While we prepared welcoming tea and coffee, Bianca confessed she was terrified of workshopping. 'I hated reading stuff aloud at school. Especially stuff you'd written yourself.'

I agreed.

'Did you do the writing task?'

'No. I'm thinking about a novel. Planning it in my head. Not actually writing it yet.'

'Cool!'

Pleased, I stored this useful stop-asking-me-about-my-non-progressing-novel excuse in my head. An excellent long-term answer for novel writers even if they might be thinking of writing another novel.

Bianca had written heaps of stuff about her main characters and their forbidden love. 'I've chosen the bit with them having sex in Rosemary's New York apartment to read at our workshop. I did what Bill said to do. I thought about a place and put my characters in it.'

'Right.'

'I've never written so much in my whole life. I'm just crazy about writing now I'm into the swing of it. Digby says I could have hyper-graphia. It's like a brain disease – you can't stop writing.'

I definitely do not have hypergraphia.

Bianca keeps a notebook at Scissors to catch her ideas. 'It's more difficult when I'm in the middle of a massage. My hands are greasy and it's hard to hold the pen.'

I understood.

Bianca didn't need to worry about workshopping. The members were behaving well. We listened attentively, and gave considered but helpful comments. In other words we're terrified of another blow-up like the one between Violet and Digby. We've learnt that even the most laid-back writers are fragile and insecure, especially when they're brave enough to air their writing in public.

Bianca read her 500-plus words to her captive audience. Now and then she'd glance up with her new-look smoky eyes to focus on Josh.

Pandora said Bianca was 'spot on' with her description of New York (Pandora's lived there).

Digby grudgingly agreed. (He lived in New York for a year when he lectured at a college there.) He gave Bianca the third degree. 'How did you capture the nitty gritty of New York?'

'Easy. Josh gave me the *Sex and the City* DVDs a couple of Christmases ago. I've watched every episode about a million times! And a client lent me a New York travel guide.'

Way to go, Bianca! While she helped me wash the supper dishes, she talked incessantly about her love-struck characters, Karl and Rosemary. My young friend, hair stylist and emerging chick-lit novelist had definitely caught the writing bug.

'And I'm so glad I've found the word-count feature on my laptop.'

Hallelujah!

After supper Bill delivered his conscientious mini-lecture on using dialogue in our novels. Members left the hall clutching their dialogue-writing tasks.

Thursday 8 October

To: Adrian <bookstreet@network.com.au>

From: Gina <piececake@email.com.au>

Subject: Writers' group meeting

Hi Adrian,

A near crisis has been avoided. You stuffed up the hall booking. The quilters' club had a prior booking for their exhibition on our next meeting date. We had to hold writer's group meeting last night, or miss out on one meeting.

Fortunately we were able to hold our usual riveting meeting plus a battle over dialogue tags, specifically, the use of plain 'said'. Some members were for using 'said'. Other members were against. Bianca's against plain 'said' speech tags. She's used 'whispered', 'screamed', 'declared', 'uttered', 'exclaimed' and 'giggled' a million times. She's thinking she won't even use 'said'. And sometimes she won't use any speech tags at all – readers will just have to work out who's talking to whom.

If members don't know the writerly info Bill's giving us, they're not admitting it. They're taking it on board and boning up on the

notes. Pity you won't be able to attend a writers' group meeting
when you're here next weekend . . . and you'll miss the trivia quiz
on Friday night.
Gina

The Dog and I had a day off from child-minding. Bossy Child's relatives are visiting. I still woke early, fed the Dog, the Girls and the doves.

The Dog did some digging and I played around with one of Bill's writing tasks. What happened before chapter one? Write a 500–1000-word back story about a character in your novel.

The Dog wandered in to report on his hole-digging.

'I'm writing about an infuriatingly perfect mother-in-law, Dog. A relative you can thank your lucky stars you'll never have because you belong to the canine family.'

Then Violet called in and put a halt to my writing task.

She had a friend with her. A friend who needed writerly advice. 'We were passing and I thought you might be just the person to help Rochelle, Gina.'

'Right!'

'I'll make the tea. You talk to Rochelle. Have you any of those peanut cookies you bake?'

I smiled at Rochelle, and indicated to Violet where the cookie jar was.

Rochelle's thinking of becoming a Shelly Beach sea-changer. Like Violet, she's a member of the Secret Writers' Club. A midnight scribbler.

Rochelle was a nightclub dancer. 'Travelled the world. Didn't get married until I was well into my forties. Having too good a time.

'I've kept a diary since I was nine years old. I'm thinking of turning it into a memoir. Lots of spicy bits. There's hardly a well-known male identity of my era I didn't know – and haven't written about. I'm thinking if I can't turn it into a memoir, maybe it could be a novel.'

Violet poured the tea. 'Quite a few of Rochelle's past lovers are still around. That's the dodgy bit. I told Rochelle to write a few chapters as a memoir and a few chapters as a novel to submit to a publisher. Use false names. Do you think that's a good idea, Gina?'

I agreed. 'If a publisher decides to publish your book, the legal department will take care of the dodgy bits.'

'Well, then, that's settled. We're off to buy a kitten for Rochelle.'

The Dog and I watched Violet and her friend leave as suddenly as they had arrived. 'I'm thinking Rochelle's racy memoir will get snapped up by a publisher. Her book will take off and become a bestseller.'

The Dog thought I reminded him of a greyhound he met on death row in the animal shelter. I'm caught up chasing a cable-driven rabbit in circles. I need to concentrate front and centre on a job and somewhere to live.

'I will. I will. Soon.'

Friday 9 October

The Dog and I slaved all day to get Sea View Cottage and the garden up to *House & Garden* standard. Then we raced down to Rosa's to help Shelly Beach's loyal band of action committee members set up the back room for the trivia quiz. We didn't have to worry about the actual quiz – Rosa borrowed the quiz package from a cousin who runs 'packed out' trivia nights in his trendy city pub.

The Seagulls' Football Club team table took the prize. The writers' group table (minus Bianca, plus Bianca's mum Gail) had to lick our wounds. We answered questions on general knowledge, science, literature and history brilliantly. We missed on sport and popular topics. We missed Lee. (I missed Lee.)

Bianca had an awesome time on the Seagulls' table. Josh was

diplomatic. He could have joined the Seagulls' table but chose to sit with fellow writers.

Digby wasn't happy. 'Questions were biased towards younger participants.'

Rosa wasn't happy either. Bar takings scarcely went up. 'Everybody's thinking too hard! There's no drinking!'

Funds from the night barely totalled cash for airport parking for one celeb author. Everyone agreed it was disappointing news to deliver to Adrian tomorrow. Writers' group members hope that the speed dating night will bring in more funds.

We restored Rosa's back room to its former function as a billiard room. Trivia quiz participants from the writers' group table retired to Daphne and Charles' home. Charles had an interesting drop of parsnip wine he wanted us to taste.

Saturday 10 October

The Dog and I stood on Adrian's verandah to admire our hard work and wait for Adrian. Adrian's hole-less garden looked brilliant. We walked inside to double-check everything.

The filtered sunlight had transformed Adrian's living room to *Vogue Living* standard. The smell of boeuf stroganoff simmering in the oven filled the room.

We were spruced and preened to look our best. I decided to wear a classic pale-pink linen shirt, jeans and my red ballet flats (all preloved finds from Daphne's shop, of course). The Dog had submitted to a non-scheduled bath and was fluffed up like a show dog. He was still fussing over a turquoise ribbon on his collar (colour-coordinated with the turquoise cashmere cardigan I was wearing around my shoulders).

I was putting the last touch to a stupendous flower arrangement gathered from Adrian's garden – Hilton-foyer standard – when Bossy Child bounced in.

'Wow! The place looks great, Gina. Adrian's called. He's coming to collect you and Hugo and take you to Rosa's for lunch. He's invited practically the whole town.'

Bloody hell! 'I presumed he'd have lunch here.'

'Have you checked your email, Gina?'

'No. Been too busy.'

Bossy Child picked up my mobile. 'It's turned off!'

'Bad news always finds you.'

Rolled-eye look. 'No wonder Adrian couldn't contact you.'

She sniffed and checked the oven. 'You shouldn't have bothered cooking your fancy meat casserole. Adrian's vegetarian.' She checked the kitchen bench. 'He'll like your chocolate mud cake, though!'

Bloody hell! I stared furiously at the Dog. 'Why didn't you tell me?'

Bossy Child bounced off again, leaving a string of messages and helpful hints behind her. 'You can cook veggie burgers if Adrian gets hungry, Gina. He said to tell you he'll be sleeping at Crow's Nest Flat tonight. He hopes you don't mind if he uses the Sea View Cottage bathroom. Alf still hasn't fixed the Crow's Nest bathroom.'

Bloody hell. I turned the oven off and removed my stroganoff. The Dog assured me Adrian was a carnivore when he lived at Shelly Beach. We agreed he must've turned vegetarian while he's been in the UK.

The Dog and I waited like patients in a medical surgery until Adrian arrived in a hired car. He bounded onto the verandah and enveloped me in an enormous hug – with an extra tight squeeze.

He held me away from him. 'You look fantastic, Gina.'

Adrian with the friendly blue eyes scrubs up well. Beardless now, and slightly tanned, he looked cool in his slick father-of-the-bride suit, open-necked shirt and minus a tie.

The Dog clung to me like seaweed. Not one smidgen of affection or recognition emitted from him.

Adrian called the Dog to him. The Dog ignored him.

Adrian laughed. 'Hugo probably doesn't recognise me without

my beard. The new cologne I'm using has probably put him off my scent too.'

I appreciated the cologne. I was silently pleased the Dog was being super-difficult.

Adrian hurried us into his hired car. The Dog jumped on my lap, and we drove the short distance to Rosa's.

The place was jumping. Rosa was beaming as she greeted customers at the door. 'Lunch is on Adrian, everyone.'

Tables were full of writers' group members and action committee members (who weren't writers' group members) plus other locals of note. I even caught a glimpse of the Sea Haven vet and his Hi-I'm-Lyn wife. The Dog and I made a definite decision to avoid them.

Violet sat at our table and scanned Lorenzo's pasta menu. 'Generous of Adrian to pay for everyone's lunch. He's paying for the wine too – but it won't break his budget. Adrian's very well off. Not as rich as Digby, though. Handy to inherit from dead wives.

'My main character, Red Blaze, received a healthy inheritance from his deceased wife. Red can choose between a five-star hotel or a peasant's hut. And he's always on the look-out for a female to spice up his life.'

Conversations with Violet are tricky. Characters from her books are combined in a complicated mix with Shelly Beach locals.

The Dog was gnawing on my ballet flat under the table. I gave him a gentle nudge.

Pandora was watching Adrian as he schmoozed the tables of diners. 'Adrian has an effortless charm.'

True. He wears it like a comfortable jacket. I watched him talking to members of the – his – writers' group. 'He's practically giving a PowerPoint presentation. I guess he's short on time and has to work the room to bring everyone on board for Writefest next year.'

'It looks as if he's got Digby on side.'

We watched Shelly Beach's jousting knights in serious conversation.

Violet adjusted her hearing aid to join in the conversation. 'Never been any different with those two lads. Always competing.'

Bianca joined our table. 'Isn't Adrian awesome? He's cool – so retro. Even at his age he'd look good coming out of the sea in a soaking wet shirt.' (Bianca's into *Pride and Prejudice*. Not the book – the TV series.)

The Dog started gnawing my other ballet flat. I decided it was time to leave.

Adrian caught up with us at the door. He gave me an engaging smile and put a comforting arm around me. 'Sorry, Gina. I've had to catch up with everyone.'

The Dog and I understood.

'Do you want a lift home?'

I smiled. 'No, we're fine. We'll walk back along the beach.'

'I'll be around at 5. You're okay with me using the bathroom at the cottage?'

I smiled again. 'Fine by me.' What else can a house-sitter say to the owner of the house they're sitting?

The Dog and I left to tramp out our unease along the beach track. Bloody hell!

Back home the Dog went to dig holes. I cleared the formal dining setting away and decided I'd make toasted cheese sandwiches if Adrian required a meal. It was chilly so I lit a fire and had a shower. I made sure the daily quota of warm water was at practically zero. I applied fresh make-up and changed back into jeans and the turquoise cashmere cardigan.

I assembled writers' group meeting material, the vet's reports and biz invoices and receipts relating to the cottage and Piece of Cake on the kitchen table. At least Adrian and I would have something to talk about.

I fed the Dog and brought him inside.

At 6 o'clock Adrian arrived with a cat. A Siamese one in a cat-cage thingy, plus a basket of cat paraphernalia.

'Violet saved Princess for me. She belonged to an old lady who's passed away. I've been on Violet's list for a pedigree cat for ages. Wanted to collect a Siamese when I went to the animal shelter but it was already taken. I took Hugo instead. Didn't I, Hugo?'

Silence.

I empathised with the Dog. A second-on-the-list candidate.

'Violet said you wouldn't mind looking after Princess until I return at Christmas.'

I smiled and weakly agreed. The Dog went to hide under the couch and didn't come out until morning.

Adrian returned from the car with his overnight bag, a bag of food from Jenkins' General Store and two bottles of wine that he deposited in his antique fridge.

'I'll take a shower, Gina, and then I'll cook us omelettes.'

Bloody hell!

I smiled and found Adrian two clean but worn and shabby towels from his laundry cupboard.

Not long after, Adrian came out of the shower looking even better than before. He didn't mention the lack of hot water as he collected the bottle of sauv blanc he'd parked in the fridge. We drank the wine as we sorted through the papers and info I'd kept for him.

He had a heap of stuff he wanted to leave with me to action. Would I have time? Did I mind?

What could a house-sitter say but 'Of course not.'

Adrian cooked a reasonable cheese omelette. Doesn't everyone in Shelly Beach? Complimented me on my chocolate mud cake and made coffee. He opened a second bottle of sauv blanc, selected one of his CDs – classified previously by Bianca as retro dance music. We slow-danced together . . . and somehow we ended up in Bedroom Two having delicious slow sex.

Bloody hell!

Sunday 11 October

Adrian was sleeping when I woke. I slipped out of bed and released Princess from Bedroom One. I watched her delicately nibbling her breakfast from her crown-embossed bowl. The Dog was outside digging holes. He came inside for breakfast. He wasn't talking to me or Adrian. He'd chewed off his turquoise ribbon. Buried it. And he didn't care if he looked an absolute wreck.

I could hear Adrian showering again, using every drop of my daily supply of lukewarm water. He came into the kitchen, dressed, packed and ready to leave, and took me in his arms. He looked at me with his friendly blue eyes, ran his fingertips down my cheek and gave me a long, really good kiss.

Over toast and coffee we talked. He wants me to find three participants who'd like to do a three-day barista training course. The course comes free with the installation of his top-of-the-range coffee machine at Piece of Cake.

'I can't stay, Gina. I have to catch up with some contacts in Sea Haven and back at the airport by 6 tonight.'

I understood.

'Don't leave Shelly Beach. Don't go away. I'm coming back for you.' Another great kiss. 'I'll email you.'

The Dog and I watched from the verandah as Adrian backed the hire car out the drive and drove down Sea Spray Street.

The Dog and I are unimpressed. Adrian's left us neurotic messes – and a bloody prize cat!

Monday 12 October

The Dog and I, and the cat, were sitting on Adrian's verandah. The early morning sun was streaming through Adrian's wisteria vines. The air was filled with their exotic perfume. I was on my second cup of strong black coffee.

'I know, Dog. I know. I've stepped over the line. I've stuffed up well and truly. I need to draw a new line in the sand. Don't worry, I'll sort things out. Our boat's been blown out of the water. We need to get back on board. Chart a new course.'

The Dog was confused by my nautical references.

'I promise . . . I promise we'll get rid of the cat. I'll find someone else to look after Princess until Adrian returns to Shelly Beach.'

The Dog was relieved. Princess didn't care. As long as she was looked after in the manner due to a prize-winning Siamese cat that came complete with a bowl, litter tray, brush and comb, and five-star goose-down doona (all embossed with a royal ensign), she was happy.

Late in the afternoon Pandora phoned. 'A few of us are going for a meal at Rosa's tonight. Like to join us?'

'Yes. That would be great.' Anything to avoid thinking about Adrian with his cool smile; replace friendly blue eyes with 'sexy eyes' and try to forget his random comment: *I'm coming back for you.*

'Damn the man!'

The Dog gave me a worried look.

'I'm all right. Don't worry. I'll lock the cat in the laundry. You can be on guard. I have to get out and clear my head. I'll email Adrian tomorrow. He'll be at his daughter's place in the UK by then. I'll sort things out.'

The Dog was relieved. He didn't mind the Sometime Cat, who was an Outside cat and was now safely dead and buried. Princess was another kettle of fish. And he hates fish.

I understood and moved the conversation on. 'In a former life I frequently dined alone. Crowded cafes are great dining-for-one options for a writer. You can overhear snippets from conversations – inspiration for a whole chapter.'

The Dog's happy to dine alone but he always takes a book to read. He was pleased I wasn't dining alone tonight. It's good to dine with friends. Friends who might be potential carers for a prize cat until Adrian returns.

The few-of-us dinner invitation consisted of a small group of writerly diners: Pandora, Violet, Daphne, Digby and Bianca.

We agreed (if you like Italian food) that Lorenzo's pasta is excellent. Violet doesn't like Italian food: 'Pasta gives me indigestion.' But she approves of the price.

During his micro-visit Adrian had enthused everyone with his plans for Writefest. We were fired up. If Shelly Beach locals have anything to do with it it'll definitely happen.

After we'd eaten, our small group of obsessed novel writers turned the talk from Adrian's Writefest to writerly challenges. Writers exchanged the magical words: *What if*.

We helped Bianca with her 'What if': What if her star-crossed lovers, Rosemary and Karl, were caught in an earthquake on the way to their wedding?

We didn't get far with Violet's gruesome 'What if': What if someone fell down a well? How many days would it take before they died? And what would they die of – starvation or drowning? (Obviously not thirst.)

Digby's into 'why's. He still can't decide whether he'll write his memoir or a novel.

'Why – when you write an authentic memoir consisting of absolute truths – do you risk being sued?'

Pandora gave excellent advice. 'Disguise the truths as fiction. Go for the novel. There might be some publicity. Good for sales. It's highly unlikely you'll get taken to court.'

After this encouraging advice, Digby was happy to move on and join in the writerly exchange about plot points.

Josh's band Ellipsis (a name in progress, apparently) began another set.

Bianca sent Josh a smile and a wave of her pencil-filled hand. 'Josh's painting quotes from *Romeo and Juliet* on his van now. He's offered to help me set up viral marketing for Scissors.'

Bianca gave another wave to Josh, then turned her attention to her writer's notebook, capturing a plot point to be included in her page-turning novel. 'I'm just loving ellipses. They're my fave punctuation.'

Our plot points flapped overhead and flew off.

'Who wants to order coffee?' I grounded my writerly friends with the minutiae of daily life.

Tuesday 13 October

All night I'd been awake composing an email to send to Adrian. The Dog watched while I sent it off.

To: Adrian <bookstreet@network.com.au>
From: Gina <piececake@email.com.au>
Subject: Writers' group meeting
Hi Adrian,
I'm very unfamiliar with the protocol of one-night stands. Although our night together was a most enjoyable experience, I must move on, put it out of my mind, and get back to our professional relationship. I'm happy to continue with our contract until you return at Christmas – and of course undertake any administration or assistance connected with your properties. I do hope you had a pleasant flight home and your UK family is well and you are prepared to forget our one-night stand ever happened.
Gina

To: Gina <piececake@email.com.au>
From: Adrian <bookstreet@network.com.au>
Re: Writers' group meeting
Had a terrible flight home. Couldn't get any rest. Can't stop thinking about you. I understand your position and am happy to get our relationship back on a professional basis – until I return.
　　Do you mind checking something with Alf? Ask him when the

coffee machine is going to be installed so you can get training for baristas underway.
Adrian

Bloody hell!

The Dog's annoyed that I didn't mention a word about getting rid of the cat. I promised him I will.

We vented our angst in Adrian's garden: weeding, digging and filling in holes to a background of building noises created by Alf.

I called Alf for a tea break. He'd been working on the roof of one of the bungalows. A positive outcome of providing tea breaks for Alf is that he stops his absent-minded whistling. Alf's endless whistle-while-you-work is definitely not cheery Seven Dwarves' whistling.

Alf was up with the barista training news. 'Fancy coffee-machine guy rang, Gina. Adrian will lose his deposit if he doesn't get the coffee machine he ordered installed in the next two weeks.'

'Right.'

'And he'll lose his free installation and staff training offer.'

'Right.'

'Forgot to ask Adrian if he'd like Potholer and his sons to work with me. They finish the Thomson house this week. Can you send Adrian an email?'

'Right.'

The cheerful Potholer and his multiple sons are well known in Shelly Beach as a reliable building team. I'm guessing Adrian will be happy for them to work with Alf.

Alf was lingering in the kitchen. Something was worrying my weather-worn friend.

'Are you busy?'

'Not particularly.'

'Beryl needs help with her finger-reading.'

'Finger-reading?'

'You know. When you read and point to the words with your finger.'

'Right.'

'Beryl can read. She taught herself years ago. She's mad on Fred Astaire. When Adrian called in on Sunday he gave her a great book – *The Life Story of Fred Astaire* – for her birthday. But she's having trouble with some of the words. She wants to read the whole book before Adrian comes home at Christmas.'

Alf can't help. 'Well, I could – and I have – but the lifesaving season is starting.' Alf trains the young kids (Flippers) two nights a week. 'I'm dog-tired when I get home.'

The Dog had just fallen through his pet door into the kitchen. He was dog-tired too. He thinks people have no right to use his adjective.

I ignored the Dog and concentrated on Alf. 'I'll have a chat with Beryl. See what I can do to help.'

Alf's happy. He left to work on the bungalows. Whistling!

Wednesday 14 October
To: Adrian <bookstreet@network.com.au>
From: Gina <piececake@email.com.au>
Subject: Fred Astaire
Hi Adrian,
What made you give Fred Astaire's biography to Beryl? Did you
know she has trouble reading?
Gina

To: Gina <piececake@email.com.au>
From: Adrian <bookstreet@network.com.au>
Re: Fred Astaire
Yes. That's why I chose the book. It's mostly photographs.
And I refuse to forget our sexy night together.

To: Adrian <bookstreet@network.com.au>

From: Gina <piececake@email.com.au>

Re: Fred Astaire

Yes . . . but! There are captions and text sections to be read and understood. Beryl will probably get through it before you arrive home. Don't let on you know that I've been helping her.
Ignoring reference to our one-night stand.

Coffee-machine news:

1. Gaggia (coffee-machine company) have contacted Alf as you may or may not know. If you don't accept delivery of coffee machine in next two weeks you'll lose deposit, plus free installation and no-cost training sessions for three staff members.

2. As per your direction I shall do my best to locate three locals who would like to do barista training.

3. Alf wants to know if you'd like to employ Potholer and his sons to help him work on the bungalows. With Potholer plus a son or two, your bungalows could be completed by Christmas.

Gina

To: Gina <piececake@email.com.au>

From: Adrian <bookstreet@network.com.au>

Re: Coffee machine

1. Miss you.

2. Tell Alf to employ Potholer and sundry sons.

3. Organise delivery and installation of coffee machine and training of baristas. No obligation to work at Piece of Cake or offer of job involved.

Thursday 15 October

The Dog and I were united. We were dumping Princess. However, I'd rejected the Dog's suggestions to post her on eBay or throw said prize cat off the end of Shelly Beach pier.

'We're doing the dumping with compassion and charity, Dog. It's not like we're giving Adrian's cat away forever.

'We can tackle the barista/cat challenge, Dog. We're not going to get stressed trying to find coffee makers or a temporary carer for Princess.

'It's a heavenly spring day.' (Bianca language.) 'We'll lock Princess in the bathroom. We'll cycle around Shelly Beach to locate three potential baristas for Adrian's training course and suss out a cat carer. You can ride in the basket on the back. Just like Toto.'

The Dog wasn't impressed.

'I won't tie you in. If things get dodgy – jump for it.'

The Dog was happier.

'You have to stay where you land, though.'

The Dog wasn't happy.

'Not exactly "stay" where you land. You have to stay in a safe place. By the side of the road. You do *not* – run – away!'

I used dot points to make my potential barista list. In a former life I was very attached to dot points. In the early days of our marriage I made endless lists.

- Pick up Kenneth's shirts from the laundry.
- Pack Kenneth's suitcase for a three-night trip.
- Organise dinner party for twelve.
- Etc.
- Etc.

But anyway, moving on.

We made a list of likely Shelly Beach locals who would appreciate three days' free barista training in the city. The Dog took the list between his teeth and we were off.

We cycled up the back dirt road to Daphne and Charles' place, our first dot-point stop. The grass beside the road was covered with common yellow daisies.

'I threaded daisies when I was little. Made daisy chains,' I shouted to the Dog over my shoulder.

'Now Bossy Child and her little weed-buster friends pull up the daisies on the foreshore. She says they're weeds. They just want native plants to grow on the foreshore. We're booked to help sometime. I'll have to check our calendar.'

The Dog approves of weed-busting. He's an honorary member of the Shelly Beach Weed Busters' Club. He approves of any environmental stuff, especially when it involves digging.

The air was heavy with the smell of eucalypt and wattle blossom. 'Wattle looks lovely but it gives you hay fever.' I risked a backwards glance. The Dog wore his stretched smile: his sharp little teeth gleamed in his furry face.

'You're loving this, aren't you?'

The Dog ignored me. He'd just noticed a rabbit in the undergrowth.

'If you jump you're dead meat.'

At Daphne's we were offered standard Shelly Beach hospitality: a cup of tea, biscuits and a bowl of water. Daphne checked my dot-point list.

'Violet? No. Charles and I are a no-go. No time. Joan and/or Joan's friends?' She shook her head. 'They're all full-time working mums.' Daphne worked down my list. 'Josh? No. Beryl? No. Call at Bianca's. She might be able to come up with some names. Don't forget Pandora. I know she's flat-out with her renovations but she might appreciate a break. And don't worry about the cat. Jody Jenkins will look after Adrian's cat until he returns. She's a cat person.'

The Dog was happy with the solution to our cat problem but was reluctant to continue our bike ride. I bribed him with the promise of a bone when we returned home.

Bianca was excited at the thought of becoming a barista. 'It'd be fun. But I can't do it. Business is awesome. I've got a full appointment book.'

We understood.

'Try Mum. She's sick of cleaning. Especially cleaning for Digby. When Annette – wife number two – was alive, it was a lovely job. Now Mum says it's the job from hell. Digby's incredibly picky.' Bianca checked her watch. 'You'll catch Mum at home if you hurry.'

Once again we resumed our journey and called on Bianca's mum. Gail jumped at the opportunity.

Excellent. I ticked one name on our dot-point list.

We refused tea and water and biscuits, and set off to Pandora's. We were cycling leisurely along the back road when Pandora jogged past us. 'I'll be home in thirty minutes. Call in for coffee. I've something I want to show you.'

'Right.' We stopped and watched her jogging ahead. 'Don't you hate fit, energetic people, Dog?'

The Dog agreed. After cats his second hate is fit, energetic show dogs.

'We'll make a detour, Dog. Call in at Bill and Deb's to see if there are handouts I need to copy for the next writers' group meeting.'

The Dog wasn't happy.

'I promise we won't stop for refreshments. And if young Hunter is on the loose I promise I won't let your paws touch the ground. I'll hold you for the entire visit.'

Hunter was roving around the house, so I tucked the Dog under my arm.

'Bill's left a handout on literary devices to copy for the next writers' group meeting,' Deb explained. The Dog and I watched while she hunted through piles of papers. 'It's probably in the car. He's been working there. It's safer when Hunter's up and about.'

The Dog and I agreed.

We followed Deb outside to the garage. 'Bill's in the city. Meeting with the publicity and marketing people. They've arranged a "lunch with Bill" author tour to publicise his novel. Bill hates talking about his writing, though. He's trying to get out of it.'

We empathised with Bill.

By the time I'd pedalled to the bottom of McIntosh Hill and pushed the bike up to Pandora's place, a showered and gleaming Pandora was waiting for us. She'd set a table on her bay-view balcony with coffee cups and a basket of handmade almond biscuits. What can't this woman do?

'Brilliant view, Pandora.'

'It's spectacular, isn't it? Digby has an even better view from his place. You get a 360-degree view from there. Has he shown you the view from the tower room?'

'Not yet.'

Pandora laughed. 'He will.'

When she returned with the coffee, Pandora accepted the offer of barista training. 'I'm so over renovating and organising trades-people. A three-day break uptown is just what I need. Knowing how to pull a good coffee won't go astray.'

I thankfully ticked her name.

'Why don't you do the training, Gina?'

Why not? I'd been thinking about it. The unemployed need train-ing so they can become employed. And I liked Gail and Pandora. 'I think I will. Yes, I will.'

'I've got something you need to see.' Pandora returned with a city newspaper. She turned to the celeb social page. Under the head-ing *New Label Launch* was a photo of Kenneth and Clever Angela. Kenneth was his usual photogenic self. Clever Angela was wearing a fashion-forward lace creation (one of her own designs, according to the caption). My eyes followed the lines of the dress as it outlined a very large baby bump.

'Oh my God. She's practically due to give birth! That's why he wants the divorce hurried along.'

246

Pandora looked at me. She knows my history with King Rat Kenneth. 'Are you okay, Gina?'

I took deep breaths. 'Yes, I'm fine.' I smiled. 'I feel fine. I wish them every happiness in the world.'

'And I meant what I said to Pandora, Dog,' I shouted as I took my feet off the pedals and we flew down McIntosh Hill. 'I don't need another baby. I have my gorgeous grandson.'

After dinner, Bossy Child, the Dog and I took Princess and her belongings to Jody at Jenkins' Store. Jody was delighted to look after Princess until Adrian returned.

Bossy Child thought the Dog and I were heartless. 'You'll have to tell Adrian – and Violet!'

The Dog and I didn't care. After we took Bossy Child home we sat on Adrian's verandah and watched the sun set. 'What do you think, Dog? Can I include three-day no-cost barista training in my CV? Will it go under the heading *Technical Skills*?'

The Dog wasn't sure.

Friday 16 October

The next challenge was to find a suitable time for three trainees to attend Adrian's barista course. Problem solved. The only vacancy available was Monday 19 to Wednesday 21 – next week.

Pandora's fine. Gail's easy. 'Just as long as the dates don't clash with the speed-dating night.'

The dates didn't clash with speed dating, but they did with the writers' group meeting. I won't be back in time to open the hall for writers' group. Bloody hell!

'Here we go again, Dog. Adrian has set up another domino chain. Take one domino out and the rest collapse. First things first. I'll check with Alf and Beryl and see if they can look after you. I can be back in time to childmind Bossy Child on Thursday.'

The Dog and I walked to Alf and Beryl's. After our finger-reading session, I asked Beryl if she and Alf would look after the Dog while I was uptown for a few nights.

'Of course you can leave Hugo with us! We adore him. Don't we, adorable little dog?'

I ignored the Dog's smug look.

'He can stay with Alf during the day. I'll bring dinner over. Alf and I will sleep over.'

Over a cup of tea and a slice of moist fruit cake I confided in this comforting woman. 'Adrian will be back soon and I have to find a job. It's been over eighteen months since I've had one where you actually earn money.'

I sipped my tea. 'I think I was on the verge of meltdown when I arrived at Shelly Beach.'

'You could have been.' Beryl stirred her tea. 'But you didn't melt down, did you, dear?'

I shook my head.

'My cousin Alice had a meltdown last year. She was a beautiful knitter. Always won first prize at the Sea Haven Craft Show for her knitted jumpers.

'"Beryl," she said after her meltdown, "Beryl, I don't think I'll ever knit another jumper again."

'I said, "The trouble with you, Alice, is you're thinking about knitting a whole jumper. Just think about knitting a sleeve. A cuff. Start by knitting five rows of a cuff!" And she did, and by the end of the month she'd knitted a complete jumper. Won first prize again this year.'

Beryl gave me a Shelly Beach bear hug when we left. 'You'll be fine, dear. You're a survivor. Some people survive after a catastrophe. Some don't. You will.'

On the way home I told the Dog of my new resolution. 'When we get home I'm going to take up knitting, Dog. And I'm starting by knitting five rows of a cuff for the sleeve of a jumper.'

The Dog thought I'd completely missed the point of Beryl's story. And he wasn't happy with the fishy smell escaping from my backpack. Alf had given us two sea salmon he'd caught this morning – salmon and snapper are biting in the bay.

The Dog grumbled all the way home. He hates fish. Back home I contacted Daphne re: my writers' group challenge.

In half an hour Daphne rang back with a solution. 'We're bending writers' group by-law no. 2. Meeting is transferred from Wednesday 21 to Wednesday 28 at our place. All members are happy with the changes.'

Pandora phoned later. 'I've called in some favours for the barista training course next week. We can have a two-night complimentary stay at Executive City Apartments. I can drive us to town.'

I rang Gail. She was happy with the news. She operates on a very slim budget. Despite Pandora's generous offer, I've left my accommodation options open. I'm considering sleeping on a park bench. I'm very wary of overnight sleepovers with friends. I can't cope with being deluged with lies, secrets and confessions.

The Dog's not talking to me again. He knows I'm leaving him.

'I'm going to send an email to Adrian and perjure myself for you. I'm not allergic to cats! I'm dumping Princess for your sanity!'

To: Adrian <bookstreet@network.com.au>
From: Gina <piececake@email.com.au>
Subject: No-cost training
Hi Adrian,
Pandora, Gail and self will do three-day barista training next week. We realise no obligation or job offer is entailed.

Real estate agent confirmed bookings for Crow's Nest Flat for December, January and February. Do you want to let it for March? Should I tell agent that tenants may need to use bathroom at Sea

View Cottage if Alf doesn't sort our plumbing problems?

Hope you don't mind but Jody at Jenkins' Store is looking after Princess until you return. I've developed an allergy to cats.
Gina

To: Gina <piececake@email.com.au>
From: Adrian <bookstreet@network.com.au>
Re: No-cost training
Hi Gina
Not to worry. Jody emailed me re: Princess's transfer of care.

Hopefully Alf will sort Crow's Nest plumbing problems soon.

Give my best wishes to team re: barista training. Can you keep detailed procedural notes during your training? Useful for future employees.

Tell agent Crow's Nest Flat is not available for rental in March. Elder daughter and family are planning to use it then, all things going well.

Did I tell you that you have the most amazing green eyes?
Adrian

Bloody hell!

The Dog caught me talking to the computer screen. 'I've had ostensibly platonic lunch dates, serious and not-so-serious dalliances – not counting the short affair with Lee – and I've handled extended flirtations before, so I'm thinking I can manage an email relationship with Adrian without it getting messy.'

The phone rang and broke into my thoughts of Adrian-with-the-effortless-charm.

It was Julia. 'The nanny's sick. Our housekeeper has been off all week. I'm sick. Simon's sick. Simon's parents are sick. We can't get a replacement nanny until Monday. Can you come tomorrow to look after Barney? Stay the weekend?'

I rang Pandora. 'Is your accommodation offer for Monday and Tuesday night still open?'

'Yes.'

'Good. I'd like to accept it. I'll meet you and Gail at the college on Monday morning and come back to the apartment after our training.'

I scored massive brownie points with Julia when I told her I'd be at her place by lunch tomorrow.

Saturday 17 – Sunday 18 October

I left the Dog in Alf's care and caught the early (bloody early) bus and train to arrive at Julia's by lunch. I'd foolishly refused Julia's offer to hire a car and charge it to their business.

A panic over nothing, really. Barney was fine. The doctor said he had a head cold. I looked at Julia and Simon. They were stressed out of their brains. Too much work and not enough play, plus a slight attack of the flu and they'd hit rock-bottom. But I was hardly in a position to offer advice.

During my journey I'd decided to visit my aunt Gabby, who lives near Julia. An aunt I haven't seen in years. Correction: Gabby is more than an aunt. She cared for me after my mother died. Then after my father died, and I was at university, she kept the house I'd inherited running for me and my scatty boarders (one being Eva).

I needed to purge myself of huge guilt gained through years of non-contact with Gabby and her long-term partner Louise. In the early years of my marriage I was ridiculously influenced by Kenneth and his mother's sick prejudices against Gabby and Louise. Then as my career took off – promotions, prestige, high salaries – boxed roses, ordered online and delivered anonymously, were a coward's way of escaping my obligations.

I told Julia I'd take Barney with me to visit Gabby and Louise. 'They only live three train stations away. And then it's just a ten-minute walk from the station to their place.'

'You've got your mobile with you?'

'Yes, and I have your number.'

'Good. Ring if you get into trouble, Gina.' Julia was grateful, satisfied her mother could cope. She dragged herself back to bed again – or was she going to attempt some work? Probably spend useless hours producing an unproductive product.

With permission granted to take Barney out for the afternoon, I stowed emergency food and nappies on board his Bugaboo pram. I took a bottle of chardonnay with a well-known label from Julia's fridge, and popped it into my Mary Poppins bag in case I couldn't find a florist along the way.

The gods were with me. It was a beautiful spring day: gentle sunshine, cool breeze. The perfect day for taking a grandson on a pram journey.

I'd put in some pre-planning – a phone call. Gabby was delighted to hear from me. 'Yes. Louise and I would love to see you, Gina. It's been too long! We'll have the champagne chilled.'

I had plenty of help getting Barney in his pram on – and off – the train. I shamefully showcased my grandson to the passengers in my carriage.

'He's a gorgeous baby. Aren't you a lucky mother?'

'Grandmother, actually.'

'I don't believe it. You look so young.'

I took the compliment on board and baby affirmations were exchanged until three stations sped by and we'd arrived at our destination.

I pushed Barney in his aerodynamic pod past 1 Ashwood Street (Victorian home, circa 1890) on the way to Gabby's house in the next street.

The house on Ashwood Street didn't resemble the home I'd inherited all those years before. It had lost its garden to a townhouse, but there was still sufficient garden to give it home-magazine appeal.

Reproduction heritage gargoyles were poised on the rooftop. Refurbished tessellated tiles coated the terrace, a favourite playing space when I was a child.

How could I have allowed my father's – and mother's – inheritance to disappear to finance Kenneth's dodgy deals and bad debts?

We continued on to Gabby and Louise's home. I stared down at Barney enjoying his rock-and-roll ride. Move on, Gina.

It was a heart-warming meeting with Gabby and Louise: real hugs and tears. No need to explain anything. They were aware of my separation from Kenneth and the collapse of the Laurel-Scott Corporation. It was a brilliant idea to bring Barney. He provided a comforting conversation facilitator – and he's such a beautiful baby.

Gabby and Louise are obviously very happy together. Gabby retired from teaching two years ago, Louise last year. They travel a lot: India, China, Japan, Russia. 'We love it. And we'd love to visit you at Shelly Beach, Gina. Wherever you decide to settle. We want to keep up with your new career. Exciting times ahead.'

Bloody hell!

Gabby and Louise walked with us to the station. One visit and I'd miraculously managed to bury a gigantic guilt demon.

Back home I fed, bathed and settled Barney for bed. Next I made a light meal for Simon and Julia. They were finally up, trailing around the house in their Country Road casualwear. Simon was distracted with his BlackBerry. Julia was sitting at the kitchen table, checking emails on her laptop.

I whispered to Barney, 'Your parents can't see the elephant roaming around their house. We'll see if we can get them to take it back to the jungle, circus, zoo – wherever it belongs.'

For two highly organised people, Simon and Julia had allowed their home to slide into chaos in a matter of days. I spent most of the rest of the weekend working frantically to restore Julia and Simon's minimalist house to its minimalist order.

On Sunday, after sorting the laundry – washing, ironing and folding – I did the usual (young) grandmother stuff. It was another miraculous spring day so Barney and I went to the park and fed the ducks. We returned home in time for Barney's afternoon nap. He's no trouble, but he has problem parents. They're so stressed. And so busy.

I cancelled an invitation to have dinner with Clare, Eva and Hester. Fortunately, I had an honest excuse – while I was on the phone, Barney was crying in the background. No way did I want to dine with hidden dragons.

I made Julia and Simon another light meal. They vanished to their room, office – whatever. Their house is like a mausoleum.

On Sunday night Nanny Anny returned, glowing with a fresh tan. She didn't look too sick. She looked as if she'd spent a sexy week on a tropical island with her boyfriend.

I checked how to get to the college by public transport for barista training tomorrow morning. I rang to check on the Dog. We had a short chat. He was fine.

I couldn't operate Simon and Julia's home theatre so I went to bed and read. I need to talk to my daughter properly very soon.

Monday 19 October
Our small team survived barista training well today. Spunky tutor Tony (2010 Brazilian Champion Barista) loves training baristas and raced us through the quagmire of techniques and tips.

Tony's passionate about coffee-making. He beseeches unbelievers to bring java into their lives: 'Coffee-making is an art!'

I didn't doubt this but I'm holding back the passion. The thought of working in a cafe with high-volume work, i.e. pulling 500 cups a day, does not enthuse me.

We mastered the coffee art of creating perfect leaves and hearts on lattes. And Tony let us into top secrets such as 'Grind! Grind! Grind! Grind your own beans.' Way to go, Tony.

We used Pandora's complimentary voucher and ate out at a jazzy restaurant. And then we returned to our apartment and exchanged confessions.

Pandora began with a blockbuster. 'I'm loaded. Inheriting my father's Shelly Beach home last year was just icing on the cake.'

Gail and I glanced at each other. So much for the out-of-date Pandora goss we'd gleaned from Shelly Beach locals.

Pandora continued with her surprising confession. 'I didn't have burnout. I had payout!

'I overstepped my work boundary. Broke my golden rule. I fell madly, passionately in love with my boss. He was going to leave his wife and kids and marry me. But trophy wife no. 3, Jolene, won out. She'd had plenty of practice fighting off competition.

'My boss escaped the affair with an apology to our company. He'd displayed unbecoming conduct. He'd made a serious error of judge-ment. I don't know what he said to his wife. He's probably still living with her on payback terms.

'Meanwhile, I decided to leave the company – but I left with a golden handshake. Decided to throw myself into transforming my late father's home into an upmarket B&B, as you know. I'm nearly there. It'll be ready this summer. Then I'll think about rejoining the rat-race.'

Gail was reluctant to confide in us after Pandora's spectacular confession – but she did.

'I feel guilty because of my iffy relationship with my daughters. I spent too much time working to repay debts when the girls were little. I should have spent more time with them.'

Gail's ex-husband left her when the girls were three and four respectively. 'Took off with the budgie, our new car and Teresa, our fish-shop attendant. I was left with running the shop and paying the mortgage and a heap of debts. I worked two jobs, sometimes three, for years until everything was paid off.'

I empathised with Gail. Similar guilt. I confessed that my relationship with my daughter Julia needs a lot of work. 'I was a minus one-star mother. I should have spent more time with her when she was little. I was career-obsessed – a high-flyer.'

A second glass of wine and I was waxing lyrical. 'I should have remembered the closer one flies to the sun the greater the fall to earth. I should have been planning my future and plotting changes. Making choices before the wax on my wings melted.'

Pandora segued from my mythological confession. '*Shoulds*, *coulds* and *woulds* are banned from our conversations from now on.'

Three women, with uncertain futures, laughed the rest of the evening away. We played 'What if' (cathartic and useful if you're looking for ideas for a page-turning novel), placing people we'd known in our former lives in unlikely situations. For example: Kenneth working in Gail's Shark's Fin Fish & Chippery – without a PA.

Tuesday 20 October

In Day Two of barista training we covered health and safety issues followed by a tricky fill-the-gap test. Pandora, Gail and I topped the class, which was esteem-boosting considering the other potential baristas were disgustingly youthful and enthusiastic.

When we returned to our apartment I rang Beryl to check on the Dog. He was in trouble. 'He's been stealing the Potholer boys' lunches. Just the ham sandwiches, Gina. He leaves the salad ones.'

Beryl put the Dog on the phone so I could chat. 'Behave, Dog. Keep eating the guys' sandwiches and you won't be able to fit through your pet door when Adrian returns.'

Beryl said she thought the Dog took note of my warning. I knew he didn't care.

Bianca had texted her mum with a message for me. Gail passed it to me to decipher: *Digby + U R ofishls 4 Sped D8ng ngt.*

Bloody hell!

Shortlisted author Bill phoned. He's in town to meet with his publisher. We arranged to meet him tomorrow for lunch. Bill's unhappy. He's caught in crocodile death-rolls with the publisher's marketing personnel – trying to avoid a whistle-stop publicity tour for his new novel.

'He has to do it. I'll talk to him tomorrow.' Sound advice from Pandora. 'He needs the publicity to max his sales.'

Tony, our champion barista, asked Pandora out. She accepted. Pandora, glammed up, her endless legs in very high heels, left to paint the town red.

Gail and I ordered room-service meals, took hot baths and went to bed at a ridiculously early hour. I wrote up the barista training notes for Adrian.

I can't believe I admitted to Gail that I found city life exhausting and that I was looking forward to returning to Shelly Beach.

Wednesday 21 October

Tony dismissed the group at lunch. A smart strategy. You tell participants it's a three-day course, when really you only have stuff to cover two and a half days. You give the participants the afternoon off and they go home happy.

A quick lunch with Bill. We listened to his trials and tribulations coping with the publicity and marketing departments – hell when you're a writer who likes to hide away in an attic – or car – and just write!

Hester had arranged to meet me before I headed back to Shelly Beach. Over coffee she passed me a cheque. My eyes boggled when I read the total. 'This hasn't come from the sale of my stuff at your farm clearance sale, surely?'

Hester shook her head. 'Remember the two rings you classified as bling? Zircon cluster settings?'

'Vaguely.'

'They were diamonds. Excellent cut, colour and clarity. And reasonable carat weights.'

'Bloody hell! The rings well and truly slipped under Kenneth's radar. He'd be furious if he knew.'

Hester gave me a satisfied smile. She was looking good. New short haircut and colour – silver. It gave her a glacial look. She's always had a no-effort size-eight figure. Botoxed? Not sure.

She rummaged in a carry bag and produced a beribboned package. 'It's from Clare.'

I opened it with caution. It was a book: *The Redundancy Handbook – A Guide to New Beginnings*. I read Clare's inscription on the title page. *Hello Gina. Remember JK Rowling wrote her way to success during her redundancy. Seven books over ten years with a fairytale resolution! Love Clare.*

I left the redundancy handbook on the coffee-shop table. It will be invaluable for a writer of magical tales.

To: Adrian <bookstreet@network.com.au>
From: Gina <piececake@email.com.au>
Subject: Barista training
Hi Adrian,
Successfully completed three-day barista training. We have the certificates to prove it! Arranged for your coffee machine to be installed tomorrow.
Gina

To: Gina <piececake@email.com.au>
From: Adrian <bookstreet@network.com.au>
Re: Barista training
Hi Gina,
Well done. Did you keep a procedural manual?

Can't stop myself thinking about a red-headed house-sitter I've met. Can't wait to get home and hold her in my arms again.
Adrian

The Dog watched me shut down the computer. 'I need time to think of a reply for your owner. Loose lips sink ships.'

I've lost the Dog again with my nautical metaphor.

Thursday 22 October

A strong wind (more like a gale) blew us along Beach Road as we journeyed to Jenkins' General Store with our basic supplies order: flour, sugar, tea and coffee.

We were pleased to hear that Princess was settling in well and exchanged weather-speak with Jody. 'Shelly Beach gets strong winds come spring. Do you want a lift home, luv? Arnold's delivering orders in about half an hour.'

The Dog and I refused Jody's generous offer of a lift home, but we stopped for a cuppa, ginger-snap biscuits and a bowl of water. We drank our tea and water standing under the store's awning and watched the choppy waves on the bay.

Foolishly I'd promised the Dog we'd walk back home along the beach. The Dog enjoys ferreting through the washed-up banks of seaweed on the sand. He loves hunting for dead marine animals.

'If you roll in anything rotten you'll have to have a bath when we get home.'

The Dog ignored me.

We diverted from the beach to collect Bossy Child from school. As soon as she got in the door, she started marking off the days on Adrian's calendar.

'Not long to go, Gina! How did you go with Barney?'

'We had fun. We went out both days. The first day we visited my aunt, and the next day we went to the park to feed the ducks.'

'And Julia let you do this?'

'Yes.'

'And did you do the other stuff too?'

'Excuse me?'

'Did you feed Barney? Change his nappy? Play with him? Bath him? Put him to bed?'

'Yes. Yes. Yes. Yes. Yes.'

'Cool.' Bossy Child was compiling a potential job list for me. 'You could be a nanny, Gina – but you'll need more practice with kids Sam's age.'

'Excuse me?'

'When Mum left Sam with you last week to check she'd turned off the iron, Sam flushed Snuffy down Adrian's toilet.'

I hushed the Bossy Child as Alf walked into the room. He was attempting to unblock Adrian's toilet because a certain toy rabbit had accidentally fallen into the toilet and was lost in the depths of Adrian's sewerage system.

'Can't fix your bathroom plumbing, Gina. I'll get the plumbers from Sea Haven in the morning. You'll have to use your neighbour's facilities.'

I smiled my thanks to Alf.

Bossy Child resumed her composition of my job list. 'You could work in a coffee shop, a library, be a conference person and a nanny – but only with babies. There you go . . .' Bossy Child counted her list. 'Four jobs. All you have to do is look for vacancies in the paper and on the internet. Then you apply for jobs and do some interviews.'

Joan arrived. She had a message from Bianca for me. 'Can you make it at 6 tomorrow night at Rosa's? The action committee wants to run through the speed-dating rules.'

'Right.'

Bossy Child showed her mum my potential job list.

260

'Add chef to the list, Terri. Gina's got great foodie credentials.'

I smiled a tight thank-you smile as Bossy Child was ushered out the door by her mother.

'Don't forget to use the timer when you shower at our place, Gina!'

I gave Bossy Child a cross-eyed look.

The Dog and I went to Piece of Cake to check out the new just-installed coffee machine and then headed back to Bossy Child's to use her bathroom.

Friday 23 October

Life at Shelly Beach can be surreal. In one day I've been on two seal watches, topped off by a night of speed dating.

The day began with an alarming 5 a.m. phone call. 'WHASH calling!'

'Excuse me?'

'It's Sylvia from WHASH, Wildlife Helpers at Sea Haven. Can I speak to Adrian?'

'He's left the country!'

'It's a WHASH emergency. A fur seal is stranded on Shelly Beach. Adrian's the area coordinator. He usually organises round-the-clock watches.'

'Right.'

'Has Adrian organised a replacement to do his job?'

'No.' Saint Adrian has slipped up this time.

'Can you do it? At least get the operation started?'

Silence.

'Just for the first hour shift?'

'Starting . . .?'

'Six thirty. The ranger's been on duty all night! He has to get home to feed his kids.'

Bloody hell! How could I say no?

'Make sure the *Keep away*, *Don't disturb*, and *Don't feed the seal* signs are in place when you leave. And we need a fifty-metre area roped off around the seal until it goes back into the bay – or dies.'

'Right.' I didn't ask what to do with the seal if it died on my shift.

'Can you arrange for other locals to take over after your shift? Ring if you have any problems. Thank you.'

Bloody hell! No time to ask bossy Sylvia why she wasn't doing her bit to help the stranded seal. Probably staying in bed all day and writing a novel.

I called Daphne, left the seal-watch organisation in her competent hands and went to do my shift, calling in at her place on the way to drop the Dog off. He was keen to come but it didn't sound like a good idea. Daphne agreed to keep him with her. 'No dogs allowed, Hugo!'

The sea was calm and pale grey in the early morning light. The Sea Haven ranger was relieved to see me. He was keen to get home to his family. The fur seal was lying on the sand; his body moved gently up and down with each breath. The seal fastened his big brown eyes on me. He was tired. Needed time to rest. I understood.

I checked that the signs and rope barrier around the seal were in place. During my two-hour watch the seal and I engaged in a time-killing chat. Fortunately he'd never had to balance a ball on his nose, and he'd never had to clap his flippers. He could flap his flippers, but not clap them. He'd heard of seals that had to perform tricks such as this – and worse.

Our seal had led a life crammed full of risk-taking, and it had taken its toll. He'd had to dodge sharks and toxic algae, and he'd been known to get free fish feeds by leaping into trawler nets. Leaping out was the challenge. All he needed at this moment was rest – chill-out time so he could return to where he came from.

I sympathised. Everyone needs chill-out time in life. Then you can move on. Maybe return to where you were before you chilled out.

Daphne relieved me for the next shift. She passed the Dog gently into my arms. On the way home I explained to him that even though he was a very small dog, he could scare the life out of the seal. 'And if you annoyed the seal he might bite you. Knowing your luck, you'd get an infection. Then you'd have to go to the vet again.'

The Dog ignored my warning but he was interested in my conversation with the seal. He didn't think there was anything peculiar about a dog-sitter chatting to a seal. Thank God!

During my second shift later that afternoon, the seal dragged itself off the sand, slid into Shelly Beach bay and swam out to sea – just in time for me to make speed dating. (Alf and Beryl had been prepared to do a late-evening seal-watch shift: 'Speed dating isn't our thing.')

The night turned out to be quite a little money-spinner. Rosa was enormously happy with her bar takings. Digby and I were time-keepers. Participants had an eight-minute window of opportunity to talk about themselves with a partner. Then we rang a bell, and the guys moved while the girls stayed put.

'Just like an old-fashioned barn dance!' Violet said. She was in charge of collecting the entrance money.

Digby read the riot act before the action started. 'No propositions. Polite eight-minute conversations. If you like someone, tick his or her name on your card. Participants hand their cards in at the end of the night, and Gina and I will check the cards. Speed daters will be notified of participants who'd like to date them. Participants can follow up their own hits.'

During the evening Digby and I chatted on and off. He was glad he's abandoned the idea of a tell-all memoir in favour of a novel. He'd written a novel before – in the eighties.

'My first wife deleted it from our primitive computer. Caused the first crack in our marriage.'

I was stopped from finding out other causes of cracks in his marriage by the need to ring our eight-minute bell.

Shelly Beach male participants were shy and retiring – until it was their turn to talk to Bianca, a woman who likes to hit the waves. Bianca's magic formula to transform local males into nonstop talking charmers? Simple: 'Talk about surfing.'

After our speed daters had finished, Digby and I worked out who wanted a date with whom from the individual scorecards. Bianca was an all-out winner.

She wasn't interested. 'I've grown up with the guys. No way am I going on a date with any of them.'

We binned names of potential dream lovers for Bianca.

Digby drove me home and tempted me with an invitation to a gallery opening in Sea Haven next week, with dinner after.

I accepted. Digby's charm cards are hard to beat.

To: Adrian <bookstreet@network.com.au>
From: Gina <piececake@email.com.au>
Subject: WHASH duty
Hi Adrian,
You forgot to organise a WHASH replacement before you left. If any more seals, whales, penguins, etc. turn up on Shelly Beach, who would you like to be your replacement?
Gina

To: Gina <piececake@email.com.au>
From: Adrian <bookstreet@network.com.au>
Re: WHASH duty
Hi Gina
Sincerest apologies. Can you handle the WHASH duty until I get back? And how much did we make from speed-dating night?

Did I tell you I keep dreaming about you?
Adrian

To: Adrian <bookstreet@network.com.au>

From: Gina <piececake@email.com.au>

Re: WHASH duty

Not sure of takings from speed dating. Violet was in charge.
Probably enough for a pair of flippers and snorkel for celeb author
to swim to Shelly Beach.

Desperately time-poor but I'll be stand-in volunteer for your
WHASH duty until you return. Advise you to take sleeping pills to
stop dreaming.

Saturday 24 October

The action committee was providing a free breakfast barbecue on
the foreshore. Pandora called in and we walked down together. There
was no shortage of conversation starters among the attendees. The
speed-dating night and the safe return of our seal to the sea were top
of the list.

Young businesswoman Bianca was victorious. 'Takings for the
speed dating are awesome. We captured the youth market!'

Daphne and hubby Charles were happy. 'Great result. It's difficult trying to raise funds in Shelly Beach. You ask people to donate
their time and money to give an event legs, and the same people turn
up every time.'

No option in Shelly Beach.

Daphne and Charles are Bianca's ideal couple. 'They're so awesome.'

Gail agreed. 'I've never heard them argue.'

Violet joined us. 'If Charles joins the writers' group next year,
Daphne says she's divorcing him. And she's definitely not joining the
fourth wives' club.'

We were confused.

'They've been married three times. They have huge breakups and
then get back together again. Charles likes being married. Daphne
doesn't care.'

Digesting this stunning goss, our small writerly group moved on. We engaged in writers' chat over charred sausages and overdone eggs in bread rolls.

Pandora's decided that if and when she gets around to writing her novel, her main character will be a high-flying female who has the proverbial rug pulled out from under her during a madly passionate affair with her boss.

The Dog thinks Pandora will be writing a bit close to the bone.

Bianca's having trouble with paragraphs. She's got pages and pages, chapters and chapters, of straight-from-the-brain, let-it-flow (but numbered) pages of writing. 'Of course I've got sentences! I just need to get my sentences into paragraphs. Short paragraphs. I hate long paragraphs in books.'

I promised to look in at Scissors during her down time tomorrow and help with her paragraph challenge.

And I'm still thinking about writing another novel.

Sunday 25 October

To: Adrian <bookstreet@network.com.au>
From: Gina <piececake@email.com.au>
Subject: Speed dating
Hi Adrian,
1. Reasonable takings from the speed-dating night. Confirming enough cash for a one-way economy fare for one celeb author. Flippers and snorkel will be required for return trip. Have you thought of throwing in free accommodation at Crow's Nest Flat to tempt celeb authors?
2. Action committee is hoping to pull in huge profit from the collector's fair Digby's organising in the first weeks of November.
3. Good news from Kingston Council. We can keep our trees. They're also building a new bus shelter (the one that got

kicked down by Sea Haven louts), and renovating the old band pavilion and toilet block. Obviously council elections are looming.
Gina

To: Gina <piececake@email.com.au>
From: Adrian <bookstreet@network.com.au>
Re: Speed dating
Hi Gina,
Appreciate the feedback. Heard you and Digby did a great job at the speed dating. Still dreaming of a fantastic night spent with a creative, beautiful, intelligent woman with green eyes and red hair.
Adrian

To: Adrian <bookstreet@network.com.au>
From: Gina <piececake@email.com.au>
Subject: Dreamless sleep
Get some sleep. Drink a cup of warm milk before you go to bed. A man of your age needs a good night's sleep in order to look after grandkids.

Monday 26 October

Adrian's mulberry tree looks magnificent. The filigree branches are crammed with heart-shaped leaves, and at the junction of each leaf-cluster tiny green mulberries are forming. I was thinking I'd send a 'how great your mulberry tree looks' email to Adrian but changed my mind.

We were having coffee when Sally the poodle arrived, dragging her chewed leash behind her. 'She's got a crush on you, Dog.'

The Dog dismissed my assumption. He said Sally was upset. She's missing Henry Shepherd. Sadly, Henry had another heart

267

attack a few days ago and is back in hospital. Sally's staying with Henry's daughter and young family. Hating it.

We walked Sally along the beach back to her new home. Another idyllic day. The waves lapped gently at the edge of the sand. The crunch of shells under our feet made rhythmic noises.

On our return journey, we met Digby. I received a Shelly Beach bear hug, an illicit kiss on the lips and an invitation to lunch at Rosa's.

Our social calendar had a gap so I gladly accepted Digby's invitation. He was hyped up. He'd just received confirmation that his bid to buy the old draper's shop next to Piece of Cake was successful. Digby has great plans for his new property. He's going to pull down walls and extend out the back to make an art gallery and gift shop.

The Dog was not particularly happy with my decision-making, i.e. accepting a spur-of-the-moment lunch date with Digby. He thinks I should be careful in case I make another decision like the one I made with Adrian. That decision has only complicated my already complicated life.

The Dog thinks I need to get into my 'calm zone' – channel jobs and a cashflow. The Dog's been hanging around Daphne's yoga-on-the-beach classes. I complimented him on his downward dog position. Not bad for a dog with short legs.

To: Adrian <bookstreet@network.com.au>
From: Gina <piececake@email.com.au>
Subject: Digby's art gallery
Hi Adrian,
Digby's bought the old draper's shop next to Piece of Cake. He's going to renovate – extend out the back – and turn it into an art gallery. He's having trouble thinking of a name for his gallery.
Gina

To: Gina <piececake@email.com.au>
From: Adrian <bookstreet@network.com.au>
Re: Digby's art gallery

Hi Gina,

I'm aware of this development. I'm negotiating with the council for the remaining three empty shops on Beach Road. I'm sure you'll be able to assist Digby with an appropriate name for his gallery. How are the bungalow refits coming along?

Adrian

Tuesday 27 October

Alf showed me through the empty interiors of Adrian's bungalows.

'They'll be classy and stylish open-plan places – made with all-natural materials. Leonda, Adrian's architect friend, designed the new fit-out. She designed the interior for Piece of Cake and Crow's Nest Flat too. She's a well-known "green" architect. We're using recycled and repurposed materials wherever possible.'

I was impressed. When I left, I noticed Alf was answering an email from Potholer on his phone.

Now that the area has reliable internet providers, Shelly Beach locals have embraced technology. They are social-networking and entering internet portals with enthusiasm.

The Dog said I'd be amazed at the number of Shelly Beach inhabitants who are using cyberspace to communicate. I don't doubt it. Bianca, who couldn't locate her word-count feature a few months ago, now has a website, is collecting friends on Facebook and gathering an online Jane Austen community with her blog.

Due to my financial status I've adopted a Luddite attitude. However, I have learnt the value of Shelly Beach's nonverbal communication.

The Dog agrees with me that to survive in Shelly Beach you need to embrace its silent language. You can't beat the face-to-face stuff for getting a message across, i.e. Bossy Child's cross-eyed look, Daphne's raised eyebrow, Violet's thin-lipped grin and Pandora's raised-arm victory signal. The Dog thinks my green-eyed mean look is very expressive too.

I ignored him.

The Dog regrets the decline in the art of letter-writing. In a former life, terrorising the postman on his daily deliveries was the highlight of the Dog's week. But the Dog's not afraid to adapt to technology. He likes the idea of keeping a blog. Maybe in the new year when his life is more settled.

We both agree that tweeting is unnecessary in Shelly Beach. One-hundred-and-forty-character messages are constantly exchanged at Jenkins' Store when you buy your bread, milk and dog food.

I suspect Adrian is gaining spy info on me via Shelly Beach tweets. That could explain how he knows what I've done before I even think about doing it.

To: Adrian <bookstreet@network.com.au>
From: Gina <piececake@email.com.au>
Subject: Bungalow refits
Hi Adrian,
Your bungalow refits are not progressing very fast. Alf showed me the amazing plans your cyberspace friend-slash-green-architect Leonda designed for your properties. They're excellent. Have your heard from her recently? Alf says she's overseas.
Gina

To: Gina <piececake@email.com.au>
From: Adrian <bookstreet@network.com.au>
Re: Bungalow refits
Hi Gina,
Leonda is a business colleague. We have a professional relationship.
I believe she's trekking in the Andes.
Adrian

'Good. Glad that's sorted. If I were thinking of an ongoing relation-ship with Adrian . . .'

Alarmed look from the Dog.

'After our professional relationship is completed . . .'

Relieved look from the Dog.

'I wouldn't tolerate real or cyberspace competition. Can you get eaten by a bear in the Andes? Maybe fall into a volcano?'

The Dog wasn't sure.

Wednesday 28 October

We had a subdued writers' group meeting this evening. Bill had just arrived back from the city again. Another meeting with the marketing and publicity people. Bill was on one of life's downers.

Bianca whispered, 'Deb says Bill's not sleeping. He's not coping well with the thought of the publicity stuff coming up to launch novel no. 2.'

We waited while Bill shuffled through his bag. 'Sorry, everyone. Lost my notes.'

'Lost the plot,' Violet whispered.

Josh stepped into the breach.

'It's his innate teacher thing,' Bianca said. (Innate is Bianca's word of the week.)

Josh shared his flow chart for the setting and plot of his sci-fi novel: an elaborate diagram filled with lines, arrows, boxes, circles, and masses of tiny printed detail. And he'd drawn all his characters! Awesome. Members were seriously impressed.

Since he's been a member of the writers' group, Josh's written 20 000 words. 'The way my novel's progressing it'll be well over 150 000 words.'

Then Josh confessed, 'I did the planning and wrote the first 30 000 words at university to gain a creative writing module credit.'

Struggling-to-get-a-word-on-the-page writers felt better after this confession.

Digby uses blank index cards, scissors and tape to construct his plot. He sticks the cards on the wall of his study. 'I'm thinking of purchasing a whiteboard. I miss having a whiteboard.'

Members understood.

During supper Digby said he'd appreciate my input into his plot. 'With complimentary Moët of course!'

I promised I'd look in some time. Thank goodness the Dog was out of earshot.

Digby's opted for multiple viewpoints – as you do when you're writing a complicated novel full of complex characters. Multiple viewpoints give him freedom to explore the emotional and psychological behaviour of his characters. Way to go, Digby.

'How's your writing going?'

(Had I, in a Moët-induced moment, talked about writing another novel?)

'Not! I've got a vague plot outline. Some structure in my head but I'm nowhere near ready to begin writing yet.'

Our learned tutor said, 'Writers find their own way. Some need structure, others flexibility.'

I'm into flexibility. Heaps of flexibility.

Violet handed copies of her final draft – *The Compost Caper Murder* (new working title) – to the group. 'I've spent a fortune on photocopying. Members need to read my draft before next meeting. I'm ready for constructive criticism. Pick up any spelling or grammar issues you can find.'

Bill discovered a sheet of editing symbols from his magic how-to-write-a-novel folder. 'I'll make copies for members.'

Violet doesn't want huge dollops of scribbled marginalia on her practically final draft. 'Don't use a red pen! Pencil will do. It's easier to erase.'

Struggling-to-write-a-first-draft members agreed to read Violet's novel of 80 000-plus words – editing where necessary. Reading Violet's whodunnit takes pressure, stress and guilt off emerging writers procrastinating over their own novels. Editing a member's novel is easier than writing your own, it seems.

Members discussed procrastination – a writer's disease. Pandora's waiting until her last goldfish dies (she's got a pondful) before she starts her novel.

Daphne waited while I locked the hall. 'I've kept aside a pair of paprika-red wedge sandals for you at the shop, Gina. Collect them anytime.'

I thanked my fashion-stylist-slash-conservationist. The sandals will look good with the Saba denim three-quarter-length jeans Daphne sourced for me last week.

To: Adrian <bookstreet@network.com.au>
From: Gina <piececake@email.com.au>
Subject: Writers' group meeting
Hi Adrian,
All members attended the writers' group meeting tonight. Not much happening. Bill's depressed with marketing stuff he has to do to sell his novel.
Gina

To: Gina <piececake@email.com.au>
From: Adrian <bookstreet@network.com.au>
Re: Writer's group meeting
Hi Gina,
Thanks for the detailed feedback. How's your job search progressing? Constantly thinking about you. Can't get you out of my head.
Adrian

To: Adrian <bookstreet@network.com.au>
From: Gina <piececake@email.com.au>

Subject: My brilliant career
Wonderfully. I'm considering job offers in the library/information technology field, plus event management and one or two outside-the-square offers. Ignoring comment about me being in your head. It's not a good place for me to be.
Gina

The Dog read my email with amused interest.

'I've used a few white lies like I did when I emailed Adrian about being allergic to cats. Alf's cousin's sister told him she's retiring in the new year – after she gets her holiday pay. She's the Sea Haven children's librarian, so there'll be a vacant part-time position at the library. Hester and Eva mentioned they're starting a business and they'd have a position for me, and Pandora said she might have a project we could work together on.'

The Dog was pleased I was in the job zone. He thought I should go for a platform job. Something to keep me going until I got my career on the rails again.

Thursday 29 October
I assisted Bossy Child with her pelican project: a model plus inter-pretive sign. Due in tomorrow. We were having issues with the legs. The bloody pelican wouldn't stand up.

Bossy Child should have heeded the wise woman and chosen a sensible bird like a penguin. 'Penguins don't need legs. They have firm flipper-type feet to rest on.'

Rolled-eye look from Bossy Child.

I was holding on to a pelican leg that was refusing to stick to a saggy papier-mâché body when a taxi drew up in Adrian's driveway.

'You've got visitors, Gina!'

Bloody hell!

Bossy Child gave a commentary while watching from Adrian's

front window. 'It's a woman with a baby and lots of luggage. She's paying the taxi driver. The taxi is backing out. It's driven off!'

'What!' The pelican collapsed. Legless.

I rushed outside and took Barney from Julia.

Julia was in tears. 'I've sacked Nanny Anny. She's been sneaking her boyfriend into the house. He's been living in the nanny flat with her! And Simon's away on a business trip. For three weeks! We've got serious problems, and I'm not sure if I want to stay with him when he gets back. And Barney never stops crying! He hates me! He wants Nanny Anny back!'

I held my gorgeous grandson in my arms. He stopped crying, gurgled and smiled at me.

'Let's get you inside.'

Bossy Child was dragging one of the suitcases up the verandah steps. I looked at the stack of baby equipment and Samsonite cases in the drive. Julia was planning on a long stay. Bloody hell!

Barney had fallen asleep in my arms. I looked at my distraught daughter. 'Don't worry, Julia. Everything will be fine. I'll make some tea. Have you eaten?'

'No. I just want to sleep.'

'What about Barney?'

'His bottle and mixture are in the blue bunny bag.'

I whispered to Bossy Child, 'What do we do now?'

'Put her to bed. In Bedroom One.'

Thank God the ceiling had been repaired. Carrying a sleeping Barney, I shepherded Julia to Adrian's minus one-star bathroom. Bossy Child held Barney. I made the bed while Julia stripped down to her underwear and washed the tear-streaked mascara off her cheeks. As soon as I finished making the bed, Julia collapsed into it. I tucked her in and she was asleep by the time I left the room.

We set up Barney's portable cot in my bedroom. Joan answered our SOS and came over to suggest a routine that I could follow. She promised to call in after work tomorrow and see how things are progressing.

I negotiated with the Dog to get him to sleep in the living room. Hopefully it'll only be for a few days.

I lay awake listening to Barney's soft, even breathing. I'm good at concentrating on small sounds in the night – it prevents too much thinking. When I was a child I kept silkworms in a box in my bedroom. I'd lie awake and listen to them munching on mulberry leaves. Tonight I'm happy to lie awake and listen to baby noises coming from my gorgeous grandson.

To: Adrian <bookstreet@network.com.au>
From: Gina <piececake@email.com.au>
Subject: Accommodation
Hi Adrian,
Julia and baby grandson Barney have arrived at Sea View Cottage
for a week – maybe more. Is this okay and if so, how do you want
their rent to be paid?
Gina

To: Gina <piececake@email.com.au>
From: Adrian <bookstreet@network.com.au>
Re: Accommodation
It's fine. Don't worry. Forget about rent.

I've been contacting publishers. I think I've struck it lucky
and will be able to book two international authors for the spring
Writefest next year (timing their visits with a major writing festival
up north).

And I've located a UK publisher who's interested in your
manuscript.

To: Adrian <bookstreet@network.com.au>
From: Gina <piececake@email.com.au>
Subject: Manuscript
My manuscript? My novel? WHO GAVE IT TO YOU?

To: Gina <piececake@email.com.au>
From: Adrian <bookstreet@network.com.au>
Re: Manuscript
YOU GAVE YOUR NOVEL TO ME!

Don't panic. I understand you're rattled with your daughter and grandson arriving so suddenly. Remember you showed me your manuscript and cancelled contract? When I was leaving for the airport I asked if you'd like me to take your novel and see if I could get a UK publisher interested in it.

Bloody hell! The Dog was watching me implode at the desk.

'I agreed?'

The Dog nodded.

I took ten deep breaths, lowered my shoulders and tackled the keyboard again.

To: Adrian <bookstreet@network.com.au>
From: Gina <piececake@email.com.au>
Re: Manuscript
Of course I remember. That's fine. Go ahead. Thank you.

Friday 30 October

The Dog and I have reached a new understanding since Adrian outed himself as a cat-lover. The Dog is happy with the loyalty clause in our new agreement. The best-friend and devotion clauses are still to be negotiated.

I hope the Dog realises the loyalty clause translates as 'the Dog cannot run away until Adrian returns'.

I looked around Adrian's living room. Baby gear and suitcases were stacked in every available space. The Dog has no hope of getting near his favourite sitting-and-sleeping spot in front of the fireplace. The kitchen table and all bench space are now too crowded with baby apparatus. This will test the I-will-not-run-away clause in our new agreement.

I took Julia and Barney to the medical centre at Sea Haven early this morning. The doctor gave them both a clean bill of health but Julia's obviously exhausted. She needs rest. If she's still depressed and exhausted after her stay with me, the doctor advised her to go to a therapist.

The rest of the day passed with us trying to get some kind of routine working in Sea View Cottage. Barney's easy: sleeps, wakes up, eats, smiles and sleeps again. I hate to say it but Nanny Anny must have had a few clues about getting babies into routines.

Late in the afternoon I remembered I'd planned to go to the gallery opening with Digby tonight. I phoned: 'Sorry to cancel tonight. I'm exhausted.' I had the perfect excuse – Barney noises in the background as evidence.

Half an hour later Beryl drove into Adrian's driveway. 'Digby asked me if Alf and I could help you out, dear. Alf's coming later. We'll do a spot of daughter-minding and babysitting so you can go to the gallery opening.'

Bloody hell!

Julia emerged from the bedroom looking tousled and weary.

Beryl introduced herself. 'You poor exhausted young mother. I've brought a lovely sea salmon for you. Freshly caught this morning. A light fish supper, early to bed and you won't know yourself.'

My Julia actually gave a weak smile.

Beryl shifted her focus to Barney. 'What a gorgeous baby.'

Julia beamed.

Bossy Child arrived. 'Mum sent me to tell Beryl if she needs any help she can ring Mum. Can you help with my pelican, Gina? I've been given an extension on my project.'

Beryl took control. 'Gina can't help you tonight, dear, but Alf and I will.'

Then to me, 'Run along and get ready, dear. Digby said he'd be here by 6.'

I took a deep breath, and gave Beryl instructions on Barney's feeding routine.

The Dog looked at me.

'I know,' I whispered. 'It's all right. Beryl's had six kids. She knows what to do with babies.' That wasn't what the Dog meant. I was leaving him. Again. And with strange people. Our new agreement was being seriously tested.

'Sorry,' I whispered. 'You'll be fine. You know Beryl. She'll look after you. I won't be late. You owe me, remember. I got rid of the cat!'

The Dog escaped through his pet door. Probably to dig a hole.

In twenty minutes flat I showered and appeared in Adrian's cramped living room. I wore my preloved Armani suit with a nippy little top, plus war paint and product-mooshed hair.

Julia looked startled, 'You're going out, Mother?'

'She's got a date. With Digby. He's a bit old!'

Thank you, Bossy Child. 'I'm going out with a friend to the opening of a local gallery. We're having a quick meal afterwards.'

'She'll be home late. Don't wait up,' Bossy Child added.

Digby aka King Arthur arrived in time to rescue me from further murky questions. I quickly introduced him to Julia and Barney. Digby didn't complain as I pushed him out the door. Attempting dating stuff with an adult daughter, grandson, Bossy Child and Beryl crowding around is not easy.

Everything was quiet and peaceful when I arrived home at the pumpkin hour. I took over the feeding of Barney. 'The baby's been an angel, Gina,' Beryl said. She and Alf left quietly.

The Dog and I discussed my date with Digby.

'I had a pleasant time. A very pleasant time! The gallery opening went smoothly. Digby made an entertaining speech. Dinner was great. Digby likes women. He knows their ways . . . he likes their company. He's excellent company. A good listener. We've a lot of stuff in common.'

Barney had fallen asleep. I guess I was talking too much about King Arthur. Trusted Dog had snuck off during the nappy-changing operation to do his possum patrol.

I was making myself a cup of tea when he returned. 'I bought a brilliant painting, Dog. All swirly blue sea and sky. Digby knows the young painter. He thinks he'll go far.'

The Dog wasn't interested. He feels he's verging on a meltdown.

Saturday 31 October

To: Gina <piececake@email.com.au>
From: Adrian <bookstreet@network.com.au>
Subject: Dinner
Heard you dined with Digby at The Palms. Great view and sensational sizzling seafood platters. I eat there frequently.

To: Adrian <bookstreet@network.com.au>
From: Gina <piececake@email.com.au>
Re: Dinner
Were the sizzling seafood platters served with or without Leonda?

To: Gina <piececake@email.com.au>
From: Adrian <bookstreet@network.com.au>
Subject: Ancient history
Ignoring comment re: my past. Will you dine with me at The Palms when I return?

To: Adrian <bookstreet@network.com.au>
From: Gina <piececake@email.com.au>
Re: Ancient history
If I'm still residing at Shelly Beach I'd be happy to accept your invitation.

I nearly broke my ankle falling over the tangle of baby equipment crowding Adrian's living room when I went to get the Dog's breakfast.

I phoned Carol to collect one renegade dog, Sally the poodle. 'She arrived late last night. I'll meet you at Bianca's, about 10, and hand her over. No problem. Having a manicure.'

Walking with two dogs and a pram is not easy. The Dog's learnt the correct protocol for walking beside a baby in a pram. Sally the poodle is hopeless. She creates a tangled mess of dog leads when she stops to investigate smells. I tied the two dogs outside Scissors – with complimentary water – and pushed sleeping Barney in his pram inside.

As she buffed my nails, Bianca segued (her new word of the week) from the importance of not letting your hands and nails fall into disrepair to dreams. 'I'm using my dreams for ideas to put in my novel.'

If I put my dreams into print it'd make a nightmare picture story-book. A book about a Templeton-type black rat called Kenneth. A big furry rat who sits on the end of your bed and spooks you out.

Carol turned up to collect Sally the poodle, with news that Henry is thankfully home and recovering well from his heart attack.

I made the Dog promise he wouldn't bring Sally home via his pet door at night without prior warning. 'And she's banned from sleeping with you on my bed. She's another cause of my rat nightmares.'

November

Thursday 5 November

I watched the Dog exit through his pet door, enter through the kitchen door, and exit through his pet door again: a nonstop circuitous route. I caught him before he started another loop and tucked him under my arm. We needed a break in the garden.

Adrian's spring garden is lush: new foliage, flowers, smells and amorous bird calls. The combined perfume of lavender and wisteria has overpowered the salty smell of the sea. I released the Dog. He raced off to check out the bungalows. No sign of Alf, Potholer or his sons. The Dog returned to my side when Barney's hungry-baby cry carried on the air into the garden.

'I know it's tough, Dog. You're stressed. I'm stressed. But it's getting better.'

The Dog gave me his fake grin; the one that highlights his sharp little teeth.

'I can't believe it's only seven days since Julia and Barney arrived. Things are working out reasonably well, though. I've been able to care for Barney while Julia's caught up on lost sleep. Julia actually seems to enjoy being with Barney now.'

I flipped back through the pages of my journal. I'd missed four days.

'Captain Bligh of the *Bounty* kept a detailed journal for the six and half weeks he was at sea with fifteen men in a very small boat. And they only had rations for five days. That's what I call serious journal-writing, Dog.'

The Dog agreed. He watched while I wrote up the four missed days.

Sunday 1 November
Julia and Barney are still at Sea View Cottage. We're helping to care for Barney. The Dog and I are stuffed.

Monday 2 November
Ditto.

Tuesday 3 November
Ditto.

Wednesday 4 November
Ditto.

Sally the poodle, a chewed rope attached to her collar, struggled through the pet door and landed with a soft thud on the kitchen floor.

'Bloody hell!' I looked at the Dog. 'You forgot to tell her she'd be in serious trouble if she left home without a leave slip.'

The Dog ignored me and went to greet Sally.

I gave the renegade Sally water, a serve of the Dog's breakfast pellets and phoned Carol. We arranged to meet at school.

Carol was apologetic when I handed Sally over. 'We're hoping she'll settle down soon. She's finding a house full of kids and other pets difficult after her quiet life with my dad.'

I agreed. I knew the Dog agreed.

Bossy Child made me promise to save the calendar ritual until tonight. She was bringing her two best friends for the unveiling of November even though it was four days late.

November's feature photo was revealed by Bossy Child to a drum roll on one of Adrian's cooking pots: a shot of weatherworn Alf, Bossy Child and two best friends (wearing their red and gold lifesaver gear) in front of the one and only Shelly Beach lifeboat.

'It was freezing. We had to wait for ages until the sun came out from behind a cloud and the photographer could take our photo.'

'Can't see one goosebump. You look cool.'

Cheerful Potholer in his work gear called in with building news. Complimentary comments were made about Alf's starring role in November on the calendar.

'Having trouble getting plumbing supplies for the bungalows, Gina. Can you let Adrian know? Advise him there'll be a delay.'

Building stuff-ups are not my problem, but I promised to notify Adrian. Potholer left after he had a cuddle of Barney. 'Babies are precious things.'

Indeed they are.

Later that evening the Dog and I grabbed a quiet star-gazing moment. Only eight weeks until his owner returns. The Dog agreed that I need to seriously think about getting a job – and somewhere to live. He thought I needed a Plan A and B. Maybe even a Plan C.

The Dog was worried. He hasn't got a plan.

'You don't need a plan. All you need to do is keep your four little paws firmly planted in Shelly Beach until Adrian returns.'

To: Adrian <bookstreet@network.com.au>
From: Gina <piececake@email.com.au>
Subject: Stop work

Alf and Potholer cannot proceed with work on the bungalows.
Waiting for plumbing supplies.
Gina

To: Gina <piececake@email.com.au>
From: Adrian <bookstreet@network.com.au>
Re: Stop work
No problem. My daughter is recovering well. I'm thinking my
grandparenting skills will not be needed much longer. How are
you coping with your daughter and grandson? Can't stop thinking
about you.
Adrian

To: Adrian <bookstreet@network.com.au>
From: Gina <piececake@email.com.au>
Re: Stop work
I'm coping well. Glad your daughter is recovering and
grandchildren are well. Barney and I saw an amazing beetle in
your garden this morning. Fashionable black with orange spaghetti
decoration on its back.
   Ignoring other comment.

Friday 6 November
To: Adrian <bookstreet@network.com.au>
From: Gina <piececake@email.com.au>
Subject: Extra dog
Hi Adrian,
How do you feel about having two dogs in your life? Henry
Shepherd's moving to his son's farm and he's not taking Sally
with him. Too much trouble for her to get into on the farm.
However, Sally keeps escaping and turning up here. (She's been
living with Henry's daughter Carol in a home that's already

brimming over with kids and pets.)

I haven't mentioned this to Carol; however, the Dog and I feel Sally probably – note 'probably' – would be happier in a quieter household with an older male owner and another small dog (and a prize Siamese cat in the new year).
Gina

To: Gina <piececake@email.com.au>
From: Adrian <bookstreet@network.com.au>
Re: Extra dog
Ignoring 'older male owner' tag. Two dogs no problem. Get Sally's registration papers changed. Buy dog basket – whatever necessary. Must go – organising grandkids' bath time. Dreaming of having a sexy bath with you at Sea View Cottage.

To: Adrian <bookstreet@network.com.au>
From: Gina <piececake@email.com.au>
Subject: Adopt a dog
Will check with Carol first to see if dog adoption is okay with her family. Then I'll proceed with the legal bit.

Any activity in your dodgy bath in Sea View Cottage's minus one-star bathroom can never be sexy.

Saturday 7 November

Adrian's Sea View Cottage is bursting at the seams. It now holds two women, one baby and two small dogs. Carol was relieved when I suggested Adrian adopt Sally. We arranged full visitation rights for her and the children.

The Dog's happy with the arrangement. I've told him to explain to Sally that things are chaotic at the moment but it will probably be quieter when Adrian returns and Princess moves in.

Julia and I were drinking our coffee on Adrian's front verandah when Bianca drove into the driveway. She brought her car to a stop with a squeal of brakes and bounded onto the verandah, brandishing a sparkler on the fourth finger of her left hand.

'Can you believe it?! Josh proposed to me again. He got the ring back from Mum. She knew all along.' Bianca was glowing. 'We're getting married soon – in about three weeks. It's sudden but we know it's the right thing to do. Only taking a two-day honeymoon because Josh has to finish the school term.'

Bianca took a breath. She did that flappy fan movement with her hands that the Dog so hates. And then she continued.

'I'm moving into Josh's house – as soon as he ditches the disco ball and smoke machine from his bedroom. We've decided to work at Sea Haven Resort over the holidays. Josh is doing the kids' holiday program. I'm doing massages and nails. We'll try to pay off his mortgage as soon as possible!

'Isn't it unbelievable, Gina? It's so romantic. Just like a novel. Probably better.'

I agreed with my writerly young friend. Sometimes life can be better than a novel.

'Mum said you're awesome at organising stuff. Would you be able to help me plan our wedding? We want a fairytale wedding at budget prices.'

The Dog overheard this comment and raised a hairy eyebrow. He followed me to the kitchen while I made coffee.

'How much time does it take to help plan a budget wedding and assist at a collectors' fair? Maybe I'll need to get a Plan D up and running in case I run out of time for plans A, B and C?'

The Dog hadn't a clue how much time it takes to help organise a collectors' fair *or* a budget fairytale wedding. He thought some people use doing stuff for other people as an excellent excuse to put off doing really important stuff for themselves, like finding a job, a place to live and writing a novel.

The Dog thought if you kept avoiding stuff one day it would come back to bite you.

Small dogs can be so annoying. Flea-picking!

Julia and Bianca were engrossed in the bridal magazines Bianca had brought with her. We spent the remainder of the evening brainstorming and planning a budget fairytale wedding that's to take place in a little less than three weeks.

Bloody hell!

To: Adrian <bookstreet@network.com.au>
From: Gina <piececake@email.com.au>
Subject: Wedding
Hi Adrian,
Good news! Josh has popped the question – again. And of course Bianca said yes. She would love it if you could give her away, but they're getting married on 27 November. Obviously you won't be back by then and they don't want to delay things. Bianca asked me to send you this email because she's worried you might be hurt by this. She hopes you understand.
Gina

To: Gina <piececake@email.com.au>
From: Adrian <bookstreet@network.com.au>
Re: Wedding
Hi Gina,
Tell Bianca of course I understand. I'm sorry I'll miss their wedding but I'll hold a party for them when I return in the new year.

Speaking of partners, we make a great team. Would you consider a short-term commitment when I return to Shelly Beach? Better still, would you consider a long-term commitment? Will you marry me?

To: Adrian <bookstreet@network.com.au>
From: Gina <piececake@email.com.au>
Subject: Insane
No time to consider teamwork or commitments – short or long.
And re: your last question, WHAT KIND OF QUESTION IS THAT?
Are you *mad*?! WE HARDLY KNOW EACH OTHER. A one-night
stand and two short meetings do not constitute a sound basis for
marriage.

To: Gina <piececake@email.com.au>
From: Adrian <bookstreet@network.com.au>
Re: Insane
Four meetings, if you count our first meeting at your daughter's
home when you were an appealing tragic mess, the breakfast
meeting in the city, our handover meeting at Sea View Cottage and
our last can't-get-you-out-of-my-mind Shelly Beach encounter.

To: Adrian <bookstreet@network.com.au>
From: Gina <piececake@email.com.au>
Re: Insane
Whatever. Ignoring ridiculous proposal and resuming professional
communication.

Sunday 8 – Monday 9 November

Two ordinary days full of chores – washing, cleaning, cooking, walking
Barney and dogs. Although I did have an interesting writerly discussion with the Dog while I followed him around the garden as he did
his moonlight possum patrol (he's not afraid but he likes company).

'Two interesting questions, Dog. Question one: if you were writing a novel, would you create a hot older woman as your protagonist?
And question two: if you decided to make the hot older woman your
protagonist, what age would you make her romantic interest?'

The Dog hates writerly questions. He refused to answer in case it would incriminate him.

Tuesday 10 November

Barney needed more baby supplies so the dogs and I took a trek to Jenkins' Store. Shelly Beach writers don't hide their emerging talents. Standing in line at Jenkins' checkout queue (Josh in front of me, Daphne behind me) I was bombarded by details of plot points and character development.

Up till now Josh has been deeply embarrassed talking about his novel. 'Never been able to talk about it – other than getting advice from my creative writing lecturer at uni.'

Daphne and I understood.

Bianca joined the end of the queue. 'Bill came in for a trim the other day, Gina. I suggested he tell us about his writing day at our next writers' group meeting.'

'Good idea.'

'Josh and I need how-to tips to help us with our work–life balance after we're married. How can we squeeze time to write into our lives?'

A tricky question to answer. Fortunately Josh completed his purchases. He blew Bianca a kiss and gave me an isn't-she-wonderful look as he raced out the door carrying his groceries. Time for an answer to Bianca's question had passed.

'Lifesaving season has started. He's off to training.' Bianca's eyes followed her Josh adoringly as he left the scene.

Daphne and I allowed Bianca to queue-jump. 'I only need milk. I've a customer due for a Braz wax in five minutes. Gina, you have to be stand-in for Adrian at the next action committee meeting. It'll be about the collectors' fair.'

'Right.'

As she raced off to do her waxing, Bianca shouted over her

shoulder, 'Meeting's at 7, Gina, at Rosa's. Bring Barney. No one will care.'

Violet joined the queue. I did a quick vanishing act.

To: Adrian <bookstreet@network.com.au>
From: Gina <piececake@email.com.au>
Subject: Flyscreens
Hi Adrian,
Just letting you know the dogs have eaten the insect screens on your windows and doors (bottom halves). Alf wants to know if it's okay to replace them? He says you'd realise this job is a priority knowing the flies and bugs that invade Shelly Beach during summer.
Gina

To: Gina <piececake@email.com.au>
From: Adrian <bookstreet@network.com.au>
Re: Flyscreens
Tell Alf to go ahead and repair insect screens.

Any news about the collectors' fair? It'd be good to have a ballpark figure when I'm negotiating Writefest visiting author payments with publishers.

Working on a new marriage proposal to submit to you.

To: Adrian <bookstreet@network.com.au>
From: Gina <piececake@email.com.au>
Subject: Still no
It'll be rejected.

I'm going to an action committee meeting on Friday. Will fill you in. I'd hold negotiations re: payment for authors until the fair actually takes place and we can count the return.

Wednesday 11 November

Chasing my tail lately. (The Dog understands this metaphor.) Julia held the fort (baby and dogs) while I cycled to Bill's today. We had writers' group tonight and I'd got the guilts because I hadn't been in contact with our tutor recently.

Bill's wife Deb was pleased to see me. 'What do you think?'

Deb pointed to a dodgy table and a red-painted chair pushed against the wall. The table held a red tumbler of pens and pencils, book-ended writers' references and a vase of red geraniums. A stack of paper took centre stage on the table.

'I've been designing a writing place for Bill. The red accent's for energy. What do you think about the geraniums? Are they too much? Should there be a photo of Hunter and me?'

Thankfully Deb continued before I could answer. 'A city journalist is coming tomorrow to interview Bill. She's doing an article about his writing place. Since Hunter started walking, Bill writes on his laptop in the car, which isn't very photogenic. Although sometimes he writes at the ocean beach after he's been surfing.

'Bill's a shocking worrier. Adrian's been emailing him, telling him to think like a surfer. Paddle out to catch a wave. Enjoy it while it lasts. Go back and catch another. Don't waste time trying to prolong the wave, or worrying if you miss one. I'm not sure it's getting through to Bill. Do you think Bill should tell the journalist he writes mainly in our car when it's parked in the driveway?'

'Why not? Writing at a surf beach and in a parked car will make for a great feature article.'

'Yes . . . you're right. Bill's not coping with the publicity, though. He's already written a hundred pages of his third novel – he's in a good space in his head, and he just wants to write.'

We walked outside to Bill's real writing place – the family car. It was empty. Bill had left a yellow Post-it note on the dashboard: *Gone surfing*.

Deb breathed a sigh of relief. 'He always feels better after he's been surfing. I'm glad he's taking writers' group tonight. It'll take his mind off the journalist coming tomorrow.'

I thought for a moment. 'Pandora's into marketing and publicity stuff. I'll ask her if she'll help Bill with a few tips.'

Deb planted a kiss on my cheek. 'Thank you, Gina. Care for a cup of coffee? Hunter's not due to wake up from his morning nap yet.'

I thought of the chaos awaiting me at Sea View Cottage. 'I'd love one. Make it black and strong.'

Over coffee Deb chatted. She needed to have a good chat. 'It's not easy having a writer as your life partner. They have lots of downs – not many ups.

'Bill's definitely a glass-half-empty person. He's a born and bred Shelly Beacher. Very clever – introspective. You probably know his dad was the local doctor. Everyone thought Bill would be a doctor – follow in his father's footsteps – but Bill wanted to be a writer. He did his building apprenticeship with Alf. Bill figured he'd build houses during the day and write at night.'

Deb left to listen at Hunter's door. 'He's still asleep.' She poured me another cup of coffee – strong and black – and continued with her narrative.

'I'm a Kingston girl. Definitely a glass-half-full person. Went to university in Kingston. I met Bill at Rosa's. I took a summer job there before I was due to take up a teaching position at Shelly Beach. Bill came into the pub every day for ages before he plucked up the courage to ask me out on a date. I started teaching at Shelly Beach in January that year and we got married in the June.

'Bill took two years to write his first novel. Adrian was excellent. He arranged for a publishing friend to look at it – and that was that. Bill's novel was accepted. Just as well. Bill's first advance kept us going for a while. We had Hunter soon after. I stopped teaching – and Bill wrote his second novel. The one that's getting published now.'

I finished my coffee. The back story of hardworking Bill Kruger, definitely not a locked-in-an-ivory-tower author, was complete. 'I'll talk to Pandora. I'm sure she'll be able to help Bill. I must get back to Julia and the baby.'

I phoned Pandora when I returned home. 'Can you give Bill some PR tips tonight without making it too obvious? A journalist is interviewing him tomorrow. Deb says he's basically having a meltdown.'

'Not a problem. Would you like a lift to the meeting tonight?'

Julia was deep in a phone call to Simon, Barney was fretful and the dogs were charging around the garden like the hounds of the Baskervilles.

'Thank you.'

The Dog declined to accompany me to the writers' group meeting – he preferred to stay at home with Sally. When Sally's not encouraging the Dog to go on a destroy-Adrian's-cottage mission she takes dognaps. When Sally dognaps the Dog makes time for chats with me – which is nice.

The Dog was waiting up when I returned from the meeting. I made a cup of tea and filled him in on the goss. 'It was hardly a jumping-off-the-roof meeting. No one's finished editing Violet's whodunnit. Members are having trouble coping with the way the murderer disposes of the body.'

The Dog was interested in hearing Violet's plotline – but in a two-sentence pitch. He believes the story has potential. If he was a reader, and he still could become a reader in his mellow older-dog years, he'd choose to read crime fiction to relax.

To: Adrian <bookstreet@network.com.au>
From: Gina <piececake@email.com.au>
Subject: Writers' group

Hi Adrian,

Gruesome meeting. Members are editing one of Violet's whodunnits. We were sent home with Violet's nightmare content stuffed into our brains, e.g. minced dead body, frozen and packed in small plastic bags and kept in a freezer. The murderer defrosts one bag of her minced partner's body at a time and feeds it to the worms in her compost bin.

- Daphne had reasonable constructive criticism. She said some readers would have trouble suspending belief because most people know it's not advisable to put meat in a compost bin.
- Bianca said that it's going to take her yonks before she can look Violet in the eye again – get back to the woman-who-loves-cats persona.
- Pandora took part of the meeting and demonstrated her spin-doctor expertise. We roleplayed 'How to cope with your fifteen minutes of fame'. (Bill's getting interviewed tomorrow and his publishers have planned a whistle-stop tour to promote his second novel.)

Group voted to skip next meeting to attend Bill's book launch in city bookshop. Digby's organized a thirty-six-seater bus so members can attend Bill's launch.

Gina

To: Gina <piececake@email.com.au>
From: Adrian <bookstreet@network.com.au>
Re: Writers' group

Suspending disbelief and accepting Violet's plot. Great idea to hire bus to transport members to Bill's book launch. Would love to be in bus with you.

On the back seat.

Thursday 12 November

Violet hammered on the door. 'I've some more chapters of my novel for you to give to the members. Met Gail and Pandora at Jenkins'. They'll be here in a moment. I'd die for a cup of tea. Have you any of your chocolate mud cake? You look terrible, Gina!'

'With just cause,' I muttered to the Dog as I made the tea. 'So would any (young) grandmother if she was operating a basic holiday cottage with appalling plumbing, coping with an exhausted daughter, a three-month-old grandson plus two demented dogs.'

The Dog ignored the 'demented dogs' bit.

He heard me mutter under my breath, 'I'm not ill – just sleep-deprived!'

My sleep deprivation is due to hours of helping settle Barney and having lots of talks with Julia.

Last night I told Julia I was unbelievably proud of her. 'You've had a hands-off mother, a free-flow father and grandmother, and look at you. A young woman known for her amazing drive, focus and clarity of vision.'

'Really, Gina?'

'Yes. Just wait. When you get back on track – and when you want to get back on track – you'll be firing. Heaven knows how you do it.'

'Hereditary! Thank you, Mother!'

Julia went to attend to Barney.

I told the Dog that was the best compliment I'd ever received.

Violet brought me back to reality.

'You really do look like something the cat dragged in, Gina.'

'Hate Violet's sick jokes,' I whispered to the Dog as I handed her a cup of tea and slice of chocolate cake.

Gail and Pandora arrived. 'Have you checked your email today?'

'Not this morning.'

'Adrian wants to open Piece of Cake for the summer season. He wants the three of us to joint-manage it.'

298

'I was thinking about doing the nanny thing for Barney. Maybe for a year or two.'

Pandora looked horrified. 'Geen-ah! Have you spoken to Julia about this?'

I shook my head. In all our talks there hadn't been a word mentioned about my nannying.

Violet took over. 'Does Julia want you to be Barney's nanny?'

'She did earlier this year.'

Violet gave me an exasperated look and marched out of the room.

'She's going to talk to Julia, isn't she?'

Pandora nodded. 'I'd say that's what she's going to do.'

'Bloody hell!'

I poured tea for them and we drank it in silence. After what seemed like an eternity, Violet marched back into the room. 'Julia doesn't require your services as a nanny, Gina. She's coming out now to talk to you about it.'

'Right.'

'Email Adrian. You can open Piece of Cake next week.'

I took control. 'Maybe the week after, depending on the paperwork.'

We agreed that we'd be joint managers. Gail and I could do with the work. Pandora's happy to fill in time until she can get her B&B up and running.

Violet left as quickly as she arrived. 'Don't forget to distribute my new chapters to the members, Gina. They need an edit.'

'Right!'

Julia came into the room and gave me a hug. 'Simon and I have been talking.'

'How?'

'On our mobiles.'

'Right.'

'We've decided to downsize. Sell our house. Move to something smaller. No nanny! I'll stay home and look after Barney for a year.

Maybe two. Work from home. Can Barney and I stay until Simon returns from his business trip?'

'Of course you can.'

More hugs and tears. I felt a slight twinge of relief. Correction: huge twinge.

Pandora, Gail and I spent the rest of the day working out costs, menus, etc. Emails zoomed back and forth in cyberspace.

We worked out shifts to cover a seven-day week opening 10 to 4.30 – and we negotiated above-award wages with Adrian.

We were working on a simple menu – excellent coffee and tea choices, scones with jam and cream, sandwiches and cake of the day – when Julia answered the phone. 'Gina, it's the school. You forgot to pick up Terri.'

Bloody hell. I grabbed Pandora's car keys and raced out the door.

That night the Dog and I sat on Adrian's verandah and contemplated the moon. 'That's blown Plan A – to become Barney's nanny and live in a comfortable city flatlet. Now I'm left with a pear-shaped Plan B – part-time work in a bookshop cafe. However, I still have a Plan C simmering and maybe a wobbly Plan D.'

The Dog thinks working at Piece of Cake for the summer season is an excellent short-term solution. All I need to do is find somewhere to live. And I'm still Barney's grandmother.

'True. But not his nanny.'

To: Adrian <bookstreet@network.com.au>
From: Gina <piececake@email.com.au>
Subject: Job offer
You could have asked me first re: opening Piece of Cake.

To: Gina <piececake@email.com.au>
From: Adrian <bookstreet@network.com.au>
Re: Job offer

I sent a group email to you and Gail and Pandora. They read their emails. You didn't read yours.

To: Adrian <bookstreet@network.com.au>
From: Gina <piececake@email.com.au>
Re: Job offer
Right! What will you do if your three joint managers stuff up Piece of Cake?

To: Gina <piececake@email.com.au>
From: Adrian <bookstreet@network.com.au>
Re: Job offer
Not a problem! I'd race the gorgeous red-headed, green-eyed joint manager to Hawaii. We'd get married on the beach. I'd employ a new manager. Change my cafe name to Slice of Pie. Put up a sign: *Change of Management*. The owner and red-headed former joint manager would live happily ever after in a chic apartment with a 360-degree view of Shelly Beach bay.

To: Adrian <bookstreet@network.com.au>
From: Gina <piececake@email.com.au>
Re: Job offer
You've been reading too many fairytales to your grandkids!

Friday 13 November

Very little of the usual blah-blah-blah (a Bianca description) at the action committee meeting. It began with fireworks. Digby announced he wanted the collectors' fair to open with a splash on the Friday night. 'I've decided to host a black-tie benefit event – a drinks party for selected guests – at the castle. Entrance: a sizable donation.'

A stunned silence met his announcement.

'I've pulled off a package deal with the manager of Sea Haven

301

Resort. After drinks at my place, guests will be bussed to Sea Haven for dinner.'

'Can't be trusted, that man. Goes off like a loose cannon,' Violet muttered in an audible whisper.

Digby ignored concerned looks and rumblings from the members and continued to reveal his entrepreneurial money-making one-man plan.

'Sea Haven Resort is providing the services of its waiters. I've organised a donation of champagne from a local winery, and I'll donate the cash for food.' Then came his soft-sell smile: 'I was hoping action committee members could prepare the food.'

Rosa was not pleased. 'Taking trade away from locals.'

Grumbling from the seated members confirmed Rosa's opinion, however Daphne saved the day. Did her conciliatory bit. 'We can't knock a sure-fire money-maker. And it's a great introduction for out-of-towners to Shelly Beach.'

Rosa could see the logic in Daphne's argument. 'Well . . . if it's only a one-time event. And I suppose people will be back at Shelly Beach for the fair the next day.'

True.

Members grudgingly voted for Digby's drinks party to proceed.

Pandora whispered in my ear, 'Digby forgets he's working with volunteers.'

I agreed.

For the remainder of the meeting committee members went into detailed planning: publicity, parking, allocation of stalls for sellers etc. and, most importantly, the number of sausages needed for the sausage sizzle.

'Not much time left for marketing,' remarked Pandora. 'But we'll manage.'

As we were leaving, Violet tossed Digby an extra fundraising idea. 'How about your guests hire heritage costumes from the Sea Haven

Theatrical Company for your party? The costumes are cleaned at the end of every production.'

Digby graciously declined Violet's offer.

I left to return to my overcrowded cottage.

To: Adrian <bookstreet@network.com.au>
From: Gina <piececake@email.com.au>
Subject: Collectors' fair
Organisation for collectors' fair is bubbling along. Digby's planning a drinks party at his castle with help from Sea Haven Resort, a local winery and voluntary labour from action committee members. Asking a hefty donation from guests. He's done a deal with Sea Haven Resort to provide a collection fair package. Package includes two nights' accommodation and use of the facilities at the resort. Hopefully guests will return during the weekend sometime for the fair. With a bit of luck this event – last one – should help fill your coffers for celeb author/s.

To: Gina <piececake@email.com.au>
From: Adrian <bookstreet@network.com.au>
Re: Collectors' fair
Sounds promising. Would love to be there with you.

Saturday 14 November
Bianca's team of wedding planners – Bossy Child, Joan, Daphne, Gail and self – arrived to discuss the wedding. The glamorous, romantic, once-in-a-lifetime fairytale wedding – with a very short planning time. I set the table. Bianca arrived soon after with Sea Haven pizzas.

Over coffee Bianca stunned me with an out-of-the-blue invitation. 'Will you be my chief bridesmaid, Gina?'

Bloody hell! I took a deep breath. A tactful answer was required. 'I presumed you'd ask your sister to be chief bridesmaid, Bianca.'

Mother-of-the-bride jumped in. 'Unfortunately Crystal can't make it back in time for the wedding. She's working up north.'

'Unfortunately! Fortunately! I'm not having Crystal anywhere near my wedding.' My sweet-natured Bianca was breathing fire. 'It'll be murder if Crystal shows up!'

My writer's brain instantly formulated a sensational plotline for a crime fiction novel: *Chief bridesmaid's multiple-stabbed body found on church altar*. Or an alternative plot: *Best man found strangled in the vestry*.

'Bianca doesn't really mean it, Gina.' Mother-of-the-bride was rubbing her daughter's back.

'Right!' I concentrated on the task at hand. 'You don't want to ask a friend from school, Bianca?'

'I wouldn't know which friend to ask. All my friends are best friends. We've all been together since grade one. You can't have ten chief bridesmaids, can you?'

'Well, you could.'

I acknowledged frantic, negative body language from the wedding planners.

'It's probably a too-hard call. It could be a challenge to find preloved colour-coordinated wedding gear for ten bridesmaids – and at short notice.'

I noted relieved body language from the wedding planners.

Stressed bride-to-be, oblivious of said language being sent back and forth across the room, continued, 'Terri is going to be junior bridesmaid. She's a perfect match for Josh's young brother: right age, right height.

'We thought, considering your height, Gina, you'd be a perfect match for Josh's best man Kevin. He's the drummer in Josh's band. Don't worry about the age difference.'

Bossy Child was staring at me.

I nodded, smiled, and accepted defeat. 'I'd love to be your chief bridesmaid, Bianca.'

Sighs of relief from the wedding planners. Bianca beamed. Bossy Child nodded her approval and gave her Cheshire-cat grin. We exchanged kisses and hugs, swung into high-powered wedding planning, and got stuck at no. 1 on my list – the bride's and attendants' frocks.

It was decided that Bianca, Gail and Daphne would trek to the city on Monday. Mission: to find dresses for the wedding party. Daphne had already rung her contacts in the vintage wedding gear trade. 'I have the addresses of several shops. We're sure to pick up some gorgeous preloved wedding gear.'

Julia joined us from the bedroom. Barney was settled for the night. The rest of the evening was spent looking through bridal magazines ad infinitum.

'Would you like to come with us on Monday, Gina?'

'I'd love to, but the health department guys from Kingston Council are coming to give the okay to open Piece of Cake.'

Everyone understood.

Daphne took my measurements. 'You've lost even more weight, Gina. You're a size eight now.'

(The Dog is positive the walking has been the cause of my weight loss. I'm not allowing him one smidgen of credit.)

'What do you think, Dog? If the chief bridesmaid gets murdered, can she change from a minor character to a major character?'

The Dog thinks it depends on the back story – for example, how much does the reader know about the chief bridesmaid before she gets the chop?!

To: Adrian <bookstreet@network.com.au>
From: Gina <piececake@email.com.au>
Subject: Vegetable plot
Checking your house-sitters' manual. Not sure what you mean by 'plant spring vegetable crop in first weeks of November'. Do you want me to employ a gardener?

On second thoughts, a gardener would be useless. Sally the poodle has joined the Dog in transforming your back garden into a dinosaur excavation site.

Gina

To: Gina <piececake@email.com.au>
From: Adrian <bookstreet@network.com.au>
Re: Vegetable plot
Don't worry. We'll plant out a vegetable plot when I return.

To: Adrian <bookstreet@network.com.au>
From: Gina <piececake@email.com.au>
Re: Vegetable plot
Refusing offer of unromantic date to plant a vegetable plot when you return.

Sunday 15 November

It's Julia and Barney's last day at Sea View Cottage. Barney and I took a final stroll around Adrian's garden. He said goodbye to Adrian's Girls, helped collect their eggs and put birdseed in the doves' cote.

Barney likes watching the doves as they waddle around Adrian's verandah on their hunt for crumbs and insects. We did a last count of Adrian's goldfish. Three missing; probably an à la carte meal for Princess when she was here. I wrote a mental Post-it note: *Replace three goldfish before Adrian returns.*

After breakfast, Barney and I checked Adrian's inbox.

To: Gina <piececake@email.com.au>
From: Eva <eva@slick-promotions.com>
Subject: Job offer
Hi Gina,
Hester and I are going into the corporate team-building business.

We'll be organising professional team-building days – circus workshops, tank and jet fighter rides, meditation, etc. etc. How would you like a job as our admin guru? Starting in the new year. Excellent salary package: car, travelling and accommodation on the firm. Could you get back to us by 30 November?
Love Eva

To: Eva <eva@slick-promotions.com>
From: Gina <piececake@email.com.au>
Re: Job offer
Hi Eva,
Appreciate the job offer. Will definitely get a decision to you by 30 November.
Love Gina

I shut down Adrian's computer. 'No time for decisions today, Barney. We have to pack. You're going home with your mum and dad. You can visit Grandma for holidays when you're bigger. Grandma might be living at the North Pole by then. We can build a snowman.'

Simon arrived at 10 to collect his wife and child. This time he left his BlackBerry in the car and came inside for coffee. Julia and he have been compiling house rules. Simon's promised to be home in time for dinner at least twice a week. Way to go, Simon!

I was helping Julia collect Barney's baby gear, distributed through-out Adrian's cottage, when Digby arrived. He wanted to discuss Bill's book launch. 'We're short on numbers for the bus booking, Gina.'

Digby chatted to Simon. 'It's easy to mistake Julia and Gina for sisters.'

A flash of displeasure crossed Julia's face – but just for a brief moment. It had passed by the time Digby did his charm thing. He farewelled Julia with a bottle of his best fizz and a bunch of yellow roses. He produced a squashy blue elephant for Barney.

Well done, Digby!

Digby helped Simon store Julia and Barney's gear in the car – an incredible stack of survival equipment for one small baby.

We exchanged hugs and kisses and buckets of tears. Digby, the dogs and I waved and watched Simon's car until it disappeared down Sea Spray Street.

'Care for dinner at Rosa's, Gina?'

I looked at two angelic dogs giving me their cute puppy-dog looks.

'The dogs will be fine, Gina. They kept running away to be together.'

True.

I accepted Digby's offer and made the dogs promise not to eat another piece of Adrian's cottage. 'When Adrian returns you can eat as much as you like.'

Rosa's was the best place to recruit participants for the bus trip to the city and Bill's book launch. Bianca did the rounds of the tables and came back with a promise of thirty-four passengers for Wednesday. 'It was easy. Everyone loves Bill. They want his second novel to sell well.'

That night I told the Dog of the new job offer from my friends.

The Dog's advice is to think about the offer very carefully. He says it's no fun digging a hole if you can't get out of it.

To: Adrian <bookstreet@network.com.au>
From: Gina <piececake@email.com.au>
Subject: Cottage occupant tally
Julia and Barney have left Sea View Cottage. One female and two dogs are residing in your cottage at present. One prize Siamese cat gives us snooty looks from the window of Jenkins' Store when we go shopping. You might have a spot of canine anti-barking training to do when you return.

I'm considering a corporate job offer in the new year; however, I will be able to work at Piece of Cake during the summer season.

To: Gina <piececake@email.com.au>

From: Adrian <bookstreet@network.com.au>

Re: Cottage occupant tally

Appreciate your dedication and commitment to Piece of Cake. I'd seriously consider the pros and cons of taking a corporate job in the city. Do you want to join the rat-race again?

'None of Adrian's business, Dog,' I muttered as I shut down the computer.

Monday 16 November

Pandora and I breathed a sigh of relief when the health and safety guy gave the all clear to open Piece of Cake for business. The fact that I have a job – albeit a short-term one – is a comforting thought – although I have the option of a corporate job with a better salary in the new year.

My beat-the-wedding-industry planners returned exhausted but victorious from their excursion to the city. As the dresses were unpacked and draped over the furniture, Adrian's living room took on a rosy glow. The bride will wear the palest of pink, junior bridesmaid hot pink, mother of the bride dusky-rose pink and the chief brides-maid . . . cyclamen pink.

After the wedding planners left I dealt with my cyclamen-pink anger by stomping down the dogs' holes in Adrian's garden. 'I hate cyclamen pink. Why does the chief bridesmaid have to wear cycla-men pink? It's so pink.'

The Dog couldn't get a handle on cyclamen pink. Sally the poo-dle could. In a former life Sally wore a lot of pink.

'It's pink. Very pink! Why can't the chief bridesmaid get to wear the dusky-rose pink number?'

The Dog couldn't get a handle on dusky-rose pink either. We were searching for a dusky-rose pink in Adrian's garden when the dogs were diverted. A frog had jumped out of the pond.

'I could have been like the classic frog that died because she didn't realise the water she sat in was gradually reaching boiling point.'

The dogs had no idea what I was talking about.

To: Gina <piececake@email.com.au>
From: Adrian <bookstreet@network.com.au>
Subject: Shelving
I've arranged for boxes of secondhand books I've stored at Tania's to be delivered to Piece of Cake. Can you ditch the military books (leave them in Rosa's shed) and shelve the writing how-to's in their place?

Cyberspace informs me that Bianca's wedding has a pink palette and the chief bridesmaid is wearing cyclamen pink. Wow!

'Sometimes, Dog, your owner's emails make me feel like I've put lemon juice on a paper cut. He has no idea how to play the flirting game online.'

The Dog had no idea you could flirt online. We moved on.

To: Adrian <bookstreet@network.com.au>
From: Gina <piececake@email.com.au>
Re: Shelving
Council has given us the all clear to open Piece of Cake. Are you happy if we open on Monday 23?

Will unpack new secondhand books, pack military books and shelve how-to-write books. I'll invoice you under librarian hourly rates. Ignoring unprofessional comment about the chief bridesmaid.

Tuesday 17 November
To: Gina <piececake@email.com.au>
From: Adrian <bookstreet@network.com.au>

Subject: Opening date

23 November sounds great! Uniforms – one-size-fits-all T-shirts and chefs' wraparound aprons – will be in one of the cupboards in Crow's Nest Flat.

To: Adrian <bookstreet@network.com.au>
From: Gina <piececake@email.com.au>
Re: Opening date

Found the uniforms. Black is cool. We're pretending multicoloured Piece of Cake branding on our backs is invisible.

We've changed our minds about opening date. We're happy to open cafe each day through the summer season – except for 27 November: Bianca and Josh's wedding date. Should we wait until after the wedding to open?

To: Gina <piececake@email.com.au>
From: Adrian <bookstreet@network.com.au>
Re: Opening date

Stick to original opening date and close cafe for wedding. If I know Bianca and Josh, they will have invited every Shelly Beach local to their wedding. Have you found the tablecloths and napkins?

To: Adrian <bookstreet@network.com.au>
From: Gina <piececake@email.com.au>
Re: Opening date

Alf has located crockery and tablecloths and napkins – made an executive decision to use paper napkins. Too much laundry.

All set to go. Will keep you informed.

To: Gina <piececake@email.com.au>
From: Adrian <bookstreet@network.com.au>
Re: Opening date

Thank you. All my love. Don't you dare leave Shelly Beach until I return. I want to take you dancing in that cyclamen-pink dress.

Wednesday 18 November

A crowd of excited Bill supporters gathered at the community hall in the late afternoon. Violet had organised welcoming cups of tea, coffee and sandwiches. 'It's a long trip to the city and there's no guarantee there'll be sustaining food at the other end.'

True.

'We go in hope but expect the worst.' This is Violet's realistic view of an excursion outside Shelly Beach.

Hamish, Shelly Beach's local bus driver, survived the city traffic. Just. 'Miserable fricking drive!' he muttered as he tipped us onto the pavement outside the bookstore at 7. 'If you're not standing on the pavement by 9 . . .' (Hamish's Cinderella hour) 'I'm leaving without you.'

Shelly Beach residents empathised with Hamish and accepted his deadline. When you haven't driven in the city for two years the traffic can be a nightmare.

Hamish snapped as the bus door was closing, 'Now I need a fricking miracle to find a fricking place to park!' We watched with grimaced faces while Hamish accelerated his bus and darted into the traffic.

'Like a ferret down a rabbit hole,' was Violet's comment.

Sounds of clinking glasses and the high-powered buzz of trendy black-clad publishing types enjoying free wine came from the bookstore. We collected a frozen smile from the PR chick and a publisher's bag of freebies. Bill Kruger's groupies were crossing the drawbridge into the world of the literati.

Platters of doll-sized food were on tables in the bookstore's cafe. Wine was discreetly dispensed by polite, smiling waiters.

Pandora was impressed. 'No expense spared. Amazing, considering the cuts publishing firms are making.'

Daphne and hubby Charles, members of the Shelly Beach paparazzi and fortunately not affected by tough economic times, deserted us to move through the crowd. They wanted front-row positions. Charles was taking photos to accompany Daphne's piece about Bill for the *Sea Haven Sentinel*.

Digby left us to network. He'd spotted a group of university colleagues. The remainder of Bill's groupies clung like limpets on a rock in the self-help section. Publishing aficionados, clutching glasses and standing in their allocated square centimetres of space, spilled out of the children's books section and into popular fiction.

Our Bill stared down at us from posters. Bianca and Deb were elated. They'd worked hard on Bill's styling. The single earring worked well; it added a nautical look to Shelly Beach's shortlisted author.

Bill delivered his practised two-minute grab without a hitch. Deb and Pandora were like starstruck mums at a school play, silently mouthing each word. The only sign of Bill's nerves was when his hands started shaking. He quickly shoved his hands into his pockets (Pandora's tip).

After Bill's publisher's big guns finished their spruiking, we quickly formed a queue in front of the signing table. Pandora had decided on this strategy before we left Shelly Beach. 'Everyone has to buy a copy of Bill's novel. Get it signed. Create a must-read buzz!'

We watched Pandora weave her way through the sea of black. She'd left us to work the room: 'I want to gauge the vibe for the book.'

Clad in classy city armour, exposing just the right amount of cleavage and flashing a determined smile, Pandora looked formidable. After the book signing, we voted to return to the cafe area and relocate the food and wine. Digby returned to our group. He assured us the fizz was a top vintage.

At Hamish's Cinderella hour, Bill's groupies gathered outside the bookstore. The bus appeared like a phantom out of the mist. It scooped us from the pavement at exactly 9 (Bianca language).

Violet warned Hamish, 'If you use one more swear word on the way home, I'll report you to the bus company.'

'Hollow threat,' she whispered to me. 'Hamish is the Shelly Beach bus company. Owns the two buses. It works sometimes.'

The free fizz delivered its soporific effect to Shelly Beach's passengers. As we left the city, the bus filled with dream bubbles, all containing emerging writers' fifteen minutes of fame at their yet-to-be book launches.

Digby's head was slumped on my shoulder. He was gently snoring. Every time he exhaled the left side of his top lip rippled. I wondered if King Arthur had ever snored. Probably not. Too busy fighting the good fight when he wasn't chatting up Queen Guinevere.

I jiggled my shoulder but Digby's head stayed firmly glued to it until we arrived at Shelly Beach community hall.

To: Adrian <bookstreet@network.com.au>
From: Gina <piececake@email.com.au>
Subject: Bill's novel
Hi Adrian,
Bill conquered his nerves. His book launch was a success. How do you feel about selling signed copies of Bill's novel in Piece of Cake? We could build a display around them in the book section: *Shelly Beach's Successful Local Author!*

To: Gina <piececake@email.com.au>
From: Adrian <bookstreet@network.com.au>
Re: Bill's novel
Good idea. Get signed copies – however many you think we can move. I'm glad Bill conquered his nerves. He still has unhealed wounds from the author signing for his first novel.

To: Adrian <bookstreet@network.com.au>
From: Gina <piececake@email.com.au>
Re: Bill's novel
Have asked locals who bought a signed copy at the launch to resell to Piece of Cake. Will re-order when necessary.

Aware of Bill's author-signing debacle. He told us how he sat for two hours and signed two books while the celebrity cookbook author sitting next to him signed hundreds of books. Pandora says this is about average if you write literary fiction. Cookbooks with good visuals always sell well. Fantasy ten times more than science fiction. Definitely planning to write fantasy if I decide to write another novel.

To: Gina <piececake@email.com.au>
From: Adrian <bookstreet@network.com.au>
Subject: Zzzz
Bill's a fortunate young author to have mentors like you and Pandora. Received a cyberspace photo of the launch. Thought you'd like to know that I don't snore.

To: Adrian <bookstreet@network.com.au>
From: Gina <piececake@email.com.au>
Re: Zzzz
Neither do I.

To: Gina <piececake@email.com.au>
From: Adrian <bookstreet@network.com.au>
Re: Zzzz
You do.

Bloody hell!

Thursday 19 November

Pandora, Gail, and I negotiated our bulk supplies for Piece of Cake from Jenkins' Store. Jody is anticipating trouble in sourcing supplies of low-fat soy milk. 'I'll give it a go, luv.'

We organised the kitchen area of the cafe so we could satisfy customers in the blink of an eye, and grabbed the opportunity to do practice runs with coffee and toasted sandwiches for Alf, Potholer and sons. They like to linger over their lattes – 'Takeaway coffees bounce around and spill in your truck.'

True.

Digby undertook some coffee sampling: flat white, long black, mocha, macchiato and espresso. Verdict: 'Great coffee.' We have coffee muscles to prove it.

The dogs and I collected Bossy Child from school for a serious try-on of the bride's and bridesmaids' dresses at Daphne's. There were ooos, aahhs and tears as we gazed at Bianca in her floaty fairytale dress.

Bianca's dress was a meringue of pale pink tulle plus added metres from the frothy train and veil – dangerous territory for bridesmaids. Bossy Child was loving herself to death in her dress – another tulle concoction guaranteed to immediately transform the wearer into a princess barbie doll.

My cyclamen-pink satin number was a wearer's nightmare.

Daphne gave me instructions. 'Stand correctly, Gina. Shoulders back, stomach in. Concentrate on your posture for the ceremony and photos. You can relax at the reception.'

Thank you, Daphne.

Joan arrived to collect her child and the dogs. The remaining wedding party retired to Rosa's for a meal.

Writerly confidences again. Topic: URST. Daphne and Bianca's shared tome on writing romantic fiction has numerous chapters on URST (translated: Unresolved Sexual Tension). Evidently when you write a romantic novel you need to keep the frisson frissoning.

Daphne was happy with the URST she's created for her characters: Charity (virginal young bride) and Giles (titled, handsome roué). She's included longing glances and secret dalliances in her Regency romance.

Bianca has completely written URST out of her novel. Her book is more animal lust. Hot and steamy rolling around in the sheets stuff. She had interesting writerly questions. 'What if your protagonists have it off behind the sand dunes on about page twenty-one? What can you write about in place of URST?'

Daphne suggested Bianca place her URST (haunting glances, brooding stares, quivering lips, charged meetings, etc.) into a short story and send it off to the *Women's Weekly*.

Pondering Bianca's URST challenge, we retired to our homes and a night with or without animal lust.

I couldn't sleep. I kept replaying the hot and steamy, rolling-around-in-the-sheets stuff with Lee. I avoided thinking about Adrian's A-list one-night-stand sex.

I got up to make myself a cup of hot milk. The Dog joined me while we moonwatched on Adrian's verandah. The Dog was happy to discuss job stuff – but not romantic stuff. We moved into a discussion re: my job offer from Hester and Eva. My Plan C.

'These are serious questions, Dog. If I accept Plan C, will I become addicted to my job? Will I once more become a suit with a flash drive, magic stick, USB, whatever – my life's backup dangling from a strap around my neck or captured in cyberspace?

'Will Hester and Eva supply me with a BlackBerry or iPhone to keep me in contact with them 24/7?

'And will I get burnout before I earn enough money for my old age? Can you get burnout if you're having fun? Can you have fun in the corporate world in tough economic times?'

The Dog said these were good questions. He needed time to think about the answers.

The Dog thought I should seriously reconsider entering the rat-race again. Did I want to commute to work on public transport? Did I want to spend too much money on takeaway black coffees? Did I want to be trapped in a windowless office under fluorescent lights all day? Did I want to dig the same old holes every day?

I'm considering the Dog's questions.

Friday 20 November

Action committee members worked all day in the castle kitchen, preparing bite-sized morsels of food. Daphne set the menu agenda: 'We prepare ten choices, allow ten pieces per person.'

When we finished we raced home to shower and change for Digby's 'fling', as Violet calls it. I wore a classy (preloved) Dolce & Gabbana black number Daphne sourced for me. It had a short flirty skirt and a beaded spiderweb back. I felt good.

Digby's castle was ablaze with lights – inside and out – when I returned. The drawbridge was down, the portcullis up. A seething buzz of conversation greeted me as I entered the main room. Josh was at the grand piano playing smooth jazz. He winked at me as I walked past. White-coated waiters served champagne and the team's finger food on faux-silver platters to guests who were paying an outrageous price per head for the privilege of being in Digby's castle.

Digby was in his showman role – at his most charming, disarming, silver-tongued best. He scooped me up to meet Alice, Tristan, Sarah and Lionel – his black-tied and frocked-up select group of friends.

Digby placed a possessive arm around my beaded spiderweb back. 'Meet Gina. She's dabbling with a sea change. She and her friends are opening a bookshop cafe next week. It's the place on the corner of Beach Road. They're producing excellent coffee. I've been chief taster.'

I smiled and accepted Digby's twist on the truth. Digby continued his wrap on me. 'Gina's taking a sabbatical. She's coordinator of our writers' group, and keeping an eye on the organisation for our Writefest next year.'

Now Digby's high-profile guests were paying attention.

'You're a writer?'

'I'm working on a second novel.' (Lie.) 'My first is with a UK publisher.' (Thanks to Adrian, this is not a lie.) 'Outlining at the moment. I like to have a very detailed outline of my plot before I begin the actual writing.'

After this comment the eyes of Digby's colleagues fastened on me and an angst-ridden writerly conversation began.

Lionel lost his novel when his laptop was stolen from his office at the university. Sarah left her partial manuscript on a train travelling between Rome and Venice. Alice's unfinished novel is trapped (hopefully on the hard disk of her computer) in an IT repair shop. And Tristan has a novel inside him just waiting to get out. 'Finding the time to write is the problem.'

We understood.

Pandora joined the group and entered our writerly conversation. Instantly she started talking up her B&B, 'the Write Place – a perfect writer's retreat'.

As we discreetly slipped away from the group to trawl the room, Pandora gave me a stack of her business cards and whispered, 'Mention the availability of laptops, printers and connection to the internet.'

'Right.'

We mingled with Digby's high-profile guests, promoting Pandora's B&B (now reclassified as the perfect writers' retreat), pitching next year's Writefest and Adrian's bookshop cafe.

As much as the action committee members were enjoying the evening, we abandoned the party scene early.

'Big weekend ahead,' Alf reminded us.

Back home the Dog was interested to hear how the evening had gone.

'Digby pulled it off brilliantly, Dog. He managed to attract his influential colleagues, along with other well-to-do sorts, to an inconvenient destination. They now know that he is well and truly alive. Still king of the castle.

'I'm thinking the proceeds from the collectors' fair towards Adrian's Writefest will be substantial. Digby's guests paid handsomely for the privilege of partying in his splendid castle with the breathtaking view.'

The Dog heard a noise in the bushes and darted off.

To: Adrian <bookstreet@network.com.au>
From: Gina <piececake@email.com.au>
Subject: Digby's do
Hi Adrian,
Digby's black-tie function was a huge success. Exhausted.
    Going to bed. I'm sizzling sausages for the remainder of the weekend.
Gina

To: Gina <piececake@email.com.au>
From: Adrian <bookstreet@network.com.au>
Re: Digby's do
Just received a cyberspace pic. That beaded dress is some dress!
    I'll dream of you sizzling sausages in your LBD.
Adrian

Saturday 21 – Sunday 22 November

I'm combining two entries in my journal to cover the collectors' fair – a major letdown after Digby's party. I just managed to survive Day One. Living in a climate-controlled environment in a former life, I found sizzling sausages under an awning in a record-breaking November heatwave way outside my comfort zone.

Day Two improved slightly. Pandora had done a brilliant job with her short but effective media campaign to bring visitors to Shelly Beach. Treasure-hunters sailed in from all parts of the globe.

Fergus (Digby's celebrity antique expert and valuer) had a constant queue in front of his table. Everyone wanted a valuation – at a price – on their valued and hopefully valuable possessions. We heard one success story. Fergus sent the Jenkins family home with the knowledge that their great-aunt's old china teapot is worth over $2000.

Bianca gained her word of the week from Fergus: 'Patina – old ingrained dirt on antique stuff.'

The Dog was impressed with my sausage sizzling know-how and he took note of my marketing tip: 'Keep onions cooking constantly. The smell of onions wafting on the air is an unbelievable sales tool.'

I explained my late return to the Dog. He was expecting me home about 6. 'After the fair closed the action committee retired to Rosa's. Rosa was happy. She had a good trading day. It was the weather. Everybody flocked to the pub for drinks.

'Violet hasn't a final figure yet, but she says we've made a healthy profit. Alf and Potholer made a sizeable amount from parking, then there was the entrance fee, a charge to operate a stall, a charge to get a valuation and $4 to buy a sizzled sausage! When Digby adds the proceeds from his black-tie benefit, the action committee should have a sizeable amount of cash to get Adrian's Writefest off the ground next year.'

The Dog thinks I've done well. My contractual obligations to Adrian have just about been met.

To: Adrian <bookstreet@network.com.au>
From: Gina <piececake@email.com.au>
Subject: Collectors' fair

Hi Adrian,

Digby's collectors' fair has been a success. I've spent two days of my life in a haze of barbecue smoke (not sure if skin and hair will be permanently permeated with the smell of fried onions and sausages) and I don't wish to ever repeat the experience! Unsure of exact amount of takings but I'd say you can go ahead and book at least two overseas authors for your Writefest. Feel confident that your authors will not have to swim home.

Gina

To: Gina <piececake@email.com.au>
From: Adrian <bookstreet@network.com.au>
Re: Collectors' fair

Well done, Gina! Pass on my congratulations to Digby and the committee members. Best of luck for the Piece of Cake opening tomorrow.

Wish I was there with you.

Monday 23 November

Piece of Cake is now officially open for business. Business was brisk although we did have a sizeable lull in the afternoon.

As Gail said, 'How many free cups of coffee and cupcakes can Shelly Beach locals consume?'

During our lull, Piece of Cake staff discreetly put their feet up, drank herbal tea and took time out to catch up with the book-industry goss Pandora had dug up.

In her previous life as a spin doctor, Pandora had worked with Delvine, Bill's publicist. 'A shark in disguise. She's very experienced and diligent. Delvine handles the big overseas authors. Not long ago a Booker-prize author cancelled her tour because she'd been admitted to a health clinic, so Delvine was free to take on Bill. He's landed on his feet. He'll get the best possible publicity.'

Bill's appearing at a major writers' festival plus is booked for a string of radio, TV and print interviews. He's had a huge case of cold feet so Deb decided to travel with him.

Writers' group members are familiar with Bill's recurring nightmares connected to his previous appearance at a major writers' festival. He had to give a reading to a scattered audience of ten in a giant auditorium – and with a broken sound system.

Deb's mum called in with some posters to promote Bill's novel. She's looking after young Hunter for the week. 'I'm desperate for a coffee. A strong coffee.'

She had to leave her coffee to capture Hunter. He was rearranging books from the how-to-write section.

Pandora held Hunter in a stranglehold while Deb's mum drank her coffee and chatted. She was in no hurry to leave. 'I've never understood why Deb and Bill called their child Hunter. Especially when they're vegetarians. But there you go.'

When Deb's mum finished her coffee, Pandora released Hunter at the front door. 'We need to install child-height barbed wire around the book section,' Pandora muttered.

Pandora's definitely not a young-child person.

Bill's fans, aka the writers' group, arrived at different times of the day to sell the pristine-condition signed copies of Bill's novels (temporary purchases to create a buzz at the launch) to us for resale in the cafe.

I put my conversation on replay. 'Yes. The hardback edition is expensive. Yes. The paperback edition will be cheaper when it comes out. Yes. It's probably cheaper if you buy it online. Yes. It is in ebook format. Yes. I'm sure you'll be able to borrow Bill's novel from Sea Haven Library.'

We decided to keep a front-of-store promo for Bill's signed books all summer after hearing Pandora's dispiriting info: 'There's no way you can return a signed book to a publisher.'

Digby called as we were closing. 'This is the number of an old colleague – my former tutor, actually. He has a 1990 Mercedes-Benz for sale. It's definitely worth looking at, Gina. You did mention you needed to buy a car?'

'Yes I did.'

I felt like Captain Hook. A crocodile had swallowed a ticking clock and was stalking me. Time was running out. After the wedding, I had to focus on getting a job in the new year and somewhere to live.

The Dog said it's not the hole I have to conquer but myself.

I ignored the Dog.

Bossy Child arrived at the cafe and we headed off to Bianca's salon for hair trials for the wedding. Fortunately my favourite hair-stylist hates it when bridal parties follow overseas celebs' latest hairdos: 'We're sticking to an *au naturel* look.' Hallelujah!

Back home the dogs watched while I soaked my feet in cool water. Josh called in for the book club wine. I sent my apologies.

'Members understand, Gina.'

I smiled and watched Josh stack the wine in his car.

Later that night I told the Dog about Digby's academic friend who has an old Mercedes-Benz to sell.

'It's the usual story, Dog. Digby says the car's been kept in moth-balls for years.'

The Dog thought I should look at it (Alf's promised he'll check any car I'm thinking of buying), considering Adrian will be returning soon and will want his car back.

To: Adrian <bookstreet@network.com.au>
From: Gina <piececake@email.com.au>
Subject: Piece of Cake
Hi Adrian,
Piece of Cake is now open for business. We did the celebratory thing this morning. Streamers in the cafe, floated balloons with

dangly strings in the book section. Free cupcake with cup of coffee promo pulled in loyal Shelly Beach customers. Daphne is writing up the opening (Charles took photos) for the *Sea Haven Sentinel*. I'd resign myself to running at a loss for at least the next month.

To: Gina <piececake@email.com.au>
From: Adrian <bookstreet@network.com.au>
Re: Piece of Cake
I thank you from the bottom of my heart for sellotaping my Shelly Beach life together in my absence. I'm forever in your debt.

Tuesday 24 November

Today was hardly a packed-to-the-rafters day for Piece of Cake trade, but this is to be expected. The good news was I was able to leave early. I posted my CV to Sea Haven Library re: a part-time children's librarian position and visited Winston, Digby's old tutor, to check out his Merc.

The car deal is the real thing. Winston's moving into a retirement home. 'Can't tolerate my son's second partner. I'm selling everything I can before the Wicked Witch gets her hands on my property.'

I spent nearly an hour with the eccentric Winston, discussing life's ups and downs (Winston is definitely on one of life's downers). When I returned home I found Bianca in tears on the verandah. My always joyful Bianca was joyless. Cause: the one-special-day stuff. 'My wedding's going to be a horrorfest!'

A cup of tea and several phone calls were needed to sort out the potential horrorfest wedding. Bianca was returned to her cheery happy self. 'I'm keeping my single name, Gina! Not taking Josh's surname. Josh says it's cool.'

I smiled as I watched her drive off. Smart young woman, is our Bianca.

'There you go, Dog. Problem sorted and I never mentioned the five-letter word: *elope*. Based on two particularly unpleasant weddings I've attended, I'd definitely go for an elopement.'

The Dog's ears pricked up. He's a schadenfreude fan. Very keen to hear about my tragic wedding experiences.

'Well, my wedding was a let's-make-the-best-of-it wedding. I remember a nervous bride coping with morning sickness, squeezed into an over-the-top bouffant dress, and carrying a huge bouquet to disguise a four-month pregnancy.

'I remember a wedding organised by future mother-in-law Martha, mother to the handsome young groom – Kenneth. A wedding where the bewildered young bride was the owner of a Victorian home on a choice piece of retail property and possessor of a considerable share portfolio. A wedding where it was understood that the young bride (once baby Julia was born) would resume her career and provide a respectable salary to sustain the groom in his business schemes and deals.'

And . . .? The Dog wanted to know about my second tragic wedding experience.

'It was Julia's wedding. I remember a mother of the bride in a designer outfit of cyclamen-pink lace and satin. I remember an outrageously extravagant event planned by Julia, Kenneth and a team of wedding planners. A wedding where the mother of the bride with her unfamiliar face and outdated hairstyle had nothing to do but smile politely.'

I decided to move my depressing conversation on and shifted to discussing writing techniques. 'Can flashbacks provide insight into a character's motives?'

The Dog was unsure. However, if he was a reading dog, he thought he'd like reading flashbacks. That way he'd have some idea about stuff that happened before the novel actually began.

To: Adrian <bookstreet@network.com.au>
From: Gina <piececake@email.com.au>
Subject: Wedding disaster
Feel pleased with myself. In one phone call I removed Bianca's worry
that the wedding guests would have slow and painful deaths. Rosa's
new chef's romantic choice of 'freshly foraged wild herb salads'
for the wedding breakfast menu is not composed of poisonous
weeds gathered from the Shelly Beach foreshore, but salad greens
purchased from the Sea Haven fruit and vegetable suppliers.

Worried about your turtle dove count, which is declining
rapidly. Cause of the demise of your doves could be pedigree cat
visits.

To: Gina <piececake@email.com.au>
From: Adrian <bookstreet@network.com.au>
Re: Wedding disaster
Well done. I'm inspired by your negotiating skills.

I'd check Lorenzo's menu re: my depleted turtle dove count.

Miss you.

Wednesday 25 November

During my lunch hour, I paid another visit to Digby's old tutor. I
received an abrupt welcome. 'Digby said you were a researcher. Can
you research historical documents for me? I'm thinking of writing a
book. I'll pay well.'

I looked at this frail old man with keen grey eyes and a sharp
brain. 'Yes, I can do that.'

'Good. You'll have to visit me at the Blue Seas Retirement Home,
though. I'm moving next week. Do you know where it is?'

'No, but I'll find it.'

'Good. Now let's see if we can solve your transport problem.'
Winston pointed to the garage at the back of his house.

I raced back to Piece of Cake with my transport problems solved. The cafe was buzzing. Locals popped in all day for coffee and to discuss wedding details. Daphne and Charles are taking official photos (they're giving the album and DVD to Bianca and Josh as a wedding present).

Violet delivered a colonnaded wedding cake made from recycled cakes she had been planning to give friends for Christmas. 'I've scrubbed the holly and reindeers, kept the bells, added pink roses. Do you think it needs more tiers?'

It was perfect. I'll never cease to be amazed at Violet's hidden talents.

I was cooking dinner at home when Digby called in. 'I need the name of the hiring firm. I have to collect the guys' wedding gear tomorrow.'

I delivered more wedding-planner info to Digby. 'Don't forget to tie pink ribbons on your car. You've got the ribbons already?'

Digby nodded.

'Good. You're driving the bridesmaids and the bride's mother Gail from Gail's place to the foreshore. The wedding ceremony is taking place in the band pavilion. Guests are bringing their own chairs. After the ceremony, guests are carrying their chairs to the marquee, which hopefully will be erected in Rosa's backyard.'

While I cooked lasagne Digby entered his wedding-planner instructions into his BlackBerry. 'Heard you visited Winston. He likes you. He said he's solved your transport problem, and you'd bought other items from him.'

'He's wicked. He's got *For Sale* stickers on every item and piece of furniture in his home.'

'He's not happy with his son, or his son's new wife. They've pressured him to move to a retirement home.'

'I gathered that.' I took Digby to Adrian's shed. Potholer had already collected my purchases from Winston: an eighteenth-century chest of drawers and hallstand, a state-of-the-art washing machine and refrigerator.

Digby expressed his approval. 'When are you going to pick up the Merc?'

'I decided not to buy it.' I lifted up a tarpaulin and showed him my Vespa.

Digby smiled. 'I forgot Winston had a Vespa. He used to scoot around on it on campus. An excellent buy, Gina.'

Digby had a very expensive bottle of bubbly in his car. He retrieved the champagne while I collected the glasses. We sat on Adrian's verandah, and discussed life in general over his excellent drop.

Later that night the Dog and I chatted. 'Winston reminds me of an old warrior, a warrior who planned to die in battle. Instead he's been exiled to live the rest of his life in the Blue Seas Retirement Home.'

The Dog has no concept of retirement homes and he doesn't approve of the Vespa for a temporary two-dog owner. However, as I'm moving out – and on – he can see the Vespa's value in delivering economical mileage for a no-dog person.

Thursday 26 November

Josh phoned from school when Gail and I were doing a trial bake of the cake of the day at the cafe. 'Gina, the dogs are racing round the playground like greyhounds. Can you come and get them?'

Bloody hell!

Gail held the fort while I went to school to collect the dogs. Walking home I delivered a dire warning to the Dog. 'Have you told Sally the poodle about the Lost Dogs' Shelter? The place where wicked, runaway dogs end up? Where all that's left of the wicked, runaway dogs are collars kept in a basket?'

The Dog says Sally is fearless. She doesn't care.

Gail suggested I keep the dogs in the yard at the back of the cafe. 'At least we'll know where they are.'

True.

The Dog's upset at being banned from Adrian's cafe. 'Canine intrusion is not accepted by the snarky health and safety guy, Dog. One secret visit when he spots you sniffing a ham toastie going past, and Adrian's cafe will be closed down. Do you understand?'

The Dog didn't understand. He'd prefer the sign Pandora wanted to erect outside Adrian's cafe: *Beware. Our dogs eat small children. But only one at a time.*

My mobile rang. It was a serious call. I answered it out of earshot of friendly snoopers. The Dog understood. He acknowledged my sign-language message to him. YES! I've an interview at Sea Haven Library (I've passed step one in my application for the part-time position as children's librarian commencing in the new year. Step two is getting the job).

Friday 27 November

Bianca's wedding day was a 'reach for the tissues and umbrella' day. We spent a damp morning accomplishing wedding-planning dot points.

- Decorate the band pavilion with a combination of ivy – real – and flowers – faux. Pink, of course! (Emergency decision-making put a halt in moving to second dot point. A large quantity of waterproof flooring was needed to prevent wedding guests becoming bogged during the ceremony. Alf and Potholer were sent on a locate-waterproof-covering mission.)
- Transform Rosa's dodgy marquee with fishing nets, fairy lights, balloons, and roses – use a pink palette.
- Decorate tables in the pub's dining area. Distribute candles, glitter hearts and flowers – use a pink palette.

- After lunch, wedding party meet at Gail's for make-up and hair, and to don wedding gear designed around a pink palette.

Dot points accomplished.

As if by divine direction the grey sky cleared over the Shelly Beach foreshore just before the wedding ceremony was due to start.

There was one down moment before the ceremony when the Bossy Child whispered to me, 'I think I'm going to throw up, Gina.'

'You're not going to throw up. I forbid you to throw up.'

Thankfully whatever was coming up went down, and the moment passed.

We were granted one and a half hours of cloudless, wishy-washy blue sky – just enough time for the ceremony and to take photos. Daphne's Charles took edgy (and dangerous) shots of Josh and Bianca balanced at the end of the pier, Bianca's pale pink veil billowing over the sea.

I concentrated on breathing in and preventing my needle-heeled gold shoes from slipping between the cracks on the pier. Smiling was unbearably difficult due to tightness of dress.

After the wedding ceremony and photo session I was given permission to breathe out.

Bossy Child and I were able to keep Bianca's mountains of pink tulle reasonably mud-free. Once we'd walked across the road to Rosa's we whispered to her that her mountain of pink tulle was now her responsibility. 'Don't spill anything on it! Watch it when you dance!'

Lorenzo's menu was excellent in spite of conflict in the kitchen. The staff's shift had finished but dessert hadn't yet been served. Rosa wanted staff to stay on but was refusing to pay overtime rates. Lorenzo and staff were refusing to work unless they got paid overtime rates. Result: Rosa agreed to pay some overtime, but guests splashed through puddles to the marquee taking their dessert and coffee with them. Later they moved to Ellipsis's musical beat – minus Josh.

The radiant but damp bride and groom left later for their idyllic weekend honeymoon. When guests were no longer able to stand up under Rosa's leaking, hot-air balloon marquee, we departed to continue partying at Daphne and Charles' place.

To: Adrian <bookstreet@network.com.au>
From: Gina <piececake@email.com.au>
Subject: Wedding
Bianca's wedding was a great success in spite of the rain. Your congratulatory email was read out. Bianca and Josh proposed a toast to you – with a special thank you for providing them with a romantic weekend honeymoon at Sea Haven.

I'd check Rosa's marquee for leaks if you plan to use it for Writefest next year. And I'd definitely avoid hiring the dodgy smoke machine from Rosa's cousin for future celebratory occasions.

To: Gina <piececake@email.com.au>
From: Adrian <bookstreet@network.com.au>
Re: Wedding
I heard you handled conflict in the kitchen with ease. I've seen great pics of you and Digby performing a star turn on the dance floor.

To: Adrian <bookstreet@network.com.au>
From: Gina <piececake@email.com.au>
Subject: Si parla Italiano
My tourist Italian was useful in procuring peace in the kitchen, and desserts for guests. Lorenzo and staff wanted extra wages for working past their shift. Rosa and Lorenzo looked like they were going to kill each other.

Wearing a cyclamen-pink satin frock leaves you with very few inhibitions!

Saturday 28 November

Pandora and I opened Piece of Cake by ourselves. Gail, now officially a mother-in-law, needed a recovery day. I was studiously turning out a crisply decorated latte for Pandora when she called out, 'Check this guy and his hot car, Gina.'

I looked out the window.

Bloody hell! It was Kenneth. I watched him get out of a ludicrous convertible yellow Ferrari and enter Piece of Cake. He strode across the polished floorboards, briefcase in one hand, to the sales counter.

'Hello, Georgy. You look fantastic.'

Pandora sent frantic I-can-save-you body language.

I whispered to her, 'It's all good.' I did my calm-and-focused thing. I've always been good at calm and focused but I'd had to relearn it without any money in the bank.

'This is a surprise, Kenneth. Would you like a coffee?'

I concentrated on making myself a skinny cappuccino and a flat white with an extra-special swirly pattern on the top for Kenneth.

'We can sit here.' I indicated a table near the window with a Shelly Beach view.

I looked at Kenneth. He was his usual shiny self. Shinier – full of buzz and energy. He was smiling, but the smile where his top lip was stretched tight and gave a slight side-twitch every now and then. I can read Kenneth's body language like a book. Kenneth was buzzy but not happy.

I took a deep breath. I was in charge. This was my territory. I'd earned it. I had a feeling I knew what he wanted, and I'd catch his verbal cues and return them to win: game, set, match to Gina Laurel.

'What brings you to Shelly Beach, Kenneth?'

I watched him put three spoonfuls of sugar into his coffee and stir it slowly. Kenneth has always taken three spoonfuls of sugar – strange how the mind hangs on to redundant information.

I stared at his teeth. Had he had them whitened? He looked

worried. Cash flow problems? No. He'd be able to negotiate loans from Angela's father.

'I've made a huge mistake, Georgy. I miss you. We were a great team. I've lost my best friend, and the woman I loved. I want you to come back. We can start again.'

So this was what he thought I wanted to hear. I was almost tempted to reply, 'I've been waiting for you to say this, Kenneth, and I want to come back.' But I played to Kenneth's rules . . . for the last time. I returned the answer he expected. 'You don't really mean that, Kenneth.'

Kenneth smiled his still-charming boyish smile. I could see his relief.

'You need to be with Angela. You're going to be a father again. And you know our marriage is over.'

Kenneth's mobile rang. Mumbled urgent-type conversation took place with the anonymous caller. He finished the call, turned off his mobile, took a sip of coffee and smiled at me. 'Do you feel like you have closure, Georgy?'

(Clever Angela has sent him to therapy.)

'Yes, I have closure, Kenneth.' Whatever the hell that means. I was shell-shocked, then I was mad, and now I just don't care.

I read Kenneth's body language, trying to figure out what the real purpose of his visit was. He smiled and took some papers from his briefcase.

Bingo! He needed to tie up legal stuff before he could start a new company.

'I wanted to see you again, Georgy, but there are also a few more papers to sign so we can finally shut down our company. Can you sign them as soon as possible?'

'I'll have my lawyer check them first.' (Lie. But it felt good.)

Kenneth shrugged and handed me the papers. And then he lifted out my long-forgotten laptop and placed it on the table.

'I found your laptop, Georgy. Thought you might need it. Your novel's still on it.'

I retrieved my laptop from its protective cover and stroked its smooth grey surface. I might need it to write my next novel.

'That's thoughtful of you, Kenneth. It'll be useful. You needn't have worried about my novel. I have hard copies and electronic copies. My agent has pitched it to a big-time UK publisher. They're very interested.'

(Thank you, Adrian.)

'I'm glad, Gina.' Kenneth finished his coffee and stood up. I stood up too and we waited awkwardly for a moment. Then he kissed me on the cheek, and whispered in my ear, 'Sex with an ex is always exciting. Call me when you come to the city.'

I raised an eyebrow and watched Kenneth's immaculately suited back as he crossed the floor. At the entrance he turned, called out thank you to Pandora, gave me a wink and his special salute. And that was that.

Pandora came to the window and we watched Kenneth drive away in his yellow Ferrari.

'Cool car.'

'It'll be leased under Angela's name.'

'It's going to rain. He'll get wet if he doesn't put the top up soon. Are you okay?'

'I'm fine.' I smiled. I really did feel fine. That ridiculous, simple word 'fine' expressed the feeling that flooded over me. I'd moved on. No more Kenneth games to play.

I breathed a huge sigh of relief. I'd forgiven myself for being stupid enough to hang on to a dead marriage for too long. Kenneth's ability to sabotage my life had ended. I was quite capable of sabotaging it myself.

'I think I'll make another coffee. Strong and black. This one is cold.'

I took my fresh coffee out to the cafe's dog-friendly yard. The Dog came to my side. 'I did well, Dog. You would have been proud of me. And don't ever expect me to answer to Georgy!'

Sunday 29 November

I drew the curtains. It had rained again during the night and Adrian's garden was a glistening tangle of green. From my bed I watched the birds darting to and fro.

The Dog wandered in. Time to get up. Time for breakfast. He watched me as I put on Adrian's old raincoat to make a quick dash to the henhouse to collect the eggs. Two Girls alive and well, and enjoying the worm weather.

I made myself breakfast, then showered and dressed. The dogs and I were waiting when Pandora called to drive us the five minutes to Piece of Cake. 'No need to walk in the rain.'

True.

Pandora opened the cafe while I made coffee. Over coffee Pandora read an excellent review for Bill's novel from one of the city newspapers.

'Bill Kruger's second novel – *Pets Care* – melds philosophical questions with a pacy plot. It's hard to pigeonhole his work but *Pets Care* will make an excellent Christmas read.'

'Bill will be relieved. He was terrified he'd become a one-book author. An author whose second novel sinks to the bottom of the bay.'

We browsed through the *Sea Haven Sentinel*, catching up with Daphne's feature (photo by hubby Charles): *Local Author's City Book Launch*.

Adrian's summer occupants – a pleasant young couple renting his Crow's Nest Flat – dropped in for coffee. Adrian will be pleased that his sea-change plan is taking shape. He now has paying tenants in one of his rental properties.

We could see the foreshore filling with tents and damp campers from the cafe windows. All day we did a steady trade in coffee and cake for early holiday-makers escaping from the rain.

Beryl called in for coffee. Beryl, coming from a line of original settlers, is Shelly Beach's historian. 'Campers usually start arriving about this time of year. Set up their tents and caravans for the season. The ranger says he has a record number of bookings for foreshore sites this year. It's the credit crunch. Folks are looking for a cheap holiday close to home. No money for fancy overseas cruises.'

True.

Violet, our resident writer, has set up at a window table with a bay view; sipping lattes, taking notes, writing perfect paragraphs and creating characters she can hang up until required for her mystery thrillers. 'No end to the mysterious characters entering the cafe or passing by outside.'

We agreed.

'I've bitten the bullet. I've submitted one of my Red Blaze mysteries to a publisher.'

Way to go, Violet. A manuscript has finally sprouted wings. It's escaped from the box under the cats' sofa. Violet is elated with the writerly thrill of accomplishment that comes when you submit a manuscript. I didn't tell her about the downside: when rejection emails land in your mailbox or when your contract loses its legs . . .

I wonder how many rejections it will take before Violet replaces this Red Blaze mystery with another from the box under the cats' sofa and sends no. 2 in the Red Blaze series to a publisher? Violet's a tough cookie. She won't give up easily.

After dinner this evening I chatted to the Dog. 'Serious decision-making time, Dog! I'm rejecting Hester and Eva's job offer.'

The Dog knew this a week ago.

'You're familiar with trees?'

The Dog was very familiar with trees.

'In a former life I'd climbed to the top of the professional tree. I don't want to do it again. At least not for a little while.'

The Dog understood and approved.

To: Eva <eva@slick-promotions.com>;

    Hester <hester@bizevents.com.au>

From: Gina <piececake@email.com.au>

Subject: Job offer

Hi Eva and Hester,

I really appreciated your job offer. However, I've found casual work at Shelly Beach and have decided to stay here for at least six months.

Much love,

Gina

To: Gina <piececake@email.com.au>

From: Eva <eva@slick-promotions.com.au>

Cc: Hester <hester@bizevents.com.au>

Re: Job offer

Well done! Hester and I would love to catch up with you at your charming local pub tomorrow at 12. We're chasing up a contact with the marketing manager of Sea Haven Resort. Are you free?

Love Eva

Monday 30 November

My rostered day off was a mixture of success for me, sad news for the Dog. This morning we dropped Sally at the Sea Haven vet, and raced off for my library interview.

My success? I have a job with a reasonable career path. I'm to start a permanent part-time position as children's librarian at Sea Haven Library in the new year.

Sad news for the Dog? Sally's pregnant and the Dog's definitely not the father. I murmured consoling words to the Dog while we raced back to the vet's to collect pregnant Sally. I deposited the dogs at the cafe and went to meet Hester and Eva at Rosa's.

Hester and Eva were already seated at a table when I entered the pub. My friends, perfectly groomed and wearing glam biz suits, looked liked they'd just landed from another planet. We exchanged air kisses and hugs.

Hester and Eva are impressed with Rosa's new fit-out for the bar and restaurant area, and Lorenzo's Italian menu. 'Brilliant pasta selection, Gina. And local produce. Goat and rabbit!'

I nodded. Rosa's new Italian menu has caused talk among the locals. Mysterious producers of goats and rabbits for Lorenzo's menu are unknown around Shelly Beach.

Local decision: as long as Lorenzo's food tastes good, and it does, no one is asking questions – but keeping their pet goats and rabbits locked up at night.

I couldn't resist inquiring about toxic friend Clare.

'Clare's fine. She and James should be skiing on the Swiss slopes about now. Then they're flying to the US. James is going to work with a US company for a year – maybe longer.

'Fantastic.'

We moved the conversation on. Eva and Hester are genuinely impressed with my micro-management of my finances and ability to land a job – correction, jobs. 'And I've bought a Vespa.'

'Wow!'

Over tea Hester and Eva presented me with the last fiscal package they'd salvaged from Montpellier Place. Hester took a pair of white cotton gloves from her bag and slipped them on her impeccably manicured hands. I watched as she unpacked a box and extracted a battered stamp album from acid-free paper. She turned the pages of the album with care.

'Do you remember this?'

'Yes I do!' It was another of Kenneth's extravagant buys on his short-lived crusade to acquire a posh, valuable hobby. No thrill of the collectors' chase for Kenneth. One completed stamp collection equates to one long-established hobby. And he didn't even have to lick a stamp.

Hester carefully returned the album to its box and handed it, and the cotton gloves, to me. 'Handle it with care, Gina. There's one stamp in there that's valued at about $15 000. Here's the valuator's card. Talk to him. Decide what to do.'

Bloody hell! 'Thank you.' I hugged my friends. 'I don't know what to say.'

'Say nothing. You'd do the same for us.'

As we stood to leave I stared at Eva. She always looks great. Today she was particularly radiant. I noticed a distinct stomach bulge on her carefully toned body.

'You're pregnant!'

'I told you you'd have to tell her!' Hester said. We sat down again. Hester went to order more drinks.

'How did you guess?' Eva answered her own question. 'It's getting obvious, isn't it? Baby's due next year. May.'

Hester returned with peach tea; another of Lorenzo's menu innovations.

Eva looked at me with amusement. 'It's okay. Forty-four puts me in the high-risk category, but I've had all the tests. Everything is fine. I'm healthy. The baby's healthy. I've thought about it. I'm financially secure. I'm going to have this baby. Hester's agreed to help me out while we set up our new business.'

Then Eva answered the question a good friend hesitates to ask. 'And I'm not sure who the father is.'

She saw a look of worry flicker across my face.

'Don't worry, Gina. It's probably Dominic's baby. When he returns at Christmas we can do DNA testing if he wants to. I won't be lumbering him or any other guy with my child. This is my call.

'We're working on my birth plan. I'm booked into the Pines hospital for a caesarean. I've already looked into hiring a day nanny, and probably a night nanny too for the first few weeks – so Hester and I can keep our business moving.'

Before I could think of a suitable feel-good comment, silver fox Digby strode into the pub and came across to our table.

There were raised eyebrows and smiles from Eva and Hester as I introduced Digby and he started his charm act.

'I've been looking for you, Gina. I thought the writers' group might like to have their Christmas break-up at the castle. Have a think about it and get back to me later.'

We received a smile, I was given a cheek kiss and Digby left to join another table.

Eva and Hester finished their peach teas. 'Sorry, but we have to go. We've a meeting at Sea Haven.' We exchanged hugs and air kisses again, and promises to keep in touch. And we would.

After Hester and Eva left, Digby handed me one of Henry's journals that he'd transcribed. 'Would you mind giving it a quick edit before I return it to Henry?'

I smiled my acceptance.

Digby checked his BlackBerry. 'I have a text message from Winston. Would you like his Wedgwood dinner service?'

'I couldn't accept it. It's too valuable.'

'If you don't take it, it will go with a truckload of stuff to Daphne's charity shop.'

'In that case tell Winston I'd love his Wedgwood dinner service. I'll treasure it.'

I stayed to have a glass of wine with Digby and then excused myself: 'I have to get back to take the dogs for a walk.'

The Dog's not talking to Sally the poodle, but he was interested to hear the outcome of my lunch with Eva and Hester. 'Eva's having a baby, and Hester's agreed to help care for it too.'

The Dog wanted to move on from the juggling-a-baby image. He's feeling betrayed. Living with a prize Siamese cat and a litter of pups is not his idea of dog heaven.

To: Gina <piececake@email.com.au>
From: Adrian <bookstreet@network.com.au>
Subject: Return
Hi Gina,
My daughter has recovered earlier than expected from her treatments. Her husband's taking leave now, and they're spending Christmas up north with the in-laws. The new year should see her well and truly on the mend. My job is done.

With this in mind, I booked a flight home a couple of days ago. Arriving approx 10 a.m. Thursday 3 December. Looking forward to Shelly Beach sunshine and spending time with you.
Adrian

Bloody hell!

December

Tuesday 1 December

Couldn't sleep. Spent most of last night prowling round Adrian's moonlit garden, thinking and planning appropriate emails. Resolution: I will not panic. I'm in my calm-and-focused zone. Today I would find somewhere to rent in Shelly Beach. Worst-case scenario? I could pitch a tent on the foreshore. There's a coin-in-the-slot community ablutions block (hopefully with hot water) I could access. Yes!

This morning I called the Dog in from the garden.

'Your owner's coming home on Thursday. He's broken his contract, but that's not your fault. When you get time to have a quiet word with him, tell him he's very fortunate I'm not taking legal proceedings.'

The Dog was depressed. He watched while I tore November along its perforated edge. I held November over Adrian's sink and lit a match. The flames devoured the thirty days quickly. I turned on the tap. November's inky ashes swirled and gurgled around Adrian's kitchen sink then disappeared down the plughole.

From December's page, a smiling Harold from Rupert's Butchery (wearing a Father Christmas hat) beamed at me above the thirty-one days of the month. The balloon caption attached to his mouth issued a warning: *Get your Christmas orders in early, folks!*

'Do you think I should order a leg of lion, Dog?'

The Dog gave me his hound-dog look.

'You're partial to the occasional lion chop at barbecues, aren't you?'

No reply.

'It's a joke, Dog. Harold's a terrible speller.'

The Dog ignored me and exited through his pet door to dig a hole. A very big hole. Hopefully one he can get out of.

I phoned Pandora. From her puffed hello I'd interrupted her torturous fitness routine.

'Adrian's returning on Thursday.'

'I've heard.'

Bloody hell! 'Can you do my morning shift today? I have to find somewhere to rent.'

'You're welcome to bunk with me, Gina.'

'I know. Thank you.'

'Ring Gail. Rent Bianca's old flat. No. Gail's got summer tenants coming in.'

'Not to worry. I'll find somewhere.'

Bossy Child called in on the way to school. 'Have you heard?'

'Yes, I have.'

'Adrian's coming back on Thursday! Mum says you can have my room as a stopgap. I'll sleep in Sam's room. I'll take my mice out for you.'

'Good. That's a very kind offer. I'll keep it in mind.'

'I have to go home and tidy my room in case you need it.' Bossy Child raced off.

I made myself a cup of strong black coffee and took it out to the garden. The Dog came to my side.

'Five months climbing ladders, Dog, and I've slid down a snake

345

to square one. I've changed from a woman of no fixed income to a woman with income, but I'm still a woman of no fixed abode. I need my own space. I want my own space.'

The Dog gave me his how-would-you-like-to-be-in-my-fur look.

'I know, I know. I'm well aware I have an income and I can rent my own space.'

The phone rang. It was chirpy Bianca. 'Can you believe it? Adrian's coming back on Thursday. So soon!'

I held my hand over the phone. 'Is there anyone in Shelly Beach who doesn't know Adrian's returning on Thursday, Dog?'

'Mum said you need somewhere to rent. Rosa has single rooms at the pub she rents sometimes. They're upstairs. The bathroom's down the hall.'

'Fantastic!'

'Or you could take over the rental of Deb and Bill Kruger's house. They're moving into a bigger house after Christmas.'

'How do I find out if their place is available?'

'Ring Sea Haven Real Estate. Sorry – a client has come in. Got to go. Catch you later.'

'This sounds promising, Dog.'

Two phone calls, a quick trip to Sea Haven and amazingly I'd found somewhere to live in the new year. 'Bill and Deb's house has got a spectacular view of the back beach, Dog, but I forgot to check if it has a dodgy bathroom.'

The Dog thinks I'm paranoid about bathroom plumbing. He says hot and cold water doesn't come into it when you clean yourself. You just start licking at the tip of your nose and finish at the tip of your tail.

Rosa was her usual magnanimous self when I approached her about short-term accommodation. 'You're lucky I can do you a favour, Gina. You can have the back bedroom overlooking the yard. Near the bathroom. Little dog can stay with you if he's invisible.'

Thank you, Rosa. Little dog's ears perked up at mention of his name.

'You just want to stay a few weeks?'

'Until Christmas. I'm renting Bill and Deb's old house after Christmas.'

'That's good. My family likes to stay during the summer season. I need all my rooms.'

'I understand.'

Then we negotiated further. 'You want another job? Six to eight, Friday to Sunday evenings during the summer season? Could be more hours. We'll see. I pay you good wages, Gina.'

I accepted. I was going to operate Rosa's new point-of-sale software, taking orders and relaying them to Lorenzo and his kitchen staff. Commencing Saturday.

Rosa and Lorenzo were not speaking. 'He's a pig-hearted man.'

'Pig-headed?'

'That too.'

Rosa was happy with the outcome. 'You're just the girl for the job, Gina. Now I never speak to pig-hearted Lorenzo. Just put his wages in his bank. I'll sack him after the summer season!'

On our way back to Piece of Cake the Dog and I discussed my new job. 'It will boost my savings, Dog.' And we both hoped Lorenzo would leave Rosa's before he got the sack.

I brought the Dog up to speed on my new Plan Q. When I was at the real estate agent's, I located land for sale at a bargain price, walking distance from the beach. I'm thinking of building a stylish, cosy, open-plan studio. Use a building design with a small carbon footprint. I bet Alf and Potholer can do it.

The Dog was pleased I had a new plan; however, his advice was to beware of crushing workloads. He said they upset your work–life balance – and balancing on three legs is not easy.

'I've been there, Dog. I'm focusing on hard work in the short term. I'll get to the "life" part after the summer season ends.'

When I went to Piece of Cake for the afternoon shift, Pandora and Gail were keen to hear my plans. 'I've arranged to move into a room at Rosa's tomorrow. And I've scored a job with her over the summer season. I'm storing my stuff in Adrian's shed for a few weeks. I've taken a six-month lease on Deb and Bill's old rental, starting after Christmas. They're moving to a bigger place in Sea Haven. And yesterday I found out I've landed the part-time job as children's librarian at Sea Haven Library. Start in the new year.'

Gail and Pandora were impressed. 'Go girl!'

To: Gina <piececake@email.com.au>
From: Adrian <bookstreet@network.com.au>
Subject: Accommodation
Apologies for not mentioning the subject of accommodation
in previous email. Please stay on at Sea View Cottage, or in one
of the bungalows. Whichever you prefer. I'll take the alternative
accommodation.

To: Adrian <bookstreet@network.com.au>
From: Gina <piececake@email.com.au>
Re: Accommodation
Appreciate your offer of accommodation. However, your
bungalows are minus plumbing and minus interior fit-outs.
I've arranged alternative rental accommodation for myself and
will move in tomorrow. Sea View Cottage all ready for you on
Thursday.

Piece of Cake staff are thinking we should include all-day
breakfasts on the menu. You can decide when you return. Last
writers' group meeting for the year is to be held at Digby's
castle on 9 December at 7 p.m. Digby's providing the food. BYO
everything else.

To: Gina <piececake@email.com.au>
From: Adrian <bookstreet@network.com.au>
Re: Accommodation
Glad to hear you've sorted your accommodation. All-day breakfasts
sound good. We'll discuss menus when I return. I'm delighted I'll
be able to attend the December writers' group meeting. Can't wait
to see you again.

To: Adrian <bookstreet@network.com.au>
From: Gina <piececake@email.com.au>
Subject: Bundle of joy
Apologies for not mentioning the subject of pets in previous email.
You have problems: Sally the poodle is pregnant. The Dog feels he's
been betrayed. No way could he have made Sally pregnant.

To: Gina <piececake@email.com.au>
From: Adrian <bookstreet@network.com.au>
Re: Bundle of joy
I see.

To: Adrian <bookstreet@network.com.au>
From: Gina <piececake@email.com.au>
Subject: Pet problems
My suggestion is that the Dog resides with me until Sally has her
pups. He needs time to adjust to the idea of pups and to a prize
Siamese cat living with you.

To: Gina <piececake@email.com.au>
From: Adrian <bookstreet@network.com.au>
Re: Pet problems
Agreed.

To: Adrian <bookstreet@network.com.au>
From: Gina <piececake@email.com.au>
Subject: Room of one's own
Glad that's settled. We have other stuff to sort out when you return.
I don't want to sound ungrateful, but I'm very happy to return your
Shelly Beach life to you – except for your dog. I need to have my
own Shelly Beach life. I want to have my own colour-coded folders,
pot plants, white voile curtains and a few doves.

To: Gina <piececake@email.com.au>
From: Adrian <bookstreet@network.com.au>
Re: Room of one's own
Agreed. See you at Piece of Cake for coffee on the third?

To: Adrian <bookstreet@network.com.au>
From: Gina <piececake@email.com.au>
Subject: Airport pick-up
Your daughter Tania has been in touch with me. She's unable to
meet you at the airport on the third. I'll meet you and drive you
back to Shelly Beach. I have your flight details.

To: Gina <piececake@email.com.au>
From: Adrian <bookstreet@network.com.au>
Re: Airport pick-up
On the back of your Vespa?

I looked at the Dog. Who told Adrian I bought a Vespa?
     The Dog chose not to answer.

To: Adrian <bookstreet@network.com.au>
From: Gina <piececake@email.com.au>
Re: Airport pick-up

No! Beryl's loaning me her car.

Thought you need to know that six members are happy to resume writers' group next year. However, if Daphne's husband joins the group, Daphne's out. She suggests you put an ad in the local paper to get new members. Bill's happy to continue as tutor – with or without funding.

Cancelling coffee date on third. Would you like to have dinner with me at Rosa's – 7 p.m. – on the third to discuss remaining business concerning your cafe and cottage?

To: Gina <piececake@email.com.au>
From: Adrian <bookstreet@network.com.au>
Re: Airport pick-up

Appreciate up-to-date information re: writers' group members.

Can't think of anything better than to have dinner with you at Rosa's on the third. Extremely grateful for all your help.

'Sometimes, Dog, your owner can write reasonably nice emails.'

Wednesday 2 December

Bossy Child called in to Piece of Cake after school – she's helping me move out.

She waited until I closed the cafe then we went to collect cartons from Jenkins' Store.

'Congratulations, Gina!' News of my job at Sea Haven Library is already circulating around Shelly Beach. Bossy Child and Jody agreed I'd be more successful with the homework club than Beryl's sister's cousin. I don't cry easily!

Jody was contemplating the continuing fallout of the global financial meltdown in the paper. 'Strange, but tough economic times haven't affected Shelly Beach traders. Passed us by. Trade is excellent. Locals buy what they need. Share stuff.'

True. Shelly Beach's basic fiscal strategies work. I'm amazed I've survived my own financial crisis. I've been so into buying things secondhand I've forgotten the value of things in the real world. Learning how to do more with less has not been too tragic.

One of Potholer's sons darted into the shop with a bucket of calamari. He handed it over the counter to Jody. 'Can I swap for some dog food?'

'Sure.'

Potholer's son disappeared down the pet products aisle.

'Like some calamari, Gina?'

I declined. 'Don't want to leave a marine smell in Adrian's cottage.'

Jody understood. 'Something for the freezer, Mum,' she called.

Bossy Child and I piled my empty cartons inside each other and left.

When we arrived home, Bossy Child located the boxes of Adrian's flotsam and jetsam in his shed. She found the plan she'd drawn on the night I demolished the interior decor of Adrian's cottage.

We followed Bossy Child's map and returned paintings and knick-knacks to their original positions.

Bossy Child helped me remove the metres and metres of white voile curtains I'd sewn and hung at Adrian's windows. We hung the old curtains back up – held together with safety pins borrowed from Joan.

I gently folded my filmy curtains into boxes and packed my preloved but stylish new wardrobe into the one Louis Vuitton suit-case I was taking to Rosa's.

We finished our work by replacing the pot of red plastic gerani-ums on top of Adrian's snowy TV set. We'd returned Adrian's living room to its original state.

Bossy Child then got busy with card, pink paint and glitter (left-over material from Bianca's wedding). She was making *Welcome Home* banners for Adrian.

'The room looks awful, Gina. Your decor was better.'

True.

I ran my hand over the books on Adrian's well-organised bookshelves. 'I'll miss Adrian's books, Dog. You learn a lot about a person by the books on their bookshelves.'

The Dog was sure it'd be okay to keep borrowing Adrian's books.

The Dog followed me into Bedroom Two. I reread the email Lee had sent me a few weeks ago telling me he'd resumed his medical studies, and collected the Post-it notes he'd written to me. 'Are Post-it notes and email printouts equal to letters you tie with a pink ribbon and hide in a secret place? Will my great-great-grandchildren discover them? What do you think, Dog? Can I use a Post-it note from Lee to create an interesting opening for a novel? Maybe my protagonist collects letters or email printouts written by her different lovers? Letters and emails can make useful plot points.'

The Dog was too depressed to answer questions about love letters.

I reached inside an envelope I'd been avoiding thinking about for weeks, and pulled out a key on a lanyard. It was the key to Lee's apartment – the one I'd almost thrown out. I smiled at the Dog. 'For once I'm happy for you to hide something in the garden. Bury this, Dog.'

The Dog raced off, lanyard trailing from his mouth, on his bury-and-forget mission.

'Don't tell me where you put it,' I called after him through the pet door.

I tore Lee's notes into pieces and put them in the kitchen bin.

'Hurry up, Gina. I'm hungry.' Bossy Child had almost finished her banner.

Joan had invited the dogs and I for dinner – so I didn't have to disturb the pristine-clean kitchen I was leaving for Adrian. Sally would stay there overnight – there was only room for one Dog in my new abode.

I retrieved Adrian's contract from the kitchen drawer and placed it in the centre of the kitchen table. I placed the bulky writers' group folder and the community hall key beside the basket of fake oranges I'd reinstated.

I added a Post-it note:

Hi Adrian
Can you bring the handouts for the writers' group meeting to Digby's
on 9 December?
Gina

I stuck the note on top of copies of Bill's final handout for the year: *How to submit your novel*. I balanced the handouts on top of the fake oranges.

'Hurry up, Gina! I'm starving.'

I gave a last look around Adrian's living room and called the dogs. We left Sea View Cottage and headed next door for dinner.

Later that night, I slipped into my new, temporary bed in my new, temporary room above Rosa's pub. While I lay in bed with the Dog at my feet, I explained the details of our pick-Adrian-up-from-the-airport mission. As usual in Shelly Beach, a simple operation has transformed itself into a complex mission.

'Beryl is driving us in her car to the airport to meet Adrian. I'm driving back from the airport, dropping Beryl in the city to stay with another cousin. Bossy Child is coming to the airport . . . because she just has to.'

The Dog understood.

'And so are you. You love travelling in a car, the wind blowing your fur when you stick your head out the window.'

The Dog agreed.

'Beryl will look after you in the car at the airport while Bossy Child plus pink and glittery *Welcome Home* sign and myself will meet Adrian in the terminal.

'Once we've driven back to Shelly Beach, we will leave Adrian and Beryl's car at Adrian's Sea View Cottage. Alf will drive Beryl's car home. Then you and I will walk to our new temporary abode at Rosa's.

'Tomorrow is when the nerves will kick in, Dog. We'll be running on adrenalin. I always ran on adrenalin at the peak of my career.'

The Dog understood. He gets huge adrenalin rushes when he's moving sand in all directions.

Thursday 3 December

The sky was blue, the sand golden and the sea sparkled as we drove out of Shelly Beach.

'Hard to leave.'

I agreed with Beryl.

Bossy Child and Beryl filled in the journey to the airport by chatting about Shelly Beach Christmas celebrations. Bossy Child and her nerdy friends are 'sprightly elves' in Shelly Beach's Christmas Spectacular, which is being staged on the Shelly Beach foreshore. I'm earning brownie points by choreographing the elves in a hip-hop number to support Father Christmas.

Alf had reluctantly taken on Henry Shepherd's former role as Shelly Beach's Father Christmas – a huge role to fill. As a sprightly elf, Bossy Child is taking her supporting role very seriously.

Her advice to Alf via Beryl is not to tell kids you can give them impossible stuff . . . like a new dad, a puppy or a mega-expensive game. Alf's to say, 'I'll see what I can do.'

And Alf is not to yell 'Ho! Ho! Ho!' Henry Shepherd made her little brother cry last year. Now Sam's got Santa phobia.

Beryl agreed that the worldly Bossy Child delivers excellent advice.

The Dog was quiet. He was rethinking Bossy Child's advice about promising kids a pup. In a very short while Shelly Beach will be swamped with pups.

We took a pee and water break for the Dog. I ruffled his furry head as he jumped back into the car. My stomach was churning and my heart was in overdrive. For the remainder of the journey, the Dog chatted to take my mind off my nerve-racking impending meeting with the legal owner of Sea View Cottage and the Dog.

The Dog's pleased with my efforts while in Shelly Beach. He's particularly happy with the career opportunities I've set in motion. However, he thinks there will come a time when I have to make a snap decision about which ball to jump up and catch. If that particular ball slips from my mouth, I have to be ready to catch the next one.

The Dog's happy with my 'moving forward' attitude. Otherwise it's just more chasing-your-tail stuff. And he's pleased I'm over the 'bone' thing: chewing it, burying it, digging it up and starting all over again . . . chewing it, burying it, etc. etc.

The Dog's taking his own advice. Moving on. He's reconciled to his temporary life with me chez Rosa's. Adrian's cottage has nothing but tragic memories for him: a naked female dog-sitter making dashes from the bathroom and the thought of a prize Siamese cat and puppies taking up residence in the very near future.

The Dog was happy to wait in the car with Beryl while Bossy Child and I went to meet Adrian. I'd promised him a walk when we returned to Shelly Beach. The Dog gave me a droopy half-smile. We both know the adage 'A well-exercised dog is a happy dog, and a happy dog is a well-behaved dog' is rubbish.

Bossy Child, armed with pink glittery sign, waited while I checked my make-up before I left the car. I'd decided to wear the preloved Donna Karan smoky-grey suit with matching shimmery singlet that I'd worn to clinch my library interview.

'It's too much – isn't it?'

The Dog thought my look was too professional. I should have listened to him and worn jeans and my creamy linen shirt.

Bloody hell!

We watched Adrian as he emerged from the arrivals gate looking cool and relaxed. He was dressed casually and at ease in jeans and a jacket, wearing a backpack and carrying his laptop.

I calculated when I'd discard my corporate jacket to reveal the smoky-grey shimmery singlet, which looked so good with my light Shelly Beach tan.

Bossy Child was waving her sign and bouncing like a battery toy.

One wave and he was beside us. He dropped his backpack and laptop and gave Bossy Child a gigantic hug. Then he looked at me. 'Gina. You look sensational.'

I met his friendly eyes with the crinkles around them and offered my cheek for an air kiss.

Adrian ignored my offered cheek. He wrapped his arms around me and kissed me on the lips. A long full kiss. An excellent kiss.

This wasn't working out as planned. A few pages of the story were stuck together. 'Is that all your luggage?'

'I like to travel light. I've sent books and the remainder of my belongings by sea. I've clothes stored at my cottage.'

Of course he has. They're in his linen cupboard.

'Like a coffee? A drink?'

'We need to get back to Shelly Beach. Beryl and the Dog are waiting in the car.'

He smiled at me. 'Right.'

In the airport carpark there were more hugs and kisses for Beryl.

Adrian put a protective hand on my back as he opened the driver's door of Beryl's car for me and then stowed his laptop and backpack in the boot.

He acknowledged the Dog sitting on the back seat. 'Good dog, Hugo!'

The Dog avoided eye contact.

Adrian laughed his warm, comforting laugh. 'Can't wait until we get back to Shelly Beach.'

We set off, and I allowed Shelly Beach goss to float around me as I concentrated on driving home.

We located Beryl's cousin's home in the city, dropped Beryl off and continued on our journey to Shelly Beach.

Conversation stopped when we came over the final hill and Shelly Beach bay, in all its smudgy blue splendour, stretched in front of us.

Alf was at Sea View Cottage to welcome Adrian. The Dog and I left them, with Adrian's promise to join us for dinner, and with Beryl's car (thankfully in one piece).

We walked along the beach track to Rosa's, basking in the salt air, blue skies and the seagull-decorated waves of Shelly Beach.

Rosa greeted us.

'I can't see the invisible dog, Gina. I've reserved a table for you and Adrian tonight at the window with the view of beaut-i-ful fore-shore trees and sand and sea.'

'Thank you, Rosa.'

I carried the invisible Dog up the stairs to our temporary room overlooking the yard, but next to the bathroom.

I'm happy in my skin and the Dog's happy in his hairy skin. I have a life in Shelly Beach with a dog – the Dog. A life complete with a career and friends.

And I may even find time to write a second novel.

Acknowledgements

I would like to thank the following people:

My agent Lyn Amy, publisher Julie Gibbs and the team at Penguin.

Fantastic editors Belinda Byrne, Anne Rogan and particularly Arwen Summers, who lived and breathed Shelly Beach with me – frequently rescuing characters stranded on sandbanks.

Cover designer Marina Messiha, and illustrator Kat Chadwick. I just love their work.

The supportive members of my writers' group, Glen, Lee, Diana, Pru and Carol, who in no way resemble the members of the Shelly Beach Writers' Group.

My husband and our big beautiful family, who were always available to listen to tales of the mythical Shelly Beach.

And a special thank you for the research contributed by a bunch of well-loved dogs.